JUST A TASTE

O'LEARYS 5

SHANNYN SCHROEDER

ISBN: 978-1-950640-03-4

$\mathcal{L}$iam O'Leary walked through his apartment and peeled off his sweaty T-shirt, one that smelled of grease and onion soup that a clumsy line cook had spilled on him. The kid had no idea what he was doing, couldn't keep up with the pace of the kitchen, and Liam knew the owner would have to fire him. Exhaustion tugged at every muscle. Thoughts of the line cook—Liam didn't bother learning names until one proved himself—made Liam shake his head.

He'd asked Jonathan if he could sit in on the interviews for the last round of new hires, but Jonathan refused, saying he wanted Liam to focus on running the kitchen. The man might be a brilliant businessman, but he had no idea what it took to run a kitchen. Liam had been working at Porter's for more than two years and he still didn't understand how Jonathan managed to own a restaurant.

Jonathan had graduated from culinary school, but had never taken a job in a kitchen. He bought Porter's and hired a kitchen staff. Liam had been his fourth executive chef. It didn't take long to figure out why: Jonathan didn't want to work the kitchen but wanted the credit for what happened there. He created the menu but rarely listened to new ideas.

Every now and then, though, Liam made small changes without Jonathan's knowledge. Tonight had been one of those nights. Unfortunately, Jonathan chose tonight to grace them with his presence, and the small addition of some herbs to the soup had turned into an explosive argument.

Liam stepped under the hot spray of the shower and tried to figure out what he wanted to do. He'd been thinking about opening his own restaurant for over a year now, but had yet to make a move. Unlike his older brother Colin, who would jump into anything that looked good, Liam needed to weigh his options.

One thing he knew for sure was that his time at Porter's was coming to an end.

With a towel wrapped around his waist, he went to the kitchen and popped the top on a beer. He fished his phone from his jacket pocket and checked messages. He'd heard the phone earlier in the evening, but since it wasn't a number he recognized, he bumped it to voice mail.

He carried his beer back to his room to pull on a pair of boxers while he listened.

"Hi, Liam, this is Carmen Delgado. I don't know if you remember me, Gus's daughter. I'm calling to let you know that my dad passed away."

The barest hitch caught in the girl's voice. She continued talking, but Liam no longer heard. Of course he remembered Carmen. She'd been a sweet kid who'd always played at giving him a hard time when he'd worked for Gus.

Gus.

Liam sank to the edge of his bed. *Gus is dead?*

Gus had been his first mentor. He'd given Liam his first real job, understood his love of cooking and food, taught him how to create. Liam's chest felt heavy. He took a swig of his beer and pushed it past the sudden lump in his throat.

"Here's to you, Gus." He lifted his bottle and drank again. He'd been a bad friend in recent years. He couldn't remember the last time he went to see Gus. How long had it been? Maybe once or twice since Gus's wife had died. Liam had gotten busy with his own life and few friendships survived his hectic schedule.

When they had spoken by phone, Liam knew Gus understood that. He'd lived a similar life. His last conversation with Gus flooded back into his head. A food critic did a write-up about Porter's and had said wonderful things about Liam.

Gus had called to congratulate him. Liam had heard the pride in the old man's voice. That had been over a year ago. Guilt crept into Liam for letting so much time pass. Picking up his phone from where he'd dropped it on the mattress, he pressed the buttons to listen to the message again, needing to find the information to pay his respects to a great man.

AFTER TWO DAYS of making phone calls, Carmen's throat was scratchy and her voice almost nonexistent. Making all of the other arrangements for her father had been simple enough. But the phone calls nearly did her in. She'd found herself praying for answering machines and voice mails so she could leave the practiced message instead of having a real conversation.

Everyone had loved Gus. He'd had friends everywhere. Her family arrived on her doorstep and tried to take over for her. Her aunts and uncles meant well. She knew that, but taking care of her father was her job and she couldn't let anyone else do it. Her whole house was crammed with people, just like it had been when her mother had died.

Gus had felt like they'd needed that support and it was simply the way of her family, but she wanted peace. She needed to be alone and she couldn't find space anywhere. It was part of the reason she made the wake only a few short hours on Sunday. People would attend the wake and come back to the house to share a meal. The faster they got her dad to his final resting place, the faster they would all move on.

So she could move on.

She didn't know what that even meant. The idea made her feel light-headed. She'd been taking care of her parents for so long, she hadn't been able to think about herself. For now, she pushed the heavy thought away. She had details to attend to, people to speak with, arrangements to make.

Her cousin Rosa popped into the kitchen. "Hey, girl, how are you doing?"

"I'm okay. I think all the calls are done."

Rosa crossed the room and wrapped her arms around Carmen. "Let's get out of here. Go have a drink, do some dancing."

Carmen pulled away from Rosa. "What are you thinking? I can't go dancing. What would people think? My dad just died and I'm going out to party?"

Rosa rolled her eyes. "What do you care what people— forget that. It shouldn't matter what people think. Everyone needs a break. Especially you."

"I can't. I still have things to do to get ready for the wake."

"Well, I'm going out. You have my number." Rosa swished out of the room in her super-skinny jeans and kitten heels.

As much as Carmen loved her cousin, they had never had much in common. No matter how different they were, though, Rosa was the closest thing Carmen had to a best friend. She was an excellent confidant, but Carmen could never keep up with Rosa's social life. Heck, Carmen didn't even have a social life. She was the only twenty-seven-year-old spinster she knew.

Pouring herself another cup of coffee, she reclaimed a seat at the kitchen table. Her uncle and cousins were still sitting in her living room, watching something on TV. They had all pitched in doing various things, but she craved space and peace. She was used to being alone most days. Her dad went out on the truck and she handled the house and the office end of the business. The extra people were suffocating.

With the sounds of the TV from the other room, she focused on making a list of things she still needed to do. She had to update the web site and let customers know that the truck would be out of commission for a while. Maybe forever? She hadn't thought about what to do with Dad's business. He'd loved the food truck, but Carmen couldn't imagine running it.

Maybe Pete would want to take it over. Her younger cousin often went out with her dad to work. He knew most of the operation. Pete, however, was immature and she didn't know if she could trust him to work consistently. Her uncles had already mentioned selling the truck and the house and having her move in with one of them.

As if she wasn't a grown woman capable of taking care of herself.

She forced her head back to the task at hand. No decisions had to be made right now. She added Update Web Site to her list, followed by Clean Out Dad's Bedroom. That would be a huge task. When her mother had died, Gus would only let Carmen get rid of a few things. He'd clung to every item of Inez's that he could. He hadn't been ready to let her go. Over the months, Carmen snuck and removed things her dad might not notice, but overall, she knew she would now have to clear out the belongings of both of her parents.

Those two items alone weighed her down. She knew there would be more. Her father had a will, so she would have to talk to his lawyer about that. Then the outstanding bills for both the house and the business. At least her dad had been smart enough to add her name to everything after Inez's death.

She blinked back the tears and focused on the details. She'd be able to hold her shit together as long as she had a job to do.

LIAM WALKED into his childhood home, so glad to feel the calm and comfort of family when he knew he would face sorrow later in the day. The O'Leary family dinner was mandatory at least once a month. Eileen O'Leary expected her children to share a meal as a means to keep close. It was something his parents worked together to achieve as soon as he and his five siblings neared adulthood and branched out to have their own lives.

He walked straight to the back of the house. The living room was empty, so he must've beaten his brothers to the house today. In the kitchen, he knew he'd find his mother standing over the stove. He wished she would let him help with the meal preparation, but she never would. They took turns bringing dessert because as much as Eileen loved her sweets, she didn't make them. Dinner was her job and she refused to share it.

"Hi, Mom," he called as he opened the refrigerator to slide in the cheesecake he'd made for after dinner.

She peered around his shoulder to see what he'd brought. "Don't tell your brothers and sister, but I like it most when it's your turn for dessert."

"That's no secret, Mom. I always make your favorites. That's why I'm your favorite."

She slapped a towel at his arm. "Don't say that. I love all of my children equally."

"No one else is here. You can tell the truth." He looked down at her, suddenly struck by how small she appeared.

Her face grew serious. "What's the matter?"

"What do you mean?"

"Something's wrong. What is it?"

He hadn't been trying to cover his grief, but he hadn't planned on talking about it either. "Remember Gus Delgado? He owned the Mexican restaurant I first worked at?" Eileen nodded. "He died. His daughter called and left a message. After dinner, I have to go pay my respects."

Eileen didn't say anything, but she patted his arm. As far as physical affection went, that was about it for his mom. His dad had been the hugger in the family.

She turned back to the stove. Judging by the smells, they'd have roast for dinner. "Is there anything I can help with?"

She shook her head. He heard the front door open and he went to see which siblings had arrived. Moira pushed through the door and Liam hoped she brought Jimmy with her. Although he hadn't been thrilled with his friend entering a relationship with Moira, he'd appreciate seeing Jimmy today.

Unfortunately, Moira entered alone. "No Jimmy?" he asked.

She sighed. "Don't look so disappointed. He'll be here in a few minutes. He went to check on his dad."

"I'm not disappointed in seeing you." He squeezed her hard until she gasped.

"Why are you all dressed up? What's going on?"

"Nothing." He released her.

She crossed her arms and raised an eyebrow. Like their mother, she didn't need words to call him a liar.

"I found out an old friend died. The wake is today. I'm just feeling out of it."

Her whole face changed, filling with sadness for a friend she hadn't even known. She wrapped her arms around him in a gentle hug, unlike the playful one he'd forced on her. Jimmy opened the door without knocking, assessed the situation, and asked, "What's going on?"

"Nothing," Moira answered. As she stepped away, she ran a hand down his arm in reassurance. She would understand his desire to not discuss it.

Jimmy's gaze went back and forth between him and Moira, and then landed on him, questioning. Liam smiled. "Any luck on the house hunt?"

"I thought so." Jimmy took off his coat and hung it in the closet. "Your sister's too picky."

"I am not," Moira retorted.

Before the discussion could go further, Eileen called from the kitchen, "Moira, come help with the vegetables."

She shot Liam a dirty look.

He shrugged. "Don't look at me. I offered to help when I got here. She doesn't want my help."

Moira moped out of the room. Liam knew it wasn't fair that their mother assigned traditional gender roles.

"What was the hug about?" Jimmy asked when Moira had left.

"I don't want to talk about it. Tell me about the house." Anything to keep his mind off his plans for later that afternoon. He and Jimmy didn't have long to talk alone. Before he knew it, Ryan and Quinn arrived with baby Patrick followed by newlyweds Michael and Brianna. Colin arrived solo.

Moira came out of the kitchen as Colin sat on the couch beside Liam. "Where's Elizabeth?"

"At the bar."

"Why do I get the feeling she's avoiding family dinner? Doesn't she know it's a requirement? Shoot, if I have to be here, she should too."

"You're blood. No escaping it. She likes to point out that she's not an O'Leary and is therefore not required to be here."

Moira headed back to the kitchen, but shot over her shoulder, "Then maybe it's about time you made her an O'Leary."

Liam watched Colin and smiled. He recognized the look on his big brother's face.

"What are you looking at?" Colin asked.

"Did you already buy the ring?"

"What are you talking about?"

"You go ahead and play it cool around Moira because we know she'll flap her jaws to everyone, but I saw your face change when she suggested marriage."

Colin leaned closer. "Is it that obvious?"

Liam shook his head. "Probably not to everyone. But you don't get nervous and that's what I saw."

"The damn thing has been burning a hole in my pocket for a couple of weeks now. I can't figure out when to ask. Or where to ask. It seems like it would be a big deal for a woman, you know? I don't want to screw it up."

"I've got nothing for you there, but let me know if there's anything I can do to help."

Colin picked up the remote and turned the TV on to a football game. The Bears were losing to the Packers as usual. Within minutes, all four O'Leary men along with Jimmy O'Malley were sitting in the living room, screaming at the television at football players who couldn't hear them.

· · ·

HOURS LATER, Liam drove through the Humboldt Park neighborhood, dreading his destination. He'd missed the viewing at the funeral home intentionally. He didn't want to see Gus like that. The thought alone brought too many memories of his own father's funeral. The street in front of the Delgado house was filled with bumper-to-bumper cars. He drove around the corner and searched for a spot.

The flowers he bought wobbled in the passenger seat and part of him wanted to leave. But he couldn't. It wouldn't be right. Not for Gus and not for Carmen. At the end of the next block, he squeezed into a spot. As he stepped from his car, a blast of cold air hit him. He pulled his jacket tighter around him with one hand while he cradled the flowers in the other.

He walked into the harsh wind down the block toward Gus's house. He hadn't been a guest at Gus's house often, but he'd eaten dinner there a few times. Of course, he'd been there when Gus's wife had died. He hadn't stayed long. His own grief had been still too fresh and he couldn't stand it.

It had been years and he thought by now it would be easier, but with each heavy step, his doubt increased. He climbed the steps to the porch and knocked. No one answered. The noise from the other side of the door was loud. He knocked harder and then turned the knob.

He entered the house and looked around. People packed the entire living room. He stood still for a moment, allowing the air of the room to warm him. He studied the faces and realized he didn't know anyone. No one approached him, but many looked in his direction with open interest.

Then he spotted Carmen. She bustled around, taking plates and delivering coffee to older men and women around the room. He crossed to her and followed until she went into the kitchen. He waited in the doorway.

The kitchen was empty of guests. She put the dishes in

the sink and then braced her arms on the counter and released a breath that shuddered through her. Guilt poked at him. He was interrupting a private moment and he should leave, but his feet wouldn't listen.

He cleared his throat. "Carmen?"

She straightened slowly before turning to face him. A slow smile formed on her face. "Liam."

He hadn't been sure she would remember him. "How are you holding up?"

She lifted her shoulders in answer. The question was dumb. That was one of the worst parts of dealing with people after his father had died. The dumb questions.

"Here." He held the flowers out to her. "I know it doesn't help or ease the pain in any way, but I couldn't come here empty-handed."

"Thank you. They're beautiful." She took the vase from him and looked for a free space on the counter. The entire kitchen table and the length of the counter held trays and bowls of food. The smells made his mouth water even though he wasn't hungry.

"Can I get you something to eat?" she offered after she stashed the flowers in the corner near the refrigerator.

"No. Can I help with some of this? Do something for you? You look like you have your hands full with all of your guests." He removed his jacket and hung it on the back of one of the kitchen chairs. He rolled up the sleeves of his shirt, prepared to help.

She blinked a couple of times. "Uh… In all honesty, I'll probably end up throwing most of this out. There's just too much." She turned in a circle. "Coffee. I need to make more."

Liam moved forward. The girl looked dead on her feet. How could her family not see this? He pulled a chair out from the table. "Sit. I'll make it."

"No, it's okay."

"Carmen, sit down. Take a break and relax for a minute." While not harsh, his tone was firm and she sat.

He remembered when Gus's wife, Inez, died and the house had been filled like this. Gus loved having the family here, but Carmen had hidden in the kitchen, overwhelmed. Liam had joined her then, too. He moved around the kitchen making coffee and then washed the dishes that were in the sink.

"You don't have to do that, Liam."

"I know. I like to feel useful. And I don't think anyone in your family wants to chat me up." He rinsed a dish and put it in the drain. "I came here to see you, Carmen. I don't know anyone else. Your dad was my friend."

He heard her hiccupping breath. When he turned, he expected to see her crying, but she just stared off at nothing. Drying his hands quickly, he squatted in front of her. "What do you need, Carmen? I watched you run around here, taking care of everyone. What can I do for you?"

Her focus shifted until her eyes met his. So much sadness. He wanted to wrap her in a tight hug, but they had never had that kind of relationship. They'd had a teasing, laughing one with minimal contact. And that had been years ago.

"Could you take the coffee into the living room? I just need a few minutes."

He patted her knee before rising. "Take all the time you need."

CHAPTER 2

Of all the people to see her, really see her, no way had Carmen expected it to be Liam O'Leary. She had called him out of respect for her father, but she hadn't thought he'd come. Maybe to the funeral home, but certainly not to the house. She'd escaped to the kitchen because she needed to get away from the looks and comments, the rubs against her hand meant to reassure her that things would be okay.

So many people filled her small house. The air became oppressive and she couldn't breathe. When Liam caught her in the kitchen, she felt her nerves unraveling and he'd seen it.

"Who's the white boy pouring coffee? Tia Rosalie wants to know," Rosa said.

So much for a minute of peace. Carmen turned to face her cousin. "It's Liam O'Leary. He stopped by to pay his respects and offered to get the coffee for me."

Carmen pushed away from the table. If Rosa was in the kitchen, others would surely follow. Especially if Liam drew attention. And how could he not? He didn't exactly blend with her family. Once on her feet, she swayed.

"Hey now. Are you all right?" Rosa caught her arm.

She nodded weakly. "I'm fine. A little worn out. It's a lot to take in at once, you know?"

Liam returned with the coffeepot, still half full, which was a good sign. Maybe people were planning to leave soon. She took the pot from him. "Thank you."

"What else can I do? Want me to wrap up the food?"

She glanced at Rosa. If she mentioned throwing it all away, Rosa would get nosy. "Why don't you make yourself a plate to take with you? I'll never be able to eat all of this."

"Rosa," someone called from the living room.

Rosa waited, looking at Carmen's face. "Are you sure you're okay? Mom and Dad are probably ready to go."

"I'm good. Thanks." She forced a smile that she hoped would pass the test for her cousin.

"Call if you need anything." Rosa grabbed her in a hug and added in her ear, "I mean it."

"I will," Carmen whispered back. The brief respite she'd taken had to be enough. She followed Rosa back into the living room to say good-bye to her family and walk them out. Luckily, when Rosa's family decided to leave, the rest of the family followed suit. It had taken another hour, but Carmen closed the door on her last cousin and sank against the door.

Blissful quiet.

Except not. Water was running in the kitchen. Who? Then she remembered Liam. She'd completely forgotten about him. She shoved away from the door and walked to the kitchen. In the doorway, she froze. The entire room was clean. Dishes stacked neatly on the drain and counter. Liam hadn't noticed her presence and she watched him for a moment.

He was bigger now than he'd ever been. Broader. But his

red hair and freckles hadn't changed. And those blue eyes still had the ability to mesmerize her.

A flash of memory struck her: Liam, elbows-deep in the stainless sink at her father's restaurant. Physically he'd always stood out in that kitchen, the one white guy among a bunch of Mexicans, but he fit in somehow. His love for her father's food brought him into the fold.

"Everyone gone?" he asked without turning around.

"Yes." She walked to him and leaned against the counter. "Thank you for cleaning up. You didn't have to do that."

"It didn't look like anyone else was going to help." He winked at her. "Besides, it was like old times."

"I had the same thought when I saw you standing at the sink. You're far from being a dishwasher now, though, right? My dad was always bragging about what a great chef you are." She crossed her arms over her middle. For all the details she'd handled over the days, she'd spoken very little of her father.

"I wouldn't be where I am today if your dad hadn't fostered my love of cooking." He dried his hands on the towel at the edge of the sink, then picked up a glass dish filled with food. "My to-go container. I'll return it when I'm finished."

"No problem. Thank you for your help. Really."

"I know you said you were going to throw the food away, but I broke it up into meal-sized portions and put it in the fridge. If you freeze some, you probably won't have to cook for weeks."

She shook her head with a smile. This man, who was a virtual stranger, had helped in ways that her family couldn't. They meant well and she couldn't hold that against them. But Liam let her be. She briefly recalled her dad talking about Liam's father dying. It had been while Mom was sick and

Carmen had been overwhelmed. She hadn't even really paid attention.

"I'll see you tomorrow." He gently touched her shoulder with his free hand and gave a little squeeze.

Tomorrow. At the funeral. She offered a weak nod, not trusting her voice. He grabbed his coat and left without a sound. Carmen locked up and stood in her living room, a room she'd grown up in, and the silence assaulted her.

She'd wanted the silence, the peace, but now she felt like it would swallow her whole. She turned the TV back on, found the telenovelas her mother loved to watch, and then she curled up on the couch.

DAYS PASSED and Liam poured himself into work. Jonathan had been riding him harder than usual and Liam didn't know why. Maybe another critic had stopped by. It would serve Jonathan right if it had happened on Liam's night off. He didn't need to see the receipts to know that service was down when Jonathan was at the helm. Liam had thought focusing on work would soothe him, but it hadn't.

He'd gone to Gus's funeral, suffered through it. He didn't stay after the service. The family's grief was palpable and Liam couldn't stomach it. Carmen had looked unflappable, which he found more alarming than the women crying loudly.

Brief moments of sadness and grief stole across her face, but she'd covered it well. Now he stood in his kitchen staring at the Pyrex pan he'd borrowed the night of the wake. It had been sitting on the counter taunting him. He knew he had to return it, should return it, but he was afraid to face Carmen. He knew from experience that it was easy to hold it together for the funeral, but later, sometimes days or weeks later, the grief and sorrow would catch up.

Chances were good that she would never even notice the missing pan. But not returning it would eat at him.

He grabbed the pan and bundled up against the cold night air. Just over a month until Christmas. These weeks would be especially hard for Carmen. Then the start of a new year. His personal deadline to figure out what he wanted for his future.

As he drove across town, he didn't think of Carmen, but of his own family. They'd questioned him plenty over every family dinner about whether he planned to open his own restaurant. They knew he'd been considering it. Jimmy pushed more than his siblings had, but that was Jimmy's way. Part of him wanted his own place. Being able to make his own decisions. Hiring people he knew would work well as part of his team. Trying new menu items just because he had the idea to.

But along with all the fun came the responsibility, not only for himself and his success, but people would be counting on him for paychecks. Gus's death was a reminder of the burden that came with being an owner. Even as a lowly dishwasher, he'd been aware of the lean months when Gus didn't know if he'd be able to pay the utilities.

Liam parked on the street, noting that it was much emptier than it had been on his last trip. He stared up at Gus's house. Yes, Gus had struggled, but then he'd found success. The restaurant had been thriving when Gus sold it because Inez had gotten sick. He hadn't thought he could run the restaurant without her.

More like he didn't want to.

Shoving morose thoughts from his mind, Liam stepped from the car and breathed a lungful of cold air. It felt like an early winter. Icy wind slapped at him and although no snow lay on the ground, everything was frozen.

No lights brightened the house, but he saw the blue glow of the TV, so he rang the bell. It wasn't late, so he was sure Carmen would be awake. He waited patiently, but the tip of his nose quickly numbed.

She swung the door open with a look of surprise. "Hi." Her smile was only a little forced.

"Hi. I came to return your pan." He held it up as if that somehow made a difference.

"Thanks." She paused, looked over her shoulder, and then added, "Come on in. It's freezing out there."

He followed her into the dark room and noticed the moving boxes. Was she moving out of her family's home? She clicked on a table lamp and then he saw. Gus's clothes were scattered around the furniture. She was clearing out her dad's stuff.

"I'll take that." She reached for the pan and he handed it over. "Make yourself comfortable. Can I get you something to drink? I don't have much here, but—"

"I'm good." He sat on the couch, avoiding the armchair he knew had been Gus's. When she returned empty-handed, he asked, "How are you doing?"

"I'm okay, I guess."

"Why are you doing this by yourself?" He asked with a nod toward the boxes.

"I want to." She sat slowly on the chair. "My cousin offered to help, but her solution would be to toss everything. My aunts would spend too much time crying."

He stared at this young, incredibly strong woman and his heart went out to her. "How about you take a break? Let me take you out for a drink and we can catch up."

Her eyebrows came together and she tilted her head as if he'd spoken a foreign language.

"I can see you've been at this for a while. It's my night off. Let's go out."

She stood, but tugged on her sweatshirt. "I'm not really dressed to go out."

"I wasn't thinking about taking you clubbing, just a quiet bar to talk. I think you look great, but I'll wait if you want to change."

"You know it doesn't say much for your social life if this is how you spend your night off." Her smile was small, but cocky, the same one she used to toss at him when she sped through the kitchen hoping her mom wouldn't catch her and put her to work.

"I don't know. I think I got the better end of the deal here."

Her smile broadened and she went from a grief-stricken daughter to a beautiful woman.

"Let me grab my jacket." She ran into another room and reappeared a few minutes later with a jacket on and if he looked closely, it seemed like she might've applied some makeup. Whatever she'd done, she already looked lighter, happier. Yeah, a break might do them both some good.

Liam led the way to his car. "Any place you prefer to go?"

"I don't have a preference. I don't get out much."

He pulled away from the curb and away from her house. Carmen immediately began chatting. "Where are you working now?"

"Porter's downtown."

"Swanky, huh?"

"It's okay."

"That's not a resounding endorsement. Don't you like it? It seems like just the kind of place you always talked about working at."

He focused on the street and tried to remember when he had ever mentioned plans to Carmen.

She smacked his arm. "You don't even remember, do you?"

He slid her a look but didn't answer.

"One day when my mom caught me trying to sneak out the back door, she made me help you with the dishes. As if you needed help. You were like a machine." She paused and he heard the smile in her voice. "You actually did all the work that day while I sat my butt on the counter." She laughed quietly. "Getting you to talk was like...I don't know. Except that day. I don't know what happened, but you talked about your plans for after culinary school. I was really impressed."

He suddenly remembered the conversation with her. He'd aced his courses at school and it had been the first time he knew being a chef wasn't just a silly dream, but something he would excel at. He'd scrubbed pots and pans that day and allowed his mind to wander to the possibilities.

Then he had a cute girl want to talk to him and speaking those dreams aloud didn't seem like a bad idea.

"Yeah, well, I felt sorry for you. Your mom forced you to hang out with me in the one place you seemed to hate."

"I didn't hate the restaurant. I just didn't want to work in the kitchen." Her voice faded and he knew they'd crossed into a topic she didn't want to discuss.

She stared out the window for a minute before speaking again. "You still didn't tell me why you don't like your job."

"I like it." He paused, searching for the words to explain. "It doesn't feel like it's enough anymore. When my boss hired me, I was so excited to have my own kitchen. At least that's what I thought I was getting. I didn't bother to ask why the last chef left, or any of the others before me."

"So your boss is a dick."

Her assessment made him chuckle. "Yeah. That's one way to put it."

"What do you plan to do?"

"I don't know." He pulled into a parking lot of a neighborhood bar. He had no idea what the place was like since this wasn't his neighborhood, but it looked like a sports bar, which should be safe enough.

The inside of the bar was warm with the press of bodies. He'd forgotten about football on Thursday nights. Most people were huddled around the bar and the two big TVs there, so he led Carmen farther back to a small table. A harried waitress came by quickly. He ordered a scotch for himself and looked at Carmen.

"A beer?"

"Are you not sure?"

"I told you I don't get out much. Rosa always orders beer."

"What brand?" the waitress asked.

Carmen shrugged.

"Why not try something new? A margarita? A martini?"

Something lit in Carmen's eyes. "Yes."

"Which one?"

"Let's start with a margarita. I know I like that." She slid her jacket off and hung it on the back of her chair.

Liam realized that she'd changed her shirt when she went to her room. Gone was the oversized sweatshirt. She wore a black top that wrapped in some crazy crisscross over her chest, emphasizing her breasts.

Whoa. He had never thought about Carmen as a woman. At least not one whose chest he'd ogle. She was only three years younger than him, but when he'd worked for Gus, she was still in high school, which made her off limits.

"I don't think I've had a margarita since college, but I vaguely remember having a really good time while drinking them."

He wanted to know about her time in college and what

she'd been doing since, but he didn't want to bring up a subject she didn't want to discuss. Tonight was about her having a good time, a chance to escape the sadness for a little while.

~

CARMEN STUDIED LIAM'S FACE. Always so serious. He had a permanent pinched line that ran between his eyebrows. Even when he smiled, it was just a lift of the corners of his mouth. She wondered if he ever laughed.

She couldn't remember ever hearing him laugh. The thing she remembered most about Liam was how quiet he was. He watched everything but said little.

Except that night in the kitchen of her dad's restaurant that had come like a flash to her brain. She hadn't thought about those days—or Liam—in a long time. He'd been different that night. In truth, she'd thought he was flirting with her. Not that she'd had much experience with guys flirting.

The waitress returned with their drinks and placed them on small napkins before asking if they needed anything else. The odd yellow color of her drink made Carmen question if she'd ordered correctly. She turned the glass before picking it up.

Liam raised his glass. "What should we drink to?"

"To old friends." She clinked her glass against his. Her lips touched the salted rim before the cold citrusy taste of the margarita slid onto her tongue. Yeah, she'd ordered right. This was a drink she could get drunk on. Her gaze slid to Liam. He'd let her get drunk and take care of her, take her home.

That was more than she could say with Rosa. Rosa drank

in bars to find men. If she found one, Carmen was on her own. But not tonight.

"Something wrong with your drink?"

"Nope. I was remembering how much I really like margaritas." She sipped again. "The first time I got drunk was on margaritas. I was seventeen and the busboys snuck a pitcher without my dad knowing. By the time cleanup was done for the night, I couldn't stand straight."

Liam smiled, as much as he seemed to do anyway. Lines bracketing his mouth were the only sign that it was a genuine smile. Now she really wanted to hear him laugh.

"Where was I when this happened?"

She shrugged. "It must've been your night off."

"Did your dad find out?"

"Of course he did. He had to practically carry me to the car. He asked who gave me the alcohol, but I wouldn't tell." She sipped again. She'd refused to tell because she'd liked the one boy, whose name escaped her now. He'd shown her attention and back then, she'd been desperate for attention from boys. "It was one of the few times I remember Dad being furious."

"I think I would've paid to see Gus yell at perfect little Carmen."

"He yelled a lot." She laughed.

"Not at you. You could do nothing wrong in his eyes. The rest of us, however, got used to the yelling. The only other choice was to quit. Gus was good practice for being a chef. We all like to yell."

"No way. Are you telling me that behind this quiet exterior lurks Chicago's very own Gordon Ramsay?"

"I'm not that bad, but most chefs are particular in how they want things run."

"Now I'm tempted to spy on you at work. I can't imagine you even raising your voice a little. You're too quiet."

"Yelling isn't always about an increase in volume." He was so calm and cool.

Carmen reached out and stroked his jaw. The red stubble tickled her palm. "What's this about?" He'd always been clean-cut, but he had a scruffy beard going on. It was trim enough to reflect that it hadn't been laziness, but intentional.

"I sometimes let it grow. It makes me look more my age." He drank from his glass. "This time, it also has the added benefit of pissing off my boss."

Carmen liked the feel of his face but forced her hand away. So Liam wasn't as calm and cool as he appeared. People did irritate him. He just wasn't loud about it. "I like it."

"It makes it harder to call me…what was it you and your cousin nicknamed me? White Bread?"

She hung her head in shame. Of course he would remember. Heat flamed in her cheeks. But the embarrassment didn't stop her from mumbling, "Wonder Bread."

"Hah! That's right. Wonder Bread."

It was almost a laugh. "We were snotty teenagers and we shouldn't have called you that."

"It didn't bother me. I'm definitely white."

She didn't understand. If he had ever referred to her or anyone in her family as a wetback or any other slur she'd heard over her lifetime, she'd be pissed. Definitely hurt. "It didn't make it right."

He shrugged it off. She finished the drink, and Liam already had his hand in the air to order another.

"Are you trying to get me drunk?"

"I'm not trying to, but if it happens, so be it. Everyone needs to cut loose on occasion." His glass was still near full. "I'll make sure you get home safely."

She sighed. Safe had been her whole life. Maybe she was tired of being safe. The waitress brought her second drink, and Carmen wondered what she and Liam would talk about.

The alcohol was loosening her up, but she found that he was okay with sitting in silence.

Unfortunately, she wasn't. "Are you naturally antisocial or what?"

Somewhere in her brain, she knew the question probably came out sounding rude, but she didn't have the skills to fix it at this particular moment.

"No. At least I don't think so. Why do you ask?"

"When you worked at the restaurant, it felt like you were always on your own. I'd talk with the other staff, both front of house and back, but you kept your distance." She wanted to ask why he'd avoided her, never asked her out like the other guys had. She'd never taken any of them seriously, so she'd always turned them down, but she probably would've said yes to him.

He shrugged. "I didn't feel welcome most of the time."

Liam had felt like an outsider? The thought had never occurred to her. "That's too bad. I would've welcomed you."

He smiled again, the lines in his cheeks deepening. "You were usually looking for a way to escape. Why did you hate working there so much?"

Blowing out a breath, she raised her drink to her lips. How could she explain her need to avoid the temptation of food? By the age of seventeen, she'd already been teased so much about her weight, that all she wanted was to be thin. Being in the restaurant, around her favorite foods, made it near impossible.

She looked into Liam's cool blue assessing eyes. And lied. "I didn't hate the whole restaurant. Just the kitchen stuff. I don't like to cook. It's not my thing."

"Maybe I should give you lessons."

She thought of his strong, capable hands, the roped muscles in his forearms, and suppressed a shiver. *What is wrong with me?*

"What is your thing?"

Hmm…the question was innocent enough, but she'd spent so much time with Rosa and the alcohol filtering into her brain made her thoughts not so innocent. She was beginning to think he might be her thing. "Business. That's what I majored in for college. I've been taking care of the office stuff for my dad since I've been home."

He pressed his lips together like he had to consider her answer. She drank some more. The second margarita went down even smoother than the first and she was reminded why she'd gotten drunk so easily. Liam's glass was empty.

"Do you want another, or do you have to go?" she asked.

"I'll get you another. I'll stick with water. I'm driving."

See, she knew he was one of those super-responsible guys. That's what her dad always said. *Liam is a good boy. Find a man like him, Carmen, and you'll be fine.* "My dad really loved you."

Liam froze, his arm in the air again to get the waitress's attention. When the waitress came over he ordered for them. Then he turned in his seat to fully face her. "I loved Gus, too. I'm sorry I wasn't around more."

"Shoot. I didn't say that to make you feel bad. I was thinking about him and you and stuff he always said."

"I know, but I do feel bad. We talked on the phone sometimes, but I should've made time to visit."

She reached out and rubbed his forearm. Her dark skin contrasted sharply with his pale complexion. "He understood. He liked that you were going after your dreams and finding success. You were like a son to him."

The alcohol had her babbling and she hadn't even started on her third one yet. She didn't want to stop, though. Allowing the alcohol to relax her was freeing. She didn't have to put on a brave face for anyone. She didn't have to pretend to know what she was doing or that she had her shit together.

Right here, in this moment, she could just be a halfway drunk girl hanging out with an old friend. A cute old friend, which made the evening better.

CHAPTER 3

*L*iam wished Carmen would stop touching him. He was a good guy, a respectful man, but she tempted him in ways her younger self only had a glimpse of. The alcohol worked its magic, and she had relaxed and opened up. The smiles she offered were genuine, unlike the plastered-on version he'd seen at the wake and the funeral. Her warm brown eyes laughed while she spoke, telling stories of the restaurant when they'd both been little more than kids.

She flirted with him now. He had no idea if it was the alcohol causing it, or the desperation borne of grief and loneliness, or if she simply wanted to flirt. He reminded himself that she wasn't in a good place, and she had things to figure out for herself. He had brought her out as a friend, out of respect for Gus and his love for his daughter. It would kill Gus all over again to see her suffer like this.

Carmen finished her fourth margarita and Liam suggested it was time to leave. She sighed. "Yeah, it's time. I'm feeling pretty buzzed."

She shoved away from her chair and wobbled enough

that she slapped her hand on the table for balance. Liam grabbed her arm.

"Are you okay?"

"I'm just out of practice for getting drunk, that's all." She said it with a smile, as if nothing could possibly bother her.

Her dark hair caught under her jacket as she slipped it on. He reached over and pulled her hair out. The silky strands flowed over his fingers and the backs of his hands as it trailed down her back. "Thanks," she said, and he noticed the unfocused look in her eyes.

He held her arm as they wound through the bar toward the exit. She pulled away and put her arm around his waist and leaned into him. She giggled. "I think I'm more than buzzed."

He slid his arm around her shoulder and guided her to the car. The blast of cold air zipped through him, but her soft body against him kept him warm. At the car, he turned her to lean against the back door while he opened the passenger side. She wove in place.

"Are you going to be sick?"

She laughed again. "I said I was out of practice, not stupid. I didn't drink enough to puke." She staggered to the door and plopped her butt in the seat. Looking up at him with her brilliant smile, she said, "Thanks for this. You really are a good guy."

Liam waited until she shifted her legs in and then closed the door.

By the time he got behind the wheel, Carmen had leaned her head against the passenger window and her eyes were closed. He probably shouldn't have let her have that last drink, but she was relaxed and having fun, so he didn't want to stop it. He started the car and while it warmed up, he studied her face.

Her hair cascaded across one cheek and her light pink

lips parted slightly. Even as she rested, she appeared to be smiling. Then he noticed she hadn't buckled her seat belt. Damn. He shifted his body and reached across to grab the belt, careful not to catch her hair.

She stirred, her eyes fluttering open. "Whatcha doin'?"

"Buckling your seat belt." He yanked to get some more slack and did his best not to notice how the belt ran across her chest making her breasts even more prominent.

While he focused on snapping in the buckle, she stroked his jaw again, like she had at the bar. "I like this. It makes you look different. Sexy."

Oh, man. He pushed back to his seat and shifted the car into drive. She settled against her seat again with a small sigh. The ride to her house was short and he didn't know if he should be grateful or disappointed. He'd enjoyed their night out. Carmen wasn't quite the same girl he'd known years ago, but he saw hints of the girl in the woman she'd become.

Parked beside her house, he walked around to her door and opened it. She took his offered hand. Again he wrapped an arm around her to keep her steady and guilt tugged at him. She'd probably be hung over tomorrow and feel like crap.

She pulled her keys from her pocket and studied them like she couldn't remember what she was supposed to do. Liam took them from her palm. "Let me." He held the keys and added, "Drink lots of water before you go to bed. It'll help with the hangover."

He turned to the lock and she leaned against the wall. He began to doubt she'd even make it to her bed.

While he tried to figure out which key belonged to this door, her finger traced his jaw again. "I've never kissed a guy with a beard before."

Crap. His fingers twitched with the keys and he finally

figured out the right one. He pushed the door open and removed the key. "Are you going to be okay from here?"

Her lips bunched before she spoke. "Yeah."

Sadness and disappointment reappeared. She'd expected him to kiss her. Hell, he wanted to, but it wouldn't be right. She was drunk and grieving. He couldn't take advantage of her. He also didn't want to be the cause of any more sadness. With one finger he slid her hair away from her cheekbone. Her skin was flawless and smooth. "I had a great time tonight. Thanks for coming out with me."

She tilted her face up. "Do you want to come in?"

It was an offer that intentionally didn't sound like an offer.

"As much as I'd like to"—and he really hoped she understood how much he wanted to—"it's not a good idea."

He stepped back to allow her to go through the door. "Give me a call if you need help with anything. I mean it."

She pressed her lips together and added a tight nod. Then she closed and locked the door.

Liam had the uncomfortable feeling that he'd just messed up somehow.

CARMEN WOKE THE FOLLOWING MORNING, late morning, with a pounding headache. She should've listened to Liam and drunk more water. She'd downed one glass before crawling into bed, and now she didn't feel like she could climb out to get more. The simple act of lifting her head from the pillow required great effort and caused much pain.

Her phone bleeped at her and she checked the screen. A text from Rosa:

I'm off work today, so I'm coming over.

Carmen focused on the little letters on the screen and told her cousin not to come.

Rosa immediately called. "Why don't you want me to come over?"

"Because I don't feel good."

"What's wrong?"

"I have a pounding headache."

"Are you sick or hung over?"

Carmen didn't answer.

"Shit, girl, are you sitting in your sad house getting drunk by yourself?"

"No. I went out last night."

"That's it. Now I *am* coming over. Get your ass out of bed. I need to hear who got you to go out drinking that was better than me."

"No—" It was too late. Rosa had already hung up. Carmen flipped the covers back from her body and struggled to sit up. Knowing Rosa, she had at least thirty minutes. Enough time to take a shower and have some coffee.

In the bathroom, she looked at herself in the mirror. The makeup she'd hastily applied last night had smeared. Her eyes were bleary. Part of her was embarrassed because of the way she'd acted with Liam last night. She'd flirted shamelessly and enjoyed it.

But as usual, Liam didn't react. She'd thought for a moment there at the door that he was going to kiss her. And God, she'd wanted that kiss.

Looking back now, she could recognize it wasn't a smart move. She didn't even know if she had acted that way because it was Liam or because it had been so long since she'd been on a date. She was lonely and Liam had given her some attention. It was like being a teenager again and she hated it.

She got in the shower, turning the water up hotter than

usual to beat the tense muscles of her neck and try to ease the headache.

By the time Rosa showed, Carmen felt nearly human. A second cup of coffee should fix her up. Her cousin strode in the back door and helped herself to a cup, too.

"So spill, bitch. I've asked you to go out with me a bunch of times and you keep turning me down. Who was it?"

Carmen started to roll her eyes, but stopped midroll because the motion brought back pain. "Liam O'Leary came by last night to return a pan from the wake. He asked me to go have a drink with him." She sighed and sat in one of the kitchen chairs. Rosa stood, leaning against the counter.

"So you agreed to drink with a man, but not your cousin."

"I was sorting through my dad's stuff, deciding what to keep and what to give away when he showed up. I realized I needed a break and took it with him. I didn't plan on getting drunk, but I was so relaxed. It was the first time since Dad died that I let go of everything."

Rosa took a chair across from her. "That's what I've been trying to get you to see. I'm a little pissed that you chose a guy over me, but whatever."

Carmen drank her coffee and let the caffeine hit her system. The buzz was nice, not as good as the margarita and lust buzz from last night, but it would do.

"What was that look?" Rosa asked with a smile.

"What look?"

"Did you sleep with Wonder Bread?"

"Don't call him that."

"Sorry. I didn't mean anything by it. It took me until I got home after the wake to realize who he was. And you're dodging the question."

"No, I'm not. And no, I didn't." But she would have. If he'd even hinted he was interested. She'd even gone so far as to throw out the line but wasn't able to reel him in.

"But you wanted to. You slut."

"Is it possible for you to have a conversation without calling people names?"

"You know I love you."

Carmen did know. Rosa was crass and played tough, but she knew Rosa was trying to look out for her.

"So when are you going to see him again?"

"I doubt I will."

Rosa shook her head. "It's time to move on. To live your life. Your parents are gone. You can do whatever you want. If you want to bring a guy home and fuck him in every room of this house, you can."

The thought had truly never crossed her mind. This was her parents' house. It still seemed disrespectful. Not to mention she had no one to fuck. She stood and carried her coffee into the living room to finish packing her father's things. Rosa followed, as Carmen knew she would.

"The truth is, I don't know what I want. It's been so long since I've given my life any thought. I'm so lost right now, Rosa. I'm stuck."

"I'll help unstick you. Let's start with these boxes."

Rosa was serious. The playful, irresponsible cousin who she thought would just toss everything wanted to help. Tears stung the backs of her eyes. "I think all of his clothes have to go. Except maybe the food truck shirts. I don't think I want any of his clothes."

For hours, they worked together, breaking to have lunch, and then continuing into the afternoon. By the time Rosa hugged her good-bye, an entire wall of the living room was filled with boxes ready for Goodwill.

It was hard to look at the boxes, so little to represent her father's full life, but Carmen finally felt like she'd made some kind of forward motion.

Now she just needed to figure out what to do with her

dad's business and how she wanted to proceed with her own life.

No big deal, right?

LIAM SAT in bed staring at the ceiling. He didn't have to be in to work until one and he was restless. He thought about calling Carmen to check on her, but wasn't sure it would be a good idea. Someone knocked on his front door, so he shuffled out of bed. When he opened the door, he was surprised to see Lily standing there. They'd forged a friendship after meeting at his brother Ryan's wedding last year. He never quite understood how she'd scored an invite, but he was glad she had.

Her cheeks were pink from the cold air outside, but she smiled. She looked at his bare chest and pajama bottoms. "I guess you forgot about brunch."

Shit. He had. He opened his mouth to apologize.

"We could do it some other time if you want."

"No. I'm sorry. Give me a few minutes to get dressed. It's just been a busy week."

She unwrapped a scarf from around her neck and pulled a knit cap off her head, sending her blond hair floating with static. Running a hand over her head, she asked, "Yeah? What's going on?"

"I had a funeral to go to. An old friend died. I went out with his daughter last night."

Lily's back stiffened a bit. "Anyone I know?"

He shook his head. "No, they're not from around here." He pointed at his couch. "Make yourself comfortable. I'll be back in a minute."

The offer didn't need to be made. Lily had been in his apartment many times over the last year. They'd hit it off at the wedding and stayed in touch. They had similar interests. She worked at her mom's diner and was considering going back to school to be a chef. They got together to experiment with recipes and he gave her tips.

They had an easy friendship that he enjoyed away from his hectic job. He dressed quickly and brushed his teeth.

From the living room Lily called, "Are you ever going to do anything with this room?"

"What do you mean?" He rolled his sleeves to his elbows.

"The room is pretty stark."

"There's furniture and a TV. What else does it need?"

She swooped her arm out. "Some sign that it's your room and not mine or some random stranger's. There's no personality."

He shrugged. "I spend most of my time in the kitchen. This room does its job."

"But it's not inviting. It doesn't tell people to sit and relax and stay a while."

"Maybe I don't want people to stay."

She stood and shoved his shoulder. "You talk tough, but I know you don't mean it." Then she reached up and rubbed his beard. "This is new."

"Every now and then I let it grow."

She wrinkled her nose. "It looks like you're trying to hide your face." She wrapped her scarf around her neck. "Where to for food?"

"You pick. I'll drive." He held the door open for her.

"What did you do last night? You said you went out with your friend's daughter?"

With his keys jingling in his hand, he said, "Yeah, she was bummed about her dad and she was trying to pack up his stuff. I took her out for a drink."

"Oh." Lily's eyes widened. "When you said daughter, I

thought you were being a good Samaritan and taking a little girl out for ice cream."

Liam pressed the button to unlock the car, suddenly feeling like he was being interrogated. He got behind the wheel and started the engine. He didn't know how to respond to Lily's comment.

"So was this like a date?" Her face didn't reveal much. She continued to smile as she looked out the window, as if his answer didn't matter. But he had sisters and he knew there was a right and wrong way to respond.

It hadn't been a date. At least it hadn't started out feeling like one, but then Carmen had flirted and he'd wanted to kiss her, which was the definition of a date. "No. Carmen and I were kind of friends when I used to work at her dad's restaurant."

She turned in her seat to face him. "That probably sounded bad. I didn't mean to pry."

Liam had a sinking feeling about this whole conversation and all he wanted to do was escape it. "Have you talked to your mom about the new recipes you developed?"

She sighed. "No. I don't think she'll ever give up any control in the kitchen. She likes to keep me out front as a waitress."

"Maybe it's time for you to move on. Find something different." He'd been struggling with the same feeling at his own job. The difference was that Lily was still young and finding her way. He was thirty and should've figured out his way by now.

"I can't do that. She needs me."

"Then your only other option is to make her listen. If you don't, you're just going to end up bitter and resentful."

She nodded silently. He was glad she didn't want to continue talking about Carmen.

As they neared the restaurant, Lily suddenly said, "I need you to teach me mac and cheese."

"Huh?"

"I keep trying to make some really good mac and cheese, but it comes out lumpy or worse, like glue. I need to know what kinds of cheese work best and how to make it so that it will work for the diner. If I can sell my mom on a new mac and cheese recipe, prove to her I can do it, that might work."

Liam breathed a sigh of relief. Food talk was something he could handle. He wasn't ready to examine what had transpired between him and Carmen. He certainly wasn't ready to consider why Lily would care how he'd spent his night. He needed to focus on the food. He knew what to do with food.

A WEEK AND A HALF LATER, Liam sat in his car staring at the certified letter. The past week had been crazy with trying to spend time with his family around Thanksgiving, but he always had to work on holidays. He'd gotten the notification of the letter, but ignored it for days. It wasn't until he was on his way to work that he stopped by the post office to pick it up.

Now, he couldn't believe the contents. Calling the lawyer had only confirmed the information in the letter. Gus had left him half ownership in his food truck. Although Liam had known that Gus sold the restaurant when Inez had gotten sick, he didn't remember much about the food truck. Gus mentioned it at some point, but on the occasions that they spoke, they rarely discussed Gus's business.

Gus was always asking about Liam and how he was doing. They talked about family, but Gus never even hinted at this. He had a huge family. Why would he leave the truck to Liam? What about Carmen? She would need the truck and its income. Wouldn't she? What was he supposed to do with it?

He'd tried calling Carmen a couple of times, but she hadn't answered. This wasn't something to discuss via voice mail. He looked at the time and debated whether talking to Carmen now would be a good idea. He'd worked the lunch shift and prepped for dinner, so for a change, he had the chance to be home early. She would probably be home. He needed to settle this with her. He couldn't let it sit. They would figure out how he could sign his half over to her so she could do whatever she wanted with it.

With that mission in mind, he drove to Gus's—Carmen's—house. Once again, when he pulled up, the house was dark except for the blue glow in the living room. He began to wonder if Carmen had some aversion to turning on the lights. He knocked on the front door and waited.

When she didn't answer, he peered through the window beside the porch. He saw her silhouetted against the light of the TV, so he knocked again. Then he yelled, "Carmen, it's Liam. I see you sitting there."

A moment later, she pulled the door open and the sight sent a shock through him. She stood wearing her pajamas, looking like she hadn't showered or eaten in days. In fact, she looked like she might've lost weight. She didn't even offer a fake smile.

"What do you want, Liam? I'm busy."

"You're sitting in your pajamas watching TV. That's not busy. What's wrong?"

"Nothing." She put her hand on her hip as if that would make her look tough while wearing a Hello Kitty shirt.

The information from the will must've really done a number on her. "Can I come in?"

She tilted her head, a movement she'd always done when

irritated. When he waited her out, she finally sighed and swept an arm out to invite him in.

The room was tidy, clear of the boxes and clothes she'd had scattered all over during his last visit. She followed him into the room, but didn't sit. She stood with her arms crossed.

"Why are you here?"

"I wanted to see how you're doing." Although it was a little lie, looking at her now, he knew it mattered. He should've called or stopped by earlier.

"I'm fine." She widened her eyes and lifted the corners of her mouth. Still not a smile.

He sat on the couch. "You don't look fine. Sit with me."

She dropped her arms and plopped next to him like a sullen teen. Moira had perfected that look a decade ago.

"I want to talk about Gus's will."

"I don't. There's nothing to say."

"I had no idea he was leaving me anything."

She lifted a shoulder. "I did."

"But—"

"What part of I don't want to talk about it do you have a problem understanding?" Tears welled and she blinked them back.

Liam suddenly understood that it wasn't the contents of the will that had upset her. It was simply the loss of her father catching up to her. "Okay. When was the last time you ate?"

She continued to look at him, blinking like she didn't understand the question.

"Have you eaten dinner?"

She shook her head.

"Good. I'm starving. I'll cook for us." He stood and went into the kitchen. In his peripheral vision, he saw her jump from the couch.

"You don't have to do that. I'm not even hungry."

"I like to cook for friends. Come keep me company. Tell me what you've been up to since the last time I saw you." *When you were drunk and flirtatious and happy.*

Pink spots appeared high on her cheeks. "About that. I'm sorry. I hadn't planned on getting drunk. Parts of the night are a little fuzzy. Did I do anything to embarrass myself?"

She didn't remember inviting him in? He'd known that she wasn't okay to drive, but she didn't seem ready to pass out either. "No. You were fine. I had a really good time."

"So did I." She leaned awkwardly against the counter while he rifled through her refrigerator.

The contents were pretty sparse. She had pre-portioned chicken breast and salmon pieces, a bag of broccoli, and iceberg lettuce. He didn't even see any salad dressing. He slid a glance over his shoulder. She bit her thumbnail.

"I told you I'm not much of a cook."

"You did. But Gus was an excellent cook. I'm sure he had more that I could use." He began to rummage through the freezer and the cabinets. It was fine if Carmen didn't want to discuss what was bothering her. He could even accept her not wanting to remember flirting with him. But he could offer her comfort through his food. She would accept at least that from him.

CHAPTER 4

Carmen watched Liam move around her kitchen as if instinctively knowing where to find things. The lack of food in her refrigerator embarrassed her. It was fine for her, but Liam was a chef. He created things, fancy dishes with multiple ingredients. And she had nothing to offer him.

She continued to gnaw on the nub that remained of her thumbnail. Her stomach flopped. Liam shouldn't be here. She couldn't continue her wallowing in his presence. At least he bought her story about not remembering their night. And he was kind enough to lie right back instead of calling her out.

After starting another pot of coffee, the one item she'd been practically living on, she sat at the table and watched Liam. Incredible smells filled the kitchen and her stomach grumbled.

"What would you like to talk about?" he asked.

She didn't know what to say. She didn't think she'd actually spoken in days. No one had stopped by and she'd ignored her phone. She'd even lied to her family and said that she was sick so she could skip out on Thanksgiving dinner.

He looked over his shoulder and she shrugged. How could she explain the hole occupying the middle of her chest? It felt empty yet full of awful pain all at the same time. Guilt poked at her incessantly. She should've done more.

When she tried to inhale, the air got stuck and she hiccupped. That one small sound opened the floodgates and she couldn't stop the tears, couldn't swallow them down any more. A stream flowed over her cheeks and she couldn't get more than a hitching, halting breath.

"Hey."

Liam stood in front of her. She knew it was him of course, but she didn't look up. His hands grabbed her upper arms, pulling her from the chair and into his embrace. His arms circling her made it worse and full, body-racking sobs escaped. She grabbed fistfuls of his shirt as if it would ground her.

His hands smoothed down her back in rhythmic movements and he murmured quietly on the top of her head. She didn't know what he said. She allowed herself to let go.

Carmen cried until no more tears came. Her eyes were rough and scratched against the lids. Snot ran down above her lip and she'd swiped at it so many times that she'd rubbed the skin raw. She had no idea how long she stood in Liam's arms before being able to breathe again.

He never moved other than to touch her back. He said nothing to interfere with her meltdown. Like her father had said: Liam was a good man.

She finally stepped away from him, embarrassed at her outburst and mortified that she cried all over him. His shirt was disgusting with her tears and snot all over it. She wiped her sleeve down the front. "I'm sorry," she whispered.

"No worries." He touched her jaw and tilted her face up.

She couldn't imagine how bad she looked. She was not a pretty crier. She wasn't delicate and refined. The proof of which was smeared on his shirt. She tried to pull away, but he held her fast.

"Feel better?"

She rolled her eyes to meet his. "Not really. But I think I needed that. I'm sorry I dumped on you."

He brushed a thumb down her cheek and she remembered why she'd wanted to kiss him the other night. She licked her lips and stepped away before she made a bigger fool of herself.

"Why don't you go clean up and I'll finish dinner?"

"You don't have to stay. I'm okay."

He shrugged. "I'm staying anyway."

Carmen shuffled away to take a shower and hoped she'd feel more human. The shower felt better than she could've imagined. When was the last time she showered? Days? Carmen rolled her eyes at herself. How had she fallen apart so quickly?

She kept everything running for her parents for so long that she should've been able to hold herself together without thinking. After changing into fresh clothes—she couldn't believe she let Liam see her in her ratty pajamas—she applied a little makeup to look more like herself, just a little something to erase the evidence of her crying.

Back in the kitchen, she found Liam plating food. He made it look so effortless and beautiful. It was just food for her, but for him, it seemed like more. "Can I help with something?"

He looked up, concentration filling his face. "Nope. We're all set." He placed both plates on the table and pulled out a chair for her.

Is this guy for real?

When they were both settled in their seats, she said, "You

really didn't need to go through all this trouble, but I appreciate it."

His smile was subtle, like so much about Liam. He was probably the most unassuming guy she'd ever met. Not that her social circle was extensive. She looked at the food and tensed. On her best day she didn't have a good relationship with food. On a day like today… She released a slow breath and cut into the chicken. She had to eat at least some of it because Liam had done this for her. Besides, he would never believe she was really okay if she refused to eat.

She tried to surreptitiously scrape the buttery sauce off the meat without him noticing. The first tiny bite entered her mouth and her stomach growled again, this time in appreciation. The chicken almost melted on her tongue. It was so delicious. She allowed herself one more decent-sized bite and then focused on eating all the vegetables.

"Something wrong with the chicken?"

The line reappeared between Liam's eyebrows, so deep that it could've been a scar.

"No. It's really delicious. I just don't have much of an appetite." Under his watchful eye, she ate two more bites before draining a large glass of water. She smiled brightly. "I'm full. That was a really good meal."

Liam continued to watch her as he slowly chewed his own food. "I came here tonight because I wanted to talk to you about your dad's will."

She froze. "I don't want to talk about that right now if you don't mind. I'm not ready."

He nodded and finished eating. She cleaned up her plate and filled the sink with water. By the time she had the pans clean, Liam stood next to her, putting his empty dish in the water.

"Thanks again for dinner." She didn't know what else to say. He hovered in the kitchen, not making a move to leave.

"How about a movie?"

"Huh?"

He leaned against the counter and waited for her to turn. "I'm usually working late, so I'm free and not tired. Want to watch a movie?"

"Liam, I appreciate you checking on me and letting me cry all over you. But you don't need to stay. I'm okay. Admittedly, I wasn't as okay as I thought I was, but I don't need a babysitter."

The right corner of his mouth lifted. "I don't want to be a babysitter. I had a good time hanging out with you the other night and thought you did too."

"I did. And you're more than welcome to stay if it's because you want to. I don't want you to feel obligated to stay." She rinsed the last of the dishes and pulled the plug on the drain.

"I'd like to stay, but only if we can change the channel. You had your mom's Spanish soap operas on and I don't get those. Two years of high school Spanish won't help me understand."

She laughed. "I won't make you watch the telenovelas. As the guest, you get to pick the show."

After drying her hands and making sure the kitchen was put to rights, she followed him into the living room. He sat in the dead center of the couch, arms spread across the back, as if to stake his claim. When she came into the room, he patted the cushion beside him.

She took the spot, albeit a little reluctantly. He curved one arm on her shoulder and picked up the remote in his opposite hand. As he clicked through the channels, she settled against the couch and his body. It felt so good to be touched, to be held, that she wanted to enjoy it, but she feared she was reading more into it than she should.

They didn't really know each other and he had never

expressed an interest in her. In fact, after her drunken offer the other night, he'd pretty much rejected her. Yet tonight he made her dinner and now wanted to hold her on the couch.

Time to turn off her brain. She was spending too much time inside her own head. She'd have to get used to Liam being around. Her dad had made sure they'd be tied together. She had no idea what he'd been thinking.

Liam settled on some silly comedy, stuff with slapstick humor and crude jokes. But together they laughed. And for those two hours, she didn't feel the guilt and grief.

When the movie ended, Liam shifted away from her. A huge yawn forced its way from her body. Her emotional breakdown followed by a ridiculous amount of laughter had done her in.

Liam stood. "I'm going home. Are you going to be okay?"

"Yeah. Thanks for everything tonight." She stood to walk him out and nodded.

At the door, he said, "I work the dinner shift tomorrow, but I need to talk to you about the will. Can we meet for an early lunch?"

Carmen knew if she didn't agree, he would have doubts about whether she was okay. And they did need to discuss the will. Although she'd known her dad included him, she hadn't known to what extent. She'd never wanted to talk to her dad about it. After her mother's death she couldn't bear the thought of him dying, so she wouldn't discuss it.

"Sure. Let me know where. You still have my number?"

He nodded. "I'll call you in the morning."

He lingered at the open door, cold air pushing into the warm house. She thought he might say something else, but whatever it was died on his lips and he nodded again before walking to his car.

Exhaustion hit her hard. But before she dragged herself to bed, she gathered her notes and her dad's will to take with her to lunch. Like it or not, she and Liam had decisions to make, and they would be part of each other's lives for at least a while.

~

LIAM SPENT HALF his night and the entire morning trying to figure out how to talk to Carmen. He remembered what it was like after his dad died. The depression and misery, not wanting to think about him, but not being able to put him out of his head. But this was her future. They needed to take care of it as soon as possible.

He grabbed his work clothes and drove to the restaurant. He chose a place close to Carmen's house, even though it was out of his way. He figured she'd be most comfortable in her own neighborhood. When he got to the restaurant, she was waiting outside the door.

The wind blew her hair around her face. Her cheeks were pink from the cold, but she looked a million times better than she had when he'd arrived at her house last night. When she saw him, she smiled and waved. He ushered her through the door. "You could've waited inside for me. It's cold out."

"I'm fine. The fresh air felt good."

The hostess led them to a table and handed them menus. Carmen barely glanced at the menu before setting it aside. Liam studied his choices and tried to remember what he'd be eating with the staff at the restaurant tonight. He discovered he didn't care because he wasn't very hungry. He decided on a burger to keep it simple.

The waitress arrived with two glasses of water and asked if they were ready to order. He looked at Carmen.

"I'll have a garden salad. Low-fat Italian on the side and a coffee please."

"Is that really all you want?" He looked at her face trying to determine if she was hiding something.

"Salad is a good lunch."

He ordered his burger, but in the back of his mind, something about the way Carmen talked about salad felt off. He thought about how she'd picked at dinner last night. Maybe she was still in a funk and it was affecting how she ate. Who could blame her? Her life had been turned upside down in the last couple of weeks.

As soon as the waitress left, Carmen set a file folder on the table. "You wanted to talk about my dad's will, so I brought all of the information with me. I should've had the lawyer invite you to the reading. I wasn't thinking."

"So you knew about this? You knew he was leaving me part ownership in the food truck?" He was sure she hadn't known.

She shook her head. "I knew you were in the will. I never asked him what he was leaving you."

Liam couldn't read her. He'd thought she had been upset by this information, but now he wasn't convinced. "He shouldn't have done that. I have no right to his business. What do we have to do for me to sign it over to you?"

"He wanted you to have it, Liam. You were like a son to him." She reached out and laid her hand on top of his.

He'd been a pretty crappy son as of late. "But this belongs to you. This is your future, your inheritance."

She lifted her shoulders. "What am I going to do with it?"

"You can sell it. Use the money to do whatever you want to do." He suddenly realized that he had no idea what she might want to do. Ever since college, she'd been at home taking care of her family. That knowledge reassured him that she needed the business far more than he did.

She sighed. "I can't sell it—we can't sell it. We each own half, but my father has a provision in the will saying we can't sell it for a year." She puffed out her cheeks with a breath before continuing. "We can do whatever we want, even let it sit for the entire year. The problem with that is—"

"It loses value. By then, you'll just be selling a truck and not a business, not the business your dad built. That's not a realistic choice."

She turned her palms up on the table. "I don't know what to do."

"Would you want to run it?"

She shook her head. "I told you. I'm not a cook. I do the business end: the office stuff, inventory, invoices, taxes. I have no desire to be on the truck every day. I've thought about hiring someone. My cousin Pete worked with my dad off and on. He knows the routine."

Liam watched the way she spoke about her cousin. "But?"

"But he's not reliable. The off and on part came from his inability to show up on time. He became a bigger frustration for my dad than a help." She toyed with the edges of the folder, curling them up and then releasing.

The waitress arrived with their plates. Carmen put the folder on the seat beside her. "Do you know anyone who might want to run the truck?"

Liam thought for a minute. No one came to mind. Of course, anyone who had a job might consider it, depending on the pay. "At the risk of sounding crude, is the truck profitable?"

"That's not crude—it's business. Yes, we operate in the black. We own the truck and the equipment. My dad took a regular paycheck and paid me for the office. It's part of why I'm hesitant to let it sit for a year. My dad took his good reputation from the restaurant and it followed him on the food truck." She shook her head as she dipped a forkful of lettuce into the salad dressing. "I thought he was nuts when he suggested buying the truck."

"He got in right when it was becoming a popular trend, though. Smart man, your dad."

She nodded and he thought he saw the hint of tears again. He gave her a minute to calm her emotions. Squirting ketchup all over his mound of fries, he focused on his choices. Would he want to run the truck? For all his experience in a kitchen, he knew nothing about food trucks. He bit into the cheeseburger and found it dry, overcooked. He chewed and swallowed anyway.

Carmen looked at him, her face tilted to the left. "Do you find yourself criticizing every chef when you go out to eat?"

It was like she had read his thoughts. "I try not to. I don't usually say anything out loud. Why?"

She lifted one shoulder. "You had this look on your face. I don't know. I remember seeing it on my dad's face when we would go out. Not always, but whenever the food wasn't up to his standards."

He smiled, remembering Gus. "Yeah. I remember your dad's looks. He was a crotchety man when it came to food."

This brought a laugh from her and he liked the sound. She needed to remember to laugh with memories of Gus. He'd been lucky because he'd been surrounded by his siblings after his dad's death. Whenever one of them felt down, someone else had a funny story.

As her laughter faded to a smile, she said, "I guess you would see him that way. He rarely showed me that side. But I saw it sometimes in the kitchen when he talked to the staff."

Liam reached back in his mind for other stories about Gus to share with her, to help her feel better. For the next hour, they laughed together over tales from the Mexican restaurant where they had both done some growing up. Her salad plate was clean, his burger only half-eaten, but he wasn't hungry. He was enjoying himself too much.

With a glance at her watch, Carmen looked up at him

with wide eyes. "Am I making you late for work? I wasn't paying attention to the time. I'm so sorry. I forget that other people actually have jobs and stuff to get to."

"I'm fine. Speaking of jobs, what are you going to do?"

Her shoulders lifted with her inhale, like she needed additional oxygen in order to form an answer. "I guess it depends on the truck. I'll have to help whoever we hire. I'll continue the office. If we can't find someone, I guess I'll look for another job. In all honesty, I haven't given it much thought."

"I was just wondering. I'd hate to see you turn into the crazy cat lady of your neighborhood," he joked.

She threw a balled-up napkin and hit him on the forehead. He tossed it back and it landed in the V of her shirt, nestled between her breasts. She smiled and shook her head.

"Need me to get that for you?" The words slipped out before he thought. He shouldn't be flirting with her. She was grieving. He didn't know if she had a boyfriend. But if she had, he surely wouldn't have left her alone this long, would he?

She pulled the napkin out and tucked it under her plate. She sighed and he couldn't help but notice the rise and fall of her chest. To cover his obnoxious thoughts, he reached into his pocket for his wallet and waved the waitress over.

As he handed his card to the waitress, he said to Carmen, "You should come to Porter's for dinner one night. You could see where I work."

Damn, was he trying to set up a date with a girl who was now his business partner?

"I wouldn't want to bother you at work."

And she shot him down. After signing the receipt for lunch, he said, "I'll think about people to hire, but it might be easier if I knew more about the business. Will you have some time to go over things, give me a crash course?"

"Sure. Whenever you want. I've updated the web site so

customers know the truck will be off the road for a while, but we don't want to stay out too long. We'll lose some of the best spots going into winter. Although another option is to close for the winter. Some trucks do that. They run during nicer weather. The winter can be brutal. Profits are always down."

He stood. "Let's think about it. If Gus ran it over the winter, he must've had a reason. We have your cousin as a backup, right? We'll work on it and figure it out."

Liam walked her to her car and waited until she pulled away. She wasn't the only one who needed to make some decisions about life.

CHAPTER 5

Three days later, Liam walked out of Porter's after what had to have been his worst night as a chef ever. Jonathan had changed the specials without telling Liam. He hadn't even asked Liam for input this time. Then he managed to purchase the cheapest cut of beef possible, all in the name of saving on the bottom line.

The dining experience of customers for that evening had been worse than if they'd gone to a corner coffee shop. And he knew he would take the blame. No one ever said the owner was responsible if the cut of meat was tough or it was the wrong cut for a particular dish—no, the chef always took the blame. He couldn't even deny it. He should've fought harder to do something different, to make it work, but his heart wasn't in it.

Too many other things were pulling at him. He'd spent his free time looking over the web site for the food truck and some spreadsheets Carmen had emailed him. They'd spoken briefly a couple of times about the truck, and although she sounded better, they'd kept the conversation simple and business-oriented.

And now, the weight of the certified letter stared at him from the passenger seat in his car. He'd stopped by the post office to pick it up before work and had assumed it was paperwork from Gus's lawyer needing his signature. That had only been part of it. A letter from Gus was included. Liam hadn't opened it yet, knowing he needed to focus at work.

As he drove away from the heart of the city, the small white envelope taunted him. He drove to O'Leary's Pub, hoping one of his brothers would be there. He didn't want to be alone when he read this. After parking in the lot, he grabbed the envelope, tucked it in his pocket, and entered the bar.

The warm air wrapped around him as he was transported to the safety of his family. Whenever he felt overwhelmed by anything, he could step into this space, even more than in his childhood home, and feel calm.

It had been in this kitchen that he'd first experimented. It was here that he drank his first beer. Here that he mourned the passing of his father. Patrick O'Leary's presence filled the space even though it had been years since his death. Liam pushed forward toward the bar.

About an hour until closing and a crowd still filled the place. Ryan had taken over the helm of the business and done right by their family. Before taking on O'Leary's, Ryan had already built his own bar in the suburbs. Liam marveled at how he'd managed. Wondered where the courage came from to strike out without fear of failing. Ryan had always been sure of himself.

Colin, not so much.

The two oldest O'Leary brothers had taught him plenty. Colin, as the oldest, should've taken over O'Leary's, but he tended to rush into things without thought. Ryan had been the steady one. Right now, Liam would appreciate advice from either of them.

He sat on a stool and waited. Jenna popped the tops on a couple of beers before she smiled at him in recognition.

"Hey, Liam. Haven't seen you around in a while."

"Been busy. Are either of my brothers around?"

"Yeah, Colin just ran into the back for a minute. Want me to find him?"

"Nah, I'll wait."

"Can I get you something?"

"A Guinness."

She set a full glass in front of him. He hadn't had a Guinness in a long time either. The thick brew always reminded him of Dad. Jenna went to deliver drinks and Liam inhaled the rich scent of the stout before sipping.

Another drink and then he pulled the envelope from his pocket and flipped it over between his fingers. He heard Colin before he saw him; the guy was always whistling or singing if he wasn't talking. And he liked to talk. Liam had somehow skipped out on the talking gene most of his siblings had.

He smiled thinking that his younger sister Moira had gotten his share.

Colin grabbed a towel and began wiping down the bar without noticing him.

"Hey, you missed a spot," Liam called.

Colin looked up and smiled. "What are you doing here?"

"Came to see you. Or Ryan. Whichever I could find first."

"I guess you got lucky then, because we all know I'm the better bet." Colin tossed the rag under the counter and leaned his elbows on the shiny mahogany. "What's up?"

Liam licked his lips and drank more beer before starting. "Remember the Mexican restaurant I worked at while in school?" He didn't wait for Colin to respond because the answer didn't mean much. "The owner, Gus, died. He sold the restaurant a few years ago and bought a food truck. I just found out that he left me half ownership in the truck."

"Wow. Maybe Ryan would've been the better brother here." Colin blew out a breath. "I want to say congratulations, but it doesn't seem right, you know? What are you going to do? Who has the other half?"

"His daughter, Carmen, is the other half. She ran the office of the business for her dad, but she doesn't want to run the truck. She's not a cook. We've talked about hiring some-one, but…"

"Are you thinking about doing it? I thought you wanted a restaurant." Colin poured himself a glass of water and walked around the bar to sit beside Liam.

"I do. I think. But Porter's doesn't feel like enough anymore. Not for a while now. Yet this isn't something I ever considered. At the same time, Gus was smart. We can't sell for at least a year, so we have to do something with it." He held up the envelope. "And then I got this today."

"What is it?"

"A letter from Gus, but I haven't opened it yet."

Colin looked at him and waved his hands as if to ask what he was waiting for. Liam shrugged and slid a finger under the flap. With a deep breath, he pulled the letter out.

Liam,

I know you are probably surprised to receive this letter and part ownership in my company. I chose you, Liam, because you are a good man, and I know you will do right by my daughter. Carmen will be lost now that both me and Inez are gone. My fear is that my family will tell Carmen what to do. I trust you. She needs time to find her own way, to learn what she wants in life. This is her time. Help her find her freedom. Take care of my Carmen.

Gus

Liam stared at the letter and reread the words.

"Well?" Colin asked.

"He wants me to take care of Carmen."

Colin chuckled. "I bet that'll be a hardship."

Liam flicked his brother a dirty look. He refolded the letter and slid it back into the envelope. After a healthy drink from his glass he turned to Colin. "I think I need to take over the truck."

"Because of a letter? That doesn't seem like a good idea. You should explore all your options."

"This coming from the most impulsive member of our family."

"You should learn from my fuckups."

"The letter's part of it. He trusts me to take care of things. I feel like I owe him." And he knew Gus's words to be true. Carmen was lost. He didn't know if he could help her, but he could certainly ease her worry by running the truck. "Taking over the truck will buy me time to figure out what I want. And if we sell in a year, I can use the profit for my own place."

"As long as you know what you're getting into." He shoved off his stool. "Let me know if there's anything I can help with."

"You're the last person I'd come to for help in the kitchen. When I want someone to flirt with my customers, I'll call."

Colin's hand smacked his chest. "You wound me. I'm off the market now. Elizabeth might kill me if I flirted with other women."

"Nah, she knows it's in your DNA. You can't help yourself." Liam finished his beer and gave his big brother a hug. "Thanks for the talk."

"I don't feel like I helped much."

"Being here helps." Liam didn't know how to explain his need for a connection to their father. He assumed Colin would understand without the words. It was one of the reasons Colin continued to work at O'Leary's even though he had a bar of his own. They all came home.

On his way back to his car, Liam thought about Carmen again. Where would she go to feel the comfort of home? He pictured her in her house. She lived there, but it didn't strike him as the place she found peace. He drove home and then worked on drafting his resignation letter. Liam just hoped he wasn't making the biggest mistake of his career.

CARMEN SPENT the morning scanning help wanted ads, not even sure what she was looking for. She had a degree in business management. She'd run her father's business for years, but had no other practical experience. She had no idea what she wanted. So instead, she focused her energy on the house. They hadn't painted the walls in years. In fact, she couldn't remember the last time any home improvements were done.

She wandered the aisles of the home improvement store for hours, gathering paint chips and samples, picking out possible light fixtures, and area rugs. She created a long list as she walked: one page for materials, including prices and model numbers, another page for things she'd have to pay someone else to do. With a new job to occupy herself, she went home, content to produce spreadsheets for her desired home improvement projects.

Eyeball-deep in Excel, she the ringing of her phone surprised her. She answered absently. "Hello."

"Carmen? It's Liam."

The deep sound of his voice scattered her thoughts. "Hi."

"Got a few minutes?"

She shoved her laptop away. "Sure."

"I'm in."

"What?"

"I'll run the truck. I'm turning in my resignation this afternoon. I have to give my boss a couple of weeks to find a new chef. It would be a bad move to leave him high and dry. Then I'll still need time to figure out everything about the truck, so I think we'll be back on the road within a month. Will that work?"

"Whoa. Wait." She stood and paced, trying to absorb what he was saying. "What do you mean you're going to run the truck?"

"Just what I said."

"But you're a chef."

"So was your dad. And if I'm not mistaken, I'll be cooking on the truck."

Her heart kicked. This hadn't been any of the scenarios she'd imagined after the reading of her dad's will. She'd never thought Liam would walk away from a restaurant to take on the truck. After their few interactions, she'd really been counting on him as a silent partner. "Why?"

"I'm ready for a change. If I'm running the truck, we'll be in good shape until we decide what to do. When the year's up, we can reevaluate."

He sounded so sure of himself and his decision, as if this had always been his life plan. She couldn't remember a time when she was that confident about anything. "Are you really sure?" She felt the need to ask regardless of the way he sounded. She knew better than anyone how easy it was to project one image while feeling something different.

She'd done it for years with her dad. She'd done it so often sometimes she wasn't even aware she was doing it.

"I'm sure, Carmen. Are you trying to get rid of me?"

"No. I just don't want you to walk away from your life. We can figure something else out." A bit of panic rose at the thought of him giving up his dreams. At least when she'd done it, it had been for family. She was nothing to him.

"The decision's made. I'll let you know when I have things settled at work."

"Okay." It was a lame response, but what else could she say?

"We'll talk soon." He disconnected as her doorbell rang.

Carmen stood staring at her phone, unable to move. The shock of Liam's announcement settled deep in her. The doorbell sounded again and she shuffled to the living room to answer the door.

Rosa rushed past her without a greeting. Her long brown hair was pulled back into a tight ponytail. It wasn't until Carmen closed the door that Rosa said, "What took so long? It's frickin' cold out there."

Carmen noticed Rosa wasn't wearing a coat, which explained the complaint. "Uh, I was on the phone."

"What, and you can't walk and talk at the same time?" She flopped on the couch. "You should just give me a key and then you wouldn't have to let me in."

Rosa had been pushing for over a year to move into the house. She wanted desperately to get away from her family, but she didn't want the responsibility of having to pay rent. Carmen had used her father as an excuse to not have Rosa move in, but now, she'd been considering it. The house was too big for Carmen to live in by herself, but something held her back.

She wasn't sure she wanted to keep the house. She still hadn't figured out what she did want.

"Why are you here?"

"I came to visit. See what you're up to."

"And?"

"And I fought with my mom. I needed to get out of there. She's just so picky." Rosa slipped into a heavy accent. "Rosa, you wear too much makeup. Rosa, put on more clothes. Rosa, you need a better job. Find a good man, Rosa."

Carmen smiled at her cousin. "You should take that act on stage. You've got her down."

"Ugh. I always wished your mom was mine. She was so cool. I miss her."

"So do I. But she wasn't always cool. She nagged, too. Just about different things." Carmen sat next to Rosa. "Maybe your mom wouldn't yell so much if you were a good girl like me."

Rosa snorted. Sometimes Carmen had a hard time believing there was only two years between them. Rosa always seemed so much younger. Or maybe Carmen just felt old.

"So who were you talking to?"

"Huh?"

Rosa pointed to the phone that Carmen still gripped. "Oh. Liam called. He decided to quit his job so he can run the food truck."

"What?"

Carmen shook her head as she spoke as if to force everything to make sense. "We share ownership, so we discussed hiring someone to run it. But he called to tell me he's ready for a change and wants to take over."

"Fuck that shit. That's your business, Carmen. You should fight the will. What was your dad thinking?"

"He was thinking that I'm not a chef, and I don't want to be. Liam offered to sign over his half to me, but that wouldn't be right. My dad wanted him to have it. I already have everything else and it's too much." She set her phone on the table and leaned back into the couch, unable to get comfortable.

Rosa still looked angry on her behalf. "What's his story? He just shows up out of nowhere and takes half your business?"

"He moved on after working at the restaurant. He finished school and became a chef. Dad kept in touch with him. Liam was like a son to him."

"He didn't need a son. He had you."

"But I never wanted to cook with him. I did everything I could to get out of the kitchen. Liam loved being there, even if all he did was wash dishes." She didn't really know how she knew that because she'd never had a conversation with Liam about it. Maybe she was just making an assumption, but she didn't think so. It wasn't like he came into work skipping with excitement. It was more that he intently watched everything so he could learn. People didn't do that unless they were invested.

"Still think it's crazy. What's Wonder Bread know about making tacos?"

Carmen felt the need to defend Liam and her father's choice. "He went to culinary school. He's a chef. He learned from my dad. I'm sure he's capable."

Rosa sighed. "I worry about you. You're always putting everyone else first. I don't want him to take advantage."

Carmen felt the laugh bubbling up. "Trust me. He's not."

"Okay." She rolled her eyes. "I'm bored with this conversation. Let's do something."

"Like what? I have work to do around here."

Rosa stood. "I'll help. Let's go."

Carmen joined her cousin and explained that she needed to get rid of her parents' bed and decide what to do with the rest of the furniture. As usual, Rosa only half-listened because she was already turning the radio on, blaring music for them to dance to while they worked.

As stressed as she'd been, dancing through the house with Rosa felt right. They worked and laughed and at the end of the night, Carmen began to feel like she would be able to find her way back to being herself. She needed to discover who she was after the grief lifted and she only had herself to care for.

CHAPTER 6

*L*iam walked into Porter's earlier than usual so he would have time to talk with Jonathan before the rest of the staff showed. He quickly changed and then knocked on Jonathan's office door.

"Come in."

Liam entered the cramped office, suddenly nervous. He'd been so sure of this move earlier, but now, his stomach sank. "Hi, Jonathan. I need to talk to you." He reached out and handed him the paper.

"What's this?"

"My resignation. I have the opportunity to do something a little different. I inherited a food truck."

Jonathan laughed as he read the letter. Then he looked up. "You're serious?"

"Yes." When had Liam ever joked with Jonathan?

"You're leaving here, leaving being a chef, for a food truck?"

"I'm still a chef. Just a different location."

"You're going to run a roach coach. That's not being a chef. You'll have no real opportunity."

Liam took a deep breath. "With all respect, I don't feel I have much opportunity here either."

Jonathan stood, dropping the resignation on the desk. "Then go."

"I'll give you two weeks. I'm not trying to screw you and leave you with no chef."

Jonathan pointed to his chest. "*I* am a chef. You want out, pack your shit and go."

Liam strode out of the office before he did something he would regret. He didn't want to get a reputation as a troublemaker. If the food truck failed, he'd need to find a new job and couldn't afford to have Jonathan saying anything negative about him. Back in the kitchen, he packed his knives.

For almost three years, this had been his home. No, not really home. It had never been his place, but he'd spent more time here than anywhere. He would miss it. He thought about staying until the rest of the staff arrived so he could say good-bye, but then Jonathan slammed out of his office.

"Still here?"

Staying any longer wouldn't be welcome. Maybe he'd stop by the bar they liked to go to after service to say his good-byes. He'd have the added benefit of not having to do it in front of Jonathan; he never joined them for a drink.

With his knives rolled and his change of clothes in hand, Liam walked out the back door. Instead of the continued sinking feeling he'd had in the office, he felt lighter, less stressed. In his car, he called Moira to invite her to dinner. Unfortunately, she didn't answer. Busy again. That girl had a social calendar that would rival any celebrity.

Next, he called Carmen to let her know his schedule had opened up.

"That can't be good," she said. "He told you to get out?"

"He was mad. Don't worry about it. Bottom line, I'm free to get the feel of working on the truck."

"I have the information you need. I have the regulations for you to read. I also have the rest of the books."

"What time works for you?"

"Any time."

"I'll come over at nine tomorrow?"

"How about I come to you? I've been cooped up in the house and it'll do me good to get out."

"You sure?"

"Yeah. You're always coming here."

"I don't mind."

"I know. I'll bring coffee. How do you take yours?"

"Black."

"Okay. See you at nine." She disconnected, and he didn't know what to think about her wanting to come to his apartment.

He brushed aside the thought. She probably did need to get out of her house.

Driving back home, the edgy feeling returned. The added free time with nothing to do got to him, so he decided to cook. He could've called any of his other siblings and he'd probably find someone who was free for dinner, but instead he called Lily. She rarely worked the dinner shift at the diner and she was always up for a cooking lesson.

"Hey, Liam. What's up?"

"You want to come over and cook dinner with me?"

"I thought you had to work."

"I'll explain when you get here."

"Who said I was free?"

He heard the playfulness in her voice. "You always have time for me and a cooking lesson."

"You don't have to be cocky about it. I'll be there soon. Want me to bring anything?"

"Nope. I have it covered."

Thirty minutes later, Lily stood at his door with a bottle

of wine and a package. He took the wine and asked, "What's that?"

"A present." In the living room, she opened the box and pulled out a bunch of pillows and a blanket. "I'm tired of your living room looking like you don't even live here. I tried to figure out what you would like, and I thought you needed something to make the place more inviting, more comfortable."

She tossed two purple pillows on his black couch and then threw a red one on his recliner. The blanket had the Chicago Bears logo on it, so at least she got that much right. He loved a good football game. Hell, he loved a bad football game.

"I thought this would be good for curling up and watching the game." She folded it in half and laid it across the back of the couch.

"Thanks. That was really thoughtful." He turned toward the kitchen. "I was thinking we could make some pork tonight if you're up for something new."

"Ooo...I don't really like pork. Unless it's bacon. Everyone loves bacon."

He set the bottle of wine on the counter. "There's more to pork than breakfast."

She went to the sink to wash her hands, but looked at him like she didn't quite buy it.

"What kind of pork have you tried?"

"Fried pork chops. My mom makes them at the diner."

"I thought we agreed we wouldn't compare our cooking to what's served at the diner. I know you love your mom, and diner food has its place, but don't go there."

"Okay, I'm game. What are we making?"

"Carnitas."

"What?"

"Mexican pork tacos." He pulled the meat from the refrigerator. He figured he needed to brush up on his Mexican cooking. "It ties into the news I have."

"You mean the news about why you're not working?"

"I quit."

She dropped the towel she'd been drying her hands on. "You quit? Porter's? Why?"

"I have a new offer."

"That's so exciting." She jumped at him and threw her arms around him in a hug, squeezing tightly. "Where is it? I didn't even know you were looking."

"I wasn't looking. This kind of fell into my lap."

She released him and he got the remaining ingredients out. Then he told her about Gus and the food truck.

Lily still needed guidance on her knife skills, so Liam instructed her again, showing her how to hold the knife and the vegetables. He curled his fingertips in on top of the pepper and sliced the knife down in front of them, slowing his motions for her to observe how he moved.

She sighed. "I don't think I'm ever going to get this."

In truth, he was starting to doubt it too. "Here." He walked behind her and picked up the pepper and handed her the knife.

He placed his hand on top of hers, protecting her fingers, and guided her chopping. Once she had the rhythm, he stepped back and went to his own knife. He felt her gaze on him. From the corner of his eye, he looked at her. "Pay attention before you slice a finger."

"Yes, sir," she said with a smirk. "What made you decide to take over the food truck?"

"It's something Gus would've wanted. His daughter, Carmen, has a lot to handle right now."

Lily set her knife down. "Look at you, going all white knight. When does this new adventure start?"

He finished chopping while he spoke. "I'm not sure. The

truck is ready. It's an established business, so it's just a matter of getting back on the road. Before I start, I'm going to work with Carmen to understand everything."

The more he thought about it, the more excited he became. It had been a long time since he'd felt the eagerness of something new. He put the pork in the pan to cook. "We have about an hour for the meat to be done."

"Then let's open the wine to celebrate."

"A little early for wine, don't you think?"

"It's fine." She reached for the bottle, but he grabbed it first.

While he worked the corkscrew, Lily brought glasses from the cabinet. He filled their glasses and they took the drinks, along with the bottle, to the living room. Lily drank her first glass quickly and poured a second. If she kept up that pace, she wouldn't make it to dinner.

After one big gulp of her second glass, she inhaled, and blurted, "I think I want to go to culinary school."

The admission didn't shock him. Lily had shown an interest in cooking the entire time he'd known her. "Congratulations?"

She rolled her eyes. "How did that sound? I've decided to tell my mom."

He set his glass on the table and turned, pulling one knee on the couch. "I think you need to own it first. Either you want to go, plan to go, or not. If you say you think you do, she can persuade you not to follow your dream. Do you want to go to culinary school?"

"Yes."

"Then lead with that."

She blew out a breath and drank more wine.

"Why is this so hard?" he asked.

She stared into her wine. "Because I wasted so much time

doing nothing. I graduated high school and went to community college and screwed around."

"You weren't ready to figure out your life. You didn't know what you wanted to do. Where's the crime in that?"

"She'll think it's another whim."

"So prove to her it's not."

"Easier said than done." She settled back on the cushion with her glass and clicked the TV on with the remote. She put on some silly afternoon talk show and sipped her wine.

He couldn't personally relate to her dilemma because he had already known back in high school that he wanted to be a chef. He was like Ryan in that way; they both knew what they wanted and went for it. Colin had been the wanderer of their family, so it wasn't as if he had *no* experience with it.

He tuned out the yelling on the screen and thought about the food truck. Would he want to change the menu? Introduce new items? Make things fresh? He wondered if Carmen would be open to suggestions.

Lily polished off her second glass and went for a third.

"You should probably slow down." He'd known opening a bottle this early would be a mistake.

"I'm fine. It'll help me process things. So with this new job, does that mean you'll be free at night like regular people? I bet you won't have to work holidays anymore. What food trucks crawl through the city on holidays, right?"

He hadn't even thought about those perks. It had been so long since he held a normal job, it hadn't crossed his mind. "You're right."

As she sipped more wine, she inched closer, until her leg touched his. "Will you miss the restaurant?"

He thought for a moment. "I'll miss the chaos of a busy dinner service. I'll miss my staff. Even though Jonathan was the one who hired them, they worked for me. We were a team. Yeah, I'll definitely miss being part of a team."

In truth, he'd never worked alone. It would definitely be a new experience.

"I wish I could be like you," Lily said quietly. "To not be afraid to take a chance. Just jump out there and do it."

He couldn't hold back his laugh. Of all the O'Learys, he was the least likely to jump into anything. "It's not jumping in. It's a calculated risk based on something landing in my lap. If Gus didn't leave me his truck, I probably would've stayed at Porter's indefinitely."

She shook her head slowly, the alcohol obviously catching up with her. "No, you would've gone out on your own. You were just waiting for the right opportunity. You're slow to act, but when you're sure, you're all in. I like that about you."

Liam went to check on dinner. He didn't ask Lily to join him since he didn't think she was capable of cooking without hurting herself. By the time he had dinner ready, most of the wine was gone, and he knew she wouldn't be going anywhere any time soon.

CARMEN WALKED down the hall toward Liam's apartment trying to figure out what she'd been thinking by suggesting she come here. She held tight to the carrier with their coffee as her bag with her laptop and binder of information pulled at her shoulder. Besides wanting to get away from her house, she wanted to see where Liam lived. She wanted to learn more about the man whose life would be intertwined with hers for at least the next year.

Still, it would've made more sense for him to come to her house; that's where the truck was parked. He would need time to get the lay of the land if he planned to restart the truck and hit the road.

As she neared Liam's door, it flung open and a cute

blonde rushed out, calling over her shoulder, "Late for work. Call you later." As she rushed past Carmen, she swooped her hair into a ponytail with a smile on her face.

That moment cemented why Carmen wanted to come here. She wanted to know about Liam. A sudden shot of guilt hit her because she and Liam had never shared too many personal details, so she hadn't known he had a girlfriend. At least it explained why he'd turned down her offer to come into her house when she was drunk. Carmen sighed and knocked on Liam's door.

He swung it open with a smile on his face. "Hi."

She extended the arm with the coffee, and he accepted it. "I got you black, but there's cream and sugar in my bag." She followed him into his apartment. His living room was pretty bare. They would've definitely been more comfortable at her house. His looked like a showroom, except for the ugly throw pillows that didn't match anything.

He closed the door behind her. "I figured we'd work in the kitchen. That way we can spread out on the table while we talk."

She turned and faced an open layout that revealed a gorgeous kitchen. The space was everything the living room wasn't. It looked lived in and used. Even though it was filled with things she would probably never personally use, she loved it. It was the kind of place her dad would've appreciated.

Liam set the coffee on the table and swung his arm out. "This is my apartment." He pointed behind her. "Living room. This is obviously the kitchen." Then he pointed behind the kitchen. "My bedroom and bathroom are back there."

"Nice place." It was the kind of apartment she'd imagined herself living in after college. A place to call her own. But her living room would be comfortable and the kitchen bare. She took her bag off her shoulder and laid it on the table. She shook off her coat and hung it on the back of the chair. "Ready to start?"

"Yep. I've checked out the web site and read some articles on food trucks, but I still feel like I know nothing."

Carmen slid her laptop out of the bag and then handed him the binder. "This is stuff my dad put together when he was planning to buy the truck. It's filled with articles and ideas, but it also has all the regulations you'll need to learn. Screw with those and the fines are astronomical."

Liam rolled his shoulders as he opened the binder. He scanned pages while she booted up her computer. Why was it that silence with Liam felt more comforting than silence alone? Quiet was still quiet.

He flipped past the articles and went to the regulations. "Two hundred feet from any restaurant?"

"Yeah."

"Downtown is filled with restaurants."

She waited until he got to the worst part.

"No way."

She didn't have to look up to know what he was reading. "Yes way."

"Walgreens and 7-Eleven are not restaurants. They're convenience stores. Who the hell came up with these rules?"

"That's the city hard at work. The Restaurant Association has a lot of pull. Food trucks cut into their profits. We threaten them, so they don't want us around."

He flipped the page. "How do you find a good spot where people can find you?"

"Some places are established. Social media works wonders, if you use it right."

Liam chuckled. "I can't imagine Gus on Twitter."

Carmen smiled. "No. That was one of my jobs. Anything related to the computer or paperwork fell on me." She waited a beat. "I'd be more than happy to pass it on to you if you prefer."

He shook his head. "If it's working, don't mess with it."

She'd hoped maybe he would want to mess with it. Social media was one of the things she didn't enjoy. She snapped her fingers. "I was hoping to dump that job."

"Maybe we can hire someone to take it over. My sister Moira is always on those sites."

"We can think about that as we get into spring. There won't be extra money through the winter."

Liam went back to the binder and she took in her surroundings. She didn't know what she'd expected from Liam's apartment. The kitchen definitely suited him. She glanced back at the living room. The only sign of a woman's touch were a couple of throw pillows, which seemed completely out of place.

Carmen drank her coffee and questioned yet again why she needed to be here. She could've emailed the books to Liam and dropped off the binder. But as she watched him studying the information, she knew she wanted to be here because she enjoyed being with him. They didn't have to talk, but if they did, it was fun.

He suddenly slammed the binder shut. "I can't sit here and read this in one sitting. Is it okay for me to keep it?"

"Sure. I don't need it for anything."

"Then let's get to the fun stuff: the menu."

"What about it?"

"Is it always the same? It's pretty simple, so I wonder how you keep people coming back."

"Dad kept the menu consistent. A couple of times, early on, he tried to introduce new items, but they didn't sell. One of the downsides to a food truck is that people put us on the same level as fast food. When they go to McDonald's, they don't want different. They want to know exactly what to expect. They see us the same way. In addition, the price has to be competitive. Like it or not, we're competing with all of those fast food places."

Liam stared at her as intently as he had the binder while he drank his coffee. He absorbed what she said, but didn't comment. When she finished, he sat back a little and then scratched at his jaw. He'd trimmed the scruff a little, but it looked like the beard was there to stay.

"How do we change that perception? We're better than fast food. Well, that's what I'm assuming since I've eaten Gus's food. How do we convince people to try new things and be willing to pay more for them?"

"Got me," she answered. She and her father had racked their brains for months to accomplish that and nothing they'd come up with worked.

"I guess I have to stay with tacos to start then. Did you by chance get your dad to write his recipes down?"

"I tried. He wrote some down, but you know how he cooked. He eyeballed everything and tasted until it was right. He didn't follow a recipe."

"Then I really have my work cut out for me. I haven't cooked Mexican since I worked with your dad. Even then, I mostly watched." He set his coffee on the table, and his face became more serious, as if that was even possible. "How are you doing?"

"Good."

He reached out and touched her hand. "Don't give me the answer you toss out to everyone because it's expected."

Again, embarrassment flushed through her. She'd broken down in his arms. He'd seen her at her worst. Did she even thank him for everything he'd done? She nodded. "I really am better. Rosa came over yesterday and we cleared out more of my dad's stuff. I made lists of things I want to do around the house. You know, projects that have gone neglected for too long."

"So you plan to stay?"

She pulled her hand back from his. "For now. I don't know what I want. I looked at ads for jobs, but even there, I couldn't focus. It's been so long since I thought about my career and what I want that I wasn't sure where to look."

"At the risk of sounding tacky, are you okay on money?"

"Yeah, my dad made sure I'd be okay. Thanks for asking." She slid her coffee out of the way and moved her computer to face him. "Here are the rest of the books. The spreadsheet I sent you before was this year's, but I thought you might want access to older stuff, to be able to see how we've grown."

For the next couple of hours, they poured over the books and the regulations together. The information was dry, but talking through everything with Liam made it interesting and even fun. They laughed and joked, and Carmen knew that being in business with Liam would be an excellent prospect.

CHAPTER 7

*L*iam had never had a more difficult time focusing as he had during the last two hours. He and Carmen looked at spreadsheets and laughed over some of the information Gus had saved. But part of his brain kept getting caught on the sweater she wore that hugged every freaking curve she had. His hands itched to run over those curves. Then she opened her mouth, and he was reminded that she was a smart businesswoman, his partner, not a woman to get into his bed.

Although he had a basic understanding of how to run a restaurant, the more she spoke of profit and loss and tax information, he started to glaze over. How had he ever thought he'd be able to run his own restaurant just because he knew how to cook? He'd always known there was more to it, but he never looked into it since he wasn't ready to branch out on his own.

He must've been staring at Carmen because she suddenly said, "What?" Then she wiped at her face as if she had something smeared on her.

"Nothing. I was just struck by how lucky I am to have you

as a partner in this. I would be completely lost."

Her eyes darted away and a hint of pink rose in her cheeks. "It's really not hard once you get the basics down. In fact, a lot of it is the same thing over and over."

"Still. Thank you for taking the time to teach me."

Her gaze returned to his. "Thanks for taking over the truck. I hope you don't end up regretting it." She closed her computer and shoved it in her bag, obviously intent on leaving. Liam didn't want her to go.

"What's your rush?"

She lifted a shoulder. "I gave you everything I've got. You said you need time to read through the binder. Did you want me to stay and watch you read?" Her lips spread wide in a teasing smile.

"No, but I thought we could hang out, maybe do something fun. I haven't been jobless in years."

"You're not jobless. Taco Taxi is your new job." She pointed at the information spread on his kitchen table. "And you have plenty to do."

"I work well under pressure. Let's go do something fun."

"Like what?"

His brain fumbled through ideas that wouldn't sound like a date. "Let's check out our competition."

"How?"

"I bet you know where to find all of the most popular trucks. We'll drive around and sample each of them. It'll show me what we're up against. I'm sure Gus did that, right? He would want to know who he had to fight for business." He piled the binder and loose sheets of paper on the corner of the table. Then he went in search of his coat.

Carmen stayed rooted in her spot.

"Not a good idea?" he asked.

"It actually sounds like a very good idea. And I don't think my dad did that. When he started, there were only a couple of other trucks. He spent so many hours working that he didn't have much time." Still, she hesitated.

"Tasting the competition would be a business expense, wouldn't it?"

She nodded.

"Then let's go."

"Are you sure you want me to go with you?"

He slid his arms into his jacket. "Why wouldn't I? We're partners. You'll notice things I wouldn't pay attention to, like price and location."

She bit her lip and he knew he almost had her. He didn't know why she was so hesitant. They had fun together.

Finally, her shoulders relaxed and she smiled. "Okay."

He held the door open for her and he followed her out. Liam pushed aside his attraction and focused on building a strong partnership and friendship.

THE NEXT DAY, Carmen didn't know what she was doing. She and Liam had spent hours together yesterday driving all over the city to follow food trucks. In the end, they only managed to hit about five, but as anxious as she'd been about facing all that food, Liam insisted they share and sample different things. She'd only consumed a bite or two of each item and felt no guilt afterward. It had been the first time in years that she'd been able to eat out without being self-conscious and worrying about how much she ate.

Now, she found herself primping in front of the mirror like she was preparing for a date. But Liam couldn't be a date; he had a girlfriend, or something. They never did get around to discussing the cute blonde who had rushed out of his apartment the previous morning. As the day wore on, it seemed to matter less and less. Liam shared so much of his life, his love for cooking and food, and what he hoped to have one day. Listening to him made her envious because he had dreams. She no longer remembered hers.

When she got back to her car in the afternoon, Liam said he would come over today to actually get into the truck and get a feel for how everything worked. She looked out the kitchen window at the truck sitting in the driveway. Her chest tightened. She hadn't stepped foot in it since her dad died. Pete had been kind enough to clean it out for her, so she wouldn't have to.

Thinking of Pete reminded her that he'd called while she was out yesterday. He wondered what she was doing with the truck and if she needed any help. She blew out a breath. After Liam got settled, she'd call Pete and let him know…what? She and Liam still hadn't discussed anything about hiring help. Although her dad had run the truck mostly by himself, he'd always said a second person was needed.

Her doorbell rang and she wrapped a scarf around her neck and grabbed the truck keys. She opened the door to see Liam holding two cups of coffee. His smile wasn't enthusiastic, but more of a sly hello. Even though they had laughed and joked over the last couple of weeks, she had yet to see Liam fully smile, like he was happy. Instead, his smile often looked like he was holding back—like he had a secret tucked away.

Unfortunately, she never mastered such a smile and she couldn't help but respond with a grin that took over her whole mouth. "Good morning." She stepped aside so he could come into the house.

"Morning." He closed the door behind him and followed her through the house to the kitchen. It was the one room he seemed most comfortable in.

"You want to head out now, or finish your coffee first?"

"Always coffee first." He drank and she watched his throat work with the gulps.

As she sipped from her own cup, she averted her eyes. She couldn't stand any more embarrassment when it came to Liam, otherwise she'd never be able to face him for work.

"Something wrong with the coffee?"

"Nope. It's perfect," she answered still looking out the window at the truck.

"What's bothering you?"

"I haven't been in the truck since before Dad died. Pete cleaned it out for me, so it's not gross or anything, but I haven't been there. I'm trying to decide if that's because I've been busy with everything else or if I've intentionally avoided it."

Liam stepped closer and rubbed a hand on her back. "A little of both, I suspect. After my dad died, it took me a long time to be able to go back to the pub, but now, it's the one place that I go to feel close to him."

She nodded and closed her eyes, reveling in the feel of his hand stroking her back. He abruptly stopped and it was like being jerked awake from an excellent dream. She heard his coffee cup hit the trash can, so she opened her eyes and walked out the back door, still cradling her cup to keep her hands warm.

She unlocked the truck and popped the window open. She led the way into the back of the truck and flipped on the lights. Cold air blew in through the window and Carmen shivered. When Liam stepped up beside her, she began a quick tour of the equipment. Liam followed first with his eyes, but then began to move and shift to get the feel for how everything was situated. He spun and turned and reached, keeping his stance wide. The man damn near filled the entire truck. It was possible that he might not be able to have someone work with him because he took up so much room.

Then without warning, he turned and bent over, to search the refrigerated compartments and storage. His ass thrust right at Carmen and she couldn't look away from the way his jeans hugged him. Lord, what was she thinking? She shook her head and stepped back, trying to figure out where to go, how to escape. Liam straightened and looked at her.

God, did her face show evidence of where her thoughts had just wandered?

"The setup and layout are perfect. Gus nailed it. Everything is within reach if you're working alone, but there's ample room for someone else."

She huffed a laugh. "I'm going to take my ample ass back into the house to get the groceries I picked up so you can practice on the grill."

She started to edge past him, but he braced his arms across the span of the path.

"I wasn't implying anything about your ass."

Crap. Her cheeks flamed. "I know. But you also said there's ample room in here and there isn't." She inhaled slowly. "It's almost stifling."

He stared into her face for a moment and she had a hard time keeping eye contact. She didn't know what he was searching for. Her gaze wandered to his lips and she wondered what his beard would feel like against her face during a kiss. She cleared her throat and said, "Excuse me."

He flinched as if he just realized he'd been staring, and then he stepped aside. She couldn't move fast enough to get out of the truck. As she sped back to her kitchen she was struck by the idea that she made it through her first visit to the truck since her father's passing because she was too busy thinking about Liam kissing her to think about being sad.

A good distraction truly worked wonders. She grabbed the bag of food she'd hastily shoved in the refrigerator last night and then polished off her coffee before heading back outside. She had things to do in the house. She had an entire list of projects to complete.

But what she wanted to do was watch Liam cook in her dad's truck. Which meant that she couldn't. The man had a girlfriend. What had gotten into her? She hadn't had a boyfriend in so long, she couldn't remember what a date felt like, but she'd never in her life tried to poach another woman's man.

Taking the bag to the truck, she decided the smartest move would be to pass it through the window and go back to her own work. She held the bag in the air, not quite tall enough to set it on the counter inside the truck. Liam saw her, she was sure of it. She waved her arm a little and he caught her wrist.

"What are you doing?"

"Handing you the food so you can practice cooking."

He took the bag and then leaned out the window. "Aren't you coming in?"

She was struck dumb by the look in his eyes. She pointed over her shoulder as if that would tell him what her plans were. "I have stuff—"

"Stuff can wait. Keep me company."

"You don't need company. Besides, if you're going to run this by yourself, you need to get used to being alone."

One eyebrow flicked up. "What if I can't figure something out and I start a fire?"

She crossed her arms. "Don't pretend to be incompetent. We both know you can figure it out."

"Just get your ass in here. I'm cold hanging out the window like this."

She sighed, but did as he told her. Yanking on the back door, she felt the warm air from inside letting her know that he'd already figured out how to start everything. She pulled the door shut behind her. Liam looked over his shoulder and smiled as he unloaded the small bag of groceries.

Carmen leaned against the closed door and let the sensations of the truck wash over her. The heat, the smells, the sounds—they all made her think of Gus. All she needed now was to hear him yelling at her to get out of the way or to hear him cursing Pete for screwing up an order. She smiled at the memory.

"That's a nice look."

She jolted from her reverie. "What?"

"That smile was one of the rare ones. One that said you were in a good place. Can I ask what you were thinking about?"

"My dad."

LIAM CHOPPED peppers while he talked to Carmen. When she had that dreamy look on her face, he'd hoped she'd been thinking about him, and he tried not to be disappointed that she thought of Gus. He'd wanted her to think of good memories of Gus.

But he also wanted to grab her and kiss her. Before she went back to the house for the food, he almost had. If she hadn't had a shell-shocked look, he probably would have followed through. He set the knife down as she talked about her dad, and he couldn't help but look at her mouth and her full pink lips. He wanted to taste those lips.

She shoved away from the door and sauntered closer. She had no idea how sexy she looked walking toward him like that. She wore another curve-hugging sweater, but no jacket to conceal it all. A cream-colored scarf was wound around her neck three or four times in loose loops and her hair flowed in waves over it.

As she walked past him, she began to unwind the scarf, and he caught a whiff of her perfume as her hair bounced up from the movement. She tossed the scarf on the passenger seat of the truck and then leaned against the opposite wall from where she'd started.

"Are you uncomfortable in here?"

She slowly shook her head. "I thought I would be, but it's good."

He returned to chopping and tossed some ground beef on the grill. He smacked at it with a spatula and tossed seasoning over it. He dug through the bag and brought out the tortillas. He felt her eyes on him and while being watched had never bothered him, something about this made him slightly uncomfortable. It was probably because he kept thinking about kissing her instead of paying attention to the food.

Liam still wasn't sure about the whole taco thing. It seemed too simple to make a food truck successful. They were competing with the likes of Taco Bell. He shook his head.

"What's so funny?" Carmen asked.

He looked over his shoulder. "I don't see how Gus was successful selling tacos. It doesn't seem like enough. At least not different enough to make people want to keep coming back or to follow him around."

She shrugged. "People like tacos. They're good walking food. You don't need utensils. They're cheap and filling."

He flipped the nearly cooked meat on the grill. Everything she said made sense, but he wanted to be more than cheap, filling finger food. "I think we should consider expanding, trying new meals in addition to tacos."

"Like what?"

"I'm not sure yet. I haven't thought it all the way through."

Which was odd that he would even mention it to her. He never talked without thinking first.

"Before you go rushing into changes, I think you should keep it as is and give it a shot. Adding more menu items will complicate things and you haven't been on the road yet. It's a lot to handle."

Again, she had a point. The woman was a businessperson without a doubt. He heated a tortilla and scooped beef on. Then he sprinkled cheese, lettuce, and tomato. He turned to her, holding his taco. "Here."

Her eyebrows slammed together. "I'm not hungry."

"Just try it. Let me know how it tastes."

He stepped closer, putting the taco to her lips, and waited. She pressed her lips together and he nudged at her mouth with the food. This brought a smile, much like it had yesterday when she'd claimed repeatedly that she didn't want to eat anything. She opened her mouth and took a bite.

His fingers grazed her lips. Her eyes widened a fraction at his touch. He pulled his hand away, but stayed rooted to his spot, mere inches from her body.

Her eyebrows crinkled again, this time wrinkling her nose in the process—never a good sign for the chef.

"What?"

She visibly swallowed, as if it took effort. "It's awful."

He looked at her and waited for her teasing smile, but none came. "You're serious?"

She nodded.

He took a bite of the taco and before he even chewed, he realized she was right. It was awful. The meat was bland and rubbery. It had no kick at all. He reached for a paper towel and spit the food out.

Carmen nudged his arm. "That's not fair. I swallowed it."

"That was your own silly mistake." He stared at the food,

and then started scraping it into the trash. "What the hell did I do wrong?"

"I have no idea. I'm not a cook, remember?"

She stood close to him and her perfume wafted up as a cold breeze swept through the open window. She picked at a leaf of cilantro and sighed. "My dad always said part of why his food was so good was because of the love he had for it. Maybe your heart's not in it."

While he'd always been passionate about cooking, he didn't believe that not having his heart in making tacos would ruin them. Shit, anyone could follow a recipe and have it turn out decently. He looked down into her dark, soulful eyes. He lost all train of thought and leaned down to brush his lips across hers.

Her sudden intake of breath hitched a little, but she relaxed against him as he put his hands under her hair. His thumbs stroked her jaw as he tilted her head up for better access. She was soft and smooth and he inched closer to feel more of her.

Carmen grabbed at his shirt on his chest, bunching the material, but then she flattened her hand and gave him a push. He took a small step back, but didn't release her face.

"What are you doing?"

"I'm kissing you. Did you not like it?" He knew the answer, but as a gentleman, he had to ask.

"Yes. No. What about your girlfriend?"

Now he did drop his hands. "What girlfriend?"

She sidestepped him in the small space. "The one who rushed out of your apartment yesterday morning?"

Yesterday? Ahh…Lily. "I don't have a girlfriend. That was Lily, and while she's a girl and my friend, she isn't my girl-friend. We hang out together and cook sometimes."

"But she spent the night?"

"On my couch. She had too much to drink before dinner the night before and passed out. "

"Oh."

What did that mean? He gave Carmen a minute, but she added nothing. Maybe that was answer enough. He thought he'd read all the signals she'd sent over their last few meetings. This was what he got for not thinking things through.

He pointed over his shoulder toward the grill. "I should get back to cooking if I want to get this truck on the road by next week."

She reached out to him, her fingers brushing his shirt at the waist. "Wait. Uh. I liked the kiss. A lot. I'm just not sure about this."

He smiled. "No pressure." He flipped off the grill off. "I'm going to go back to the store for more food to figure out these recipes."

"It might be easier to get the recipes right in a regular kitchen and then adapt for here."

"Nah. I'd rather figure it out where it needs to work. Are you okay with me staying around to cook?"

She smiled brightly, the relaxed smile he loved to see. "Of course. We're partners. *Mi camión es su camión.*"

"Translation?"

She winked at him as she headed out the door. "My truck is your truck. See you later."

Yes, indeed, she certainly would see him later.

CHAPTER 8

Carmen walked back into the house in a bit of a daze. Not only had Liam kissed her, but then she flirted as she left. She didn't even know where that had come from. And without a drop of alcohol to boot.

She still felt the tickle of his mustache against her lip and his firm grip on her head. Her skin warmed with the memory. She'd wanted to continue, but she pulled back. She wouldn't kiss another woman's boyfriend, but he was single. Did that mean she wanted it to happen again?

Her stomach fluttered with the thought. She hadn't had many boyfriends in her life. A couple of brief relationships in college and a few random dates since moving back home. The thought of starting something with Liam didn't seem smart. They were partners for at least the next year, so if things fizzled between them, she'd still have to face him daily for work.

Plus, he would probably want to move on as soon as they could sell the truck. What would that mean for them?

She was getting ahead of herself. It was a kiss. Even if it happened again, maybe it wouldn't go any further.

She went to her parents' old bedroom, which was now empty of everything, and popped open the can of paint. She'd work through her thoughts about Liam, weigh the pros and cons while she painted the room. The process would take care of two problems simultaneously.

Too bad Rosa was working. Having her input on Liam would help. She understood guys much better than Carmen did. Rosa had experience. Just thinking about her lack of experience made her stomach churn again. She grabbed her paint pan and swiped the roller against the wall.

LATER THAT DAY, when she checked her mail, she was hit with another surprise. An envelope from her dad's lawyer containing a letter from her dad. She'd know Gus's messy scrawl anywhere. She didn't know how long she stared at the envelope before determining she couldn't open it. Not yet. She tucked it into a drawer and went back to painting.

The pale blue made her smile. Her parents had always kept every wall in the house some shade of white. As if white really had different shades. She'd begged for color in her room as a teenager, but they refused. Of course, she'd also asked for black, during her brief goth phase, so it wasn't surprising that they'd said no.

But now, especially, she needed color, vibrance, to beat back the nagging sadness. She turned on the radio and danced through the job. Before she knew it, two walls were done, she had streaks of blue on her arms and her jeans, but she felt relaxed. The color definitely worked its magic.

She took a step back and surveyed her work. She probably wouldn't ever get work as a professional painter, but the results pleased her. After putting the lid on the can of paint, she cleaned the roller in the bathroom sink while singing and swaying to the music she had blaring from the living room.

Even the music made her inordinately happy. Her parents never let her blast music either. Guilt battled with her joy. She felt such freedom in the absence of her parents, which intensified the guilt. She missed them. Every moment, every day. But this was the first time since she'd left for college that she'd been on her own, and she was loving it.

A throat cleared behind her and she jumped, spinning around with the wet roller in her hand. Water sprayed across the bathroom wall, leaving a splatter of watery blue as it dripped. A few spots flew out at Liam, who stood in the doorway.

She froze in shock. She set the roller in the sink. "Gosh, I'm sorry. I didn't hear you and when I did, you totally took me by surprise. Here." She grabbed a towel and blotted at his shirt.

His hands caught hers. He leaned close to her ear to talk. "It's okay, Carmen. You left the back door unlocked, so I let myself in."

Having his body so close reminded her of their kiss. She pulled away before she acted on her stupid hormones. "Hold on," she said. She hurried into the living room and turned off the radio. "Sorry about that. I didn't even know you were still here."

"I'm here all right. The truck is clean. The food is all in the trash. Maybe you were right. I'm going to try again in my kitchen."

"You threw everything out?"

"I had some uncooked food that I shoved in your refrigerator, but everything I cooked got tossed. It wasn't as bad as the first batch, but it was nothing special either." He shook his head. "I haven't been this stumped since my pastry class in school."

He needed help. She closed her eyes and sighed before

offering the one thing she didn't think she could do. "I'll teach you."

"What?"

Reopening her eyes, she stared into his intense blue gaze. "I'll teach you to cook like my parents."

"I thought you said—"

"I'm not a cook, but my mother taught me everything she knew." Turning back to the mess in the sink, she said, "Give me a minute."

He backed away from the bathroom and she immediately began to regret the offer. Images of cooking with her mom flooded her head. Not long after her mother had been diagnosed with cancer, Carmen had moved back home. Even in her weakened state, Inez insisted on cooking every day.

She wanted to make sure that Carmen could cook. Inez believed it was a skill every woman needed, especially if she wanted to get and keep a man. Carmen still rolled her eyes at that one. When the roller was clean, she leaned it against the edge of the sink and looked at her reflection in the mirror.

She hadn't cooked since her mother died. Well, she cooked in order to eat, but not like she had with her mother.

Back in the kitchen, Liam had already gotten the remaining groceries out of the refrigerator. Carmen licked her lips as nervousness swamped her.

"Show me what you got," Liam said lightly. His teasing was just what she needed to move into action.

She went into the freezer and pulled out one of the few containers she'd kept. "This is mole sauce. Maybe you've heard of it. We don't have the time or the ingredients for me to start a new batch, so we'll save that lesson for another day."

After popping the container in the microwave to defrost it, she set to work chopping more peppers and onions. She wasn't nearly as skilled as Liam, but she managed to get the job done. "Get some chicken out of the fridge."

He grabbed a couple of chicken breasts, ones that would've been her dinner for later in the week, only now instead of being baked plain, they would be slathered in sauce and seasoning like the food of her childhood. She almost groaned at the thought.

She worked on instinct, her hands moving by rote after having cooked with her mother so much. With every slice and chop, she remembered her mother's plump hands correcting Carmen's. As she dumped everything into the pot on the stove, she could hear her mother's words, "Always taste as you work, so you'll know if you need to fix things."

Before she could act on her thought, Liam was at her elbow with a spoon in hand, dipping it in. He tasted and smiled. "Pretty good."

She smirked. "You ain't seen nothin' yet."

Teasing and playing with Liam kept her mind off memories of her mother. She was able to focus on the task at hand. Liam needed to cook like a Mexican. He stood watch over every move she made. He said nothing. He didn't comment or correct, even though she knew he would do things differently. She could almost see him taking mental notes.

With the flame doing its job of cooking their food, Carmen turned to him. "While that cooks, why don't you tell me what you want to do to the menu?"

"I told you I didn't know yet."

"And I think I know you well enough to know that while you were destroying recipes out in the truck, you were also thinking about other possibilities." She sat down at the table and put her feet up on the chair adjacent. Until that moment, she hadn't realized how tired she was.

He picked up her feet and sat in the chair, repositioning her legs across his. Something about the motion made her uncomfortable, like the gesture was too intimate, which was silly.

"At first I was thinking maybe we go gourmet—"

She couldn't stop the cringe.

He patted her calf. "But then I realized that would never work. So then I thought what if we went to the opposite direction? Instead of trying to make tacos fancy, what if we make everything on the truck traditional?"

"Tacos are pretty traditional. So are the rice and beans."

"But they're not street food. When I think about Chicago street food, the first thing that pops into my head is elotas."

This time she laughed. "Are you kidding me? My father is probably rolling in his grave to hear you suggest that. The whole idea of him creating the food truck was to get away from the image of the street vendor pushing a cart through the neighborhood."

"But people like it. I remember running errands for the bar with my dad and if we saw an elotas cart, I begged him to stop. Even at the age of ten, I wanted to know how to make it. And what about churros? Who doesn't like a sweet cinnamon dessert? It's all walking food. People can grab it and go."

"I don't know, Liam. It's a risk. People could also look at our truck as though it's worse than fast food and walk on down the street to find a burger."

His face lit with excitement, which was an unusual look for him. "We won't let them. We just have to make ourselves irresistible. Word will get around, like it did for your dad when he started the truck."

She pulled her legs down and stood, the aches returning tenfold to the arches of her feet. Her thighs burned and her shoulders tightened. The painting and running around had caught up with her. She went to the stove and pulled the chicken out and began to shred it.

"Are you going to tell me what you're making?"

"A non-walking food—enchiladas." The spicy scent of the mole sauce hit her and she was reminded once again of her mother. Her dad's mole sauce had been a great temptation for her as a kid. She'd pour it on anything. Spooning the sauce carefully over the chicken, her mother's voice rang in her head again, "Not too much, Carmen, you want to be able to taste the food."

Once the chicken was ready, she filled the tortillas and rolled them. Again, Liam said nothing. He simply watched. She wondered what he was thinking. With the tortillas in the pan, she spread sauce and cheese on the top and put it in the oven. "It's almost ready. Now you can tell why I don't cook. It takes forever. When it's time to eat, I just want to get it over with. The prepping and cooking and waiting make me crazy."

"A math test is something you want to just get over with. Not a good meal. How did you miss that one important lesson from your dad?"

She hadn't. No matter what they had going on in their lives, her family always ate at least one meal a day together, even if it meant they ate at the restaurant while on break. But all of those meals contributed to her battle with her weight her entire life. It hadn't been until she reached college that she felt in control and she'd been hesitant to loosen that control, especially since being back at home.

"Every meal can't be special. In fact, most aren't. It's fuel for your body. Yes, there are times when the effort makes a difference, but for everyday eating? Simple is the way to go." She returned to her chair and sighed. She was going to be so sore tomorrow.

"Simple doesn't have to be plain or tasteless."

"Who said I eat tasteless food?"

"I've seen your refrigerator, remember? I've eaten lunch

with you and I've seen the nasty salad masquerading as a meal."

Her cheeks flushed. Of course he would notice. "I ate with you at food trucks yesterday," she pointed out.

"Only after I coerced you."

She shook her head, desperate to change the topic. "Back to crappy street food. How do you suggest we convince people to part with their money for some elotas and churros?"

He leaned back in his chair. "I haven't worked that part out yet. I'm not suggesting we roll out with this next week. I need to get the hang of the truck and develop a plan."

The enchiladas baked in the oven and the smell made her stomach grumble. She'd skipped lunch in her excitement to get her new room painted. The upside would be that she'd actually eat the meal she'd created.

Liam stood and went back to the refrigerator. "Got any wine or beer?"

"Maybe. Rosa often brings stuff and leaves it."

He popped up with a couple of bottles of light beer and handed her one. "If you prefer, I can run to the store for something else."

"This is fine. Not much of a drinker, remember?" Her cheeks warmed again at the thought of what happened last time she drank with him.

"Dinner smells about done."

She moved to stand, but he held up a hand to stop her. "You cooked. I'll serve and clean up. You look beat."

Instead of arguing, which was her initial reaction, she sat back and propped her feet on his chair again. This time it was her turn to watch as he moved around her kitchen. She liked the way he moved, so sure and confident. He plated the food, giving her far too much like he did every time, but her stomach growled so she didn't complain. She would be back to plain chicken breast or salmon tomorrow. Tonight, she would indulge.

As Liam put the dish in front of her, she looked at his mouth and thought she'd like to indulge in that some more, too.

LIAM BROUGHT the food to the table and wanted to do more. Carmen looked tired and stressed, but not unhappy. When he'd walked in on her painting the bedroom, he was surprised. He'd gotten used to her being a businesswoman and sometimes he caught glimpses of the teasing girl she'd been, but while she danced around a half-painted bedroom, he saw yet another side to her.

He liked it.

He'd wanted to catch her swaying hips and kiss her again, but wasn't sure how well that would've been received, so he'd backed out of the room. As much as he wanted to kiss her again, he wouldn't push. She was still dealing with a lot and it probably wasn't the best time to start a relationship, especially since they were partners.

As he sat at the table with his fork in hand, he thought about Colin and Elizabeth. They had met and their relationship developed because they were business partners. While it hadn't been perfect, they made it work.

He dug in to the enchiladas, not sure what to expect. Carmen had repeatedly told him she couldn't cook, but he'd watched her efficiently assemble the meal as if it was second nature. As Gus's daughter, it probably was. He took his first bite and the melted cheese scalded his mouth. Ignoring the pain, he closed his eyes and savored the flavors that filled him.

The smoky, spicy peppers were softened by a hint of

chocolate in the mole sauce. He let the food sit on his tongue for a moment before chewing. The taste, the texture, everything was perfect. He opened his eyes as he swallowed. Carmen stared at him, her plate untouched.

He pointed his fork at her. "You've been holding out on me."

"No, I haven't." She ducked her head and took a bite of her food.

"You told me you don't cook, that you don't like it. This is not a meal made by someone who hates cooking. This is delicious. I might even go so far as to say it's perfection."

"Thank you," she whispered.

He lost her again in that moment, but he didn't know why. She curled into herself and ate a few bites in silence. He gave her space and waited for her to let him in. He devoured his enchiladas in record time, while she continued to poke and eat slowly.

Shoving her dish away, she suddenly jumped away from the table. "Sorry. I can't do this. I thought I could."

Liam caught her arm as she tried to escape to the living room. Turning her to face him, he saw the sorrow on her face again. "What is it?"

She shook her head. He did what felt natural and pulled her to his chest. With his arms wrapped around her, she settled in. She didn't cry, but her body was filled with tension.

"Tell me why dinner upset you."

He felt her chest fill right before she pulled away. Instead of letting her run, he held her hand and pulled her toward the table. He sat in her chair and tugged her onto his lap.

She gave a sad laugh. "I'm not going to sit on your lap."

"You already are. And I like it. Now talk."

She wiped both hands over her face. "It's stupid. I *know* it's stupid."

Liam's hand rested on the curve of her hip and the other held her hand in her lap. He stroked her fingers to get her to continue.

"When my mom got sick, she wanted to cook. Like all the time. Even when she was too weak. I cooked with her because it was important. I knew she needed to teach me in a way that I wouldn't listen to when I was a kid." She sighed and settled her head on his shoulder.

"But I never actually ate with her. By the time the food was cooked, she was always worn out. I'd save a plate for her to eat later and I'd toss the rest."

He remembered her talking about throwing out all of the food at Gus's wake. He'd thought it was wasteful, which was why he'd made individual portions. Now, he knew there was more to it. "Why?"

She sniffed, but still hadn't started crying. "I don't have a good relationship with food. I was a fat kid. It took until college to lose the weight and be able to control my life."

He'd known her as a teen. While she was never model-thin, she hadn't been obese either.

"Coming back home, I was just so afraid that I'd fall into the trap again. My mom's favorite pastime was feeding people. It's how I grew up. I didn't want to go back to being that fat kid."

"You weren't really fat. You know that, now, right?"

She snorted at him.

He shifted her so he could see her face. "You were a pretty teenager. All the kitchen staff—at least those under the age of thirty—talked about you. You were fun and full of life and your body was killer." She started to look away, to dismiss what he said, so he grabbed her chin. "It's even hotter now. I don't know how some guy hasn't snatched you up."

"I have no social life. Hard to meet guys when I've spent all of my time taking care of my dying mother."

What about in the years since? he wanted to ask, but didn't. The reason didn't matter.

She patted his cheek and then stroked along his beard. The idea of keeping the beard was growing on him. She stood. "I realized when I finally sat here to eat her food what a huge chance I missed out on with her. I should've eaten with her. I should've made every meal a big deal, but I was too selfish to see that."

"Eat with me now. Start fresh."

A smile eased onto her face as she looked at his empty plate. "I think you finished."

"I can suffer through another helping if it means you'll sit with me."

She took his plate and filled it. When she returned to the table, he stood and grabbed her hips. The small gasp that escaped her lips urged him on. He lowered his lips to hers and brushed against them. Then he angled his head and nudged her lips apart, wanting to taste her.

He loved how soft and warm she was. He deepened the kiss on her sigh and pulled her body closer to his. His blood raced as his hands roamed over her curves. His dick perked up and his fingers dug into her hips before he released her. The look on her face gave him a sense of satisfaction. A lusty haze filled her eyes. He brushed his lips across hers one more time and then whispered, "You are all kinds of sexy."

As they took their places back at the table, Liam came to the conclusion that while he was willing to take his time getting to know Carmen all over again, he would definitely push for more than friendship.

CARMEN SAT at the table and stared at her plate of food. A swarm of emotions rolled through her. Giddiness topped the list after Liam kissed her again. She couldn't quite process his words about her being sexy. Never in her life had she felt sexy. He made her want to believe.

The guilt and sadness over her parents hung on tightly. Liam seemed to understand, which was a blessing in itself.

He nudged her plate closer and she ate. For the first time in a long time, she ate a home-cooked, satisfying meal from her childhood, and she allowed herself to enjoy it. Tasting her dad's mole sauce made her wish for him to be standing at the stove over the stockpot making a new batch. She only hoped she could deliver on her promise to Liam, that she really could replicate the sauce.

Liam smiled at her over his plate, which he was nearly halfway finished with. Where the heck did he put all that food? She ate her mostly cold enchiladas and washed them down with her warming beer. At some point, she'd get this whole how-to-have-a-meal thing down. She wanted to be normal and not freak out about the calories or what her body looked like. Liam treated her like she was normal.

"What do you have planned for the rest of your night?"

His question made her heart pump double time. After the heat in his kiss, she had no idea what to expect from him. "Nothing. Maybe I'll finish painting, but I'm kind of tired. I don't know if I have the motivation. How about you?"

"I was supposed to be working tonight, so I have nothing going on. Want to go see a movie?"

"Uh…" Was this a date?

Liam reached over and took her hand. She loved the feel of his large, rough hand against hers. His was a sign of strength and competence. "Carmen, I like you. A lot. I'd like to go out with you. Judging by your reaction to our kiss, I think you'd like that, too. But if you're not ready, say the word and I'll back off."

Not ready? Had she ever been ready for any man, much

less one that had this kind of effect on her? She licked her lips. "I don't know what ready feels like, but I like you, too."

"Is that a yes?"

"I guess it is."

Liam smiled. An honest-to-God, real smile. The creases on the sides of his lips deepened and his eyes brightened. The beautiful sight captured her. She was so used to his serious countenance, and his half smiles, where he lifted one corner of his mouth, but this was something. This smile was like a weapon. No wonder he didn't pull it out often.

She stood to clear the plates, but his hand covered hers. "I'll get these. You go get ready. I'll check movie times."

She was hesitant to move her hand because she liked his there. "Okay."

"Anything you want to see?"

"I'm not too picky, but nothing sad."

He nodded and turned to the sink with the dishes. Carmen went to her room to pick out clothes. Nervous flutters hit her again. How was she supposed to dress for a date? Rosa would tell her to wear something tight that showed cleavage. Carmen rolled her eyes. It would be dark in the movie theater. Her clothing choices didn't matter. And this was Liam.

That thought led her to thinking about the end of the date. Would he want to spend the night? She didn't know if she was ready for that. In fact, she knew she wasn't. Jeans and a sweater and ugly underwear. That would make the decision to keep her clothes on easy. Undressing in front of a guy was hard enough for her—past experiences didn't do wonders for her self-esteem—but she would be mortified if a guy saw her ugly underwear.

After piling her hair on top of her head, she went to the bathroom to shower. Even after scrubbing, she still had a few paint streaks on her arms, but the rest of her was clean and relaxed. She dressed, applied makeup, and checked the time. She'd taken a little longer than she planned and hoped Liam didn't mind. She let her hair down and debated between adding curls or straightening it. Straightening would take longer, so she heated the curling iron and used it to add some waves. Satisfied, she shook her hair out and smiled at her reflection.

She found Liam in the living room, her laptop on the coffee table, and he had the TV on.

"Sorry I took so long."

He looked up and the smile returned. "It was worth the wait."

Wow. Just wow. He might not be much of a talker, but when he did, he knew what to say. "Thank you. Did you find a movie?"

He handed her a slip of paper. "I like this one." He pointed to a romantic comedy that she'd been wanting to see.

"Really?" No man wanted to see a romcom.

"You said nothing sad. This fits the bill. Plus, we have extra time before it starts, so we can sit in the back row and make out."

Now he thought like a typical man. And she liked the way his brain worked.

Hours later, Carmen sat in Liam's car wondering what would happen next. They had arrived at the movie theater early and while Liam had kissed her, they didn't have a full makeout session. He talked and asked questions about college and what she wanted to do with her life. Now, as they drove back to her house, she thought about *what next.*

When they walked to the car, he'd put his arm around her. He held her hand as he drove. And man, did she want to kiss him again. He pulled into the driveway and turned the car off. Her heart jolted. He didn't plan to just drop her off.

"Let me walk you to your door."

She nodded and stepped out of the car. The temperature had dropped and the wind kicked her hair up. Liam met her on her side of the car and put his arm on her shoulder again. They walked to the door in silence. When she pulled out her keys, she said, "I had a really good time."

"So did I."

He stepped closer, placing one leg in between hers. A subtle shift in his weight and she wanted to cling to him. He slid an arm around her waist and pulled her close as he lowered his mouth to her lips. He started slow and soft, but then his tongue sought hers.

He pressed her body against the door, cradling her head with his hand. Although she felt the cold air around them, her body was hot as her blood raced. This felt so good. She couldn't ever remember a time when a man did this to her.

Liam eased away from her and she immediately missed his mouth. She tilted her head up, but he leaned his forehead against hers. "You should probably go in now."

His words made her heart hurt. What had she done wrong?

He swallowed hard. "If we don't stop now..." His words were more strangled this time.

She realized that he was as turned on as she was. She hadn't done anything wrong. She'd done something very right, so she smiled. "What if—"

"Stop right there. You weren't even sure you were ready for a date. I'm not rushing you into anything."

Her dad was right. Liam was a good man. She pulled his face back to hers, and pressed a closed-mouth kiss to his lips.

"Thank you. I'd like to do this again. I'd really like it."

He chuckled and stepped away. Even in the dark, she

couldn't help but let her gaze wander down the length of him. She didn't know what that did to him, but he groaned and gave her a little push.

"Go inside now, Carmen. I'll see you tomorrow."

"Good night," she said sweetly.

When she closed the door behind her, she stood there until she heard Liam's car start up. She finally understood what Rosa enjoyed about teasing men she met at the bar. It was a great sense of power to know she could turn on a man like that. Liam entering her life was causing a ripple effect and changing so many things.

As much trepidation as she had in forging ahead, the thought of new things excited her. Before she went to bed, she sat and thought about all the dreams she'd held on to after college. All the things she'd thought she'd want to do or accomplish. Then she made a list. It was time to move on and have her own life.

For the rest of the week, Carmen and Liam worked side by side, in her kitchen and on the truck. She taught him what she could about cooking her dad's recipes. One thing she learned about Liam was that he didn't like being told what to do. Every time she corrected something he did, he'd scowl and the line between his eyebrows deepened. The man was used to being in charge. Long gone was the meek dishwasher in her dad's kitchen.

By Friday afternoon, they'd had enough—enough Mexican food, enough recipe tweaking, enough sexual tension. After they'd cleaned up last night, Liam had suggested taking a break from the truck and business for a day. They needed to relax, to get away before they ended up hating what they were trying to achieve.

His words made sense, and in truth, she liked the idea of spending time with him without worrying about work. He'd done nothing more than plant steamy kisses on her all week. He touched her all the time. A rub, a pat, a stroke. But not once did he attempt to take it further.

For the first time in her life, she felt ready to take it

further. A new kind of nervousness invaded her body, but she pushed it down. Things were going well and she wanted this with Liam. No other guy ever made her feel safe and cared for the way Liam did. She knew that was because she'd had crappy taste in guys when she was in college and since coming home, she hadn't given any man the chance to make her feel anything.

Liam made her feel.

She'd ventured out to the mall and bought new underwear, a matching bra and panty set to wear on her date. Although she suggested they go out to dinner, Liam offered to cook for her. She barely ate anything all day so she could enjoy everything Liam offered without guilt.

Standing in front of his door, preparing to knock, her nerves attacked full force. She shifted the bottle of wine she'd brought and inhaled slowly. This was normal. A new relationship would be full of firsts. She needed to learn to embrace them. Maybe even enjoy them. She knocked lightly and Liam answered quickly, as though he'd been standing by the door waiting for her.

"Hi."

"Hi." His gaze coated over her, warming every inch as it went. He opened the door wider, gesturing her in. As she passed, he leaned over and kissed her cheek. "You look great."

"Thanks."

Her heart thumped as she looked at him. Had it really only been a day since they'd been together? He took the bottle of wine from her hand and helped her out of her coat. Again, his gaze raked over her like he hadn't seen enough the first time. She was glad she decided to wear a feminine skirt instead of her usual jeans. Her stomach knotted at the thought of him staring like that when they were naked.

Darkness. It was already evening. As long as the lights

were out, she'd be fine. She swallowed hard at the lie she told herself. She didn't need to see him to feel his eyes on her.

"Something wrong?"

"Nope."

He hung her coat on the coatrack near the door. "Come into the kitchen. Dinner will be ready soon. We can enjoy a glass of wine while we wait." He paused midstride. "Unless you want to sit in here. I can bring the glasses in."

"The kitchen's fine." She followed him and the wonderful smell of something delicious caught her. Her stomach growled. She probably should've had something to tide her over. She didn't want to act like a pig at the trough.

The kitchen table was set. He even had a couple of candles waiting to be lit. She took a stool at the counter and watched Liam open the wine. "What's for dinner?"

"Lamb and polenta."

He poured her a glass of wine and then went to the stove and began whisking whatever he had in the pot on the flame. The rhythmic sound of metal on metal soothed her. These were sounds she'd grown up with. The radio played in the background, something smooth and jazzy. If this was Liam's seduction technique, he knew what he was doing.

She sipped from the wine, well aware that she was drinking on an empty stomach. "Anything I can help with?"

"You can grab the salad from the fridge," he said without looking up.

Carmen walked to the fridge and nearly had to pick up her jaw when she looked inside. Ruthlessly organized, the entire thing was filled. How much food could a man who lived alone eat?

She grabbed the glass bowl, which was prettier than anything she owned, and asked, "Salad dressing?"

"Already on. It's ready to eat."

She placed the bowl on the table between the two place

settings, which were adjacent instead of across the table from each other. She liked the way Liam did things. By the time she returned to her spot at the counter, he'd pulled a pan from the oven and her stomach grumbled again. She swallowed a gulp of wine to quiet it.

"Hand me the plates from the table." He suddenly looked up. "Please."

She smiled because she knew that in any other kitchen, pleasantries were tossed aside. There was no time to waste on please or thank you. But for her, he altered his speech. She set the dishes beside his work station and watched as he plated the food. It was like viewing an artist at work. The dinner was photo-ready and almost too pretty to eat.

Liam wiped his hands quickly on a towel and then picked up the plates. He put them on the table and turned to her. Instead of telling her to sit, he grabbed her hips and pulled her in for a devastating kiss. His lips were impatient and his tongue swiped against hers, pulling a moan from her chest. He pressed her body fully against his and shifted the angle of the kiss.

Carmen became light-headed. She couldn't tell if it was the wine or Liam's kiss, but it was wonderful. He slowly pulled away, but his fingers tightened on her hips. "I've wanted to do that since you walked in the door, but I didn't want to ruin the polenta. Timing is everything."

She was a little short of breath. She didn't think a man had ever wanted her like this. It was a heady feeling. "Burnt polenta might've been worth it."

He let go of her body and smirked. "You've never had my polenta."

He turned and pulled her chair out for her. She rolled her eyes. "I can get my own chair, Liam. You don't have to try to impress me."

As she sat, he lowered to her ear and whispered, "I like doing things for you."

A shiver raced down her back. He pulled away and took his own seat. Carmen stared at the plate in front of her. Liam reached over and added some salad to her dish.

A small smile accompanied his words. "I know how much you like your salad." He added a bit of salad to his own plate and then looked around. "I forgot my wine."

He walked to the counter to get his glass and Carmen studied her plate. She had no idea where to start so she started with what she knew: the salad. The leafy greens held a hint of balsamic vinegar, but the taste woke her mouth. Liam returned to his seat with his glass and the bottle of wine. He topped off her glass and then lit the candles before picking up his silverware.

"Do you do this all the time?"

"What?"

"Go all out for dinner? It seems like a lot of work for two people. Even more so if you're eating alone."

He gave a careless shrug and lifted the corner of his mouth. "When I'm eating alone, I don't light the candles." He scooped up a bit of polenta.

She watched his lips close over his fork. The man made eating look sensual. "I'm serious."

"So was I. Kind of. I like to cook. I usually ate at the restaurant, so I don't cook every meal at home, but when I do, I want it to be something I like. I believe in eating well."

Those were words she'd grown up with. Eat. Eating well for her meant an expanded waistline. She shoved the thought aside. Liam made this fabulous meal for her and she *would* enjoy it. She followed his lead and scooped some polenta into her mouth.

She'd never had it before although she'd heard of it. The thick texture coated her tongue. An earthy taste followed.

She swallowed, but savored the flavor. She had no idea how he made a pile of mush taste good, but he did. This was the same guy who couldn't get tacos right?

If the polenta was that amazing, she could only imagine what he could do with lamb. She cut a piece of meat, which took little effort because it was so tender. The rosemary was a perfect match to the meat that practically melted on her tongue.

"Is it good?"

She realized she'd closed her eyes while eating and when she opened them at Liam's question, he was staring at her again. "Good doesn't begin to describe this. It's amazing. What's the flavor?"

"Truffle oil." Her compliment earned her a warm smile.

Truffle oil. One more thing she knew nothing about. Except that it tasted great. She went back to eating, but took her time. One thing she'd learned about herself over the years was that rushing only made her eat more. More than she needed.

The further she got into the meal, the more a nagging thought poked at her. Liam was too good of a chef to be working on a food truck. Her dad had been a cook, a good cook, but he wasn't a trained chef. Gus was all about family food, stuff to eat on the go, that was homemade. Liam was an artist when he cooked.

He would never be happy slinging tacos forever.

She took a gulp of wine to push down the fear. They'd agreed to give it a year. At that point, they would probably sell. Liam had bigger dreams than the Taco Taxi.

LIAM WATCHED CARMEN EAT. Part of him knew it would make her uncomfortable, but he couldn't help himself. The woman looked like she was making love as she thoroughly enjoyed the meal he'd made. He was glad he opted to use the good stuff regardless of price. She was worth every penny. If he always got that reaction, he'd cook for her every freaking day. He was so turned on that he couldn't taste the food himself.

She made it difficult for him to follow his plan. He didn't rush into anything, and when he decided he wanted a relationship with Carmen, he also knew that he'd take his time. They had no hurry to move things along, especially since she had so much going on in her life. But every hour they spent crammed into that damn truck or even standing over the stove in her kitchen, he was acutely aware of how much he wanted her.

Now, watching her revel in the food he'd created, he wanted nothing more than to clear the table and take her right here. Which went against everything he ever did.

Ever since coming back in contact with Carmen, he'd been different but he couldn't explain why. It was part of why he'd suggested they take a day off. A day away from the business and away from each other, but he couldn't get her off his mind. Less than twenty-four hours and he couldn't wait to see her again.

They ate, but didn't talk. It was one of the many things that made Carmen so attractive to him. She didn't require him to talk all the time. If she wanted to speak, she would, but she didn't push him. Silence never seemed to bother her, though. But then again, she rarely needed words to convey what she thought.

Her body language spoke volumes and her eyes even more. He could easily get lost staring into her dark eyes.

Carmen pushed her plate away. "That was phenomenal. I couldn't eat another bite."

He looked at her plate. She'd eaten little more than half of what he'd given her. "Hmm. That's too bad because I made cheesecake for dessert."

She bit her lower lip.

"House rules are that you don't get dessert if you don't finish your dinner."

She leaned her forearms on the table. "If I finish all that food, I wouldn't be able to eat dessert either."

"How about a few more bites and then we'll take a break? Go sit on the couch, finish our wine. The cheesecake will be fine until later." What he wanted was to take her to his bed and work up a whole new appetite.

She must've gotten his intention because she blushed, just a slight hint of pink on her golden skin.

Scooping up another bite of polenta, she turned her fork over, and keeping her eyes locked on his, she swirled her tongue over the fork. He swallowed hard and leaned closer. Screw dinner. If she wasn't hungry, he could think of more interesting things to do with her tongue.

He reached out and cupped the back of her neck, pulling her closer. Even with the corner of the table between them, his mouth met hers. He tasted the truffles and her wine. His jeans became tighter as his dick hardened, but he would be happy to continue feasting on her mouth.

Her fork clanged against the dish between them, startling them both. Carmen jerked back. She breathed heavily and he watched the swell of her breasts rise and fall. Her pulse fluttered against his palm.

She pulled away from him and stood. "We should clean up the dishes."

He jumped up and grabbed her again. Her ass leaned on the edge of the table as he pressed his body to hers. He wanted to push her back onto the table and strip her, but he knew she wouldn't go for it. Liam trailed openmouthed kisses down her neck. Her breath hitched.

He shifted again so his thigh pressed between her legs. She gasped with a high little squeak, and then gripped his shoulders as she began to wiggle her hips. In his head he pictured her dancing through her bedroom, hips shaking in rhythm, and how much he'd wanted to be up against her. Feeling her writhe beneath him quickly became a top priority.

Dragging his mouth away from her skin, he cleared his head. When he spoke, his voice was gravelly with need. "Do you want to stop?"

"Huh?" Her eyes fluttered open.

His dick throbbed against his zipper, making coherent thought more difficult. "Carmen." He waited until she focused on him. "Do you want to stop?"

"No," she answered quickly. She leaned forward and kissed him again.

He grabbed her hand and pulled her through the apartment to his bedroom, flipping on lights as they went. In his room, he kicked a pile of dirty clothes out of the way so she wouldn't trip. In his head, he heard his mother scolding him for being a slob. But then he turned to Carmen and pulled her back into his arms and all thought fled.

Liam began unbuttoning her shirt, kissing his way down, when Carmen's hands stopped his. He looked at her in question.

"Before we go any further...I..." She closed her eyes. When she reopened them, she looked scared.

Crap. That was never a good look in the bedroom. "What?"

"I don't really know what I'm doing."

Whoa. "Are you a virgin?" He scanned his memory for any mention Gus had ever made about her having a serious boyfriend and he came up empty. Was it possible that she'd made it to her late twenties without sex?

"No, but I don't have much experience. I just…don't want you to expect, I don't know." She collapsed on the bed and flopped back, throwing her arm over her face.

For as sexy as she'd been all night, he looked at her now and saw that she was pretty damn cute. She had performance anxiety.

Liam crawled over the top of her until his thigh was nestled between hers. He stayed propped on an elbow and with his other hand shoved her arm aside. He traced a finger down her cheek. "Do you want to do this?"

She nodded.

Thank God. "Then don't worry about it. Just do what feels right." His hand trailed a path down her neck, over her shoulder, and then down the side of her body. She trembled beneath him and he wanted so much more. "If I do something you don't like, say so and I'll stop. And if there's something you like that I'm not doing, tell me." Not that he could imagine not doing everything to her.

She cringed. "That's just it. I don't even know what I like."

"Then we'll figure it out together." He lowered his head and kissed her as he tugged her shirt out of her skirt. Warm smooth skin greeted him. He really needed to get rid of all these clothes. He reared up and yanked his shirt over his head and tossed it in the pile on the floor.

Then he reached down and finished unbuttoning her shirt. Beneath the simple black top was a scarlet satin and lace bra. The cups barely held her breasts. Lying under him, skirt barely keeping her decent, she was sin personified and he was more than ready to go to hell.

CHAPTER 10

Carmen couldn't breathe. She watched Liam unbutton her shirt and although instinct made her hands twitch with wanting to stop him, she held back. There was something fascinating about his pale white skin against hers. His hands, always so strong and capable, were incredibly gentle.

He stared at her chest and she was so grateful that she'd splurged on the new underwear, something that made her feel sexy under his scrutiny. But she was painfully aware of the stretch marks marring the skin on her abdomen. His tongue traced along the top edge of the bra and her skin pebbled with goose bumps. He inched his way down until he stood next to the bed. Still staring at her, he tugged off her cute pumps and ran his hands over her feet.

"Uh, Liam?"

"Hmm?" His hands wandered up her leg. Her skirt was at her hips, so she knew he was looking at her new red panties.

"Can we turn out the lights?"

He froze. His gaze shot to her face. "Why? I want to see you."

She closed her eyes and drew a slow breath. How could she explain this? He would think she was a total freak. A shadow crossed over her as the mattress shifted with his weight. She felt his body next to hers.

Again, his fingers traced over her face. "There's nothing to be nervous about."

This went so far beyond nervous that she didn't even have words. This was self-consciousness and loathing for her own body. As content as she'd become with her body and she believed she'd come to terms with it, she wasn't ready to reveal it to him. Certainly not on their first time. Beyond the stretch marks, she was jiggly after not having time for the gym in longer than she could remember. She didn't have a toned, athletic body. She wasn't just curvy, she was plump.

He sighed, kissed her cheek, and then he was gone.

Yeah, he thought she was a freak. But then the lights beyond her eyelids disappeared. She opened her eyes to the darkness of the room. And then Liam was back, cast in shadow from the hall light. He'd turned off the lights for her. The tightness in her chest loosened a bit and she smiled.

She scooted back on the bed as he neared. His silhouette filled her vision as he climbed on the bed, his jeans rubbing against her bare thighs. Moonlight filtered through the windows and lit his face enough for her to see his grin.

"Better?"

"Much." Her whisper was harsh to her own ears. Her pulse picked up again as Liam's hands got busy.

He spread her shirt wide and palmed her breasts. His hard thigh nestled between hers, applying a glorious pressure that made her want to purr. His mouth found hers while his right hand squeezed her breast, lightly pinching her nipple. What had been smooth comforting satin now felt far too restrictive. His hand left her breast and pulled her skirt up.

He stroked her through her wet panties. Her hips began

to move against him. She fisted her hands in the blanket, unsure of what else to do with them. Liam sucked at her neck, sending tingles through her and coalescing where his hand met her body.

Again, Liam pulled away and her immediate thought was that she'd done something wrong. She followed him up, forcefully pushing her body to sit. Her shirt slid down her shoulders. He stood before her, shoving his jeans and underwear off. His dick sprang free.

Her eyes widened and she hoped he couldn't see. It had been so long since she'd seen a naked man. Even when she'd had a boyfriend, she'd been too nervous to really look. His skin, so white in the moonlight, practically glowed. He reached down and tugged her sleeve until the shirt came away from her body.

It took another second for her to realize he wanted her naked. She reached around her back to release her bra. He leaned down and whispered, "Let me."

He bit down on her earlobe. With one quick flick, he had her bra unclasped and drew it away from her. Her boobs drooped without the support of the cups and Carmen wanted to cover them. Liam, on the other hand, appeared to be fascinated. He knelt in front of her and took a nipple into his mouth.

The warm, wet pleasure of his tongue caressed her and her head lolled back. She wanted him to do this everywhere. Nothing had ever felt so good.

He eased her back against the mattress and then pulled at the waistband of her skirt. She lifted her hips so he could remove it. Like with his own clothes, he took the skirt and underwear simultaneously. She was completely bare and her stomach churned. She wanted to tug the blanket over her, but that would require movement and she was paralyzed.

When he covered her body this time, the silky, hard length

of his dick poked her thigh. He kissed her again and the same wonderful dizzy feeling filled her. Her brain overloaded as Liam's hands went everywhere. He said nothing, but an occasional pleased groan slipped past his lips. She had a hard time believing those sounds were in response to her body.

He made his way back up her body and his face hovered over hers. His eyes lasered on her. "Are you okay?"

She still couldn't talk, so she nodded.

"You're sure you want to do this?" The question sounded a little strangled.

Liam, always the gentleman. As if she would stop now. She was enough of a weirdo without being *that* girl. And she did want this. "Yes," she whispered.

He reached over to the nightstand and she heard a wrapper. This was it. She was going to have sex with Liam. Every muscle in her body tensed. When he came back to her, she spread her legs wide to make room for him. He settled between her thighs and she braced for his push, for the weight of his body against hers.

Instead, his hand found her again and stroked her and he went back to kissing her neck. His skin was hot against hers. She reached up and touched his chest, her hand dark in the shadows of the room.

His breath was ragged against her as she moved her hands to his head and then down his shoulders. The tingling built and coiled in her when the shock of his fingers entering her caused a gasp. She tilted her hips up.

More. She wanted more of this.

Forcing her voice to work, she said, "I'm ready, Liam."

Without a word, he moved his hand and shifted his weight. She felt the head of his dick pressing against her. Once he was in place, he curled his arm beneath her and held her close as he pushed into her in incremental bits.

Please screamed through her head. She rocked her hips, bringing him closer and deeper.

"Fuck." His word came out harsh and shaky. He didn't move, just nestled between her, covering her, penetrating her.

She felt so full and overwhelmed. And then he began to move. He pulled out and slid back. He kept his face buried in her neck.

Carmen lifted her knees and awkwardly tried to hook her legs around his hips, but there was nothing for her to latch on to and they kept slipping away. He grabbed her right thigh and held it at his hip and drove into her faster. Their skin became slick with sweat.

She waited for the coiling to go away, for some explosion to tell her this was right, that it was good. Her mind raced ahead telling her what she should be doing. *Raise your hips. Move your hands. Moan.*

Breathe.

But she could do none of that. Liam rose on his forearms and kissed her. Pulling a mere inch from her lips, he said, "Relax."

She squeezed her eyes tight. God, didn't he understand? She couldn't. And she wanted to more than anything right now.

He stopped moving and she felt his penetrating gaze boring into her. Tears pricked at her eyes.

"Christ." He leaned his forehead against hers. "Do you want me to stop?"

She refused to open her eyes. She shook her head no. Because she didn't want him to stop.

"Carmen."

She finally opened her eyes.

"I don't want to do this if it's not good for you."

"It's good. It is." She inhaled deeply and felt his chest hair rub against her nipples. "It's okay…to finish."

"Crap." He started to roll away.

Her arms and legs wrapped tightly to hold him. She tugged until he was on top of her. She could never talk if she had to look into his eyes. Hoping her voice would last, that her words wouldn't crack, she talked. "It feels good, Liam. Please don't stop. I *want* this. I just can't get where you're going. But it's good."

A slow breath released from him, fluttering against her hair, and he began moving again. She closed her eyes and enjoyed the feel of him moving against her, his muscles bunching and flexing.

When his whole body went rigid and he shook, a new sensation filled her. She did this, brought him this pleasure. It was a different kind of satisfaction.

He collapsed against her and she smiled as she stroked his back. It only lasted a moment, but it was a moment longer than she'd had with other guys. He rolled away, taking all of his warmth with him. Through the slit in her eyes, she watched the rise and fall of his chest, still faster than normal.

He groaned as he sat up. "I'll be right back." He stumbled as he walked away.

She shot up and began looking for her clothes, which was difficult in the dark, but she wasn't about to turn the light on. Feeling with her foot, she encountered clothing. As she bent to see if it was hers, Liam groaned from the doorway.

"That's a beautiful sight."

She shot straight up again, her hands moving to conceal everything, unsure of which part would be the worst to leave exposed.

Liam stepped closer and grabbed her wrists. "Come back to bed."

"I was looking for my clothes."

"I know what you were doing." He tugged her, but she didn't budge. "Carmen, I swear I can do better than that. I can't go down in your book as your worst lover ever."

A laugh burst out of her. Once she started, she couldn't stop. Tears streamed down her face. All the tears she'd held back now flowed. When she looked at Liam's face, she tried her best to sober, but when she saw the total consternation deepening the crease between his eyes, another round attacked her, but she swallowed it and forced a calming breath.

"Liam, I told you I have very little experience." She pulled her hand away from him and touched his cheek. "You are, by far, the best lover I've had."

"Sweetheart, that isn't saying much. You didn't come. Shit, you didn't even have a fake orgasm."

"But that's not on you."

"Yeah, it is."

She knew he wouldn't understand. She shook her head and bent to retrieve her clothes.

"I don't want you to leave."

She hadn't thought about it, but leaving wasn't the first thing on her mind. She didn't have a plan other than covering her naked ass. "Okay, but I can't walk around naked."

"Why not? No one else is here."

"I would never feel comfortable like that."

"I'll get you something comfortable to wear. Hold on."

As he rummaged through his dresser, Carmen imagined all the beautiful women on TV and how they all looked incredibly sexy in their man's shirt or boxers. She glanced at Liam's body and then down at hers. No, she wouldn't look like that. His shirt wouldn't hang halfway down her thigh, showing just enough to make him want to look. Most of her would probably still be hanging out.

Sticking with her own clothes would be her best choice.

He turned from his drawer and handed her a T-shirt and a pair of sweatpants. She eyed them. They both looked baggy. Not sexy, but definitely comfortable. Looked like he wanted to cover her up as much as she wanted to cover up.

"Thanks." She slipped the clothes on quickly. Liam pulled on a pair of boxers and nothing else.

"Ready for dessert?"

"Huh?"

"I have cheesecake, remember?"

"Shoot. We didn't clean up. Your kitchen's a mess." She moved past him to go clean up.

"Carmen." His tone was serious, so she turned. "We'll clean up, but then we're bringing dessert back here."

Something in his voice caused a shiver to race down her back. She'd avoided dessert for more years than she'd care to think about. He made her crave dessert.

Liam made her want a lot of things, and that made her all kinds of nervous.

∽

FRUSTRATION FILLED LIAM. His reputation for being single-minded served him well in the kitchen. He never considered himself selfish in bed, but that's exactly how he felt at the moment. Things between him and Carmen were hot. There was no denying the chemistry. But she held back. She wasn't comfortable, and he blamed himself.

He followed her back into the kitchen and devised a plan for the rest of their night. She was already scraping food into the trash and filling the sink. "I have a dishwasher."

Her head popped up from where she concentrated on dishes. "Oh." She turned the water off. He watched her move around his kitchen, piling dishes and wiping down the counter, anything to avoid the elephant in the room.

That damn elephant sat on his chest, suffocating him.

She continued to move as if he wasn't even there. She came around the corner of the counter to pick up their wineglasses.

"Stop." His sharp words made her freeze. She cautiously looked at him. "Just stop, Carmen. What are you doing?"

"I'm cleaning—"

He snatched the wineglass from her hand and slapped it back on the table, shattering the stem. Shards of glass sprayed out. "Fuck!" He glanced at his hand. No cuts. "Don't move," he said to her.

Before attempting to clear the broken glass, he inhaled deeply. He needed to get his frustration under control. He couldn't deal with her avoiding the fact that he—they—had sex, and it was lousy for her.

Only she'd said it wasn't. What else would a woman say, though? Unless she was a nasty bitch, which he couldn't imagine Carmen ever being, she would give him a pat and say it was okay.

"Liam?" Her voice was small, and he hated to think he'd frightened her.

He took a wide step over where glass might lay to get close to her. He took the other glass from her hand and set it gently on the table. "Come here." He pulled her toward the living room.

Once in front of the couch, he nudged her to sit. She sat with her hands in her lap, fingers entwined and twisting. He squatted in front of her and placed his hands over hers. "If this is going to work, Carmen, we need to be honest."

She bit her lip and nodded, but continued to stare at her hands like she was bracing for something bad.

"It's making me crazy that you're acting like what just

happened in the bedroom was not only okay, but that it was good for you. We can't make it better if you're not honest."

She looked up into his eyes. Her throat worked with a swallow. "I am being honest." Her eyes fluttered closed. "I told you I didn't have much experience and you shouldn't expect much."

"I expect you to enjoy yourself." He stroked his palm on her cheek.

"I was." She reopened her eyes. "I've never had an orgasm from sex. I don't think I can. That doesn't mean it doesn't feel good or that I'm not enjoying everything."

He couldn't argue. Being near her, touching her, kissing her, being inside her was a pretty incredible feeling. He still wanted her to come, though. "Have you ever?"

"Ever what?"

He was almost afraid of the answer. "Had an orgasm?"

"Yeah, I think so."

Jesus, Mary, and Joseph. She wasn't even sure. What the hell kind of guys had she slept with?

She pulled her hands away and tried to stand. "I can't do this."

He stood, blocking her path. With his hands on her hips—he loved the curves of her body—he held her in place. "Why not? Talk to me."

She laughed a small chuckle. "You are the least talkative person I know. It's one of your better qualities."

"But I talk when it needs to be done. We need to talk about this, Carmen."

She rested her head on his chest. He kissed the top of her head and inhaled the floral scent of her shampoo.

"It's hard. I'm not used to talking about this stuff."

"Then let's start with the obvious. The guys you've slept with were jerks. Or they didn't know what they were doing."

He felt her lips curve against his chest. "Screw the dishes. Let's grab the cheesecake and go back to bed."

She might relax in bed, as long as he didn't ask her to get naked. She stiffened at his suggestion, though.

"We'll talk. Share dessert. Figure this out. I'm a man on a mission now, and I don't give up easily. "

"Okay."

He thought he'd have to convince her to stay, but her acquiescence came easily. If only everything worked like that.

"But not the whole cheesecake. One piece to share."

He slid his hand into hers. "That's barely a taste. It won't be enough."

She rolled her eyes. He surveyed his kitchen, which was basically trashed. Dirty dishes piled up, the broken glass on the table. He held in his cringe, knowing that a conversation with Carmen was far more important, but he *never* left his workspace looking like that. He took the cheesecake out of the refrigerator and compromised. He sliced a really big piece and put it on a plate.

"That's not a normal piece."

"Work with me. You'll be glad once you try it."

He reached into the silverware drawer and debated, but settled on one fork. He wanted to feed her, to enjoy watching her indulge.

In the bedroom, she halted just inside the door. "I've never done this."

"What?"

"Hung out in bed with a guy. I only spent the whole night with a guy once and that was because we were both too drunk to move. But hanging out in bed, talking, eating. Nope."

Alcohol would explain at least some of her sexual disappointment. He turned on his bedside lamp. A soft glow filled the room. "It's easy. Relax and get comfortable."

He yanked back the covers and gestured with his arm for her to get in. She sat with her back against the headboard, barely disturbing anything. He climbed in beside her. The sudden urge to touch her and be in contact came on strong. He sat, facing her, slid one leg beneath both of hers, and leaned closer with a forkful of cake.

She opened her mouth and took the piece against her tongue. "Mmm…delicious."

Rather than take a bite for himself, he readied the fork for her. "I know you're embarrassed to talk about this, but I want to make love to you, Carmen. I want you to explode with pleasure. I want to make you come so hard, your body will be useless."

She swallowed the cheesecake and he watched her throat work. She didn't close her eyes, which he saw as improvement. A small victory. He reached across her and set the plate on the nightstand.

"What if we lie here and just explore? We won't have sex. I want to find out what you like and if you can't tell me, we'll have to figure it out." He leaned forward and kissed her, loving the taste of creamy sweetness on her tongue. His hand slid under her shirt, but she stopped him.

"The light."

"You're still fully clothed. I see you like this every day." He kissed her lips. "Besides, you have a gorgeous body."

"I'm self-conscious about my body. Especially with you."

"Why especially with me?" Had he ever done anything to make her feel inadequate?

She closed her eyes slowly, something he realized she did to gather strength. "When you look at me, it's like…I don't know. You see more than I want you to." Her eyes opened. "You're like that with everything. So completely observant.

Like you can't miss a detail." She scrunched up her nose. "There are lots of details I'd like you to *not* notice."

He'd known girls with body image issues. It wasn't unusual, but most of them could forget about it for a while during sex. They could let go of their hang-ups to have a good time. Carmen would need to do at least that.

"So leave your clothes on until you want them off." He kissed her neck while he pushed higher under her shirt, his fingers seeking her full breasts. He palmed her breast and then lightly pinched her nipple. "Do you like that?"

"Uh-huh." She followed with a nod that had her jaw bumping his nose.

He moved his hand to her other breast. Her pulse quickened beneath his tongue. He spread his hand on her belly as he headed south. She stiffened.

"I don't like that."

"What?" He hadn't done anything. He pulled away to look at her.

"Your hand on my stomach." She rolled her eyes again. "I told you I don't much like my body. I feel fat. Your hand on my stomach makes me feel fat."

He had no idea how to change her mind. "You're not fat. I like touching your skin. So soft."

Against her lips, and with a smile, he asked, "Where is good for touching? Boobs, yes. Hips? Ass? Pussy?"

"Uh..."

"I'll take that as all yeses." He snaked his hand below the stretchy band of the pants he'd given her to wear. "When you orgasmed before, was it by yourself?"

She nodded.

"I don't suppose you'd be willing to show me?"

"God, no. I couldn't do that."

She could and at some point, he hoped she would. He dipped his fingers down her slick slit and stroked.

CHAPTER 11

Oh, God, does that feel good. Carmen allowed her eyes to flutter closed and tried to ignore the fact that Liam was watching her and that her head was resting rather uncomfortably against the hard wood headboard of the bed. She took slow breaths and willed her body to relax.

Clearing her mind, she focused on every touch and movement Liam made. Women did this all the time without feeling awkward. Big women, bigger than her, had guys coming onto them. Maybe what Rosa said was true: Guys didn't care what you looked like as long as you were naked.

But she wasn't naked and Liam hadn't given up. From beneath her lashes, she stole a look at him. His shoulder muscles curved and bulged as he shifted. Whatever he just did with his hand was amazing and she forgot to breathe.

His free arm wrapped around her, underneath where she lay. "You might be more comfortable if you lay down." He tugged until she scooted lower, which caused a delicious pressure when she collided with his palm.

"Oh." Her eyes widened.

"Clitoral stimulation is a guarantee. Hard?" He pressed

against her clit. "Soft?" He circled his thumb over and around it. "Fast?" He picked up the pace and she saw stars against her eyelids. "Slow?" He moved his fingers in a snail-like fashion.

"Yes."

"To which?"

"Any." She was breathless and had to remind herself to inhale. Tension coiled and spiraled through her. She threw her arm across her eyes to block out any acknowledgment of Liam and rode the pleasure he offered.

His head dipped down and he sucked her hard nipple into his mouth through the shirt. Wet cotton stuck to her and rasped against her sensitive skin, but it increased her enjoyment of everything. Her hips began to move, to meet Liam's ministrations. He pushed one long finger into her, followed quickly by a second, stretching her, but it didn't feel like enough. Not like when he was inside her.

With his fingers curled inside her, pumping in and out, his thumb pressed against her clit. Her breaths came in short gasps. This was too much. Something wasn't right, but she didn't want to correct it. She began to tingle where Liam touched her. She arched her back, pushing her chest up to meet his greedy mouth.

Her muscles began to tighten.

"That's it. Let go, Carmen."

"I can't." She was close. So close, she felt like she stood on the edge of something, clinging, afraid to fall.

Liam's hand moved faster than was humanly possible and her thighs shook. Her arms trembled and then a high-pitched squeak squeezed past her constricted airway. Every nerve in her body was on high alert.

Then she felt it: the falling, the explosion, the magic as her muscles contracted and released. Liam's arm was still wrapped around her and he held her while she came down.

He stopped moving, but his hand hadn't left her. The position was so intimate, amazing.

When she moved her arm, she realized her cheeks were wet. Had she actually cried? She was afraid to open her eyes to face Liam's blue stare. But he had more patience and she knew he would outwait her. She opened her eyes and hoped she didn't look like she had been crying.

"I told you I'd get you there." He wore a smile of smug satisfaction.

"Wow." She had no other word. Of course she'd heard tales of sex being like that. Volcanoes and fireworks and explosions. But she never thought it would be real for her.

Liam finally pulled his hand out from her pants, and embarrassment struck her again knowing that his hand was wet because of her. He smirked and put his finger to his mouth and licked it.

Her jaw dropped. He did *not* just do that. Did he think he was in a porno or something? Guys didn't really do those things.

"I like the way you taste. There isn't a damn thing to be embarrassed about."

He read her every thought. That was why she crumpled under his watchful gaze. He kissed her then and she tasted a hint of herself on his lips mixed with his sweat in his beard. It was then that she realized how turned on he was. He'd carefully kept his hips and groin away from her, but when she nudged her thigh over, there was no mistaking the bulge in his underwear.

"We could finish, you know."

"You did finish, and I said no sex. I meant it. If I jump on you right now, it would be like that was just a prelude to what I could get out of the situation. That's not what this was."

But her body yearned to have him inside her again. How

could he not know? Even without an orgasm, the way he stretched and filled her felt good. She opened her mouth, but had no words.

"Will you spend the night?"

"I didn't bring anything."

"You don't need anything."

She wanted to, but she didn't know if she could. She'd never slept away from home. Not ever. What if she rolled over him or stole all the covers?

"You're thinking too much. Do you want to sleep here?"

"Yeah, but—"

"No buts. Stay. We can curl up here and watch TV. Finish our cheesecake." He held a finger to her lips and she smelled her sex on it. "Before you argue, you just expelled enough calories to afford dessert."

He made everything seem so simple. Life was never this simple. But for now, maybe she could pretend.

LIAM WOKE in the morning and slipped out of bed without waking Carmen. It was early and while he never liked mornings, he'd gone to bed much earlier than his usual routine. Not to mention the dirty kitchen had been nagging at him all night. He cleaned up the mess from dinner and started breakfast. He knew Carmen would balk at eating a real meal because he'd watched her swill nothing but coffee every morning this week.

He wanted her to enjoy food the way he did instead of seeing it as the enemy. He wished he could make something special, like French toast, but settled for omelets. He chopped up some peppers and ham and shredded some cheese. While the pan heated, he whisked the eggs and sipped coffee that was still too hot.

She came from the bedroom just as he poured the eggs into the waiting pan. "Wait."

Carmen stopped. She had her hair piled messily on top of her head and she wore the clothes she'd arrived in yesterday.

"I didn't finish cleaning up the broken glass. I didn't want the vacuum to wake you. Don't move."

Instead of standing still, she moved around the opposite side of the table. He flipped the eggs and then started the vacuum where he'd left it waiting. She moved around the counter and poured herself a cup of coffee. He caught her eying the pan of eggs.

"I made breakfast. I have a family thing today, but maybe we could get together later?"

She nodded. He'd thought about inviting her to dinner, but with the O'Learys, you only brought someone to dinner when you were serious. He didn't know what to think of his relationship with Carmen. He liked her and cared about her, but he wasn't sure yet how serious they were. She still had a lot in her life to figure out. Besides, he needed to tell his family about quitting his job to run the food truck.

"I'm not really hungry."

"Too bad. I cooked. You can eat a little." He slid the omelet onto a plate and split it in half. He tilted his head toward the table to get her to follow. She glanced around the kitchen and then joined him.

"I would've helped you clean up. You should've woken me."

"It was fine." He began eating, but she didn't, so he handed her the fork. "How are you feeling?"

Her cheeks grew pink with her smile. "Good, thanks. How did you sleep?"

"Excellent." And he had. He enjoyed having her in his bed to wrap his body around all night. The only thing that would've improved the experience was if she'd been naked. "What are your plans for today?"

"Prepping for the truck. Making a fresh batch of mole so you'll be ready for tomorrow. Updating the web site. Trying to get word out on social media. Exciting stuff." She shrugged and put a bite of egg into her mouth. She sighed as she chewed.

"If you wait, I'll do the prep with you. Write down the social media stuff. My sister, Moira, is always doing something online. When Colin opened his new bar, her big mouth spread the word, and they filled the place. I'll have her work her magic for us." He paused in eating, hoping she would eat more. She did, which made him inordinately happy.

They finished breakfast together, and Carmen started to look twitchy. "Something wrong?" he asked.

"No."

He reached out and grabbed her hips to pull her close. "So, about tonight. I was thinking if we're prepping the truck and I have to head out early, it might be a good idea if I spend the night at your house."

"Liam, are you angling for an invitation to my bed?"

"Of course, but I didn't want to be presumptuous. We have a lot of work to do." He nuzzled her neck, loving the smell of her and the uptick in her pulse.

"Work?"

"The truck. I need to be ready to hit the ground running." After a second, her question hit him. He pulled away. "Did you think I was talking about us being work?"

She tilted her head a little to the side to let him know that's exactly what she'd thought.

"Babe, being in bed with you is all pleasure." To help her understand, he captured her mouth and kissed her. When his blood was pumping, he pulled away before he dragged her back to bed. "Any questions?"

She shook her head with a lusty look.

"I'll see you after I'm done with my family."

"Okay." She was still breathless, so he winked at her.

She grabbed her coat and left.

Liam took a shower and thought about how to tell his family about his life changes.

~

LATER THAT AFTERNOON, Liam sat at the dining room table with most of his family. He still didn't know what to say. He cleared his throat and said, "I have news."

Everyone at the table quieted, which was quite a feat for this group.

"I quit my job at Porter's." He let that sink in and then continued. "I quit because I inherited part ownership in a food truck. Starting tomorrow, I'll be running Gus's Taco Taxi."

"Oh, my God." Moira shoved away from the table and rushed at him. With her arms wrapped around his neck from behind his seat, she added, "Congratulations!"

Colin said, "So what helped you make up your mind?"

Moira's eyes narrowed at Colin as she made her way back to her seat. "You knew?" She smacked Colin's arm and then turned to Liam. "Why did he know, but I didn't?"

Before Liam could answer, she sat back at her seat next to Jimmy, and asked, "Did you know about this?"

She was getting mad at being left out of a secret, and Liam laughed. "No, Jimmy didn't know. I talked to Colin when I found out about it. It's not like running a food truck is my dream job, but I talked with Carmen, that's Gus's daughter and my new partner. We can't sell for at least a year and it's a good business. It'll be something new for me."

"Congrats, man," Jimmy said from across the table.

"Thanks." He returned his focus to the bland roast his mom made for dinner. He felt her looking at him, but she said nothing. Eileen O'Leary was like that. She often kept her mouth shut, at least until she couldn't.

"As long as I have your attention," he said to Moira, "I was hoping you could use your social skills to spread word about the truck. Gus did a strong business, but since his death, it's been off the street. Carmen has the web site updated and she has Facebook and Twitter accounts, but if you could give us a shout-out, it might help."

"No problem. Get me the info."

He shifted his weight and pulled the sheet of paper from Carmen from his pocket and handed it to her.

"Tell us about Carmen."

Liam shrugged. Leave it to Moira to start asking questions. The damn reporter brain. "What do you want to know?"

"Really, Liam? You're going to try to dodge?" She sighed heavily as if being totally put out. "How cute is she?"

He choked on a piece of meat and washed it down with water.

"Heh. I knew it. You guys are all the same. So it's just the two of you working in that small truck *all* day long, huh?"

"No, actually. I'll be out on the truck myself. She runs the office part of the business. She doesn't cook." The lie almost died on his lips. She did cook, and she was damn good at it; she just resented it.

"You still didn't tell me how cute she is."

Liam stood with his plate to take it to the kitchen. "Pretty damn."

"Liam." His mom's sharp tone whipped out.

He was a grown man still getting scolded for cursing. It wasn't like he'd said she was fucking smokin' hot. "Sorry." But he couldn't help but wink at Moira, whose mouth hung open. He rarely talked about his personal life and Moira was always bugging him about it. She hadn't expected him to answer at all, so he enjoyed stunning her.

Of course, that gave her fuel and she propelled into the kitchen right behind him. "Pretty damn cute. Does that mean you like her?"

"Of course I like her. I wouldn't be able to work with someone I don't like." That wasn't entirely true; he'd managed to work with Jonathan for a long time without really liking him.

Moira nudged him with her elbow as she scraped her plate. "You know what I mean. Are you dating?"

"Yes. And that's all I'm going to say. It's new. I don't know where it's going. She's got a lot happening in her life and I don't need you freaking her out."

She set her plate on the counter and put her palm over her heart. "I'm hurt. What makes you think I would freak her out?"

"Because you're scary," Jimmy said from the doorway.

She glared at him.

Liam watched as she stood on tiptoe to kiss his friend. He was glad he didn't fight their relationship more than he had at the very beginning when the shock of Jimmy being with his sister caught him off guard. They were good together. They balanced each other out. It was something each of his brothers had found as well.

As he filled the sink to start the dishes, he thought about Carmen. Did she balance him? They weren't really opposites, not like the other couples sitting around the dinner table in the other room.

Jimmy joined him at the sink with a towel to start drying.

"You're not on dish duty."

Jimmy shrugged.

"Moira conned you into doing dishes for her."

Jimmy smiled. "No, actually, I volunteered. I figured you'd rather have me in here than her. Want to talk about it?"

"What?"

"Anything. Last time we talked about your job, you weren't happy, but you weren't doing anything to change it. You never mentioned wanting a food truck. It's not really what I pictured you doing." He picked up the first plate and dried it.

"This fell into my lap, but it'll be a good challenge."

"And your partner's hot."

"Hell, yeah, she is."

Ryan came into the room with an armful of plates. "Heads-up. Quinn is on her way with the rest of the glasses."

Liam was grateful for his brother's warning about his sister-in-law. She could be almost as bad as Moira at digging up information. He rinsed the silverware in his hand as Quinn quietly placed glasses on the counter. She studied him a moment, but said nothing.

When she left the room, Liam lowered his voice. "I knew Carmen when I worked at her dad's restaurant. She was cute but she was still a teenager and I was in culinary school, so I couldn't think about her like that. But then I saw her at the wake and in the days since." He inhaled deeply. "She's hot, but she doesn't know it. She lacks confidence and even though I don't have her whole sexual history, I know she's had crappy lovers."

"Makes it easier for you then. You come across like a god."

He certainly hoped so.

"Is it serious?"

"Like I told Moira, I don't know yet. We just started dating a week ago. I don't know how much of the relationship is because we really like each other or if it's simply proximity." He said the words to stay rational, but they didn't feel right. He believed he would still date Carmen even if they each had different jobs. He could imagine cooking for her when she came home from work or in the morning before she headed out.

Of course in that scenario, he couldn't imagine what other job either of them would have. That was the crux of the problem. They both had a lot to figure out.

"I can understand," Jimmy said. "I'll try to keep Moira off your back."

"As much as I'd enjoy that, I doubt you'll be successful."

"Little you know. I've been successful for months. She was talking about *helping* you with your love life last summer."

Liam scrubbed the pot his mother used for mashed potatoes. It was one of those hand-me-down pieces that had been in the family forever. He couldn't remember his mom ever using anything else when it was time for potatoes. He wondered if he would have a similar piece in his kitchen.

"Hey, while we're alone." Jimmy's voice was barely audible. He looked over his shoulder to watch the door. "I need your help."

"Anything."

"I plan to buy Moira a ring for Christmas. I don't think she has any idea, since we haven't talked about it, but that also means she's never mentioned what the hell kind she likes."

Liam pulled his hands from the soapy water and slapped his friend on the back, leaving a trail of suds and murky drops. "Congrats."

"Shh. That woman has ears like a dog." He stole another look at the door. "I need you to help me pick one out."

"Have you thought about how you're going to ask?"

"Yeah. I've got that covered."

Just then, Quinn reentered the room, eyeing them both. "I'm here to grab dessert. Moira said it's in the refrigerator."

Jimmy opened the fridge door. "We grabbed pastries from Blackstone this morning." He handed her the box, the string already broken.

Quinn raised an eyebrow.

"Talk to Colin. He snagged something before we hit the kitchen."

"Hurry with the dishes or there'll be nothing left." She walked back to the dining room with the bakery box.

Liam drained the sink. "Tomorrow's my first day on the truck. I don't know what to expect or what the rest of my week will look like, so I'll give you a call and we'll figure a time to get together."

He dried his hands on a towel as his phone buzzed in his pocket. A message from Lily.

I know you have dinner with your family, but I need to see you. Stop by after? It's important.

"Your hot partner calling already?"

"No, it's Lily. She wants me to stop by."

"Lily?"

"She's a friend."

"Hmm-mm. Better not let Carmen hear."

"Carmen knows."

"Tread carefully, man." Jimmy draped his wet towel along the counter.

"What's that supposed to mean? Lily's a friend. We met at Ryan's wedding. We hang out and cook together sometimes. You're friends with Gabby. Moira's okay with that, right?"

"Yeah, but Gabby's my partner. Moira has seen us together. Besides, no one does to me what Moira does."

"Dude, that's my sister you're talking about. I don't want to hear it."

Jimmy chuckled. "Yeah, I guess those days are gone."

Liam checked the time. "I need to get going. I'll call you in a couple of days."

CHAPTER 12

Carmen stood over the stove with her dad's stockpot waiting for ingredients. She'd watched her dad do this for years. She knew how, but she'd never put in the effort to really do it. She closed her eyes and envisioned her dad. He talked through the process every time, as if he needed the words to get it right. She knew now that he did it to share with her even though she wasn't ready to hear it.

With a deep, fortifying breath, she went to the refrigerator, now fully stocked for at least the day, and pulled what she needed. When a knock sounded at the back door, she checked the time. She wasn't expecting Liam for a couple of hours. She looked out the window to see Rosa waving her arms. The girl never wore a coat and then bitched that she was cold.

"What took so long? I knew you were home, but you didn't answer at the front."

"I didn't hear you. I'm busy."

Rosa stopped her foot-stomping and the rubbing of her arms for warmth. "You're cooking?"

Rosa knew about Carmen's aversion to cooking. "Liam's

taking the truck out tomorrow. As good of a cook as he is, he knows nothing about Dad's mole, so I'm making a batch."

"Ooo…Look at that. Carmen's finally getting her groove back." She snapped her fingers and dropped into a hip-wiggling dance.

Carmen couldn't help but laugh. If Rosa only knew—but then, in a few minutes, she would because Carmen was never good at keeping secrets from Rosa.

"Wonder Bread is really going to run a taco truck. I can't believe it. What are Gus's customers going to think?"

"I told you to stop calling him that. Liam is a trained chef with excellent experience. We serve tacos. If anything, he's way overqualified for the job." She heated the pan with a bit of lard. The blob turned her stomach a little, but this was her father's recipe.

"Can he speak Spanish?"

"Pete ran the truck with Dad all the time, and he barely speaks Spanish."

"You know what I mean."

Carmen turned and folded her arms. "No, what do you mean?"

"Liam might be a good guy—"

"He is," she snapped.

"Oh, shit. You really like this guy." Rosa crossed the room and stood beside the stove. "When the hell did this happen?"

Carmen shrugged. "We've been hanging out a lot while getting him ready with the truck. Then he kissed me. It evolved from there."

The smile formed on Carmen's lips before Rosa asked another question. Turning back to the pan, she added the various peppers that would give the sauce the heat she liked.

Rosa whistled. "You slept with him too? Now I need details."

While the peppers browned and got crunchy, Carmen

thought about how to explain things with Liam. "We're dating. He makes me feel good, Rosa. It's so different from other guys I dated. And he's patient, if you know what I mean."

"No wham-bam for the Irish boy, huh? I guess that earns him some points. Is he good?"

"Very." The word was inadequate, but it would do. She didn't want to reveal how much of an impact Liam had had on her. She and Rosa often talked about sex. Well, Rosa talked, and Carmen mostly listened. She couldn't imagine how good it would be with Liam if she could learn to be as uninhibited and carefree as Rosa.

"One word is not a detail."

"You know I don't kiss and tell."

"You barely ever kiss. I tell you everything."

Carmen laughed and looked at her cousin. "Believe me. There are some things I could do without hearing."

"I'm going to the store to get us drinks. Alcohol will loosen those details."

"There's beer in the fridge."

Rosa reached in the fridge. "You never have beer." When she pulled back with two bottles, she added, "And you have a bottle of wine."

"Liam brought it." Along with other food he left at her house. He claimed it was left over from his experimenting, but she knew that her lack of food drove him crazy.

Rosa twisted the caps off and handed her a bottle. "Drink up."

"It's two in the afternoon."

"So what? We're not going anywhere. I'll even help cook." Rosa moved around the kitchen easily and Carmen envied her comfort. Her cousin was comfortable everywhere.

"Chop the onion."

"Figures," Rosa grumbled. Before starting, she moved to

the radio. "We need some tunes." Rosa believed everything was better with music. Her hips began to sway to the rhythm as she picked up a knife.

Carmen pulled the peppers from the pan and added the next round of ingredients. "He's sneaky," she told Rosa. "He's quiet and gentle and soothing. It's like he knows what I need before I do. It's kind of unnerving, but also nice."

She thought about the way Liam looked at her, with desire burning in his blue eyes. A shiver skated down her back. "He looks at me with this intense expression. It's such a turn-on. Like he can't get his hands on me fast enough. But then he's never fast. He's methodical."

Rosa dropped her onion in the pan. "I wouldn't mind that kind of attention. He got a brother?"

"A bunch, actually."

Rosa nudged her. "So hook me up."

"I don't know his family. I just know there are like six kids. I think he said most of his brothers are married, though, so I think you're out of luck."

"Maybe when you're done with him." Rosa wagged her eyebrows.

Her immediate reaction was *hell no*, because she couldn't imagine being done, but she said, "Gross. I would never date one of your exes."

"That's because they're all losers."

Carmen stirred the ingredients in the pot and drank her beer. She'd have to keep it to just the one so she wouldn't be drunk when Liam showed up. She looked at the clock again. What was the likelihood Rosa would leave before Liam arrived?

Rosa heaved a sigh. "Fine. I get it. You don't want to share. Besides finally getting laid, what else is going on? You've been scarce for weeks."

"At first, I couldn't be around people."

"I'm not people. I'm your best friend."

"I know. I needed to get used to Dad being gone." But Liam had been there with a kind word or gesture. "I'm still sorting stuff out. The truck is dealt with because Liam is handling it. I've started looking for a regular job, but I don't even know what I want to do. I also started three different projects around here. I got the bedroom painted, though." It was her turn to sigh. "I feel scattered."

"I know that feeling."

Uh-oh. Carmen knew that tone. "What happened?"

"I got fired. Again."

Rosa spent most of her life scattered. No, more like unfocused. She liked to party and she liked men, but other than that, she flaked on everything else: school, jobs, hobbies. "Do your parents know yet?"

"Nope. I'm hoping to find something tomorrow so they won't know. Or at least when they find out, I'll already have a job."

"What happened this time?"

"I was bored and screwing around on company time."

"Please tell me you weren't literally screwing around, like with your boss or something." She added the remaining ingredients and put the peppers back in. When the chicken broth began to simmer, she added the touch of chocolate.

"No. I was surfing the Internet when I was supposed to be typing up some stupid report."

Carmen felt relief. Rosa's parents would keel over if she had gotten fired over her sex life.

With everything in the huge stockpot, she sat at the table and kicked the chair next to her for Rosa to join her. "Sounds like we both need a plan."

"You have a job. Working for the truck is what you've been doing for years. Plus, you don't have to pay rent or nothin'."

"I still have bills. The truck was never supposed to be my life. At first, it was to give me something to do while I took care of Mom. Then after she died, I stayed on to help Dad. I don't know that this is what I want to do forever. It's not really a career. Definitely not the one I planned on and worked for." But that had been so long ago, she wasn't sure she even remembered those dreams.

"At least you have a plan, something to try to get back to. I got nothing."

"Find something you like, something you're passionate about." She smiled at her cousin. "Something other than a guy."

Rosa rolled her eyes.

"You have to want it enough to stick with it." Liam was a chef who wanted a restaurant. What if he didn't stick with the truck? Carmen shoved the thought aside. She'd deal with that if it happened.

"Too bad I don't have any ideas."

Carmen pushed up from her spot. "Then in the meantime, you can help me paint. This house hasn't had any work done in too many years."

Before following Carmen to the living room, Rosa dialed up the volume on the radio and grabbed a couple more beers.

Liam rang Lily's bell. Why she wanted to live above her mother's diner, he would never understand. Kind of like Colin and Ryan had both lived above O'Leary's Pub. When he was done with work, he wanted to get away, into his own space.

Lily opened the door with a bright smile and handed him a glass of wine.

"What's this for?"

"We're celebrating."

He followed her into her apartment, which was really just a studio. She had a small love seat in front of a chest that held her TV. In the corner, her bed was situated beneath a window. Her kitchen consisted of a miniscule counter, an apartment-sized refrigerator and stove. The pots he'd given her last Christmas hung from a rack.

He shrugged out of his coat and laid it on a folding chair. They sat on the faded couch.

"I talked to my mom. I told her about culinary school and how much I want it. She listened, Liam, like really listened. She didn't blow me off with 'I taught you how to cook. If it's good for us, it's good for the diner.' It was like the first time she got that I want more than the diner."

He patted her leg. "Congratulations. I told you it would work out."

"It wouldn't have happened without your help." She jumped at him and wrapped her arms around his neck. Her actions knocked his wine all over his shirt.

"Shoot. I'm sorry." She pulled away and grabbed a towel from the kitchen.

A red splotch spread across the middle of his torso. Lily returned and began blotting the spot.

"This isn't working. Take the shirt off and I'll see if I can get it out."

Liam unbuttoned the shirt. He had a matching spot on his undershirt. Lily watched his movements.

"Give me that one, too."

"It's fine."

She took his shirt to the kitchen sink and ran water on it. She scrubbed furiously. "I'm so sorry about this. I just got excited. I wasn't thinking." She held the shirt out and examined it. "It might be ruined. I'll buy you a new one."

"It's not a big deal. Forget about it. Come back and tell me what your mom said."

Lily trudged back to the couch, gripping his ruined shirt. She moved his coat and hung the shirt in its place and then joined him. "I told her I want to go to culinary school. At first, she thought it was a joke. When she saw I wasn't laughing, she listened. I told her about you and how much you'd already taught me."

"I haven't done much."

She reached out and covered his hand with hers. The movement, which she'd probably done before, suddenly felt different to him. "Yes, you have. Don't sell yourself short."

Her hand didn't move and she scooted closer. "Without you pushing me to talk to her, I probably wouldn't have. Thank you."

She leaned in again. Before Liam could process what she was doing, her lips made contact. She tilted her head and opened her mouth, shoving her tongue past his lips. Liam blinked in shock and then grabbed her shoulders. Gently pushing her back, he asked, "What was that?"

She smiled, her blue eyes soft. "I get that you're a cautious guy. I do. And I've been waiting forever for you to make a move. I guess I got tired of waiting."

"Oh, uh." He leaned farther back into the couch. "I'm seeing someone."

She sank away from him. "You are? Since when?"

"It's kind of new." How the hell was he supposed to answer this without hurting her? He'd never looked at Lily as anything other than a friend. In fact, she was like another little sister.

"Oh." The single syllable held pain that he hadn't wanted to cause.

"I like you, Lily, but we're friends."

"I know, but..." Her voice trailed off, as lost as he felt at the moment.

He'd missed all the signals from her. He'd been so caught up in his own life for the past year that he didn't pay attention. Looking back now, he never remembered her having a boyfriend or even a date. She usually wanted to hang out at home with him. He'd attributed it to her wanting to learn more about cooking, but now he saw it.

"I should head out," he said as he stood. "I have to get the truck ready for tomorrow."

"Okay." She stood beside him. "I'm sorry. For your shirt, for throwing myself at you."

"You didn't throw yourself. It was a kiss." One that did nothing for him, but he couldn't tell her. "No big deal. Friends?"

"Of course." She smiled, but it wasn't real.

She looked like she wanted to cry, which just made him want to leave faster. He tugged his wet shirt on and threw his coat over it, buttoning up so the wet spot wouldn't turn to ice outside.

"I'll call you later in the week."

"Sure."

He walked out of Lily's apartment and wondered if it was possible to be friends with a woman who clearly had feelings for him. If he had continued to be blind to the attraction, of course, but now that she'd made it known? He wasn't sure.

Liam drove to Carmen's house. For a change, lights were on in many rooms, including the kitchen. He parked and grabbed his bag. He'd planned to be there earlier, and knowing Carmen, she probably started the prep without him. From the front porch, he heard the thumping music.

He knocked with his fist, hoping she'd hear him over the radio. The music quieted slightly and the door swung open. Carmen's cousin Rosa smiled up at him with a beer in her hand. "Hey."

"Hi," he answered, tucking his bag behind his back a little.

He didn't know if Rosa knew he'd be spending the night. Carmen didn't give him the impression she talked a lot, unlike Moira, who told everyone everything.

Rosa stepped away from the door, allowing him entrance. Her eyes stayed on him, but she called over her shoulder, "It's Wo—Liam."

"Good to see you again, Rosa." He stepped aside and let her close the door.

Carmen stood in the middle of the living room, where all of the furniture was now located. "Hi," she said.

"Sorry I'm late. I got caught up."

"No problem. Mole is on the stove. We got busy here."

He dropped his bag next to the door and followed Rosa into the room. "Busy doing what?"

Stripes of various colors streaked the walls.

"We were going to paint, but Rosa didn't like the color I picked, so we went back to the store and got some samples."

He edged closer, wanting to grab her and kiss her, but not sure if she would welcome it in front of her cousin. "What did you decide?"

"We haven't. As usual, Rosa and I can't agree on anything. How was your family thing?" She didn't step closer, so he figured she wanted to play it cool with Rosa in the room.

"It was dinner with my family. We try to do it once a month. Get everyone together." He took off his coat.

"What happened to your shirt?"

He looked down at the blotch covering most of the front of the shirt. "Long story."

Carmen came closer. "The stain will probably never come out now. Why didn't you treat it right away? Give me that."

Before he could say anything, she was stripping it from him, clucking like his mother would. She shot him a look when she saw the undershirt. "That one too." She held out her hand like she wouldn't take no for an answer.

"I planned to just throw them away. I don't think they can be saved." But he did as he was told.

Rosa stood on the other side of the room snickering.

He looked at her over Carmen's head. "What so funny?"

"I don't think I've ever seen such a white boy, unless you count that vampire in the movie." Carmen glared at her as she left the room. Rosa gulped more beer.

Beer he'd brought to the house.

Rather than continue to stand shirtless in the middle of the room, he went to his bag and pulled out a fresh T-shirt.

"Moving in?" Rosa asked.

"No." He'd let Carmen address that. He put the shirt on with Rosa still staring. "What have you been up to besides complaining about paint colors?"

"Nothing." She narrowed her eyes. "Why are you working the truck?"

"Because it's partly mine and Carmen doesn't want to. Gus built a good business and neither of us wants it to go down the drain. Why do you care?"

"I don't. About the truck. I care about her." She angled her head toward the back of the house. "She doesn't need more heartache."

"What makes you think I'd hurt her?"

"I don't know you."

"I doubt you know all of her boyfriends. She knows me. Gus knew me. He trusted me."

"There's no accounting for his taste."

Now he was getting pissed, but he wasn't sure why. Rosa's opinion didn't matter. "What's your problem with me?"

"I got no problem as long as she's happy."

He nodded. That's all he could expect. He'd given Jimmy a similar speech. Of course that had come after he'd punched his friend. Liam understood wanting to keep those you loved safe. He wouldn't hurt Carmen.

Carmen came back and pulled up short. "What's going on?"

"Nothing," he answered.

Rosa smiled. She must've thought he'd rat her out. "I'm going home. Early day tomorrow. Wish me luck."

"Are you okay to drive?" Carmen asked.

"Yeah. I'm good."

"Call me when you get home so I know you're safe."

"Yes, Mom." She kissed Carmen's cheek and left.

As soon as the door shut behind her, Liam swooped in and pulled Carmen close. He hadn't realized how much he'd wanted to kiss her, but now that he had her in his arms, greed urged him on. Holding her close, his erection grew and his mind blanked.

She pulled away with a laugh. "Hi to you too."

"I wanted to do that the second I walked through the door, but I didn't know with Rosa…"

"She knows about us, yeah, but I don't think I want to make out in front of her."

"So tearing your clothes off would've been a bad thing."

She laughed again. "Come to the kitchen. The mole is done. We just have to chop veggies and stuff." She talked as she moved through the house. "My dad used to get up crazy early to prep to avoid the busyness of the restaurant, but I think we can do most of it now. Unless you prefer morning. The restaurant is closed either way, so we'll have the place to ourselves."

Although he listened to her, he was distracted by the sight of her ass as she bent over to look into the refrigerator. "Why not just do all the prep work on site when I set up?"

She slammed the lid from her stockpot on the counter. "You didn't read the regulations."

"I did. Which is how I know you're breaking the rules by making mole in your kitchen."

"Then you would also know that you can only be in one place for two hours max. The GPS in the truck reports your location. If you wait to make everything until you set up, you'll lose a ton of actual selling time. You need to have everything up and running in under thirty minutes. Sell for less than an hour and a half, do the minimum breakdown and cleanup and move on."

"Okay."

She rubbed her forehead. "I'm glad I called Pete. He can walk you through this."

"Carmen, I can handle this. I've run whole kitchens with service for a hundred on an average night. I can handle a small line of people brave enough to stand in the cold for some tacos. I told you I don't need Pete."

"Pete knows the routine. Running the truck should be at least a two-man operation: one for taking the orders and the money and one for cooking."

"You said Gus worked alone."

"He did, but that doesn't mean it was smart. On the days Pete worked with him, we consistently saw an increase in business. Two guys can make more happen. And like I said, Pete knows this. If you screw up, we'll get fined. A thousand dollars. There is no 'whoops, didn't mean to.'"

He tried to smooth his hackles. When it came to cooking he was never incompetent. "I won't screw up. As long as I get the truck moved in under two hours we're good. I'll make it happen."

Worry splayed across her face. He liked the living room much better than the kitchen right now. At least there, she hadn't thought him incompetent. He stepped closer and ran his hand along her jaw. "I've got this. Trust me."

"I'm trying."

He kissed her again, this time without the fervent attack. His tongue coasted over hers. She tasted of beer and something spicy. He briefly wished he'd brought the leftover cheesecake because he really wanted to taste that sweetness on her again. He nibbled on her lip and slid a hand down to her ass. He cupped a cheek and pressed her close.

Her breathing became ragged. She bumped her hips into him. He kissed his way down her throat and she moaned. Yeah, this was much better than arguing about the damn truck and stupid city rules.

"Liam." Her voice was little more than a breath.

"Hmm-mmm."

"We need to finish."

"I'm trying."

Her hand came down hard on his shoulder. "The prep work, Liam."

"It can wait."

"No." This time, she at least tried for forceful.

"Give me a few minutes. I'll change your mind." He pressed his thigh between her legs and stroked her.

"We can't."

"We can. Take a break. You said yourself we could work tonight or tomorrow."

"But…"

He eased his face away from her delectable neck. "But what?"

Her eyes were wide. "Last night, I could barely move when we were done."

The amount of satisfaction that burst through him was unnatural. "Then you can nap and I'll prep."

She bit her bottom lip like she was still considering. He squeezed her nipple and her eyes slammed shut. She nodded and before she could change her mind, he grabbed her hand. "Which room has a bed?"

"Around the corner."

CHAPTER 13

Carmen didn't know what had come over her. Leaving work unfinished was not how her dad taught her to run a business. But Liam was very convincing. For a guy who normally moved slowly and methodically, he practically ran to her bedroom.

They crashed onto her bed and his hard-on poked her thigh. She loved knowing she had this effect on him. Without warning, his hand shot past the waistband of her pants and he stroked her like he had last night. She was already wet from his kisses.

With a finger inside of her, he paused. "I want to go down on you."

"Huh?"

"I want to go down on you. Taste you. Make you come with my mouth."

Oh, God, she had heard him right.

"Carmen?"

"Yeah?" Her mouth was suddenly dry, but her panties were soaked. If his mouth made her wet when he kissed her, what magic would it do down there?

His smiling face filled her vision. "Was that a yeah, go ahead?"

She nodded.

Again, Liam moved fast. He yanked her pants off in one smooth movement, exposing her to the chilly air of the bedroom. She didn't have time to get self-conscious about how she looked half-naked on her bed because Liam didn't stop to look. He disappeared down her body. He nudged her thighs wide and settled his broad shoulders between them. His bare shoulders. When had he taken off his shirt?

His beard bristled softly against her inner thigh, sending tingles through her system. He kissed her thigh and inched upward. She held her body still against all instinct to wiggle and move. Her heart thundered in her ears.

And then he kissed her and licked her. Her entire body began to hum. This was so much better than anything she'd ever experienced. When he sucked on her clit, her hips jumped into the air. She felt his laugh as a vibration against her while he followed her movement.

Liam was relentless. Need clawed at her and she had no idea how to satisfy it. Liam's fingers joined his mouth, but it wasn't enough. Tension coiled and her thighs trembled. She was on the edge of something she couldn't claim.

Then it happened again. Her body went rigid beneath him as she became overwhelmed with the sensations. She struggled for breath.

Liam rose above her with his hips pressing against her. He slid into her and she knew what she'd been missing. This. Him.

He entered her as far as he could, and she automatically wrapped her legs around him. She sighed at the way he filled her.

He lowered his face and she smelled herself on him, in his beard, mixed with a scent that was Liam, and it made her pull him closer. He kissed her and their mingled scent and taste was heady and wonderful.

Beyond that moment, Carmen was lost. Liam could've done anything he wanted and she wouldn't have cared. The haze of lust and pleasure overrode everything.

Carmen had no idea how long she lay there. Her brain was long empty as her lungs filled with oxygen. She was still fully clothed above the waist and Liam had pulled the blanket over their bottom halves. He lay half on top of her, his breath blowing against her hair. As her senses all came back to normal, guilt and worry assaulted her. She knew she'd had a great time, but she had no idea if Liam did. The entire experience had been a bit of a blur.

"You're not supposed to be thinking yet."

"I can't help thinking."

He nuzzled her neck. "I must not have done a good enough job if you can think already."

"You did more than a good enough job. You were amazing."

"Can I get that in writing? Maybe on a T-shirt." He kissed her neck and then pushed up to look at her face. "What are you thinking?"

"Was it as good for you as it was for me? I have no idea, and I feel like you keep doing all the work, and I'm not sure what you're getting out of this."

"Hell, yeah, it was good for me. I told you before, you're not work. Your body is all about pleasure." He slipped his hand under her shirt, but didn't grope her. His fingers settled against her ribs. "Want to take a shower with me?"

She didn't know how to answer. She still hadn't been completely naked with him, at least not where he could see everything. Under the harsh light of the bathroom, exploiting every imperfection? Not a good idea.

The corner of his mouth lifted and he shook his head a

little. "Sooner or later, I'm going to convince you to be stripped bare in front of me and you're not only *not* going to be embarrassed, but you'll enjoy it."

She snorted. That would likely never happen.

He left the bed and she watched his naked body. It wasn't perfect. She knew that no one had a perfect body. At the door, he turned and winked at her. The playful gesture was so different from the Liam she was used to.

When he was gone, she flipped back the covers and grabbed some sweatpants.

LIAM WOKE while the sun wasn't even a thought in the sky. Carmen scooted closer again and as much as he wanted to stay in bed, he needed to make sure he was ready. He made a pot of coffee and read through Carmen's checklist of items.

She'd written down Gus's routine. Some of Gus's plan didn't make sense. It seemed inefficient. He finished his first cup of coffee and began his own plan of attack. He settled at the kitchen table with Carmen's big binder of information. He had read it. Admittedly, there were parts he skimmed. The food truck was a small kitchen. Kitchens were all the same. Food safety regulations didn't change.

He glanced at his phone. The temperature reading for the day was only supposed to be a high of fifteen degrees, not accounting for wind chill.

His best hope was that with only twelve days until Christmas, people would be out in force to shop. Shopping made people hungry. Or so he'd heard.

The thought of shopping reminded him that he still needed to get his grab bag gift. With a family of six siblings, now growing to include spouses, they'd decided that a grab bag made sense. He'd gotten his sister-in-law, Quinn. He wasn't sure what to get her. He'd have to think fast, though. The idea of shopping a day or two before Christmas made him sick.

He remembered Jimmy wanted him to go shopping for a ring for Moira. He'd get Quinn something then. He pulled out his phone and made a note to call Jimmy and set something up for the weekend.

A sweet thought occurred to him. The taco truck was a Monday through Friday business. His weekends were free. And his holidays. And his nights.

With each passing thought, he was liking the truck more and more. At seven o'clock, Carmen joined him in the kitchen and drank her coffee in silence, but he saw her watching the clock. He needed to be on the road by ten to claim his spot, and they hadn't heard from Pete.

"I'll come with you to the restaurant and help you get ready." The unease on her face and in the line of her body was unnatural.

"What's wrong?"

"I don't go to the restaurant."

"Ever?"

"I haven't stepped foot in the place in years. Since before Mom died."

He opened his mouth, but nothing came out. How could she not be part of the restaurant?

She fisted her hands. "When my dad bought the truck, it was so he would have more time with my mom. He sold most of the business to his brother in order to make that happen. The restaurant is our commissary location. Our official kitchen as far as the city is concerned."

He had no idea that she had such a problem with the restaurant. "Why?"

"The place brings back too many memories. I wasted my

entire adolescence avoiding the kitchen and my mom. I guess it's guilt more than anything."

"If you're not ready for this, I can go alone. Give me the key."

"No. It's about time I handled it. Besides, the truck belongs parked over there. I'm surprised my neighbors haven't called and reported me already. You drive the truck and I'll follow in my car. I'll meet you at the end of the day and pick you up."

At the restaurant, Liam felt like he was sucked into a time warp. It had been about a decade since he'd worked there and not much had changed. The kitchen was tiny compared to the one at Porter's. He stared at the sink that had been his station longer than he'd liked. His fingers almost pruned just thinking about it. He'd come a long way since then. He glanced at Carmen. So had she.

Carmen taught him about all the hookups and necessary details for cleaning the truck after shift. For someone who had no desire to run a kitchen, she sure knew a lot. She'd be amazing running any business.

He kept an eye on her as they prepped the food. They decided to keep it minimal today to see how busy they were. The cold and the weeks away would take a toll, but there was no way to know what he would face.

Carmen masked whatever emotions hit her upon walking in the kitchen. She clipped invoices to a clipboard and showed him the section of the walk-in cooler that was reserved for the truck's inventory.

They worked together to load the truck and secure everything. Pete still hadn't called or shown up. The silence was filled with tension. Liam had little patience when it came to people being irresponsible, especially when it affected him and his performance. Carmen disappeared out the back, and through the open door, he saw her talking on the phone. Her body was rigid while she spoke and when she disconnected, she kicked the tire of the truck.

Looked like she was as pissed at Pete as he was. Well, Liam had neither expected nor wanted Pete's help.

When she walked back into the kitchen, she said, "Pete will meet you on site." Her words were clipped. She closed her eyes before continuing. "I know you didn't want him to help, but he knows the truck. Use him at least until you have a handle on things."

"Whatever." He couldn't hide his irritation anymore.

"I'm trying to make it easier for you, Liam."

"I'm fine. I need to get going."

"Call me if you run into problems or have any questions."

"I will." He leaned over and gave her a quick kiss.

CARMEN WATCHED Liam drive off in the truck. He was pissed about Pete and he had every right to be. She still worried about him on the truck, though. Working alone had played a part in her father's death. It didn't matter that Liam was younger and stronger. Overworked was overworked.

She turned back to the kitchen. Now that Liam was gone, the full force of being back there hit her. The cool metal of the stainless steel counter reminded her of leaning against there, hoping her mom would forget she'd come in the back door. She'd always preferred the back of house, the kitchen to the front with the customers, regardless of what she'd said to Liam.

The noise and pace and smells made her feel at home.

But standing in the silence, only memories flooded her brain. Her dad yelling at the counter, ringing a bell to announce an order up. Memories of her dad reminded her of the letter she still had tucked away. She'd been feeling better, and she knew the letter would make her cry. She was tired of crying.

She looked around the kitchen. Gus's restaurant was a huge source of pride for the family. Her uncle Johnny had kept up the tradition. Business was still good, as evidenced by the books. Sadness weighed on her heart. She felt so disconnected from everything: her family, her business, her life.

She leaned her forearms on the table like she had as a teen. The chill sent a shiver up her arms. It had been so long since she'd thought about her life that she had no clue what she wanted. Getting through each day was all she could handle for so long. She'd forgotten how to stop and have fun, enjoy what was happening around her.

Pushing off the table, she resolved to take the time to do that now. She didn't have to decide her life plan at the moment. She had income and a place to live. Stepping back to enjoy life was an option. She just needed to figure out how.

With a last look around, she sighed. Of course, Liam had left everything spotless, like he hadn't stepped foot in the space. She turned off the lights and locked up. The blast of cold air had her burrowing deeper into her coat.

Maybe she'd wait until it was a little warmer to enjoy outside. Thoughts of warmer weather made her think about warmer places. She hadn't had a vacation since...she really couldn't remember. She unlocked the car and sat on the cold vinyl. While the engine warmed up, she considered a vacation.

As a kid, her parents had taken her to Wisconsin Dells. Disney World had been out of their reach. Her dad had taken her to Mexico once to show her where he'd grown up. A vacation would give her a nice escape from having to make decisions and plans.

Then she thought about Liam. He wouldn't take a vacation with her. He'd just started on the truck after quitting a good job. He was too focused on being successful to step back and screw around. Could she go somewhere alone? Rosa would be happy to go, but she never had any money.

Carmen drove back to her house and tried to think about where she would want to go, but nothing struck her. She glanced at the clock. She had plenty of time. In fact, she had nothing but time. When she got home, she tossed all thoughts aside and took a nap.

LIAM DROVE toward the heart of the city. They had decided on the Grant Park location for the first stop. As the weather warmed, it would be a great spot for business and probably overly competitive, but in December, they hoped he could grab it without issue. At ten forty-five, he parked, glad to see no other truck in sight.

He started the burners to warm the grill and opened the windows and the awning. His breath puffed white clouds, and the air was cold enough that he thought icicles might start forming on him. Carmen had written up the menu board. Her curvy script was much neater than whatever scratch he would've displayed.

Grant Park was desolate. Buckingham Fountain stood in the distance, shut off for the season. Traffic remained constant, though, and he hoped foot traffic would pick up. Carmen had chosen this spot as one of her dad's favorites.

The sound of feet slapping the pavement caught his attention. A tall, thin Latino guy ran up to the truck. His smile was easy as he said, "Hey, I'm Pete. You must be Liam."

"You're late."

"I know, man, sorry. I overslept."

Pete stepped up into the truck behind Liam and made his way to the front. He washed his hands and tied on an apron.

"Look, we don't know each other, so let me tell you this now. You want to work, you be on time. If you're late, don't bother showing up."

Pete nodded. "You sound a lot like Gus."

"Gus knew how to run a business."

Liam got to work, partially cooking a batch of meat so orders would move faster. Pete turned on a radio and hung halfway out the window.

"Not much going on."

As if Liam needed the announcement.

Thirty minutes later, however, they had a steady stream of customers. Most were not looking to eat while they took a stroll through the park, so Liam wrapped orders up to go back to offices.

The best thing Liam could say about Pete was that he had been late.

Pete screwed up orders as he called them out. He flirted with every woman who came to the window. Liam began to question if the guy knew how to make change or if their profits were blowing away with each pickup line.

The pace was steady, but not unbearable. Then Pete joined him at the grill and started moving ingredients and utensils.

"What the hell do you think you're doing?" Liam asked.

"I just want to squeeze in here and make a couple of tacos for me and the cute chick at the window."

"You're supposed to be working, not eating."

"I skipped breakfast and she's the last one in line."

"I don't care. This isn't your personal dating service."

"You don't gotta be a dick about it."

Liam pointed to the window where another customer had walked up. He turned back to the grill and made the tacos for his order. As more orders came in, he split focus between listening to Pete and keeping track of what was popular. Basically, nothing flew out the window. Every order was a couple of tacos. Over the course of the first hour, they'd only sold one or two orders of rice.

They needed to change things up, bring people out to eat, something to spark interest. Like it or not, they were competing with fast food. He needed to find a way to make people realize that what they offered was better than fast food.

At twelve thirty, the timer he'd set rang out. Liam got a slight pleasure at watching Pete jump at the sound. They had fifteen minutes to finish the orders at hand and close up to get to the next location. This two-hour limit bullshit was ridiculous. It was like the city didn't want them to succeed.

"Last order," Liam called. He made the food efficiently and passed it through the window with a smile. As the customers walked off, Liam said to Pete, "We have exactly ten minutes to break down and secure everything to drive to the next spot. With traffic, I think it'll take about twenty minutes to get there."

He cleaned the utensils and counters and turned off the grill. "I'm going to get rid of the trash. Make sure all the food is secure and put away. Are you going to follow in your car or ride with me?"

"I'll ride with you. I'm parked in a lot."

Liam jumped out the back of the truck and got rid of the trash. When he returned, Pete had the truck closed up, windows, doors, and awning, so he climbed into the driver's seat and drove into the fray of bumper-to-bumper down-town traffic. When he got to Clark and Monroe, a cupcake truck vendor was already parked.

From his research, he knew this truck was here most days. Since they offered dessert, Liam didn't see the problem with sharing a block. He parked behind them, careful to make sure he was totally legal and away from the crosswalk.

He cut the engine and said to Pete, "Start setting up." He left the truck and went to talk to the cupcake people. At the window, he introduced himself.

"You're taking over Gus's truck?" the girl asked.

"Yeah. I'm new to this whole thing. This a good spot for foot traffic?"

"Well, this time of year is dodgy, but we do okay. I'm Lisa." She extended her hand through the window.

"Liam." He shook her hand and turned to leave.

"Wait. Take this." She handed a chocolate cupcake to him. "Welcome to the neighborhood."

"Thanks. Stop by if you want some lunch. Tacos to go can't be beat."

"Tempting, but I'm vegan."

"Oh. Then you definitely don't want anything we have on the truck. Have a good day." Liam returned to the truck as he sank his teeth into the thick layer of frosting. The top was overly sweet, but the cake was good.

"It's okay for you to flirt and eat but not me?"

Liam stepped into the back of the truck. "I wasn't flirting. I introduced myself to a fellow vendor. She gave me a cupcake. And I was on time for work this morning."

He surveyed the truck and found a mess. Pete had reorganized everything Liam had set up. He'd only left the guy alone for ten minutes. "Why did you move everything?"

"I set it up the way Gus liked it."

"I'm not Gus and I had things the way I want them."

"Whatever." Pete opened the windows.

Then Liam saw the meat sitting on the counter, exposed. What. The. Fuck. "Pete!"

"What now?"

"Why the fuck is the meat sitting on the counter?"

Pete looked at him like he was stupid. "'Cause we're getting ready to cook."

The cocky comment made Liam want to punch him. He reined in his anger and clamped his jaw before speaking. "Meat cannot sit out in the open. There are food regulations."

"I know what I'm doin'. I've worked on this truck since the beginning. It's fine."

"No, it's not fine. You can't leave food out. Even if we don't get caught doing it, it could make people sick."

"Nobody's ever gotten sick."

"In your kitchen, do whatever the hell you want. In mine, you follow the rules."

"This ain't yours. It's Carmen's."

"And mine." He pointed to the meat. "Throw it all out."

"Hell no."

Liam reached into the refrigerator and pulled out fresh batches of meat. "That goes in the trash."

"It's a waste. Gus would never do that."

"Gus put up with too much shit from you."

"Fuck you."

"Get out. You're fired."

"You can't fire me."

"I can, and I did."

"What about my car?"

"What about it?"

"I need to get it."

"So walk. I have a business to run."

Pete shoved past him and jumped out of the back of the truck. Liam set the timer to keep him on track and finished setup. A line started to form, so he donned his gloves to take orders and money before manning the grill. Within minutes, he understood why Carmen had suggested a second person, but there was no way he would put up with Pete's crap.

CHAPTER 14

*C*armen woke from a fitful nap and checked her phone. No word from Liam. She wanted to believe that meant everything was going well. She didn't know why she was so nervous about Liam running the truck. He was every bit as competent as her dad. While waiting to hear from him, she logged on to her computer and began to search for ideas for a vacation. The world was too big for her to narrow choices, so she texted Rosa.

While Rosa was far from a world traveler, Carmen knew she would have ideas. Her phone bleeped almost immediately, as if Rosa needed to shout.

CARIBBEAN!!

That's it? No other ideas?

None needed. Beaches, drinks, and sexy men. Your vacay is made. Let me know when and maybe I'll join you.

Carmen laughed. Of course Rosa would want to go, but she also knew her cousin sucked at follow-through. She sent her thanks and then looked into the Caribbean. Hours passed and she hadn't heard from Liam. He should've called by now, so she sent a text and hoped he wasn't driving.

169

Back at kitchen. Done soon.

Carmen grabbed her keys and headed to the restaurant. When she pulled into the back lot where they stored the truck, Liam had the doors open as he cleaned. Pete was nowhere in sight.

Please, God, tell me he didn't blow Liam off.

"Hey," she called as she shoved her hands in the pockets of her coat. "Where's Pete?"

Liam looked over his shoulder. "I fired him."

"What?"

"I fired him."

Crap. This was not how her life was supposed to go. "Do I want to know what happened?"

"Besides the fact that he showed up late, did little more than flirt with every female customer, and then had a total disregard for food regulations?"

No, this definitely was not how things were supposed to happen. "Pete doesn't know regulations. My dad never required it of him. He took orders and cleaned up. A pair of helping hands and not much more. Firing him was a little harsh, don't you think?"

Liam jumped off the truck with a menacing look on his face. "No, I don't think it was harsh. He didn't want to be there. He had a crappy attitude, and when I tried to correct what he'd done, he blew me off like what I said didn't matter."

Carmen listened and while what Liam said sounded like something Pete would do, she couldn't help but think this was a pissing contest between the two of them. "Do you need help finishing this?"

"No, I've got it." He climbed back into the truck and gathered the food.

"You don't have to snap at me."

"I'm not. I don't mean to. It's been a long day out in the

cold for what feels like very little. Dealing with your dumbass cousin didn't help."

She understood his frustration, but he had no right to talk to her like that. "Pete might not be the most responsible guy—"

Liam answered with a snort.

"But he was there to help. Contrary to what you might think, you're not God and you can't do it all. I'll call Pete and smooth things over."

"Hell, no. There is no smoothing this over."

"You're being unreasonable. It was a rough first day and you need to get to know each other. I'm sure if you teach Pete, let him know what you expect instead of just yelling, everything would be fine."

He stepped out of the truck, arms loaded. "Everything is not fine. Pete can't do whatever he wants and act like he runs things. I don't have time to play games. He's fired."

"What makes you think you can make an executive decision like this alone? We are partners, you know."

"Like you consulted me before hiring Pete?"

"I was trying to do you a favor."

"Trust me, I don't need favors like that." He walked past her and into the back door of the kitchen.

When the door swung open she was treated to a waft of home. The kitchen still smelled like it had when her dad ran it. Before going in to say hello to her uncle, she checked the truck to make sure Liam had followed her directions for draining everything and turning off all of the gas.

Her dad ran the truck for the last couple of years, but she didn't feel his presence here like she did that morning in the kitchen of the restaurant. Maybe that was because she didn't work the truck with him, so this was just a space, nothing special.

Liam stomped back and glared at her. Temperamental

dude. She said nothing, but went to the kitchen. "Hey, Junior, Uncle Johnny here?"

"Carmen, what the hell are you doing here? Did someone die?"

She smacked his arm. "That's not funny."

He sobered, apparently remembering her dad had just died. "I didn't mean it like that. It's just that you haven't come here since your dad sold it to mine."

The heat of the kitchen started to get to her, so she unzipped her jacket and unwrapped her scarf. "I know. I'm making sure Liam knows what he's doing with the truck."

"How's that working out?"

"Liam? Okay, I think. Today was his first day and things didn't go well. Pete was on the truck with him and pissed him off."

Junior slid a plate onto the pass-through. "Order up." He turned back to her. "Dad's in the office. He'll be glad to see you. You want to stay for dinner?"

"No, thanks. I'm Liam's ride. The truck has been at my house so that's where he started this morning. I need to get him to his car." She could've said she had plans with Liam, but she held back. Rosa knew, which meant Junior probably knew. Her cousin loved to gossip with her big brother. "I'll be back before I leave."

She walked down the hall to the small office in back. She knocked quietly on the door.

"Yeah?"

She opened the door and poked her head in. "Hey, Uncle Johnny. It's me."

"Carmen!" He stood behind his desk. "Come in. Come here." He moved toward her and grabbed her in a big bear hug.

Johnny looked a lot like her dad, only the super-size

version. If her dad had been a cuddly teddy bear, Uncle Johnny was the grizzly.

"What are you doing here? Not that I don't love seeing my favorite niece."

"The truck. We put it back on the street."

"Yeah, Rosa was telling me about that. How'd it go?" Johnny looked as doubtful as the rest of her family when it came to Liam.

"Okay. It would probably be better if Liam could get along with Pete. I don't know what happened today, but Liam fired him. He seems really pissed too." She sighed and dropped into a chair in front of the desk. Johnny took his spot across from her. "Liam's not like Dad. He's a formally trained chef. He's a little more uptight than Dad, so he doesn't have the patience for the kind of crap Pete does." She said the words, knowing they were true, but didn't know how she knew. Liam had shown nothing but extreme patience with her.

Johnny sat back in his chair. "Pete's Pete. How many times have I fired him because of his lack of work ethic? I don't know where my sister went wrong with him."

"There's nothing wrong with Pete. He's just young." She shouldn't make excuses for her cousin. Gus had fired him more times than anyone could count. Pete was irresponsible. The whole family kept hoping something would stick with him, but partying was his first priority.

"Everyone has to grow up."

"Do you know anyone else who might be good on the truck?"

Johnny raised his eyebrows.

"Not me. I can't work the truck."

"Why not? You know everything there is. Gus never understood why you wouldn't join him after your mom died."

"I couldn't." Her throat became tight. No one knew why she avoided the restaurant or why she couldn't work on the truck. At this point, she wasn't even sure she knew anymore.

"I don't have any extra staff. I'll ask around, though."

"Thanks." She rose. Hopefully, Liam would be done with the truck so she could leave.

"Come to the house this weekend. We've missed you. The girls are baking cookies, I think."

Yeah, cookies for Christmas, just what she needed. "Maybe."

She slipped back out through the kitchen, waving to Junior as she went. As hard as it had been to come to the kitchen with Liam this morning, being there while the restaurant was open was worse. Although it hadn't been her dad's restaurant for a few years, she felt his absence.

She bundled up again before pushing the heavy back door open. Liam was locking the truck. At least she had good timing. "Ready?"

"Yeah."

They walked to her car in silence. Carmen got behind the wheel and waited for Liam to buckle up before speaking. "What's your plan for tomorrow?"

"The Grant Park location wasn't great. I want to look at some of the other places."

She shivered as the engine warmed up. "No, I mean for help."

"I have no plan. I'll work alone."

"Do you think that's a good idea? You've only done this one day."

"And I finished alone this afternoon because I got tired of Pete's shit. I'll handle it."

"Whatever." She didn't know why he was pissed at her. He was probably just lashing out because Pete pissed him off, but she didn't need to take it. She pulled away from the restaurant and turned the radio up loud. Not that she needed to let Liam know she didn't want to talk; the man had little to say.

When she parked beside her house, she got out and went inside. If he wanted to join her, she wouldn't throw him out, but she wasn't going to invite him in either. In the living room, she looked out the window and saw him standing beside her car as if in a debate with himself. Rather than stare at him through the window, she went to the kitchen to make some dinner.

The quiet *click* of the front door sounded and she paused in rummaging through the refrigerator. She closed the door and turned to face Liam.

"Leaving your door unlocked isn't safe."

Like she needed a lesson in safety. She stared waiting for more, hoping that hadn't been his sole purpose in coming in the house.

"I'm sorry I snapped at you. It was a rough day. Pete irritated me before I even laid eyes on him, and it went downhill from there. I shouldn't have taken it out on you."

"No, you shouldn't have." She took in his appearance. He'd shed his coat somewhere else in the house and for the first time, she noticed he wore a chef's jacket. It struck her as odd. Her dad always worked in a T-shirt. Liam looked formal, but overworked. The front of the jacket was splattered, and he had the top buttons undone.

He stepped closer, reaching for her. She swallowed hard as he grabbed her hips and pulled her to him. "Can you forgive me?"

Before she could answer, he kissed her neck. The sensation melted any anger she had. "Maybe."

"What can I do to make it up to you?"

"I don't know."

His mouth continued to work against her skin, making

her breathless. He moved higher and kissed her mouth, his tongue teasing her with soft strokes. His fingers pressed into the curve of her hip and then he pulled away.

Every time he did that left her dazed. Was it supposed to be like that? Every time?

"Want me to make dinner?" he asked.

"You've been cooking all day."

"That's not really cooking." He stepped back and ran a hand over his head. "In all honesty, I didn't like it much. The pace was fast, but I'm used to that. I don't know what it was, but I was on edge all day. It wasn't as much fun as I'd thought it would be."

Her heart sank. Part of her knew the truck wouldn't be enough for a guy like Liam, but she'd thought it would take longer than a day for him to grow tired of it. What would they do now?

She reached for his hand. Interlocking her fingers with his, she rubbed the back of his hand with her free one. "When I was in the restaurant, I asked Uncle Johnny if he knew of anyone who might want to work the truck. I know Pete isn't easy, but he's not a bad guy. He's young."

Liam tossed a look at her that said he'd never been that unfocused.

"What do you want to do?"

"I don't know." He pulled away again, this time bracing his fists on his hips as he turned his back to her.

She ran her hands across the tense line of his shoulders. She wanted to plant a kiss on his neck, just above his collar, but she wasn't tall enough. "There's bound to be a learning curve. Like starting any new job."

"I know."

She felt his back rise with a huge intake of air. "What can I do to help?"

He let out a chuckle. "Work the truck with me?"

Her hand froze at his shoulder blade. Thoughts sped through her mind. Why was she afraid to work on the truck? If Pete could do it, she sure as hell could. She wouldn't have to cook. But customers weren't fun to deal with. She could spend the whole day with Liam. It would definitely give her a sense of whether this relationship had real merit.

Liam turned slowly and she dropped her hand. "Didn't mean to freak you out. It was a joke."

"Okay." The quiet word slipped past her lips.

Liam kissed the top of her head. "We'll figure something out."

It was time to get over her hang-ups, deal with her fear. "No, I mean, okay, I'll work the truck."

"What?" He held her upper arms and studied her face. "I thought you didn't want to."

"You need someone to work. I know the truck and the routine. I'm as invested in this business being a success as you are."

"I don't want you to do something you don't want to, something that will make you miserable." His hands slid up and down her arm in a soothing motion.

Did her touch have the same effect on him?

"I won't be miserable. At least not any more than you will be. This is our business. It's not fair for me to only do the parts I like. You can't just decide not to clean up even though it's not fun."

"You're really okay with working with me?" He smiled and his body relaxed.

Her nerves settled with his smile. "Yeah."

"It won't be forever. We'll look at maybe hiring someone when things pick up." He kissed her cheek. "I knew your dad was a tough guy, but I have no idea how he ran the truck by himself. I thought I might lose my mind this afternoon. Stubbornness was the only thing that kept me from rolling up early and leaving."

Her dad didn't really handle it alone. He'd often worked the truck by himself, but it took a huge toll on him and his health. For which a swift kick of guilt smacked her again. If she hadn't been so selfish in her refusal to work with him, maybe he'd still be with her now.

"You sure you're okay?"

She nodded before speaking. "Yeah. Just thinking about my dad."

"What do you want for dinner?"

"I wasn't kidding. You don't have to cook for me."

"I like to cook for you." Then he got busy in her kitchen like he was at home.

~

THE FOLLOWING MORNING, Carmen's eyes popped open. Liam lay next to her looking like he had no intention of moving. She nudged his shoulder.

"Uhn."

"Time to get up." She rolled off the bed and shivered. She shuffled to the kitchen and started coffee. Then she took a hot shower and dressed in layers. She knew the truck got hot while they cooked, but it was so bitter cold out that she knew she wouldn't be warm with her hands passing through the window taking money and handing over orders.

Gloves. She needed gloves. While she sucked down that glorious first cup of coffee, she rummaged through the hall closet for a pair of gloves. By the time she found a pair that had seen better days, Liam was up and grumbling about the ass crack of dawn. She smiled as she went back to the kitchen. She didn't know Liam wasn't a morning person.

When she'd spent the night at his house, he was up before her cooking breakfast.

"Good morning, Sunshine."

"It's barely morning, and I've yet to see the sun."

She topped off her mug. "It's winter. The sun waits a while to make its appearance."

He glared at her as he poured his coffee.

"So, you're not a morning person. I'll try to remember that."

"Morning people are evil."

"Not true. Get dressed."

"What's your hurry?"

"Once I'm up, I like to get moving." While he nursed his coffee, she logged on to her computer, set their locations for the day, and tweeted them so they'd get picked up by various sites. Liam had veered from the spots her dad usually worked. It made her a little nervous, straying from the known, but Liam had a right to experiment.

She ran out and started her car so it would warm up and she began to rethink the whole idea of running the truck through the winter. Who in their right mind walked around looking for lunch when it was this cold out?

By the time they reached the restaurant, Liam appeared to be awake. He still wasn't talking much, but then again, he rarely did. They moved around the kitchen doing their prep. Her knife skills couldn't compete with his, and she kept waiting for him to nudge her aside and take over. She felt his eyes on her and without looking, imagined his grimace at her clumsy chopping. She might not be fast and pretty, but she got the job done.

When the truck was loaded, Liam got behind the wheel and drove into downtown. As quiet as he was, she was glad Pete met him on-site. Pete's chattering would probably have driven Liam nuts before the first site. At ten forty-five, they parked at Clark and Monroe. Only one other truck was there and they sold grilled cheese.

Her concern with parking anywhere was the competition from other Mexican food restaurants. As soon as the truck stopped, Carmen jumped out and started unrolling. She had the windows open and the awning up while Liam fired up the grill. Although the temperature read in the twenties, the big buildings blocked what little sun they hoped to see. They were parked in the shadows and cold air sucked into the back of the truck.

Carmen stood beside the grill and warmed her hands on the meager heat.

"You're in my way."

Carmen looked at Liam. "I'm cold, and you're not cooking yet. We have no customers."

He cocked an eyebrow, so she did the same. "I'm not stopping your setup."

His jaw clenched, but he continued in his economical movements, putting things where he wanted them for the shift. Once her shivering stopped, she grabbed an order pad and set up her small station, where she'd take orders and money. From her spot, she continued to watch Liam. He was quite the distraction.

Competent and sure in everything he did. And he wore another chef's jacket. Where did that come from? Yesterday's was white, but today's was dark, like navy, and the cuffs of the sleeves were turned up, revealing part of his forearms. Man, those were sexy.

She'd never thought about arms being sexy, but something about Liam made her reevaluate that. His pale skin, sprinkled with freckles and a dusting of his red hair shouldn't make her hot, yet here she was, unzipping her jacket.

She forced her mind back to work and created the

specials board with prices to hang outside. As she completed this last task, people started lining up. Behind them, another truck had pulled in. They sold chicken or something. She should probably learn more about the local competition. She knew nothing about any of these trucks, but her dad had talked to most of them.

Before she could mention it to Liam, customers began ordering and she had no time to think. She wrote orders down, called them out, then hung the slip on a clip near Liam. She couldn't believe the steady line of people. It didn't take long for her to grow tired of smiling and chatting with people to make suggestions.

But she didn't hate it.

About an hour in, Liam was backlogged. The tickets were piling up and people were stomping their feet against the cold while they waited for food. Carmen exchanged her warm gloves for some food service ones and began laying out the components for the next order.

"What are you doing?"

"Helping you catch up. People are cold and they want their food."

"You're going to mess things up. Go back to the window."

That was it. She only had so much patience for someone being cranky in the morning. He had no need to question her abilities. With a fist on her hip and her other hand pointing at him, she said, "Look, I've been making these tacos my whole life. Don't tell me I don't know what I'm doing. I might not have your magic kitchen skills, but I know how to cook."

His face cracked into a strange smile and he burst out laughing. She'd never heard such a deep, rich sound, especially from Liam, and it startled her.

"What the hell is so funny?"

He continued to laugh as he folded and wrapped three

chicken tacos—topped with her mole sauce, she might add—and then said, "I wish you could've seen yourself. You just went all stereotypical Latina with the head weaving and finger pointing." He shook his head on another chuckle.

Then he added, "You might as well have tacked on a 'No, you di-in't'." His accent was atrocious.

She should've been angry. But all she could think was that she had sounded like Rosa when she yelled at Liam. Except Rosa would've added an insult in Spanish.

The waiting customers were watching and most appeared amused. She smiled. "You're on."

"What?"

She bumped his hip. "You cook on that half. I'll take this. We'll see who gets it right faster."

A couple of people waiting for food clapped. Carmen worked side by side with Liam, bumping and occasionally crashing into each other. They hadn't dropped any food, though. They teased and joked and customers laughed along with them. Carmen managed to take orders while cooking, so she declared herself the winner of their little competition.

Before they knew it, the timer was ringing and they had to wrap up for the next site. They waved people away, telling them that they'd be back tomorrow. They cleaned up quickly. Carmen turned to go out and close the awning, but Liam grabbed her and kissed her hard. When he released her, it took a moment to remember where she was and what she was supposed to be doing.

"What was that for?"

"For making this the most fun I've ever had at work. I don't know why you didn't want to do this; you're a natural."

She pushed away from him to go outside. Not even the wind whipping at her cheeks could remove the warmth she felt.

CHAPTER 15

*L*iam found himself smiling as he cleaned the truck and took food back into the kitchen of the restaurant. He had no idea how much money they'd made, but it felt like they'd been busier than the day before. Then again, maybe he was just enjoying how much fun he had working with Carmen.

When he'd suggested her working with him, he hadn't expected her to agree. He didn't know why she had, but he was happy about it. Working with her was a million times better than working with Pete.

The only thing that would make her perfect would be if she would stop getting in his way. Every time he turned around, she was messing with his orders. She didn't move things like Pete had, but she'd jump in and start wrapping tacos and bagging orders while he was still double-checking what he had.

It made him nervous and jumpy, but she made no mistakes, so how mad could he get?

"Did I pass your test?" she asked as she scrubbed at the grill.

He nudged her out of the way to take over the task. He pointed to the lettuce and tomato bins. "Take those to the cooler. What test?"

She answered without moving away from the grill. "Whatever test you have in your head that Pete failed."

"I'll clean the grill."

"I have it." A sly smile quirked up. "Or is that part of the test? You don't think I can clean to your standards?"

He knew no one could ever do things to his standards. That was why he preferred to do it himself. "There is no test. You didn't try to get a date with any of our customers, so there's that."

"I bet I could take orders, cook the food, and still pick up customers faster than you." Steam billowed up as she poured some water onto the flat top to help clean.

Even though he knew that part of the glow in her cheeks was due to the heat of the small kitchen space, he also saw a new sparkle in her eyes. He wrapped an arm around her hip and pulled her back against him. He lowered himself so the curve of her ass snugged against his crotch. He kissed her neck. "No way would you beat me in the kitchen, babe, unless you were picking up other men because then I'd have to stop cooking to beat the crap out of them."

She stopped scraping and leaned into him. "Jealous of some imaginary guys?"

"They're not imaginary. I saw a few checking you out today."

She shook her head like he was making it up. She didn't even recognize a guy flirting with her. Liam knew this was good for him, but it also said much about what she thought of herself. He turned and took the lettuce and tomatoes into the restaurant.

He wasn't used to people not doing as he said in the kitchen, but he had to remember Carmen wasn't part of his staff, not one of his employees. She was his partner and she knew what she was doing.

Even if it was different from the way he would do it.

That was the nagging part. He liked things to be his way.

They finished cleaning and closed up the truck. He watched Carmen work. For someone who'd insisted she didn't know about running the truck, she knew exactly what needed to happen. She drove back to her house and he followed her inside.

She dropped the money for the day along with the receipts and invoices for the food on the table and started a pot of coffee. He'd forgotten that her job wasn't done yet. She had the books to take care of.

"You want me to help?"

"What?"

"The books. It's not fair for you to have to do that on top of working all day."

"It's part of running a business."

"So it should be my part, too."

"It'll be faster for me to do it. If you have time this weekend, I'll teach you how I have it set up."

He cupped the back of her neck and brought her close for a kiss. He brushed his lips across hers. "Why wouldn't I have time this weekend? Trying to get rid of me?"

Her gaze shot away. "I didn't want to assume…"

He lifted her chin to look into her eyes. "I was kidding. And it's okay to assume. That's what it means to be in a relationship. If I had plans, I'd tell you. Right now, my plans are to spend as much time as possible in bed with you."

Her pulse throbbed against his hand. He kissed her forehead. "You do your office stuff and I'll make us dinner."

A small sigh escaped her mouth.

"What?"

"Keep it simple. I can't eat huge calorie-filled meals all the time. I don't know how you do it."

"Healthy doesn't have to be tasteless. If you eat a normal portion, you'll be fine." He took a moment to run his hands down the sides of her body, over her hips, and around to her ass. "Besides, I like your body. Everything about it. Just the way it is."

"I like yours, too," she whispered.

THE REST of the week sped by in a blur. Carmen was relaxed and comfortable. Liam had spent every night at her house. She'd had more great sex in this one week than she'd had in all of her previous experiences put together. The fact that Rosa called and wanted to go out for drinks Friday night was a good thing. Taking a small break from practically living together made sense.

Things between her and Liam were moving fast. Besides the fabulous sex, which she'd never thought she'd have, they worked together seamlessly. And they were having fun.

After finishing work for the day, Liam kissed her good-bye at her front door and told her to have fun with Rosa. Then he asked her to call him when she got home so he'd know she was safe. She looked forward to talking with Rosa and hanging out, but at the same time, she wanted to be with Liam, curled up on the couch watching TV after eating dinner.

That was probably the most surprising thing. Liam had been helping her enjoy food again. Each time a slice of panic poked her, he looked at her with desire. The guilt and fear still simmered, but she was able to eat and enjoy a meal. She hadn't even been aware how empty her life had been without real food. If she continued on this path, though, she'd have to find the time to start working out again. After years of controlling her weight via her diet, she'd have to go back to exercising like she had in college. Overall, it wasn't a bad trade-off.

Rosa arrived, dressed to kill as usual.

"I thought we were hanging out together."

"We are," Rosa answered. "But you never know who you might meet. Ready?"

Carmen shook her head at Rosa. The girl was always looking for a man. Carmen had never looked for one. They were so different. Carmen wondered why they were such good friends.

Rosa drove to her favorite bar. Carmen didn't have a favorite bar or anything else for that matter. The interior was dark. Ambient lighting scattered through the place. From the back, thumping music pounded and Rosa headed in that direction.

Carmen clamped her arm. "Let's get a table on this side. Otherwise we won't be able to talk." And boy, did she want to talk.

Rosa rolled her eyes, but grabbed a table near the center of the room. Rosa always liked to keep her options open and see what was going on around her. Carmen liked that about her cousin; it made her fun.

A waitress came by and they ordered margaritas. Although Rosa continued to scan the room, she asked, "So what's going on with you and Liam? Dad said you're working on the truck."

"I am and I like it. We're having fun."

"But working with your boyfriend? He is your boyfriend, right? You're not a friends-with-benefits thing."

"We're in a relationship, so I guess you'd call him my boyfriend."

"I don't know why I asked. You'd never be able to handle anything less."

Carmen didn't bother to argue; Rosa was right. Casual sex would never be her thing. "I like working with him, but it's…I don't know. Intense, I guess. We work all day. He's been spending the night at my house, so we're together all the time."

"That's crazy."

"I know it's crazy, but it doesn't feel crazy."

"Is he good in bed?"

Of course, as soon as the question left Rosa's mouth, the waitress arrived with their drinks. Heat flushed Carmen's cheeks. She couldn't make eye contact with the woman. She mumbled a thank-you and took a drink to cool her throat. The gritty salt on the rim followed by the bite of alcohol reminded her of the last time she'd had a margarita, with Liam. The night she'd wanted to sleep with him and he sent her off to bed alone.

"You didn't answer."

"Yes, Rosa. He's really good in bed. Not that I have much to compare him to." She sighed. "He makes me feel beautiful and sexy. Every time he looks at me, I feel his lust."

"But? I hear a big, fat but coming."

Carmen leaned close and lowered her voice. "But I don't know what I'm doing. The few times I had sex before this, it was over quickly and I wasn't really involved, if you know what I mean. I was too self-conscious to enjoy myself."

Rosa's face squinched up. "Self-conscious about what? Most men don't care about much when they're getting laid."

"You always say that, but it matters to me. I felt fat and didn't want a guy to notice."

"You're not fat."

"Not now, but I was then. I want to be different with

Liam, but I don't know how." Her shoulders sagged. "He hasn't even seen me totally naked."

Rosa put her chin on her fist as she leaned her elbow on the table. "How exactly did you have sex and spend the whole night together without getting naked? Sounds like more trouble than it's worth."

"It probably is, but he puts up with it. I'm afraid it won't last."

"You need to let go. Just have fun. Do whatever feels good for you. Trust me, he'll appreciate it."

Carmen swallowed more of her drink. If she was going to confess, she might as well go all the way. "I don't know what'll feel good. I don't know where to start."

Rosa nudged her shoulder. "Good thing we have all night. I have plenty of ideas."

THREE HOURS and too many margaritas later, Rosa dropped Carmen off at Liam's house. She should've called first, but if she did, she would've lost her nerve. Her liquid courage would only last so long.

He answered her knock wearing a pair of sweatpants and nothing else. She sighed.

"Hi. What are you doing here?"

She pushed past him and said, "I want to sleep with you. Do different stuff."

"Are you drunk?"

She squinted and held up her finger and thumb, barely spaced. "Maybe a little. But I know what I'm saying. The margaritas are just helping me say it."

"Say what?" He closed and locked the door.

She closed her eyes and blurted. "I don't want to be

boring in bed. I don't want you to be afraid of doing things with me like you have to protect me or something."

"Are you saying I'm boring you?"

She opened her eyes and stared at him. "God, no. I feel like you're holding back." She waved her hand. "I know I'm guilty of that, too. That's what I want to change. I just don't know how."

She swallowed and waited for a response. Her heart crashed against her ribs as Liam neared her.

"Get naked."

"Wh—What?"

"You said you wanted to be open, no holding back. Get naked right here in the living room, with all the lights on." He cocked an eyebrow, daring her to follow through.

She unwrapped her scarf and took off her jacket. Liam crossed his arms and waited. She kicked off her shoes and then peeled off her jeans, keenly aware of the fact that her sweater was long enough that she was still covered. Maybe not modestly, but covered.

"It's easy." He dropped his sweatpants and stood in front of her in his boxer briefs. He stepped closer still and kissed her. When he backed away, the bulge in his underwear was noticeably larger.

She licked her lips. He laughed and she realized she was staring. "Sorry," she mumbled.

"Don't be." He pushed his underwear off.

Now she really couldn't help but stare. He stepped closer again and tugged her sweater over her head. She didn't resist, but she did close her eyes. Chilled air washed over her warm skin causing a slight shiver. When she reopened her eyes, Liam was staring at her.

"The rest is up to you."

She reached behind and unclasped her bra. She let it drop to her feet. Instinct had her wanting to cover herself, but

Liam grabbed her hands. He looked into her eyes, even though she was mostly naked. Without breaking eye contact, his hands moved over her breasts, causing her nipples to pebble and harden.

She wanted his hands everywhere. Hooking her thumbs in the waistband of her panties, she gave them a shove, but Liam's fingers on her nipples were distracting.

"Allow me," he said gruffly. He slid her underwear down, kissing her stomach and along her hips as he moved. By the time she was ready to step out of the panties, he was kneeling in front of her. He looked up and she saw heat and passion in his eyes.

He kissed her thigh again and using both hands, spread her legs. He swiped his tongue over her and her knees weakened. She slapped her hand on the back of the couch for balance. As much as she loved his mouth on her, she already knew how good this was. She wanted new and different.

Taking a small step away, she said, "Come here."

He rose to meet her. She gripped his dick, felt the warm, smooth skin, and stroked him. The sound he released was somewhere between a moan and a grunt. The tip was wet and she rubbed her thumb across it, moistening the entire head. She loved knowing she made him this hard.

"I don't know if I'll be any good, but I want to try."

He gave her a look of confusion, but she sank to her knees. Rosa had been kind enough to give her blow-by-blow instructions and she hoped her alcohol-fueled brain would be able to follow them. She licked the head and tasted the saltiness. She swirled her tongue over him and then took him in her mouth until he bumped against her soft palate.

She began to bob her head. When Liam's hand landed on her head and his fingers tangled in her hair, she knew she was doing it right. Her jaw became sore and tight, but she kept going. Liam tugged her hair, startling her into letting him go.

"Stand up." His voice was strangled. He was on edge and she'd gotten him there.

Carmen felt proud enough that she'd almost forgotten that she stood naked, her nipples hard, and her sex wet.

"Let's go to bed."

"Let's finish here," she offered. She bent over and pulled out the condom Rosa had stuffed in her purse.

His hand closed over hers. "You sure you want it like this?"

She didn't know what she was getting herself into, but she nodded. He took the condom from her and kissed her hard. His dick poked into her stomach. Liam scooped her hair back and attacked her neck with his mouth, biting and sucking, making her even wetter. She whimpered.

He released her and put the condom on. Then he spun her and said, "Put your hands on the couch."

She followed his direction. Her heart beat double-time, knowing that this would definitely be different. He pulled at her legs until she took a step back, forcing her to bend at the waist.

Liam ran a hand down her back and followed with hot, wet, urgent kisses. He stood behind her. His dick prodded her ass cheeks and her thighs as his fingers skated down her spine. He reached around her hip and then he touched her clit. She was so sensitive and turned on, the simple flick almost buckled her knees.

He rubbed against her and her hips thrust up at him. He entered her from behind in one long, smooth stroke. She laid her forehead on the back of the couch and gripped the cool leather with her fingers. Liam rocked into her, but he kept one hand on her clit, rubbing, stroking, flicking, driving her absolutely crazy.

Moving his hands to her hips, he picked up the pace, thrusting into her. She felt her flesh jiggling, but she couldn't stop to get embarrassed. Her orgasm built, but it was just out of her reach. Liam's fingers tightened on her, pressing into the softness of her hips. She wanted—no, needed—his hand back on her.

"Please," she whined.

He slowed and leaned close, moving her hair off her shoulder. He was buried deep inside her and whispered in her ear, "Please, what?"

"Touch me."

He reached beneath their bodies and pinched her nipples, drawing a moan from her.

"Liam." She was breathless and he had her pinned so she couldn't move her hips, couldn't wiggle or buck even though her body screamed for her to do so.

His fingers trailed down her stomach until he reached her clit. "This?"

"Oh, God, yes." And then he took his hand away again. He was trying to kill her. She didn't know why, but she knew he was doing it on purpose.

He took her hand from the couch and pulled it back to her body. With his fingers on top of hers, they stroked her. "Keep going."

His hands moved back to her hips and he picked up his rhythm again. Her own fingers paused where he'd left her. As soon as he moved, though, the pad of her finger made contact and she shuddered. Her hand couldn't move fast enough. Her muscles tightened and clenched, but the movement didn't stop. The pressure was overwhelming and then she crashed.

Her entire body buzzed. She tried to catch her breath, but Liam pounded into her, pushing her against the couch, shifting the piece of furniture. She tried to find purchase to hold still, but her muscles were useless. He gripped one of her shoulders, holding her in place.

Then a growl came from him and he stilled. Her muscles were still pulsing around him. She didn't know how she was able to remain semi-upright. Liam slid out of her and pulled her to standing against him. His arms circled her from behind. "You okay?"

"Yeah."

He turned her to face him and kissed her. "Different enough?"

She nodded, a hint of embarrassment creeping in now that her brain was functioning again. He smoothed a hand down her cheek. "I love your body. Let's go to bed and experiment some more."

For the first time in her life, Carmen walked through a living room with a man while she was completely naked. And unashamed because he loved her body. In that moment, Carmen knew she was falling for Liam O'Leary and she was in deep.

CHAPTER 16

*L*iam stood outside the mall and cringed at the crowds. How the hell had Jimmy convinced him to go shopping a week before Christmas? And on the weekend. He saw Jimmy crossing the lot, so he waited for him.

When Jimmy hit the sidewalk, Liam said, "I hope you know how much you owe me. This place is a zoo."

"I appreciate it."

Inside the mall, they pressed through the mob of people to get to the jewelry store. As he got shoved and bumped, Liam was glad he'd ordered his grab bag present for Quinn online. Sitting in front of the computer was looking better and better.

"Nervous?" he asked Jimmy.

"Nope."

Liam looked at his friend and saw no signs of nervousness. "You're really getting married?"

"Yep."

"To Moira? Are you sure you know what you're getting into?"

Jimmy laughed. "Yeah, I do. All I need to do now is figure out what kind of ring to get her. Any suggestions?"

"What do I know about jewelry? I thought I was here for moral support."

They walked through the store, peering in case after case of rings. Liam had no idea how a guy was supposed to make a decision. He wandered to another case. They all had stones other than diamonds. "Hey, Jimmy, come here." Jimmy joined him. "What about an emerald? It's different."

Jimmy looked into the glass. "You're a genius." He pointed down at a ring. "That's the one."

While Jimmy spoke with the salesperson, Liam continued looking around. He wanted to get Carmen a Christmas present, but the idea of jewelry made him a little nervous. They hadn't been together that long, but he really cared about her. He looked at earrings and although Carmen had pierced ears, he hadn't seen her wear any. He moved on to bracelets and necklaces.

Jimmy bumped his shoulder. "Shopping for Carmen?"

"Thinking about it."

"This is serious."

Liam shrugged. "It's Christmas and she's had a hard couple of months."

"So buy her a teddy bear."

"What?" He looked up from the case.

"A girl sees jewelry as taking the relationship to the next level. If you're not serious about her…"

"I am. I care about her. A lot." He looked back at the necklaces. "I want to get her something special. She's important."

"Better plan to bring her to family dinner then."

"What do you know about that?"

"I know the O'Learys do a trial by fire. If you plan to keep her around, she needs to know what she's getting into." Jimmy pointed at a necklace. "That one."

It was a simple silver chain with a Claddagh. He liked it. He could imagine it around Carmen's neck. She wasn't Irish and probably wouldn't understand the symbolism, but it was a piece of him, his heritage. It held meaning without being too serious. He waved the salesperson over and asked to have the necklace wrapped.

With their packages in hand, they left the store. "When are you going to ask Moira?"

"I think Christmas Eve or maybe Christmas morning before we go to your mom's. I want her to have the ring before we have dinner with your whole family. I can't have her open it in front of all of you."

Liam clasped a hand on Jimmy's shoulder. "You'll make my mom very happy."

"You bringing Carmen to the family thing?"

"I don't know. We haven't talked about it yet."

"But things are good?"

"Very. We work together and spend our free time together. She's pretty fucking amazing."

"I know the feeling."

They pushed through the crowds and headed back into the cold. Before they parted ways, Liam said, "You better find a good hiding spot. Moira was always the first to snoop out where my parents hid presents."

"I'm well aware of your sister's nosy ways. I'm leaving it at my dad's house."

"Good move. See you later."

Liam walked back to his car questioning his purchase. He and Carmen hadn't talked about exchanging gifts, not that he expected one. He wanted her to know how special she was, but he didn't want to put pressure on her to make their relationship more than she was ready for.

∼

WINTER ROLLED in full force over the next few days. A storm came in and dumped a foot of snow in the city. Bad weather caused fewer people to be out, which meant the truck wasn't as busy. After two days of miserable sales, Liam was ready to throw in the towel. It didn't help that Carmen had tried to tell him not to take the truck out.

She'd refused to go with him, citing that business would be down because of the weather. She stayed in her nice, warm house and worked on the books.

When he strode through the back door on the second day, she smiled. "Good day?"

"Hell, no."

Instead of saying I told you so, like either of his sisters would've, she just said, "The weather's better tomorrow and I've been thinking about how to draw people out to see us."

"Okay." He poured himself a cup of coffee and looked out the window at the piles of snow. "Who shoveled the sidewalk?"

"I did."

He should've done it before he left in the morning. If he had, he would've been late getting on the road, though. "I would've done it."

"It's not a big deal. Anyway, remember how much fun we had when we fought over cooking tacos?"

"What?"

"When you got all mad and bossy and tried telling me I don't know how to cook."

"I never said that."

She shot him a look. "You didn't need to say it."

"You're the one who said you couldn't cook."

"I said I didn't. As in I don't like to." She walked up to him and planted a kiss on his cheek. "But when it comes to my dad's tacos, I'll outcook you every time."

"You wish." He patted her ass. "What does this have to do with your idea?"

"I'm thinking that everyone loves a competition, so we can make it one."

He leaned against the kitchen counter and tried to process what she said. "Competition with who?"

"Between us—girl versus guy, Latina versus white boy, home cook versus educated chef—however we want to promote it."

He had no idea if it would work, especially in the dead of winter, but he knew they'd at least have fun. The last two days without Carmen had been far from fun.

"Do you think your sister could help spread the word on social media? I've already crafted some tweets and Facebook posts. I'm ready to put them up as soon as you check them out."

"You don't need my approval. I trust you." He finished his coffee and called Moira.

"Hey, Liam. What's up?"

"I need your social media skills again."

"Sure. What do you need?"

"Carmen has some ideas for getting people to the truck."

"Hold on. Let me grab a pen."

"Actually, I'll pass the phone to Carmen and she can explain." He held the phone out and Carmen's eyes widened.

She shook her head.

"Just take it." He placed the phone in her hand. "I'm going to shower."

He kissed her quickly.

As he left the room, he heard Carmen say, "Hi, Moira. This is Carmen," followed by a laugh.

Forcing Carmen to interact with Moira was a good move. Carmen could explain her plan easier than he could. Then there was the added benefit of Moira's personality—his sister made friends with everyone and he wanted Moira to be Carmen's friend.

~

THE FIRST DAY of Carmen's experiment yielded decent results. They weren't insanely busy, but Liam wasn't bored. The real surprise came the following day. He didn't know if it was because the sun was shining or if Moira really did do some magic, but people were lined up and waiting.

Carmen had gotten two whiteboards and set one up on each side of the windows. One read "Girl vs. Guy—Whose tacos will win?" The second highlighted their individual experience: Liam's culinary school and Carmen's growing up in her dad's restaurant.

After yesterday, Carmen had decided they needed an actual wager. The loser of the competition would have to wear a hat proclaiming that he or she got whooped by the winner. Photos would be posted on social media.

Liam couldn't afford to lose. No way would he let Moira own an embarrassing picture of him declared a loser.

As soon as the grill was hot, Carmen started her trash talk. "Come on, everyone, let me show you what a real taco tastes like."

"How about a real taco prepared by a real chef?" he retorted.

An hour and a half later, Carmen shook the ticket bins she'd put out for customers to vote. In order to vote, a customer just had to drop a ticket into the bucket for Carmen or Liam.

The paper swished against the plastic. "I don't know, Liam. I think my bucket has more votes. Worried?"

"Hell, no." He was, in fact, a little worried because Carmen had started smiling and flirting with customers. He tried not to let jealousy ruin his attitude because he knew she was only doing it to get ahead. "Even if you're winning now, we have another stop. Maybe I'll bat my eyelashes to get a few votes."

"First of all, I don't bat my eyelashes. Second, if you want to go the sex appeal route, roll up your sleeves and flex your muscles." She shut the windows and locked up.

"You think my arms are sexy?"

She grinned. "Definitely."

As he hopped behind the steering wheel, his phone rang. Moira. She'd love hearing how successful they were with her help. "Yes, Moira, you are a social media genius. I bow to your skill."

"Liam." Her voice cracked, followed by a hiccup.

His hand stilled on the key in the ignition. "What is it?"

The phone fumbled on Moira's end.

"Moira!"

"Liam, it's Jimmy—"

"What the hell is going on?"

"It's your mom. She collapsed. She's at the hospital."

Jimmy continued to talk, but Liam heard nothing. It wasn't until the phone beeped with the end of the call that he blinked.

"Liam." Carmen shook his shoulder. "What's wrong?"

He shook his head and blinked again to clear it. His throat tightened, and a rock tumbled into his stomach. He forced the words out. "My mom. She's in the hospital."

"Oh, my God. You have to go."

He stared at his hands, unsure of his next move.

"Liam!"

He looked up at Carmen. Did she say something?

"Liam." Her hand touched his cheek. "Switch places with me and let me drive."

He opened his mouth to protest, but then realized he

couldn't drive. He couldn't focus. He opened the door and stepped down. As he passed Carmen in front of the truck, she grabbed him in a fierce hug. Tears burned his eyes and his throat closed completely. He struggled for air and couldn't swallow. The pain was too great.

Carmen patted him and rubbed his back before pulling away. He shuffled to the passenger side and got in.

The drive to the hospital was a blur. His only overwhelming thought was that he wasn't ready to lose his mother.

~

CARMEN WATCHED Liam slip from the truck. "Thanks," he mumbled.

"Do you want—"

He slammed the door and ran into the hospital.

I guess he doesn't want me to come in.

She stared at the closed hospital doors for a moment before pulling away. She drove back to the restaurant to clean out the truck. She didn't trust her ability to run the truck alone. She definitely couldn't pretend to be happy and friendly toward strangers.

Her heart hurt for Liam and his family.

She tried not to be bothered that he'd rushed out of the truck without saying much. She remembered all too well what it was like to receive a phone call like that. Instead of wallowing on the sting of hurt, she focused on thinking about how to help. She cleaned out the truck, and since they had plenty of food left because they never made it to their second stop, Carmen decided to make food for Liam and his family.

Chances were no one would want to eat, but they would need to. It would be something small she could do to show her support for Liam. Although she hadn't met Liam's family, she knew he had five siblings and most of them were married. That was a lot of people to feed.

In the kitchen of the restaurant, Junior moved around filling late lunch orders.

"Hey, Junior. I need to take over a section of the grill for a bit, okay?"

He rushed to her side and laid his palm against her forehead. "Are you sick? Not only have you been here almost daily, but now you want to cook in this kitchen?"

She swatted his hand away. "Liam's mother is in the hospital. He got the call a while ago. I figured I'd make food to take to his family."

"What happened?"

"I don't know. I didn't get the whole story, but he didn't look good when I dropped him off."

Again, the sting of being ignored as he rushed to his family hit her. She reminded herself that he was hurting and worried, and it had nothing to do with her.

"I'm slow now. I'll help. What do you want to make?"

Carmen smiled. For all of her family's shortcomings, they always came through when someone needed help. "I plan to use the leftovers from the truck to make tacos. Something easy to eat."

"Okay, let's go."

Junior helped her cook up the meat for tacos, adding more when she told him how many people she hoped to feed. As she worked with her cousin, Carmen relaxed. She'd never felt comfortable in this kitchen, but today, she was at ease. She missed her dad a little less.

"You and this Liam guy, huh?"

"What?" Carmen asked.

"You and Liam are dating?"

"I guess you could say that. We're in a relationship and I like him a lot."

"Is he good to you?"

"You sound like my dad." She smiled at the thought. Junior was her age. "Yes, he is good to me. He makes me feel cared for and wanted and…not so uptight."

"That's definitely a good thing. I was starting to think we'd place bets on how long it would take you to snap."

"My own family turning on me. Sad." She shook her head.

He bumped his shoulder into hers. "We worry."

"You can stop now. I'm doing better."

They worked to wrap the tacos and place them in a foil pan. Carmen looked at her clothes and considered going home to change, but then decided she didn't want to waste the time. The O'Learys had been at the hospital for a couple of hours already. She fixed her ponytail and wished for some makeup. This would be the first time she'd meet his family and the circumstances couldn't be worse.

She loaded the food into her car and waved at her cousin. On the way to the hospital, her nerves began to churn. Maybe she should've called Liam first and asked if they wanted food. No, he would've said no. But she wanted to do something for him. For his family.

After parking her car, she carried the tray in a bag through the doors of the hospital. She got directions and rode the elevator up. She stepped from the elevator and saw the waiting room. Even without having met Liam's family, she knew she'd found the right place. She stood in the doorway absorbing the shock of the grief in the room.

Everyone in the room was paired off. Liam stood with his back to her, a blonde rubbing his back. A surge of jealousy struck her when she realized it was Lily, the woman he'd said was nothing more than a friend. His *friend* was invited to be here, but he'd left Carmen without a word.

A short redhead came up to her when she noticed Carmen staring.

Carmen spoke quietly. "I'm Carmen, Liam's partner. I thought you guys might be hungry, so I brought some tacos."

"Thank you. That was very thoughtful. I'm Moira." She extended her hand. Her eyes were red-rimmed and her cheeks blotchy. "Nice to meet you."

Carmen wiped her hand on her jeans and then shook Moira's. "Nice to meet you, too. I wish it were under better circumstances. Any word on your mom?" She slid a glance to Liam, who still hadn't turned around.

"We're waiting for information." She watched Carmen and then called, "Liam."

Liam finally turned, but still didn't take notice of Carmen. Both he and Lily looked at Moira.

"Carmen's here."

Liam looked much like Moira. His eyes were red and her heart sank. "Hi," she offered.

"Hi."

He stepped forward, and everyone else seemed to fade away.

"I brought some food. I'm sure no one really feels like eating, but you need to. Your bodies will run down and you'll all be useless. At least try to have something." She longed to reach out to him, to touch him, to comfort him. Instead, she shoved her hands in her pockets and turned away.

"Thanks, Carmen."

She left the small room and pressed the button for the elevator.

"Carmen," someone called.

Carmen turned to see Lily approach.

"Liam's not really himself. It's nice to meet you. I'm Lily." She extended her hand, and Carmen took it.

"Nice to meet you."

The elevator dinged and Carmen put a hand on the door to keep it open.

"Thanks for the food."

"No problem." Carmen stepped into the elevator.

"Here's my number." She held out a slip of paper. "Give me a call if you need help at work. I don't know if Liam will be up to it for a while. I think his family will need him."

Carmen took the slip and held it tightly in her fist, but didn't answer. The doors slid closed and Carmen breathed a sigh. Like she would ask Liam's other woman for help. She was being unfair, but she couldn't muster enough energy to care. Lily was being nice; she didn't deserve Carmen's nasty attitude.

The truck and work were the last things on Carmen's mind right now. She hadn't come to the hospital because she was worried about Liam being on the truck. Christmas was at the end of the week. They could close for the holiday a little early.

Even if they couldn't afford to keep the truck off the street, she had her own family to rely on; she didn't need Liam's friends.

As she walked out into the cold air, the image of Liam's sad face tugged at her. She felt petty getting upset over Lily's presence when Liam had so much to deal with. He'd said that Lily was a friend. If Lily had been a man, Carmen would've thought nothing of it.

She shouldn't be jealous. She had no reason not to believe in Liam and what he said. But she couldn't help being saddened by the fact that he hadn't chosen her to give him comfort.

CHAPTER 17

"When does Maggie's plane land?" Ryan asked.

Liam heard the question, but had no idea who it was directed to.

"She was already on the plane this morning before….this. She called to remind me she was on her way. I'm supposed to pick her up at six," Moira answered.

Why was Maggie already on a plane if she hadn't known about Mom? Then he remembered she was coming home for Christmas.

"I'll get her," Jimmy said.

Liam turned and looked at the way his friend sat with Moira. She gripped his hand like it was a lifeline. Her knuckles were white. Jimmy patted her hand and kissed the top of her head. Liam ran a hand over his face and watched the rest of his siblings. They all had someone they loved to turn to in comfort.

Lily took his hand and laid her head against his arm. As much as he liked Lily, he didn't gain any comfort from the contact. He remembered Carmen standing in the room and how much he'd wanted to go to her and hold her. He didn't know why he'd stayed rooted in place, but he had. Now he regretted it.

Movement at the door caught everyone's attention. Doctor Childress came in and everyone stood. Liam's heart pounded.

"How is she?" Ryan asked.

"Your mother suffered a heart attack. We're going to run some more tests, but she's all right and resting now. There's nothing you can do. You should all head home."

"Can we see her?" Ryan pushed.

The doctor's eyes widened at the crowd around him. "Not all at once. Two people at a time. But really, there are so many of you, I would prefer if not everyone went in. She might not even wake up until tomorrow."

The siblings all looked at each other. Liam swallowed past the lump in his throat. "Ryan and Colin should go in and let her know we're all here. We'll take turns seeing her later."

Ryan made eye contact with each of them. The spouses and significant others had already taken a step back to let the family decide. Moira and Michael nodded. As the two oldest, Ryan and Colin should be the two to go in.

The pain in his chest loosened a little with the knowledge that the doctor said his mom was okay. A heart attack, though. The same thing had taken his dad almost five years ago. He didn't want to see his mother lying in a hospital bed.

Shit, he wanted a drink. He didn't often turn to alcohol, but sometimes a situation called for it. He grabbed his jacket before realizing that he had no vehicle.

"Where are you going?" Moira asked.

"I need some time away from here."

Lily stood beside him. "I'll give you a ride."

"Will you come back to Mom's later? Maggie will be home. I thought maybe we could all have a late dinner together." Moira pointed to the pan Carmen had dropped off. "At least we won't have to cook. We can eat tacos." She forced a smile that made her look almost like herself.

"Maybe. Call me if anything changes."

He walked out with Lily trailing after him. He followed her to her car, grateful that she didn't feel the need to talk.

"Where do you want to go?"

"A bar. I need a drink."

"Are you sure that's a good idea?"

"If you're not going to take me where I want to go, let me know and I'll call a cab."

She started the car and drove to his neighborhood. She pulled up to a bar a few blocks from his apartment. "This okay?"

"If they have alcohol, it'll be fine." He stepped from the car and turned to thank her for the ride when he realized she'd turned off the engine and had gotten out.

"Drinking alone is never a good idea."

He shrugged and went in. He immediately ordered two shots and downed them before ordering a Guinness. The alcohol hit quickly because he hadn't eaten all day. Lily sat beside him and ordered a pop.

"You want to talk?"

"Not about my mom."

"Okay. Tell me about work."

He took a long drink of beer. "It's slow, but it's winter, so there's not much to do about it." He thought about Carmen and realized he'd left her alone all day to work and clean the truck and prep for tomorrow. He couldn't work tomorrow. He needed to be at the hospital.

"Do you enjoy it?"

Again he thought of Carmen and how much fun he'd been having. "Yeah."

"Wow."

"What?"

"That smile was not an *I like my job* smile."

"What do you mean?"

"It's Carmen, isn't it?"

He didn't pretend not to understand. "Yeah. She's pretty amazing."

Looking at Lily, he was sorry for the sadness that crossed her face, but he couldn't help but wish it were Carmen sitting with him. He should've asked her to come in to the hospital or even asked her to stay when she did show up. But he couldn't think. Not until he had word about his mom.

And when he'd finally gotten that word, she wasn't there. Somehow, he felt like he'd fucked up.

Lily's lip trembled a bit. "Can I ask what it is about her?"

Liam took another long swallow of beer. No way would a conversation like this work out well for him.

"It's just…I thought we had something going. We've been hanging out together a lot over the past year, and I thought you were just a cautious guy. Taking your time, planning when to make a move."

That was him in most aspects of his life. But he'd never planned to make a move on Lily. How could he tell her without hurting her more?

"I like you, Lily, but I always saw you as a friend. Part of that was me being caught up in work stuff, trying to figure out my career. I wasn't looking for a relationship at all. I'm not even sure how it happened with Carmen."

She nodded slowly and sipped her pop.

Yeah, he felt like shit. The alcohol wasn't helping, but he ordered another shot anyway because it couldn't get much worse. He slugged back the shot and thought more about Carmen.

～

CARMEN'S PHONE RANG. She'd been hoping Liam would call and now he finally was. "Hello."

"Hi, Carmen. It's Lily."

"What happened? Is Liam's mom okay?"

"She had a heart attack, but she's okay. Umm... I'm with Liam at a bar."

Carmen's chest tightened. *They're friends. Friends go to bars together.* "Why are you calling me?"

"He's really drunk. I don't want to call his family. I was hoping you'd come get him."

So she wasn't good enough to drink with, but she was supposed to clean up after? "Why don't you just take him home?" The words hurt to say.

"I could. It wouldn't be an easy task, but I would. The thing is, he's been talking about you since we got here. I think he wants to see you, but he's too stupid to make the call himself. So I took his phone while he went to the bathroom."

Carmen didn't know what to think.

"Will you come?"

"Yes." She grabbed a piece of paper to write down the address.

When she got to the bar, she immediately saw Liam and Lily sitting on stools, not a cozy corner booth. "Hi."

Liam spun in his stool. His head tilted, and he looked at her through narrowed eyes. "What are you doing here?"

"Taking you home."

Lily stood behind him. "I'll help you get him to your car."

"I'm not goin' anywhere." He raised his hand. "I need another beer."

"No, you don't." Carmen shook her head at the bartender. "Let me take you home."

"Can't go home. Moira wants me at Mom's house. Maggie's comin' home."

"I'm sure they don't want to see you like this." She tugged

his jacket off the back of the chair. "How about you take a nap and then I'll take you to your family?"

He shook his head like he was considering it, but said nothing.

She pulled his arm. "Come on."

He stood and wobbled. She opened his jacket for him, and he held on to the bar for balance as he slid his arms in the sleeves. "How'd you know where to find me?"

"Lily called me."

He turned to look at Lily and almost lost his balance. "Why?"

Lily went up on tiptoe and kissed his cheek. "Because you want to be with her, not me."

"Aww…Lily, it's not like that." He reached for her hand.

"Yeah, it is." She leaned over and spoke to Carmen. "Are you going to be okay getting him into the house?"

Carmen lifted her shoulders. "We'll find out."

"I don't need help. I'm fine."

Both women looked at him.

"I can't drive, but I can walk." He stumbled past both of them and said over his shoulder, "See?"

Carmen looked at Lily. "Thanks for calling me."

Lily bit her lip before responding. "I care about him a lot. I wanted him to like me, but he's all about you. Take care of him."

"I will." Carmen squeezed Lily's shoulder and went to follow Liam.

He was weaving down the block in the opposite direction of where she'd parked.

"Hey, this way." He turned and rocked on his heels. Man, she hoped he didn't fall over. She was strong, but she wouldn't be able to pick him up. The thought had her questioning why Lily called. Maybe Lily just didn't want to deal with this.

Carmen walked over to Liam and wrapped an arm around his waist to steady him.

"I missed you today," he said.

She didn't say anything.

"Are you mad?"

"Why would I be mad?"

"'Cause I kind of forgot about you. I didn't, but I wasn't thinking right." He sighed. "I wish you were at the hospital with me."

"It looked like you had that covered." Even though she knew better, she couldn't keep the resentment from her voice.

"I know I fucked up. Just yell at me or something."

"I'm not going to yell at you."

"Wish you would. Then we could have makeup sex."

She laughed and leaned him against her car while she dug out her keys.

"Makeup sex is good," he added. He pulled her hips to bring her closer. "We've never had makeup sex."

"We haven't really fought."

He blew out a heavy breath. "I'm sorry."

"You don't have anything to be sorry for. Your family needed you." She stepped away and pressed the button to unlock the door. "Do you need help getting in?"

He ran his palm across her jaw. The skin on his fingers was rough, but his touch gentle. She closed her eyes and enjoyed the contact.

"I love you," he whispered.

Her eyes shot open and her lungs froze. Before she could even think about forming a response, he fumbled with the door handle and swung the door open. He bumped her as he moved to climb in.

The sound of his door closing snapped her attention. Love? He loved her? Did he know what he was saying or was it the alcohol taking charge of an emotional situation? She took her time walking around her car. No man had ever said he loved her. Liam was giving her lots of firsts, but she was trying hard not to read too much into this.

As soon as she started the engine, he leaned against the passenger side window and dozed off. Carmen drove him to his apartment and shook him awake. "We're at your place."

He fumbled for the handle to get out of the car. Carmen rushed around to meet him. Instead of pushing her away, he slung an arm over her shoulder and leaned into her. She liked the feeling of him leaning on her.

She patted the pockets of his jacket to find his keys. Once inside, she helped him to the bedroom.

He flopped back on the mattress and slapped his palm next to him. "Come here."

"Go to sleep, Liam."

"We're supposed to have makeup sex."

"First, we didn't fight. Second, you're in no shape for sex."

He pushed up on his elbows. "Are you saying I can't get it up? Trust me, I can."

She smiled. "I'm sure you can, but what you need is sleep. Your family is expecting you."

He lay back again. "I meant what I said. Drunk or not. I love you."

She pressed her lips together, still unsure of how to respond. Within seconds, his breathing settled into the deep rumble of sleep, allowing her to escape without answering.

She went to the kitchen and made a pot of coffee. Liam couldn't sleep all night because he did need to get back to his family. If she didn't wake him in a couple of hours, he'd probably be pissed. That gave her a couple of hours to sort through her feelings.

Do I love him?

Her immediate response was yes, but that made her

nervous. They hadn't known each other all that long. She had no idea how long it was supposed to take to fall in love.

Her mother had rarely talked about her early life in Mexico, but the one story she loved to tell was about meeting Gus.

Inez's face had softened and she drifted into a dream when she shared the story. She'd been walking down the street with friends, and Gus had bumped into her. Later, she found out it had been intentional. Her mother had described that first meeting with such clarity, even when she'd been very ill. She said that when she'd looked into Gus's eyes something inside her swelled and changed. She knew she was in love.

Carmen adored hearing the story, but always thought her mother embellished a little to make it sound more like a fairy tale. But now, she believed her mother's words.

Carmen had never believed in love at first sight, but she understood that elusive feeling of looking into someone's eyes and feeling different. Liam did that to her every time their eyes met.

Her greatest concern was that maybe it wasn't love. Maybe it was a huge case of lust. How would she know the difference? She had no experience with either.

She didn't want to push anything, especially now, with everything happening with his mom. His focus needed to be on his family. Things between them could wait.

She puttered around his house while he slept. She sat in his living room for a bit, but felt uncomfortable. The fluffy pillows and blanket seemed out of place for the room and for Liam. He never struck her as a fluffy blanket type of guy. Nothing about this room fit him.

At least her house felt lived in. Even without the clutter of things from her parents, her house still felt like a home; Liam's didn't. For some reason, it really bothered her.

LIAM HEARD something above the thundering of his head, but he didn't know what it was. He lifted one eyelid a fraction. *Fuck, that hurts.*

Something clinked near his head, and he turned toward the sound. The pounding turned to piercing pain, and he winced.

"Sorry," Carmen whispered. "You've been asleep for a couple of hours, and I thought you'd want to get back to your family. I made you coffee and toast."

He forced his eyes open again. The room was dark except for the light coming from the hall. Her cool fingers touched his forehead. She'd stayed to take care of him. He grabbed her wrist and pressed a kiss to the palm of her hand.

"I feel like shit." He struggled to sit up. The smell of coffee made his stomach turn. He blew out a breath and then realized how badly he needed to brush his teeth.

Carmen sat on the edge of the bed. "Is there anything I can do?"

"I need to take a shower. God, why did I do this to myself?" Thoughts of his mother immediately invaded his brain and grief struck him.

"We all do stupid things when we're scared and worried about people we love. You want to talk about it?"

He swung his legs over the side of the bed and pulled his shirt off. He didn't want to talk about it, but then Carmen held his hand and kissed his shoulder. Tears built up in his eyes again.

"I don't know if I can handle my mom dying. I'm not ready for it." The words croaked out from his tight throat.

"You'll never be ready."

Of course, she knew better than anyone.

"It was hard when my dad died. He was the foundation of

our family. But my mom…" He swallowed and searched for the words. "She's the heart and soul. She keeps us together and going strong."

"Lily said your mom was okay."

"She is, but who knows really?"

Carmen leaned closer and hugged him. He held her tightly. He envied her strength. She'd faced both of her parents dying, and she was still one of the happiest, most friendly people he knew. He was grateful to be on the receiving end of all that love.

"Will you come with me to my mom's house? We're all supposed to meet there tonight to come up with a plan." He didn't want to let go of her again. Not ever.

She pulled her body away, but went back to holding his hand. "Whatever you need. But…are you sure? It seems like making plans about your mom is a family thing. I don't want to intrude."

"I want you with me." He stood then and went to the bathroom to try to feel more human. He needed to get his shit together for his family. Having Carmen with him made it easier, made him feel stronger.

After a shower, two cups of coffee, and the toast Carmen had made, he felt marginally better. He checked his phone. A text from Moira had come in letting him know that Jimmy was on the way to the house with Maggie. Colin had stayed at the hospital, and everyone was meeting to develop a plan for Mom.

Carmen sat quietly at his kitchen table the entire time. After reading the text, he kissed the top of her head, once again, so grateful that she'd stayed. "Ready to go?"

"Yeah." She hesitated. "Are you sure you want me to come with? I can drop you off and pick you up later. I don't mind."

He touched her cheek. "I'm sure. I want you to meet my entire family. I want them to know you. I need you with me."

He thought speaking such words would be hard, but it wasn't. Honesty was something he'd always valued, something his parents taught him was important, but he'd never been big on discussing his feelings. Carmen made it easy. He wanted her to know how he felt.

Somehow, he knew she needed to have every reassurance because she didn't have faith in herself. He needed to have enough belief for both of them until she understood.

Carmen drove to his mom's house. The street was lined with his siblings' cars. They strode up to the door, and Jimmy had it opened before they could knock. In the living room, Moira sat on the couch, holding Maggie, who was sobbing. Liam had hoped to miss this scene. He nodded at Moira and walked away.

Ryan, Michael, and his wife, Brianna, sat at the dining room table. Liam went to the kitchen to make more coffee. Ryan's wife, Quinn, was already there with the pot brewing. "Need any help?"

She turned and looked at him with the same tired, puffy eyes everyone else had. "No. Go sit with Ryan. I'll bring the coffee when it's ready."

Liam paused for a minute and turned to Carmen. "Quinn, this is Carmen, my girlfriend." He grabbed Carmen's hand and tugged her forward.

Quinn smiled. "Nice to meet you. Thank you for bringing food. We all needed it."

"It was the least I could do." She gripped Liam's hand tightly and he wanted to continue to reassure her.

He pulled her back toward the dining room. Before taking a seat, he introduced her to his other siblings. From the far side of the room, Moira stood and smiled. Maggie was no longer with her.

Everyone greeted her and then Ryan said, "Take a seat. We need to figure out what to do about Mom."

Liam pulled out a chair for Carmen, who sat hesitantly, before he sat beside her.

"Colin called and said the doctor will probably release Mom by the end of the week. She'll be home for Christmas Eve. You all know she'll still want everyone here, but—"

"I'll take care of the meal. I'll cook everything so she won't have to worry about it," Liam offered.

Ryan smiled. "That's what I was hoping for." He glanced at his other siblings. "She'll want the tree decorated."

They all looked to the living room, where the tree should be standing. Mom usually decorated well before Christmas week.

"We also need to take turns at the hospital until she does get out. Quinn is on break, and she's already agreed to fill in wherever we need her. Maggie's home."

Just then Maggie bounded down the stairs like she'd never left. Her face was still tear-streaked, but she was calm. "Yes, I'm here." She slid into a seat across from Liam. "Who are you?" she asked Carmen.

Liam looked at his baby sister. She still had a habit of being rude. "Maggie, this is my girlfriend, Carmen. Carmen, my youngest sister."

Maggie stared at Liam. "I thought this was a family meeting."

Carmen's jaw clenched, and Liam laid a hand on her thigh. "I asked her to come with me."

"Maggie, stop being rude," Ryan said.

She rolled her eyes. Liam wondered if Jimmy had gotten a similar comment. Quinn and Brianna were technically family now that marriage was involved. He'd never thought Maggie would be so much like their mother.

Carmen pushed away from the table. "I'll help Quinn in the kitchen."

As soon as she was gone, Liam leaned forward on the table. "You're being a brat."

"I'm being a brat? My mother is in the hospital, and you brought your little hoochie mama to hang out in our house. There are more important things than getting laid."

Liam shot out of his chair, but Ryan rose slowly. Everyone in the room was silent.

Ryan spoke first. "We're all upset about Mom, Maggie. That doesn't give you the right to be a witch to anyone."

"Watch what you say about Carmen. She's not some girl I'm fucking. I love her."

Again silence filled the room, except for Jimmy, who snickered in the corner.

Ryan took his seat and added, "Well, then, we'll expect to see her at Christmas dinner."

Over the next hour, they squabbled over a schedule and who would do what to make sure Mom wouldn't be left alone while she recovered. Then they argued over what should happen after the holidays. Without more information, they couldn't decide what else they needed to do. Maybe their mom would need someone to move in to take care of her, maybe she wouldn't. Only time would tell.

But for now, Liam settled in with the knowledge that she was okay. She was coming home.

CHAPTER 18

Carmen listened to the O'Learys bicker and fight for hours. How were they not all exhausted? While they had argued, she warmed up food to feed them and kept the coffee flowing. No one had spoken to her since Maggie's outburst, but Liam acknowledged her with small touches. He held her hand, put his arm around the back of her chair, squeezed her knee while it was tucked under the table.

The family dynamic amazed her. As much as the fighting could've been ugly, she never doubted the underlying love and respect they had for each other. Part of her longed for that kind of relationship, but another part of her was grateful that she hadn't had to face the decisions they were facing.

As Carmen moved from the kitchen back to the dining room, most of Liam's siblings offered curious stares; Moira flat-out smiled. But Maggie continued to shoot daggers. Carmen stayed out of the family discussion and focused on feeding them and then cleaning up. It wasn't much, but it was all she could think to do to help. As she worked, Ryan's comment about expecting her for Christmas gnawed at her.

She and Liam hadn't discussed the holidays, except for

talking about when to have the truck on the street. Things just seemed to be moving so fast. Even though she'd been in the kitchen, there had been no mistaking Liam's declaration of love in front of his entire family. The sentiment warmed her and scared her all at the same time.

She loved knowing the words were real, not just some drunken comment, but the thought of them rushing things wouldn't leave her.

In the kitchen, she ran the water and filled the sink to wash dishes.

Moira came up next to her. "You don't have to do the dishes, too. You've done enough."

"It's okay. I don't mind." And she didn't as long as it kept her away from the conversation in the other room.

"So you and Liam are serious, huh?"

Carmen offered a slight shrug.

"What does that mean?"

"It means I'm not sure what we are."

Instead of attacking Carmen, as Maggie might've, Moira laughed. "Liam is kind of intense."

"That's an understatement."

This only made Moira laugh harder. "One thing you can count on with Liam, though, is that he won't play games. If he says he loves you, it's the real deal."

Carmen's heart sped up.

"Do you love him?"

Carmen plunged her hands into the hot water. "I've been asking myself the same thing all afternoon. I think I do, but I'm not sure."

Moira picked up a towel and began drying the dishes Carmen put in the drainer.

"Don't you need to get back to the conversation?" Carmen asked her.

Moira lifted a shoulder. "They're fine without me. Right

now, I like this conversation better." She paused for a minute. "Liam's a serious guy. He's been a little distracted for a while, trying to decide what he wants. But when he sets his sights on something, there's no stopping him."

"Is that a warning?"

"Nope. An observation. Maybe a piece of information for you to tuck away. I want you to know that Liam doesn't make a move unless he's sure. So he must be really sure of you to bring you here."

Carmen and Moira finished the dishes in silence. Moira's information helped, but at the same time it didn't. Carmen believed Liam was sure about them, she just didn't know *how* he could be so sure. But she wanted to let go and trust and believe. Which meant committing to coming to Christmas with his family.

She hadn't thought about a gift for Liam. She'd figured she'd get him something small because they were partners and all, but spending the holiday together as a couple meant she needed to get something better, more personal. It only took a minute before she knew what she wanted to get him. Unfortunately, she would need help.

She looked at Moira and went for it. "Can I ask a favor?"

Moira smiled. "Shoot."

"I need some help with Liam's Christmas present."

"Ooo...I love secrets."

"Don't believe her for a minute. She can't keep a secret to save her life," Liam said from the doorway.

"Shows what you know. I won't tell you what Carmen and I talked about." She turned back to Carmen. "Give me your phone. I'll program my number in and you can call me later."

Carmen pulled the phone from her pocket and handed it over.

Liam walked over and slid an arm around her shoulders. "Should I be worried?"

"I don't know. Should you be?"

"Anything involving Moira causes some worry." He kissed the top of Carmen's head. "Colin called. Mom's awake. We're all heading over to the hospital."

Moira said, "Are you both going?"

Carmen shook her head. "I'll drop Liam off and go home. Your family takes up enough space all on your own. I don't think you need extra people."

She waited for Liam to argue, but he didn't.

"Hey, Moira, can I ride with you? Save Carmen the trip?"

"Sure." She left the room.

Carmen pulled the plug from the drain and dried her hands on a towel. "Give me a call if you need a ride home. I'll come get you."

"Like you said, my family is big enough. I'm sure someone can give me a ride. Are you okay?"

"Me? Why wouldn't I be?"

"Maggie was rude. I'm sure you heard everything."

"Let's face it. Emotions are running high. I'm sure she didn't mean anything by it."

"Doesn't give her the right to be nasty."

Carmen simply held on to Liam's words. "It didn't matter."

"But then you cooked and cleaned and took care of us like you're the maid. I didn't bring you here for that."

"You needed to talk with your family. I wanted to help. Did you feel like a maid when you washed dishes and cleaned up after my dad's wake?"

He shook his head.

"You do what you need to do to take care of family." She reached up and kissed his cheek. "Go see your mom."

"Can I come to your house after?"

"I'd like that."

She followed Liam back through the house and said a brief good-bye to everyone before bundling back up to go out. By the time she reached her house, she was exhausted. This had been one of the longest days of her life, and it hadn't even been her family drama. She curled up on the couch and enjoyed the quiet peacefulness of her house.

LIAM SAT in the uncomfortable chair in the waiting room while his siblings went to see Mom one by one. Maggie had charged into the room and hadn't left the bedside, so everyone else took turns. Since Colin had been there most of the day, he stayed in the waiting room. He took a seat beside Liam.

"I hear I missed a big announcement at the house."

Liam looked at him. "What?"

"You and Carmen? Not only do you pop up with a surprise girlfriend, but you're in love?"

Liam rubbed his palms on his thighs. "You know how it is. When you're with someone all the time, working together, hanging out, making plans, things happen."

"Yeah, I know exactly how that goes."

"Where is Elizabeth anyway?"

"She's at the bar. She told me to stay with the family and she'd handle everything. I don't know what I'd do without her." Colin leaned his elbows on his knees. He looked as beat as Liam felt, and he hadn't gone on an afternoon bender.

"You okay?"

"Yeah. This place gets to me. I fucking hate it here."

Liam thought back to when their father had been here. Colin had taken it harder than anyone expected. "How is she doing really?"

He was afraid of the answer. He knew everyone said their mom was going to be okay, but something like this changed things. He needed to brace himself for whatever he'd see in the bed.

"Surprisingly well. As soon as she woke up, she started barking orders. The poor nurses. I almost felt bad for them, except I knew that if she was snapping at people, she really was okay."

Liam released a relieved breath.

"Be prepared, though. When Moira walked in, I heard her bubbling with gossip. I'm pretty sure she's telling Mom all about your love life."

Liam shook his head. "Let's hope Maggie doesn't put her two cents in." He still couldn't believe Maggie's attitude.

Ryan poked his head in the door. "Your turn."

Liam stood and stretched. Moving slow wasn't going to change things, so he forced his feet forward. The hall was quiet as he walked toward the room. Moira leaned against the wall opposite the door and Jimmy had his arm around her. Liam pushed the door open.

Maggie sat on a chair beside the bed and held Mom's hand. Machines bleeped and whirred. Mom was sitting up and smiling as she gripped Maggie's hand.

With the exception of her hair being a mess, Mom looked like herself. A little pale without her minimal makeup, but happy with Maggie's company.

"Hey, Mom." He made his way to the bed and leaned over and kissed her cheek. "How are you?"

"For the fortieth time, I'm fine. A bad spell is all. The doctors won't listen."

"You had a heart attack, Mom, not a bad spell."

She waved him off. "I guess a stay in the hospital is what's needed to bring the family together."

"Don't talk like that," Maggie said.

"We have dinner together all the time. Sometimes, we even talk to each other when you don't make us," Liam added.

"You're not sayin' much to me, though. I have to hear from your sister that you have a woman in your life. That you're in love?"

Maggie glared at him. He took the seat across from her.

"Carmen is a nice girl, Mom. I told you about her. She's Gus's daughter, and we work together on the food truck."

His mother's piercing gaze hit him. It was like being interrogated without words.

"What?" he asked.

"Seems all of a sudden."

"Isn't that the way love happens? All of a sudden?"

Maggie patted Mom's hand. "What Mom means to say is that it happened awfully sudden with someone who isn't a nice Irish girl."

"What?" In the back of his mind, he supposed he knew his mom held some strange desire for him to marry an Irish girl from the neighborhood, but she hadn't actually said it. She certainly hadn't brought up the heritage of any of his siblings' significant others.

But they were all white.

The idea struck him so hard and fast that it was painful. He'd known his mother to make inappropriate remarks occasionally. He'd always attributed it to her age, but he never thought of her as a racist.

He stared at her. She looked at her hand locked with Maggie's. He shoved away from the chair and stood. "I'm glad you're feeling better, Mom."

He left the room before he said something he would regret and that would most likely upset their mother. She was still recuperating and needed to remain calm. Liam was nowhere near calm right now.

Leaving the room, he asked Jimmy to drive him to Carmen's house. Jimmy said nothing until they were in the car.

"Want to tell me what happened?"

"I think my mom is mad that my girlfriend is Mexican." Saying the words left a bad taste in his mouth.

"It's a different generation. You know that. Look at my dad. He still mumbles crap about my partner, Gabby. I tell him to shut up. You can't change that mind-set."

"But you're not in love with Gabby."

"Got me there."

"My mom just had a heart attack. I can't start a fight with her and tell her to shut up. I also can't bring Carmen to the house and expose her to my mom's attitude. What the fuck am I supposed to do?"

"I wish I knew what to tell you. Maybe you need to give it time. Let her get to know Carmen. You have your brothers and sisters on your side."

"Except Maggie. I don't know what got into her."

"She's just upset like everyone else. She's been gone a long time. It's hard when you come back and think everything's going to be the same, but you find out people have moved on and things have changed. Add your mom's heart attack and it's a lot to handle."

Liam hadn't thought about that. Jimmy had been gone for years in the army. They'd talked plenty and visited a few times while he'd been gone, but Liam didn't think about what it must've been like to return and have everything be different. Maybe he needed to cut Maggie some slack.

It sure would be easier if she were giving everyone else as hard a time, though.

They pulled up to Carmen's house. "Thanks for the ride. And for taking care of my sister."

"No problem."

"You still going to propose?"

"Why wouldn't I? I think now's as good a time as any. By Saturday, she'll be my fiancée."

Liam ran to the front door and knocked. He needed to ask Carmen for a key. It was too freaking cold to stand on a porch unnecessarily.

She opened the door with a sleepy look on her face. All of the anger and frustration fled his system.

"Sorry if I woke you."

"That's okay." She welcomed him into her arms, and they went to bed.

AFTER A FABULOUS NIGHT OF SLEEP, Carmen woke early to get the truck ready. Rosa had called to chat last night and when Carmen had told her about Liam's mom, Rosa offered to work the truck with Carmen.

Carmen hesitated, but she really didn't want to take the truck off the street. They'd finally started building momentum again and taking days off would make them unreliable. People wanted to know when and where the truck would be. She knew that was how to build a solid customer base.

She loved her cousin, but Rosa was unpredictable. Could she be any worse than Pete had been? And really, it was only for a few days. She hoped. Liam needed time to handle things with his mom, but he wasn't going to walk away from his whole life.

Standing in her kitchen, she checked the weather. Another miserably cold day, but at least the sun was out. With any luck, that would be enough to draw out the last-minute shoppers. She sipped her coffee and posted their schedule for the day before heading to the restaurant.

Liam continued to sleep like he had no intention of waking. She grabbed a key from the drawer and left a note by the coffeemaker. His car was parked in her driveway since they'd been using her car to get to and from the restaurant. He could sleep in and then be with his family.

She checked the clock, poured a coffee to go, and hoped Rosa would be on time. No way did Carmen want to run the truck alone. When she arrived at the restaurant, Rosa's car was already parked.

As Carmen stepped from her car, Rosa met her.

"Damn, girl, I was hoping you'd be here before I actually had to leave. I didn't expect you to be early enough to help prep. I'm in shock."

Rosa rolled her eyes. "You should have more faith in me. I said I'd be here."

Inside the kitchen, Carmen began gathering supplies before she thought about the fact that Rosa had no idea what she was doing. Carmen stopped and thought about the process. She and Liam had formed such an easy relationship that their routine was seamless. After gathering her thoughts, Carmen made a list of what needed to happen.

Rosa nodded and then grabbed an order pad and wrote things down. Yet another surprise.

As they loaded the truck, her phone rang. "Hello?"

"Where the heck are you?" Liam asked.

"I'm at the restaurant getting the truck ready."

"Why didn't you wake me? Give me ten minutes to get dressed."

"No. It's okay. I have Rosa working with me. You were exhausted after yesterday and you need to be with your family. We have this handled." She set the tomatoes and onions in the cooler.

"You sure?"

"Yeah." At least she thought so.

"I miss you."

Her heart fluttered, but she said, "I've been gone less than two hours and you were unconscious when I left."

"But the bed is really cold now."

"It must be time for you to go to the hospital to spend time with your mom then. Coffee's ready and I left you a key to lock up."

"A key, huh?"

"Well, I don't want my house left unlocked."

"I think you just want me to be able to come over whenever I want."

She rolled her eyes like Rosa had. "You do that anyway."

She'd been a little worried that he might think she was pressuring him into something by leaving him a key, but like with everything, Liam took it in stride.

"I like being able to surprise you."

"Yeah, you're pretty good at that."

"Hey, now," Rosa called from behind her. "No sex talk on the job. We have work to do."

Carmen laughed and so did Liam. "She's right. About the work, I mean. We have to get going."

"See you for dinner?"

"You might be busy with your family. I'll call you." She disconnected and avoided making eye contact with Rosa.

"Shit, you got it bad."

"What are you talking about?"

"You are so hung up on him."

"You sound like a teenager. We're adults in an adult relationship."

"And you get all moony-eyed when he calls. Some adult." Rosa slid the last of the food onto the truck and slammed the door.

Carmen couldn't respond intelligently. She wanted to

stick her tongue out at Rosa, which wouldn't make her feel any more adult, so she did nothing.

It took longer than usual to leave the kitchen, but once they hit the road, Carmen felt better. Rosa didn't slack off during prep, and when they got to the site, she took directions and they were able to open on time.

Carmen stood over the grill and braced herself. Cooking with Liam had been easy and fun. She didn't have to take it seriously because he was serious enough for the both of them. But now it was all on her. She had to be *the* cook. This was what she'd wanted to avoid.

She glanced at Rosa and wondered if Rosa could handle the cooking. Then she shook her head. Avoiding difficult things was not the way to live her life.

Rosa leaned against the window and peered outside. "It's damn cold out there. Are you sure people are gonna show up to eat?"

"I hope so."

For the rest of the day, at both their first stop and their second, Carmen and Rosa worked steadily. Carmen's hunch had paid off; many people were on the streets for Christmas shopping. Rosa worked the window professionally. She was friendly and a little flirty, but not obnoxiously so. She was just being Rosa.

Carmen found her cooking rhythm easily enough. She just thought about what it had been like cooking with Liam. She missed the teasing and joking she had with him, but Rosa was fun. By the time they rolled up after the second stop, Carmen was tired, but satisfied.

As she drove back toward the restaurant, she said, "You did a really good job today. Thanks."

"Shhh…don't tell my dad. He might expect me to work at the restaurant."

Carmen laughed. She remembered thinking the same

thing as a teen. "You might miss having the chance to work with your dad. Why don't you like the restaurant?"

"Same reason you don't."

Carmen knew that wasn't true. She hated being at the restaurant because it had been a constant reminder of her weight. She felt fat and then she was surrounded by food, so she ate, which made her feel fatter. It was a never-ending cycle. She'd convinced herself if she stayed away from the restaurant, she'd feel better.

It had taken years for her to realize that wasn't the case. And now it was too late.

"You're really good with customers, though. I'm sure your dad would love to have you on staff."

"Uh-uh. I like your customers. They're around for five minutes, tops. In the restaurant, I have to hustle and be nice and *hope* to get a good tip. I can't stand it. Here, the pace is faster. All I have to do is chat for a few minutes, make them smile, and they're on their way." She smiled. "And I don't have to stand over that hot ass grill."

Carmen pulled into the lot. "Works for me."

"So we're done."

"Not quite. We have to empty and clean out the truck so it's ready for tomorrow."

When she parked, Junior poked his head out the back door. "No way. I heard a rumor that my sister was actually working, but I had to see it to believe it."

"Ha-ha," Rosa said.

"She worked her ass off today and did a great job. I'm impressed."

Rosa made a face. "What is with you people? I've held jobs before. I know how to work."

"You need help?" Junior asked.

"We got it," Carmen answered. She'd been isolated from her family for some time, and it felt good to get back into their lives. Ever since her mom had gotten sick, Carmen pulled back. No, it had been even earlier. When she left for college, she backed away from her family while she tried to figure out who she was.

She'd tried to reinvent herself and thought her family had been part of the problem. Over the last month, something had shifted and changed within her. She felt new and revived. She credited her relationship with Liam. With him, she'd learned to open up and experience life again. Part of it was his love for his family and the connection they had. Carmen had been missing that. Until her dad died, she hadn't even realized how much she missed it.

She grabbed containers of food and rushed into the kitchen. "Hey, Junior." When he looked up from the grill, she said, "I'm having a New Year's Eve party this year at my house. Pass the word on to everyone."

He frowned. "You sure you're up for that?"

"Definitely. I want to be with my family." Maybe she'd even convince Liam to bring some of his family. Unless they had plans. Now that she was in a relationship, this was probably something she should've run by him first. But it was a party. Who didn't love a party?

As she wrapped up her work for the day, she began to compile a mental list of what she'd need to do over the course of the next week to get ready for the party. Her dad would be thrilled to see her now. She wished she'd been smart enough to have these realizations a long time ago.

CHAPTER 19

*L*iam worked with his brothers and sisters for the next few days getting their mom's house ready for Christmas. He'd spent a little time with Carmen, but not nearly enough to take the edge off his emotions. Mom hadn't said anything more about Carmen, but he felt like the other shoe would drop at some point. She hadn't denied Maggie's accusations and that troubled him.

He didn't know what he'd do if his mom couldn't accept Carmen. It was Christmas Eve, and Colin and Ryan were at the hospital while he and Moira finished decorating the tree. They laughed over some of the ornaments that had seen better days, but their mom refused to get rid of because one of them had made it as a kid.

"Are we all set for tomorrow?" Moira asked.

"I guess."

"You have all the groceries? You need us to bring anything?"

Liam smiled. When had his sister become an "us"? "Everything's in the fridge. You have a plan to keep Mom out of the kitchen?"

"I got something, but I don't know how well it'll work."

"What?"

"I'm going to mass with her."

"Talk about taking one for the team."

"And you all better appreciate it." She went to the wall and plugged the lights in. The tree lit up. "Carmen is coming tomorrow, right?"

"We haven't talked about it, so I don't know."

Moira studied him.

"Your looks don't scare me."

"Mom shouldn't scare you either. You're a grown man, and Carmen seems really nice. I like her. Mom will get over it."

Liam bent over and packed up the empty boxes from the ornaments to take back to the basement. "First, Mom doesn't scare me. However, I don't want to start a fight and upset her. She's not one hundred percent yet. Second, I've been so busy here and Carmen's been running the truck that we haven't talked about plans for Christmas. She might need to be with her family."

"Mom is stronger than any of us give her credit for. If she wasn't, she wouldn't have commented on Carmen at all. Bring Carmen. Show Mom how great she is." Moira picked up a box and followed him to the stairs.

"How do you know how great Carmen is?"

"Besides the fact that I see how happy she makes you? We've talked a little."

The thought of Moira and Carmen conspiring made him uneasy. He never knew what kind of trouble his sister might be causing. He walked down the steps to the musty basement and shoved the boxes in the corner. Moira tossed her box next to the rest.

She cocked a hip and crossed her arms. "You need to

make sure Carmen knows how important she is, especially if Mom cops an attitude."

"She knows."

"You sure?"

"I told her I love her. It doesn't get any simpler." He turned to go back up the stairs. Even though he was an adult, the basement still creeped him out.

Moira caught his arm and spun him into a hug. "I'm happy for you. Don't screw it up."

He patted her back. "We're talking about me, not you."

She smacked his arm. "I didn't screw things up with Jimmy."

"I know. I'm just yanking your chain."

They clomped up the steps and surveyed the living room. It looked the same way it did every Christmas. The artificial tree stood in front of the living room windows so people on the street could see the lights. The shelves beside the TV held knickknacks: small statues of Santa, snowman candles, and various bells.

Then they moved on to the bedroom, where they changed the sheets and Moira threw in a load of laundry so their mom wouldn't have to worry about it. When she came back to the living room, Moira said, "You know we're wasting time. She's going to walk in and criticize what we did and how it's not right."

"That's Mom. But at least we tried."

The front door swung open, and Ryan came through carrying Mom's small bag. He was followed by Maggie and Mom with Colin pulling up the rear.

"Maggie, I'm not a frail old woman. I can walk by myself."

"The front walk was slippery. I didn't want you to fall."

"We're in the living room. My floor is not slippery." She yanked away from Maggie, and Liam smiled.

Moira was right; their mom was stronger than anyone

gave her credit for. Mom took off her coat and shoved it at Maggie before looking around. "Who put up the tree?"

"Moira and I did," Liam said, stepping forward and giving her a kiss on the cheek.

She pressed her lips together and gave a stiff nod. He smirked at Moira, who rolled her eyes.

"You want some tea, Mom?" Moira asked.

"Oh, yes. They didn't know how to brew a cup in that place." She settled on the couch and everyone stood watching her. "What are you all standing there for? Don't you have lives to lead? I'm not goin' anywhere."

They all let out a collective sigh and then laughed. Mom really was okay. Liam went to the kitchen to do some prep for tomorrow's dinner. Moira stood at the counter readying the teapot.

"Told you she'd appreciate the effort we put in."

Moira turned to look at him. "The only reason she didn't complain was because you said you helped. If I told her I did the decorating, she would've made corrections. She sees any effort from any of you boys as an unbelievably great thing. You can do no wrong."

"Don't be jealous."

"Shut up."

"So what did you get Jimmy for Christmas?"

Moira pulled out a plate and set three cookies on it for their mother. Mom was definitely a creature of habit. Everything the same, no matter what.

"Nothing you really want to hear about." Her cheeks grew pink and he regretted asking.

"You're right. I don't want to know. I'm going to head out in a little bit. Maggie staying here by herself with Mom?"

"Yeah. She knows to keep Mom out of the kitchen?"

"Yep."

Liam opened up the bread he'd gotten at the bakery and

laid the slices out to harden overnight for the stuffing. He'd toss them in the oven first thing in the morning if necessary. Then he finished chopping the vegetables for the salad and double-checked to make sure he hadn't forgotten any ingredients before washing his hands. He gave Moira a quick hug and said, "Have fun with Jimmy tonight. See you tomorrow."

"See you. Tell Carmen I said hi."

CARMEN FELT bad about dodging Liam's calls earlier. She went to her aunt and uncle's house for Christmas Eve dinner. Although there would be another dinner tomorrow, she could get away with participating in only one. Things had been so hectic that she and Liam hadn't talked about their holiday plans, so she hadn't invited him. They'd only been dating about a month, and it seemed early for the whole meet-the-entire-family thing, plus it was a major holiday.

She was a total coward and sent him a text when she sat down for dinner. She hoped he wasn't mad so they could meet after. She wanted to be able to give him his gift while they were alone. In addition to the collage of pictures she'd framed with Moira's help, Carmen also bought some slinky lingerie with Rosa's help. She wanted tonight to be about them.

As much as she'd decided that she wanted to spend more time with her family, a big family meal was still difficult for her. Her aunt insisted on dumping more food on her plate as if Carmen couldn't decide what to eat for herself. Then came the poking and prodding, with comments like "Eat up." Her stomach threatened to revolt.

All of the progress she'd made by eating regular meals with Liam, real food with taste and texture, things she could enjoy, had not prepared her for this. She ate about half of the food on her plate and felt ill. And fat.

By the time she said her good-byes to her cousins and aunts and uncles, her only thought was that she wanted to pull on some sweatpants and crawl into bed.

She hadn't heard from Liam, and then she remembered his mom was being released from the hospital. She figured she'd call him when she got home to make sure everything was okay, but when she pulled into her driveway, his car was parked there.

She went into the house, tossed her keys on the kitchen table, and went to the living room. On her table sat a small Christmas tree with twinkling lights. She didn't have the energy to decorate the house this year, so the little tree made quite the impact.

Liam sat up where he'd been sprawled on the couch. "Hey, you're home."

His face lit with a smile that she returned and all of the stress and anxiety she'd felt over the last few hours disappeared.

"What's this?" she asked, pointing to the tree.

"I needed somewhere to put your present." He slid a small box off the table. "Merry Christmas."

She sat beside him and kissed him. She held his head, running her fingers through his hair, loving the brush of his beard against the soft skin of her lips.

"You okay?" he asked when he pulled back.

"I've missed you."

"How was your night with your family?"

"The usual."

"What does that mean?"

"It means I wish I had been here with you. How's your mom?"

"Good. Back to complaining about all the usual things."

He paused and took her hand. "I want you to come with me to my mom's house tomorrow, but I feel like I need to warn you."

She let out a slow breath. "About?"

"My mom." He tightened his grip on her hand. "She's...well..."

"Jeez, Liam, spit it out."

"She's disappointed that you're not Irish."

Carmen waited, sure there must be more. She considered what that meant. "Is she upset that I'm not Irish or that I'm Mexican?"

"I'm pretty sure it's that you're not Irish, but I can't be sure." He rubbed a hand over his head. "In all honesty, I think it's because you're not white."

She slid her hand from his grasp. She let it sink in and tried to determine how she felt. Part of her thought she should be angry, but she wasn't. Deep down, she knew she wasn't because she had feared the same reaction from some of her family members. It was why she hadn't invited him to Christmas Eve dinner.

He reached for her again. "You know I've never even thought about it, Carmen. And the rest of my family couldn't care less. But my mom is..."

"Old, out of touch, set in her ways." She settled next to him on the couch and reveled in the feel of his embrace as he brought her closer. "I get it. My family's the same. It was my cousin who used to call you Wonder Bread, remember?"

His fingers played with the ends of her hair. "Is that why you didn't ask me to come with you tonight?"

She nodded. "I'm not embarrassed to be your girlfriend. But it's still so new that I didn't want to chance anyone attacking it."

"My mom won't attack. She probably won't even be cold toward you. She'd most likely be overly friendly because she would never want anyone to accuse her of being racist, but I didn't want to bring you into the fray without warning." He kissed the top of her head. "I know that once she gets to know you, she'll love you."

Carmen didn't respond. She wanted to fit in with Liam's family, but she didn't want to cause a rift with anyone. "If you're sure, I'll give it a try."

"Good."

"Do I get my present now?"

"Absolutely." He sat up to grab the box. "I would've given it to you even if you decided not to go tomorrow."

She jumped up from the couch. "Hold that thought. I'll be right back."

"Where are you going?"

"I have to get your present."

She raced to her bedroom to grab the picture frame. She looked at the lingerie she bought, but couldn't bring herself to put it on. Emotionally, she felt battered and taking that extra step to put herself on display would be too much. Another day.

For now she hoped the photos would be enough.

LIAM STRETCHED out on the couch and waited for Carmen to return. He was still nervous about giving her jewelry, but he hoped she liked it.

Standing in front of him, she held out a neatly wrapped package. He held out hers. "You first," he said.

"Let's do it at the same time."

"Okay."

They swapped presents and she ripped into the paper while he peeled it away.

"Jeez, are you a grandma looking to save the paper? Tear

into it," she goaded him. She didn't wait for him to catch up, however. She flipped the top off the box and then ooohhed over the necklace.

He stopped unwrapping to watch her face.

"It's beautiful, Liam." She traced her fingers over the design. "What is it?"

"It's a Claddagh. The crown represents loyalty, the hands, friendship, and the heart, love." He took it from the box and shifted so he could put it around her neck.

She lifted her hair. "It sounds distinctly Irish."

"It is. I bought it last week, before anything happened with my mom. I wanted you to have something from me that would be personal."

After he clasped it, she turned back to face him. The necklace was beautiful against her golden skin.

She pushed at him. "Your turn. We were supposed to be doing this together."

He removed the paper and flipped the frame over. What he saw amazed him. The picture frame was filled with photos of his entire family.

In the center, was a candid shot that Carmen's cousin had taken of Liam and Carmen in front of the truck. It had been freezing out and in the photo their breath puffed like smoke, but they both looked happy. He took a few minutes to study the other photos.

"Do you like it?"

"How?" He was filled with so much emotion. No one had ever given him such a personal gift filled with so much love.

"I wanted to give you something that was important, to let you know how much you mean to me. This is what I asked Moira to help me with. Every time I'm in your living room, I feel like I'm in a stranger's place. I wanted something to make it yours."

"It's amazing. I love it."

She stroked his jaw. "Good. "

He kissed her. "I love you."

"I love you, too."

He stood and pulled her off the couch. "Time for bed."

He planned to spend the night showing her how much he loved her. Regardless of what anyone else said about their relationship, they belonged together.

CARMEN ROLLED over the following morning and groaned. She stretched and enjoyed the soreness of her muscles. A slight ache all over reminded her of her long night with Liam and she smiled. She reached out next to her, but the bed was empty.

Liam rarely got up before her. She rubbed her eyes and sat up. As she did, Liam came through the door with a cup of coffee.

"Good morning." He handed her the cup. "I was going to make you breakfast, but I overslept. I have to get to my mom's. Moira called to let me know they're headed to mass soon."

Carmen took a sip of coffee and tried to understand. "What does mass have to do with you?"

"Moira's getting my mom out of the house so I can start cooking. My mom is still under the delusion that she's well enough to cook Christmas dinner." He kissed Carmen's cheek.

"Do you need me to get ready?"

"No. You stay and I'll come back for you after I get everything started. When I get back, don't let me forget the cheesecake in the fridge."

Her mouth watered at the mention of his cheesecake. She'd gone for years without any dessert at all, but one taste of his cheesecake and she had thoughts of throwing away her scale. Of course the memory would permanently be linked to the first amazing orgasm of her life.

He smirked. "I know what you're thinking."

She blushed and drank from her cup.

He leaned and whispered in her ear, "I made a second cheesecake for us for later."

She shivered and felt a pulse run through her body. She licked her lips.

Liam pressed a kiss to her mouth quickly. "Don't do that. I really have to leave. I'll call when I'm on my way back."

"Do you need me to bring anything?"

"Nope. We have it covered."

"What should I wear?"

"Whatever you want."

She looked at him. He wore jeans and a black sweater. "Will you be changing?"

"Nope. The O'Learys are a casual crowd." He backed off the bed and left the room. A few minutes later, she heard the front door click shut. As soon as she knew Liam was gone, Carmen grabbed her phone and called Rosa.

When her cousin answered, Carmen said, "I need some advice."

"Since when am I the advice giver?"

"Since I know you've encountered some parents who didn't like you."

"What are you talking about? Everyone loves me."

"Listen. Liam wants me to come to Christmas dinner with his family, but he warned me that his mom is not thrilled with the fact that I'm Mexican."

"Fuck her."

"That's helpful."

Rosa sighed. "If she thinks you're not good enough for her little boy, you're probably not going to be able to change her mind. I say screw it. Walk through the door rattling off everything in Spanish. Make her crazy."

"I don't know why I called you. You're not helping. This is important. Liam is really close with his family. Today is a big deal. Plus, the poor woman just got out of the hospital. I have to be nice." She walked to her closet and flipped through the hangers, looking for the right thing to wear.

"What if it doesn't work?"

"What do you mean?"

"What if you do everything in your power to make the woman like you and she still won't accept you? Then what?"

"I don't know."

"Well, *chica*, that's a conversation you need to have with your man. If his family is as important to him as you say, he might have to choose. Is he man enough to choose you?"

Crap. This was all getting way too intense. She just wanted to have a nice dinner with Liam's family. She wasn't looking for a lifetime commitment. She didn't even know where things were going with them. That was a lot of pressure.

"Score one for Rosa. I made Carmen speechless."

"Yeah, whatever. I have to go. I'll call you later. We're still on for Monday?"

"If you need me, I'll be there, but won't Liam be ready to get back on the truck since his mom is home?"

"I'm not sure. A few more days can't hurt. They're all trying to figure out who's going to check on her and help her out and stuff."

"Enjoy your dinner. If you need backup for a fight, you know who to call."

Carmen laughed and disconnected. After deciding on a dark green sweater and her black jeans, she took a shower and tried to come up with an adequate gift to bring Liam's mom. She should've planned better. She usually did, but Liam had a way of throwing her off balance.

Hours later, she stood in her living room, armed with a fruit basket, which seemed really lame, and stared at Liam's cheesecake. She'd give anything for him to come to the door right now and whisk her off to bed instead of dragging her to a family dinner. A family *holiday* dinner.

Liam opened the door like he lived there, and her heart lurched. It was so natural to see him walk through her front door that it took her by surprise. His cheeks were red from the minute run between the car and the house. While she slept, snow had fallen again, coating the old iced-over brown muck. The scene was picture perfect for Christmas Day.

"Ready?" he asked.

"I guess." She handed him the cheesecake and followed him out. "Did Moira's plan work?"

"As much as we could expect. As soon as Mom walked in after church, she started telling me how to cook. Luckily, she needed a nap, so she went to bed." He quieted as he climbed into the car.

He had the heat blasting and the space filled with warm air. He turned it down and she buckled up.

"How is she feeling?"

"Honestly, none of us know. She won't say. I think if a truck ran over the woman, she would tell us it was just a scratch and she was fine."

"Parents are like that."

They said nothing on the remainder of the drive, which allowed her nerves to go crazy. She'd never had to meet anyone's parents before. When Liam parked the car, he said, "It looks like everyone else is already here. There are a lot of us, but we're friendly."

"A lot, like how many?"

"With us, thirteen, not including the two babies."

She chuckled. "That's nothing. Thirteen doesn't even cover one side of my family."

"We just stick with immediate family for stuff like this. Weddings and funerals bring out the extended family." He opened his door and cold air rushed into the car.

She climbed out and met him on the sidewalk. He led the way up to a brick bungalow that looked like every other bungalow on the block. She hadn't paid much attention last time because she'd been worried about Liam. He held the cheesecake in one hand and put his other arm around her shoulder. She didn't know what to expect, so it was hard to prepare herself. He hadn't told her what they did for Christmas other than eat dinner. Plus, his mom didn't like her.

At the top of the concrete steps, Liam released her and pushed the front door open. Once inside, he handed off the cheesecake to Quinn and took Carmen's coat to hang up. Christmas music played in the background, and she surveyed the situation.

From the living room she saw the dining room table covered in a red linen cloth. A smaller card table was set up in the corner. She prayed she'd get stuck at the kiddie table. She could handle herself with only three other people.

With his hand on her back, Liam led her a few steps into the living room. People sat on the couch and love seat. Although Carmen had met most of them the other day, there were a few new faces. Liam pointed at people down the line and offered introductions. He saved his mother for last, where she sat on an armchair like a queen presiding over court.

Carmen went forward with her lame fruit basket. She almost felt like she should bow. She extended her hand. "Hi, Mrs. O'Leary. It's nice to meet you."

To her surprise, Mrs. O'Leary stood to greet her. "Same to you."

"I brought you this." She handed her the basket and received a tight smile in return.

Mrs. O'Leary took the gift, turned it slowly in her hands inspecting it, and then nodded. "I remember as a girl getting oranges in my stocking Christmas morning. It was the best treat imaginable."

Maybe her fruit basket wasn't so lame after all.

"I'll put this in the kitchen for you, Mom." Moira took the basket from her mother.

The room had quieted with her entrance, which made Carmen feel self-conscious again. Someone needed to talk, so she did. "How are you feeling, Mrs. O'Leary?"

"Call me Eileen." Then she sat back down in her chair. "I feel fine, regardless of what my children will have you believe. I'm strong as a bull. How's this business you roped my boy into?"

Carmen could almost hear the collective intake of breath in the room. Liam had disappeared from her back, but from the corner of her eye, she saw him making his way back with a folding chair.

She accepted the chair from him and sat before answering. Liam said, "I have to check on the food. I'll be right back."

She didn't know if Liam had heard the question, but she knew she needed to respond. "Well, Mrs.—Eileen, the truck is a solid business. My dad spent years making it successful. And for the record, I didn't rope Liam into it. My father left him half of the business. No one said he had to run it. That was his choice."

Carmen almost faltered under the woman's stare. She thought about Liam and everything they'd done over the past few weeks. "But I have to say I'm glad he made that choice."

"You don't have an accent."

Carmen wasn't quite sure how to take the statement. "No. I was born and raised in Chicago."

Whatever she said, it was enough for Eileen to offer a curt nod and maybe a hint of a smile. If that was the worst of the grilling, Carmen had no worries. The noise around her picked up again and Moira grabbed a chair and sat next to her.

"Thanks again for all the help you've given us with spreading the word about the truck. Your brother was right, you have the social media stuff down."

"It's easy. It's just chatting."

From across the room, a big guy leaned forward. "And if anyone loves to *chat*, it's Mouthy Moira."

Moira shot him a smirk. "That's Jimmy. He loves to hear me talk. Isn't that right, sweetheart?"

"Boyfriend?" Carmen asked.

"Fiancé," Moira said and held out her left hand. "As of last night." She wiggled her fingers, and Carmen stared at the beautiful ring.

Instead of the usual diamond, an emerald sparkled on her finger. Moira's face lit with a gorgeous smile. From the corner of her eye, Carmen saw Eileen lean back in her chair slightly. For a moment while watching her daughter, she looked completely thrilled.

"How exciting! Congratulations!" Carmen said. "Liam didn't say anything."

"I'm sure Liam knew before anyone, but he doesn't give up secrets."

"Not surprising. He's a quiet guy."

Moira leaned closer. "How the hell do you work with him? Doesn't it make you crazy?"

Carmen thought about it. "He's not terribly quiet when he's working. In fact, he barks a lot of orders."

"That sounds like Liam."

"But you know when we were competing earlier this week? The guy versus girl thing? He spent the whole day talking. Not conversation, but trash talking and teasing nonstop. It was a lot of fun."

"I forgot about that. How did it work out? Who won?"

Carmen shrugged. "We decided it needed another day to really take effect. We did our first stop and I was way ahead in the votes, but we never made it to the second stop. You know..." She looked over her shoulder to Eileen and lowered her voice. "That's when you called about your mom."

"Excuse me, Carmen. Can I get you a drink? We have wine, beer, water, pop..."

Carmen looked up at the man in front of her and tried to remember which brother it was.

Moira spoke first. "Ryan is putting on a good show. He never plays host for anyone, so lap it up. I'll have a beer as long as you're going that way." She swung a look to Carmen.

"That would be fine for me, too. Thanks."

He stepped away and Carmen asked, "Do you have a date set yet?"

"No, we're waiting for Colin and Elizabeth to decide since they got engaged first. And with him being my older brother, it's probably the right thing to do..." As Moira talked, Carmen settled in. Liam's family wasn't all that different from hers. She could totally handle this.

CHAPTER 20

*L*iam stood at the kitchen counter drinking a beer and waiting for the potatoes to be ready for mashing.

Ryan came in and grabbed three bottles of beer from the fridge. "Your girl is doing well out there."

"I figured she would. How's Mom?"

"Quiet as usual." Ryan popped the tops off the beers. "So it's really serious between you and Carmen?"

Liam shrugged. "I think so. It's hard to tell, though, since we've been dealing with so much. First, her dad, then setting up the truck, then Mom. If life was normal, would we be together?"

Ryan smirked. "One thing I've learned is that there's never a good time to fall in love. It happens and you either accept it or you don't. Your choice. There is no waiting for a better time."

Liam accepted the words. Ryan knew what he was talking about. He'd almost given up on Quinn a year and a half ago. Now they were married with a baby. Liam knew he loved Carmen, and he didn't care that it had happened fast. His life was moving forward, which was what he'd wanted.

He just wasn't sure if Carmen wanted the same things.

"Does Mom seem to like her?"

"You know Mom. She won't say much. But don't worry about Carmen. She's talking with Moira. She'll be fine. Remember when I brought Quinn here the first time? It'll all work out, especially if it's right. I need to go deliver these before Carmen and Moira come looking for me."

Ryan left and Maggie came in. She looked at Liam for a minute and then said, "She's okay."

Liam leaned closer and put his hand to his ear. "What was that?"

"I said, Carmen is okay. I shouldn't have been so judgey."

"You come by it honestly." He pulled her into a quick hug. "Just be nice to her."

"I will." She stepped back. "Need some help? It's all touchy-feely couply out there. Damn, I haven't been gone that long, but all of a sudden, everyone's in looooove."

He chuckled. "It happens."

He pointed to the potatoes, which were finally boiling. "You can mash those." He polished off his beer and checked the oven. "I have to run downstairs and grab the roast out of that oven."

When he returned, he peeled back the foil and sniffed the roast. It was perfect. He'd tried for a positive mix of his recipes and his mother's. Although she wasn't a horrible cook, her food tended to be bland. And sometimes overcooked. Seeing pink in the roast might send Mom into a tizzy.

He covered the roast again and began pulling the rest of the food out. Just when he thought he'd escaped, Eileen came into the kitchen. She moved slower than usual, but she was as nosy as ever.

"Did you get the vegetables on in time?"

"Yes, Mom."

"I don't think you had the roast in long enough. People don't want raw meat."

Liam sighed and struggled for patience. "Mom, you do know I'm a chef, right? I know how to cook. I might do things a little differently than you do, but I know what I'm doing."

"Bet you did some fancy thing to the stuffing as well."

He turned to look at her with a smile. "Actually, the stuffing was one thing I didn't change at all. Your recipe is perfect." Simple and reminiscent of her early life of poverty, but tasty. The stuffing had become one of the foods he associated with family holidays, so he couldn't change it. He would probably never serve it in a restaurant, but he'd always make it for his family.

"Go sit down, Mom. We've got this taken care of."

"I've done nothing but sit for days. It's not good for a person."

"The doctor said you needed to rest."

"I'm rested. Now I'm ready to do."

He handed her a basket of dinner rolls. "Take this to the table and sit. Send in everyone to help carry the rest."

She left the room and Liam went to task getting everything else on plates and in bowls. He carved the roast and then the turkey as his siblings all filed into the small kitchen to grab the waiting food.

As he plated the meat, Liam suddenly realized this was the first time that he'd been in charge of not just cooking the meal, but carving the turkey. Their father had always done it, and when he passed, their mother took over, even though all of the boys were capable. Somehow this occasion felt momentous.

Until Colin came into the room and slapped his shoulder. "Let's go. The army is starving out there."

Liam hefted the platter of turkey and when he walked

into the dining room, his family greeted him with cheers. Comedians, all of them.

He set the plate at his mother's elbow and took his seat. Carmen was already beside him, and he looked over his shoulder to the small table where Michael and Brianna and Moira and Jimmy sat. He briefly wondered how they determined who'd get stuck there.

Eileen held out a hand to Liam. She nodded at Colin, who sat at the other end of the table, where their father used to sit. "Colin, say grace."

Liam took Carmen's hand. He bowed his head while Colin spoke, but he kept his gaze on Carmen. She was calm, unfazed by his rowdy family. He really did love her. When Eileen released his hand, it was his cue that the prayer was over. He squeezed Carmen's hand before grabbing the plate of turkey to pass.

He loaded his plate and picked out a couple of pieces of white meat and set them on Carmen's plate. The corner of her mouth lifted, and she passed the plate to Maggie.

Even though it seemed like everyone spoke at once as they passed food and made requests, Liam was completely in tune with Carmen, knowing what she would want on her plate and what she wouldn't. At one point, Maggie did shoot him a look in question, but no one said anything, other than to include her in conversation.

Liam couldn't remember any of his siblings bringing a date home for dinner without a complete interrogation happening. Not that he'd complain about this.

CARMEN PUSHED BACK from the table and stood to help clear the dishes. She followed Liam into the kitchen and began to fill the sink.

"What are you doing?"

She glanced around. "There is no dishwasher, so I figured the dishes needed to get clean somehow."

He turned the faucet off. "We take turns doing dishes around here. I cooked, so I don't have to wash. And since you're my guest, you don't have dish duty either."

Maggie bounced into the room. "Time for presents!" she announced. She sounded more like a twelve-year-old than a world-traveling twentysomething.

Carmen had not been looking forward to this part of the night. Other than the fruit basket, she hadn't bought gifts for anyone. She didn't even know anyone well enough to think about a gift. How awkward would it be to sit around and watch everyone else open theirs?

Liam held her hand and led her into the living room. He sat on the floor with his back against the arm of the couch. He patted the spot between his legs for her to sit. Instead, she sat beside him. Sitting between his legs felt much too intimate for a family gathering. But she looked around and saw that while Jimmy sat on the couch, Moira sat on the floor, between his feet. His hands rubbed her shoulders and played with her hair. Quinn sat across from her with a baby in her lap as did her sister. Carmen wondered if they intentionally timed their pregnancies to coincide.

Colin plopped on the love seat beside Maggie and pulled his fiancée, Elizabeth, down onto his lap. Although the woman laughed and slapped his chest, she didn't move.

This family obviously had no issue with PDA.

Ryan grabbed packages from under the tree and tossed them at their recipients. Sometimes, the gift was too heavy, so he actually had to walk it across the room. No one attempted to unwrap anything as they were delivered.

Much to her shock, Ryan called her name and then tossed a small box at her. She caught it and looked at Liam, who shrugged. They had exchanged gifts last night, but maybe he saved something small for her to open with his family so she wouldn't feel left out.

The two babies had a mountain of presents in front of them in a matter of minutes. Carmen felt bad for their mothers, who would get stuck opening all of them. The babies were barely old enough to sit by themselves.

Ryan called her again and tossed another package.

What the heck?

While the passing continued, Carmen looked at the tags stuck to the gifts. One was from Moira, which shouldn't have surprised her because through their brief conversations, Carmen had already discovered that Moira was one of the most open and friendly women she'd ever met.

The other gift was from Eileen. How had she been able to get Carmen a gift? The woman had been in the hospital yesterday. Before she knew it, two more gifts were passed to her. Tears sprang to her eyes. She'd wanted to be accepted by Liam's family because he was important to her, but she hadn't expected gifts.

She blinked rapidly, and Liam put his arm over her shoulder, pulling her close. "Getting presents is supposed to make you happy."

"I am." She leaned over and kissed his cheek. "I love you," she whispered.

He smiled one of those rare smiles that filled his face. He brought her mouth to his and captured it in a passionate kiss. Gifts fell off her lap as she twisted to deepen the kiss. She forgot all about being in a room full of O'Learys. Liam's kisses transported her to a place where no one but them existed.

A sudden, sharp whistle pierced the air, and Carmen jumped back from Liam. Heat flared up her cheeks, and she wanted nothing more than to be swallowed up by a sinkhole. Liam turned back to face his family.

Jimmy called out, "I want to know what kind of present gets a thank-you kiss like that one."

"That wasn't a thank-you. She kisses me like that because she loves me," Liam responded.

"Get a room," Maggie yelled from her perch on the couch.

Moira jumped in. "Don't be jealous Magpie. You'll get your chance." Her voice was sickeningly sweet, and Carmen couldn't hide her smile.

This family was a lot of fun.

The last presents were handed out and everyone tore in simultaneously. She took her time, relishing in the love she felt in the room. The presents she received weren't expensive or terribly personal: a scarf, a pair of gloves, some chocolate from Ireland (a shocking present from Maggie), and a pair of beautiful earrings from Moira.

Carmen took a few minutes to look around at everyone. They chatted as they held up presents. It looked like most people only had a couple of things to open. Then she heard them chatting about grab bags and who had who. Quinn and her sister, Indy, were still unwrapping presents for the babies while the dads watched with cameras poised.

Her heart squeezed at the sight.

"Griffin, what is this?" Eileen asked, holding up a piece of paper.

"We hired a cleaning service for you," Indy's husband answered.

"I'm capable of cleaning my own house."

"We know you are, and you've done it for many years. It's time for you to relax, and let us take care of you."

"No one ever does it as well as you do it yourself."

Griffin smiled. "If you're not happy with something, all

you have to do is point it out and they'll redo it. They'll work until you're happy."

Judging by the look on Eileen's face, that would take some doing.

"You like your presents?" Liam whispered in her ear.

"Yes. Not as much as I like what you gave me, though." She fingered the necklace at her throat.

Quinn handed her son off to Ryan and stood, gathering pieces of wrapping paper. "I hope you all know that there will be payback. You all chose the noisiest toys possible. Someday, you'll have children, and I'll get my revenge."

She waved scraps of paper as she spoke. No one took her seriously, or they didn't care, because they all continued with their conversations. Carmen pushed off the floor to help collect the trash.

Ryan stood with the baby. "You had to know that would happen. You and Indy gave birth to the firsts: granddaughter, grandson, niece, nephew. No one's used to having babies around."

Carmen's heart gave another squeeze. Her parents had never had the joy of holding a grandbaby. The thought saddened her.

"Yeah," Jimmy said. "It gives us a reason to go to the store and play with toys. Just wait until he gets bigger, and I get him his first football and teach him how to throw it."

Quinn sighed but smiled.

As Carmen scooped up ripped paper, she thought about how spoiled her child would've been if she'd had one before her parents had died. A few other people began crawling along the floor to grab trash. Then of course, a couple of the brothers balled up paper and began to throw it.

Eileen stood. "Enough of that. You'll scare the babies." She bent over to take the baby from Indy, but Griffin was at her side in a flash.

"Have a seat. I'll bring her to you."

"I don't need to be coddled. I carried babies around for years." She smiled at the infant. "And this little thing isn't much."

Indy passed the baby up to Eileen. Griffin helped his wife off the floor and pulled her into an embrace. Carmen had no idea how long they'd been married, but they acted like they were still on their honeymoon. Carmen's parents had been like that.

It was a special forever kind of love. She stole a glance at Liam and wondered if they would have that.

Then she mentally shook herself. She was getting caught up in the excitement of the holiday. Liam was the first real relationship she'd had. There was no need to push it to be anything else. Besides, who knew where they'd be in a year? Most likely, they'd be parting ways because they'd be able to sell the truck.

Liam had mentioned he wanted to open a restaurant, that the truck was a stopping point on his journey. She very well might be just another stopping point for him. As she filled a trash bag with paper, she looked over the room again and decided she could live with that. A year of this kind of happiness after so many of sadness was well worth it.

AFTER A LUXURIOUS DAY in bed with Liam on Sunday, her week began with an argument with him about the truck. She'd told him she already had Rosa scheduled to work so he would have time with his mom.

"My mom is fine. What am I supposed to do, sit and watch her?"

"I'm sure there are appointments with the doctor or trips to the grocery store you can help with. Your mom had a heart attack. It's not a cold. Take all the time you need to be with her." Carmen got ready and poured herself a cup of coffee before heading out into the cold.

Liam followed her into the kitchen. "What do you want me to get for the party on Friday?"

"Nothing. I'll figure it out later. Did you invite your brothers and sisters?"

"Yeah. Moira has a work thing she needs to do. Ryan and Griffin are both staying at home because of the babies. Colin has to run his bar. Maggie said she'd come, and Michael might, unless he has the chance to pull an extra shift at the firehouse."

Carmen tried not to be disappointed. It was a little last minute, but after they'd all been so nice to her this weekend, she really wanted to include them.

"What are you thinking about serving?"

She sipped her coffee. "Pizza?

"Forget it. I'll plan the menu."

"I don't need you to play chef, Liam. It's just a casual party with my family. Trust me, they aren't picky."

He pulled her close. "I don't get to do chef-like things too often. Let me do this."

She smiled. Working on a taco truck was a step down for someone like him. Sometimes she forgot. "Fine. But nothing too weird."

By the time she got to the first stop with Rosa, Liam had called her three times with reminders about the food or the menu or the grill. All things she knew how to do on the truck. Didn't the guy know how to take a day off?

He claimed that he could multitask. He called her while running errands for his mom. The whole day reaffirmed her knowledge that Liam was the kind of guy who liked to run things.

They weren't as busy as they had been the previous week,

but not slow enough to consider closing early. Although Rosa and Carmen worked well together, it wasn't as much fun as working with Liam.

As they closed up at the first site and readied for the second, Rosa asked, "So where did you decide to go on vacation?"

"Huh?"

"You said you were going on vacation. What did you finally decide?"

"Nothing. I had some ideas, but then everything happened with Liam's mom and it didn't seem like such a good idea anymore."

Rosa stared at her, but didn't say anything.

What was she supposed to do? Leave Liam and the truck when his mom was in the hospital? Even if she put the business aside, she cared about Liam. He needed her here. But she had no way to explain that to Rosa. Rosa had never been in love.

Carmen smiled thinking about how much she loved Liam. She started the truck and pulled out into downtown traffic.

"What's that smile for?"

"Nothing."

"Liar. You're thinking about getting it on."

"Am not."

"Then what?"

"I love Liam. I really do." She sighed. "I dreamed about finding some special guy one day, but it was always somewhere down the line, in the future, never now. It's like I looked up, and he was just there. It's better than I thought it would be."

"He like this, too?"

"Like what?"

"All mushy and shit."

"He told me he loves me, if that's what you're asking. I spent Christmas with his family. Even I know a guy doesn't do that unless he's serious." She rounded the corner near Monroe and slowed. A truck was already in the spot they usually took. Crap. Now they'd have to go somewhere else.

She tossed Rosa her phone. "Check the food truck finder site and see if this guy is on there. We already posted we'd be here today, and he swooped in and stole our spot."

Rosa clicked away on the phone. "Nothing."

Carmen sighed. She didn't know what to do in this situation. She drove at a snail's pace down the block and considered a different location.

"Let's try farther north," Rosa suggested. "Why stay in the middle of downtown? There are some spots on the Northside we can try."

"Yeah, but those spots are usually taken."

Rosa's focus was on the phone's screen. "There should be a spot opening on Lincoln. One of those cupcake trucks will be leaving soon if they haven't already."

Carmen turned the truck and headed to Lake Shore Drive. With any luck, they'd get to the next stop before someone else took it. Although it wasn't required for anyone to report where they were going, it was courteous to other vendors and it helped customers know where to find the truck.

"While I'm driving, post to Facebook and Twitter about the change in plans. Then text Liam and see if he can log on to the web site and update it." She thought about whether the web site would have an impact. She couldn't decide if it would be worth bothering Liam. Ultimately, she figured it couldn't hurt.

Within minutes, her phone rang again, so Rosa answered it. "*Hola*, Carmen's phone."

There was a pause, then Rosa said, "She's driving. Okay."

She pressed a button and Liam came across on speakerphone.

"What's going on?"

"When we got to the Monroe location, someone else was already there."

"They can't do that."

"Yeah, they can, Liam. We don't own the spot."

"It's a dick move."

"It might be, but that's the way it goes." She could almost hear him pacing.

"What truck was it?"

Carmen bit her lip, not liking the way he asked. "Why?"

"Because if they want to play that game, I'll make sure I win."

"Liam, it's just business. Not a big deal."

"The hell it's not. We've been at that spot for over a week. Our customers count on it. They're trying to poach our customer base."

Rosa smiled and jumped in. "It's the Heavenly Buns truck."

Carmen swung at her cousin, but Rosa had anticipated the move and scooched closer to the door.

"What the hell is Heavenly Buns? Sounds like a strip club."

Rosa broke out in a fit of laughter. "Maybe they shake their asses and wear thongs while cooking." She made herself laugh so hard, she started to cry.

"It's a sandwich place. They sell sandwiches on buns." Carmen inhaled deeply. "We'll talk about this when I'm done today. I need to get to the Northside. I'll call you later."

"Bye." Liam didn't sound happy, but what was she supposed to do?

"Do not encourage assinine behavior," she said to Rosa.

"What'd I do?"

Carmen shook her head. When she got to the spot on

Lincoln, no other trucks were in sight. She parked and they set up. Customers began to trickle up to the truck, but business wasn't as good as she'd expected with downtown shoppers out to do gift returns and exchanges and hit after-Christmas sales.

When they returned to the restaurant, Liam was waiting for them. He helped them unload the truck and clean up, all the while grumbling about buns. Carmen tried not to laugh, but the whole thing was ridiculous. Liam couldn't understand that the food truck business was competitive. He acted like he never had to face competition.

They stood in the kitchen of the restaurant washing the remaining pans.

"It's like this," she tried to explain, "when you worked at the restaurant, you couldn't do anything if three more restaurants popped up on your block. This is the same thing."

"No, it's not. This is more like someone moving in to use your kitchen."

"You're wrong. We don't own any spot. No one does."

"Would you do this?"

Carmen thought for a minute. "Probably not, but that's because I wouldn't want a confrontation. My dad did it. It's how you establish yourself. Get good spots consistently."

Rosa watched their interaction. "I'm with Liam. They're assholes. How do we get even?"

Carmen looked back and forth between Liam and Rosa. "You guys can't start trouble. It'll be bad for business, and with your luck"—she pointed at Rosa—"the police will be involved."

"We'll play by the rules," Liam responded.

Somehow, Carmen didn't believe either one of them.

CHAPTER 21

As long as Liam had some time away from the truck, with Carmen's insistence he take more days, he went to visit his mom and maybe cook for her. One thing he'd noticed was that she rarely cooked for herself. She always made a full meal when any or all of the kids were there for dinner, but on days when she was alone, she thought it was a waste to cook.

Times like these made him glad Maggie was home, even if it was just for the week. Maggie provided Mom with company and someone to cook for.

Liam walked through the back door and heard the kettle whistle. He turned the knob on the stove and yelled, "Hey, Mom. It's Liam."

"No need to holler. I'm right here."

Without thought, he grabbed her teacup and readied her drink.

"Why aren't you at work?"

The hint of brogue in her voice let him know that she was in a bad mood. He had no idea what set her off, but she sounded ready for a fight. "Carmen is working the truck with her cousin. She wanted me to have time with you."

"I told you all. I'm not an invalid. I don't need constant watching."

"I know, Mom. But you scared us. We just want to make sure you're okay."

She sniffed and pursed her lips.

He handed her the cup and said, "It was really nice of you to get Carmen a present for Christmas. I appreciate it."

"It was your sister's idea."

He'd already figured Moira had a hand in that, but his mother needed to know it made him happy. Running the risk of the fight he wanted to avoid, he asked, "So what did you think of Carmen? She's really great, right?"

"She was fine."

He looked at his mother and wished he could get into her head for a few minutes. "I really care about her."

Another sniff.

"What's the problem?"

"Your father'd be rolling in his grave. He wanted you to marry a nice Irish girl." She sat at the table and sipped the tea.

Liam knew his father wouldn't have cared who he got involved with. And no one mentioned marriage at all. This was his mother planting her seeds of doubt and loyalty to her heritage. Rather than call her on it, he changed tactics. "Carmen is a nice girl, Mom. So what if she's not Irish."

"She's not American either."

He sighed. "She is American. She was born here. Her parents were immigrants, just like you and Dad."

She didn't respond. He began to question why he thought he'd be able to talk to her about Carmen, to get her to accept Carmen as part of his life.

~

THE REMAINDER of Liam's week flew by in a blur. Between checking in on his mom, who was growing more irritated by the day, and preparing for Carmen's New Year's Eve party, he had little time to plot revenge against the Heavenly Buns truck. With everything set for the party, he demanded to work the truck on New Year's Eve.

Carmen had been able to grab the spot on Monroe on Tuesday, but Heavenly Buns beat her to it on both Wednesday and Thursday. When Carmen had beaten them to the location, they rode by jeering at her. Not that Carmen had told him. All of his information came from Rosa, who was developing into quite the loyal employee.

Liam was determined to be there on Friday to see what would happen. He had Carmen wait to update the web site and social media until he was already on the road. If Heavenly Buns was trying to take his spot, he planned to make it as difficult as possible.

As if warning him to behave before he left the house wasn't enough, Carmen called him just as he and Rosa were setting up. He tossed the phone to Rosa. "Talk to your cousin and tell her we're fine."

Rosa's eyebrow lifted. "Like she's gonna believe me?"

Rosa answered his phone, and Liam stood outside the truck while the grill heated. He heard Rosa explaining that nothing had happened and that it was business as usual. Then the Heavenly Buns truck rolled up on them. It crept by, with the driver and passenger staring at Liam.

He smiled and waved. They returned the one-finger salute. Game on.

Carmen had tried to convince him it wasn't personal, but those two were making it personal.

Rosa laughed pretty hard and handed him the phone.

"Hey, Carmen."

"What happened? Rosa's laughing like crazy."

"Nothing much. The Buns truck isn't very happy. I want to test a theory."

"Liam…"

"What's the worst location your dad ever worked?"

"I don't know."

"Can you find out from some other trucks? There's got to be a spot that everyone avoids. Find out what it is and then let everyone know that's where we'll be this afternoon." Liam climbed back into the truck and took off his jacket.

"Why?"

"So I can drive by and wave at Heavenly Buns as I go to our real location. If it's not personal, they won't show there. If it is, they'll have a real problem."

"This isn't a good idea."

"I have to go now. People are starting to show."

"Liam."

He hung up, knowing she'd be a little pissed, but he didn't want to discuss it. That damn truck was fucking with them, and he didn't know why. But he'd put an end to it.

In the few moments he'd spent talking with Carmen, Rosa had the rest of the truck set up, including the menu board and she was currently chatting up customers. Liam hoped she wouldn't be like Pete—all talk and no work. But as Carmen had said, Rosa was good on the truck. She carried on conversations with customers while bagging orders. She didn't make mistakes on the order slips.

And in between customers, she wanted to help hatch a plan to get even with Heavenly Buns. He told her what he had Carmen working on. Rosa's response was that they should drive by and egg the truck.

A little juvenile, but Liam understood where she was coming from.

When they finished at the first site, Liam did a slow crawl down the deserted street that Carmen had said would be their second site. Sure enough, Heavenly Buns was already there. As he passed the truck, Liam honked and waved with a smile. He drove up to the Northside to the spot Carmen had tried earlier in the week.

He pulled in behind a cupcake truck and started the setup process all over. Rosa groused and grumbled about not doing something to Heavenly Buns.

"I promised Carmen we wouldn't do anything illegal. Sabotaging their truck would just cause problems for us. I need to find out why they're fucking with us." He glanced at the halfway-prepared truck. "Can you handle this? I want to talk to the cupcake people and see if they know anything."

Rosa nodded and continued setting up. Liam shrugged on his jacket and walked over to the cupcake truck. They had a small line of customers, so he stood off to the side and waited for one of the girls to acknowledge him.

"Hey, taco man, what's up?"

"I was wondering if you knew anything about Heavenly Buns."

The woman's partner turned her head and looked over her shoulder. "Mine are pretty fine, but I don't know about heavenly." She winked at him and handed another customer a cupcake.

"Trisha, stop it." The first woman leaned on the window and waved him closer. "What do you want to know?"

"I'm still new to this business, but that truck is screwing with us. At first, we thought it was coincidence that they would show up at the spot we'd advertised we'd be at, but I just confirmed that's not the case." He pointed at the truck. "I don't know if you knew Gus, but he died unexpectedly, so it's not like he told us if there was a history there."

"Yeah, we knew Gus. Good guy." She hung her head lower. "I don't like to trash other trucks because most of us are respectful and we get along, but those people are assholes. Since the end of the summer, when they came on the scene, they've been doing this. Every few weeks, they do to a truck exactly what they're doing to you."

"What do they get out of it?"

She shrugged. "I think they're trying to figure out the best locations. The thing is, if they just asked, any one of us would be willing to help." She pushed herself back through the window.

Liam nodded and said, "Thanks," before heading back to his truck. He shared the news with Rosa while they worked. Business was as slow as it had been earlier in the week, so they cut out early to detour and see if Heavenly Buns had remained in the same location. When Liam drove by, they were packing up. He honked the horn and waved, which earned him another round of fingers.

"Angry people," he said.

CARMEN HUNG up after talking to Liam and worried about what he and Rosa might do. With Liam's temper and Rosa's penchant for causing trouble, she just hoped that they'd bring the truck back in one piece. In the meantime, she decided to go on a goodwill mission to Eileen O'Leary's house.

Carmen couldn't do anything about the color of her skin or her heritage, but she could show Eileen that she was a good person who cared about Liam. That should be enough. And if not, well, at least she could say she tried.

She parked in front of the O'Leary house and took a few slow, deep breaths. Her heart raced with nerves. Going in alone felt much more daring than having Liam at her back. Sucking up her courage and shoving down her nerves, she stepped out of her car. The wind whipped her hair around her face.

Moving across the sidewalk, she tread carefully to avoid slipping on the ice. Rock salt littered the concrete porch. Someone had stopped by to make it safe for Eileen to walk. Carmen rang the bell and bounced on her toes to keep warm.

Maggie opened the door and Carmen tried to hide her surprise. "Hi."

"What are you doing here?" Maggie stepped back from the door. "Sorry. That sounded rude. I just didn't expect you."

"I know. I didn't realize you were here. Liam's on the truck today, so I wanted to stop by and check on your mom."

"Maggie, who's at the door?"

"It's Carmen," she called over her shoulder.

Carmen said, "As long as you're here..."

Maggie pulled her farther into the living room. "You're here now. You might as well stay."

Carmen shrugged off her coat, and Maggie tucked it into the hall closet. Carmen walked into the living room and saw Eileen sitting in front of the TV watching soap operas. "Hi, Mrs.—Eileen. I didn't know Maggie was here and I thought that since Liam is working today, I'd stop by and maybe cook you some lunch."

"Lunch sounds great. Right, Mom?" Maggie was a little too enthusiastic.

"I don't like spicy food."

Carmen clenched her jaw and nodded. She followed Maggie into the kitchen.

"What she really means is make it tasteless and over-cooked," Maggie said when they were in the other room.

Carmen couldn't stop the smile. "Are you still coming to the party tonight?"

"Yeah. Is it okay if I bring a friend?"

"Sure." Then she thought about all the couples on Christmas. "Boyfriend?"

"No. My friend Shane. We try to hang out as much as possible when I'm in town." A slow smile lifted Maggie's lips. "When I lived here, I spent all my free time with him. Besides my family, he's all I really miss when I'm in Ireland."

"You live in Ireland?" Liam had never told her. Carmen rummaged through the refrigerator to figure out what to make for lunch.

"Well, kind of. I wanted to travel, and while I bounced around a lot for a year, I kind of settled with my cousins in Ireland." She leaned against the counter as Carmen started setting food out. Maggie's voice dropped. "But now, with my mom…I think I'm ready to come home."

"Wow. I bet your family's happy."

"Don't say anything. I haven't told anyone. I'm flying out tomorrow, but after I get my stuff together, I think I'll come home."

Some of the stress Eileen caused eased out of Carmen's body. Maggie was sharing secrets with her. It was nice to know that the dislike stopped with Mama O'Leary. Carmen surveyed her options for lunch and decided on a salad topped with chicken. Simple yet tasty. And heart healthy. "Anything I should know about what your mom likes or doesn't?"

"Make whatever you want. She'll eat it."

Maggie hopped onto the counter and swung her legs out while Carmen prepared the chicken. Adding only scant seasoning, she let the meat cook while she chopped lettuce and vegetables. "Traveling the world sounds interesting. Tell me about where you've been."

Maggie told her about different countries in Europe, and Carmen began to think about her own canceled plans again.

Maggie was only a few years younger than her. Why did she feel so old listening to her travel stories?

When she pulled the chicken from the oven, Carmen checked to make sure it was done, but she'd eaten plenty of plain chicken in recent years to know it was ready. She looked at the sad piece of meat and suddenly couldn't recall why she'd eaten so much of it. For over a month now, she'd been eating with Liam and not a plain chicken breast had been in sight.

And she didn't feel fat. At least no more than usual, and even that feeling fled the moment Liam looked at her. She cut up the chicken and placed it on a separate plate in case Eileen didn't want it on the salad. She looked at Maggie, who had paused in her storytelling. "Lunch is served."

"I missed this, too," Maggie said. "Meals with family. It's not like I don't eat with my aunt and cousins, but it's not the same, you know?"

Carmen understood exactly. She nodded and brought the salad and chicken to the dining room table. "Eileen, lunch is ready."

Eileen took her spot at the head of the table like she had on Christmas. Maggie dug into the food, but Carmen lost her appetite.

"It's good, right, Mom? Thanks for cooking for us, Carmen."

Eileen nodded. "It'll do."

Carmen figured that was as close to a compliment as she would receive from Eileen O'Leary.

When Liam arrived back at Carmen's house, she was running around, stressing about everything. He decided to wait to tell her about Heavenly Buns. She didn't need anything more to worry about.

"Babe, the house is fine. People are coming to drink and have a good time. They're not going to inspect anything." He stood in the kitchen and began cooking. It felt like it had been forever since he cooked, really cooked. Sure, he'd done Christmas dinner, but that was a no-brainer. He didn't have to plan a menu or think about recipes or pairings of items. Regardless of how simple Carmen said she wanted her party to be, he had a ton of fun playing in the kitchen.

The idea struck him while he cooked that maybe they should consider doing some catering. They would probably need additional licensing, but expanding the business would give them a buffer, especially in the off season. If they had parties and meetings to cater, the irritation of Heavenly Buns wouldn't have such an effect on them.

She strode into the kitchen with a bottle of glass cleaner

and a roll of paper towels. "Tell me again why I thought a party would be a good idea?"

Liam pulled her into a hug, massaging her shoulders as he did so. "You never really gave me a reason, but I was under the impression you wanted to do something fun with your family."

"Fun. Right."

He grabbed the cleaner from her and tossed it on the counter. "Go change, get ready for your party. No one cares how clean the house is. By the time the night is done, it'll be a mess all over again, and no one will notice because they'll all be drunk."

She sniffed the air. "I thought I told you to keep it simple. Chips and dip. Maybe some sandwiches."

He smiled again. "This isn't complicated, but it's different. I had fun." He pushed her from the room and hoped she'd calm down.

An hour later, guests started to arrive, Rosa being the first. Gone was her usual bun coiled tightly on the top of her head. Her hair hung down in long, loose waves. The dress she wore clung like a second skin. "Wow. You clean up good," he said.

"Not so bad yourself." She walked into the kitchen and scanned the area. "Need help?"

"No, I think I've got it covered." He hitched his chin toward the other room. "Go calm your cousin down. She's a ball of stress."

Rosa opened the fridge and bent over, causing her dress to ride up to illegal territory. He looked away, but as he turned, he came face-to-face with Carmen. "Hey, babe. You look beautiful."

He kissed her cheek. She looked gorgeous in her low-cut tank top and skirt that swirled around her knees. He imagined shoving the skirt up and bending her over the couch in his apartment.

Rosa stood from her spot, handed him a bottle of beer, and then reached out to give Carmen one too. To Carmen she said, "You need this. It's a party. Let loose."

Then Rosa strode out of the kitchen, hips swaying, looking like she wanted to find some trouble.

"I thought you said most of the guests were going to be your family."

"They are."

"Then why..." He gestured after Rosa with his unopened bottle.

"That's Rosa. She looks for men everywhere. My cousins will probably bring friends, so her chances of hooking up with someone increase." Carmen set her beer on the table and looked at him.

"Something wrong?"

"No."

He didn't believe her, but chalked it up to her being stressed. As the house filled, Liam struggled to remember the names of everyone Carmen introduced him to. The night progressed and she seemed to lighten up and have fun with her family.

CARMEN SERVED food and drinks and already consumed more alcohol than she should. Especially considering she'd only sampled one of the little meatballs Liam had made. She kept thinking she'd stop and make herself a plate of food, but people kept distracting her. A nagging voice in the back of her head reminded her that she didn't need to watch Rosa as much as she had been.

Jealousy had spiked when she'd seen Rosa in the kitchen

with her microskirt hiked up while getting a beer from the fridge. Carmen knew better. Rosa was her cousin and she would never make a move on Carmen's boyfriend. But Liam had looked. How could he not?

From across the room, she watched as Rosa recounted her day on the truck with Liam, a story she'd already told a dozen times, but which neither of them had bothered to tell Carmen. Irritation had her grabbing yet another beer. Liam joined in with some hand gestures, which kept the listeners laughing.

This was not how her night was supposed to go. She and Liam were a team, not Rosa and Liam. She sounded petty, even in her own head, but she didn't care. She popped the top on her beer. Carmen loved Rosa; they were best friends. So she *knew*, without any doubt that Rosa would knock Liam on his ass if he ever made a move on her, but Carmen still couldn't stop the prick of envy.

Rosa was everything Carmen had always wanted to be: confident, sexual, assertive. Carmen leaned over the kitchen table, reached for a chip, and bathed it in gloppy cheese dip. She inhaled it, followed by a handful more. Even as the warm, gooey mess slid down her throat, she knew she'd regret it later, but in the moment, she didn't care.

She moved on to the meatballs, stabbing one after another with a toothpick before popping them in her mouth.

Someone came into the kitchen beside her and said, "Ooo…Liam cooked."

Carmen shifted to see Maggie standing there, a huge guy right behind her. Around the mound of meat in her mouth, Carmen said, "Hi."

Maggie smiled. "I'm the same way around Liam's food. I can't help myself." To illustrate, she poked a meatball with a toothpick and ate it in one bite. The man behind her settled a hand on her shoulder. "Oh. Carmen, this is my friend, Shane, who I told you about earlier."

"Nice to meet you. Have you seen Liam? He's in the living room."

Maggie waved. "Yeah, he said hi and directed me to the food." She grabbed a plate, handed it to Shane, and then took another for herself.

A plate, Carmen. Might've been a good idea so you don't look like a total pig. But now the thought of more food had what she'd already eaten taking a spin cycle in her stomach. Someone in the living room turned the music up louder. Maggie's eyes widened at the sound. Carmen leaned over, the alcohol making her feel a little wobbly, and looked at the scene in the other room.

Her family had moved furniture and created a spot in the room to dance. Of course, right in the middle was Rosa, hands in the air, shaking her hips. What she hadn't expected, however, was Liam dancing right behind her. Carmen stepped forward to get a better look.

"Oh, jeez. Nothing worse than a guy with no rhythm trying to dance with a girl who does. I'm so embarrassed," Maggie said. "He's very typical white guy out there."

Maggie's assessment was correct; Liam couldn't dance. It should've been funny, but Carmen just got mad. She crossed the room and strode straight up to Liam. Her hand fisted in the front of his shirt, and she pulled him away from Rosa. His hands naturally landed on her hips.

He lowered his head and said, "Thank you for rescuing me."

She might not be as sexy or confident as Rosa, but Carmen knew how to dance, so she did. She wrapped one arm around Liam's neck and started a bump and grind that he likely wouldn't forget. He barely moved. He kept his hands lightly at her waist and allowed her to move all over him.

She had no idea if anyone else watched or if they were all too busy dancing, and she didn't care. This was about letting Liam know that he was hers. The song ended and she felt parched.

Liam lowered his head again and planted a searing kiss on her lips. If anyone had a doubt they were together, it would've been squashed.

"That was really fucking hot. What are the chances we can get everyone to leave?"

She smiled. "It's not even midnight."

"I'm not sure I can wait that long."

Voices raised in another corner of the living room. Carmen couldn't see past the wall of a guy who stood there, though. Then she realized it was Shane. Liam released her and went to see what the problem was. Carmen followed.

"She said she doesn't want a drink. Leave her alone," Shane said.

"Hey, man, I was just trying to get to know her, that's all."

Christ. She'd know Pete's voice anywhere. Carmen pushed past Liam and skirted around Shane. "What did you do now, Pete?"

Pete raised his arms. "Nothing. I offered her a drink, and this guy gets all in my face about it."

"You had a hard time taking no for an answer."

Maggie's eyes darted between the two men. "It's fine. No problem." She tugged on Shane's arm and led him back to the kitchen.

Before Carmen could say anything to Pete, he was already gone, skating through the crowd of cousins in the room.

"What was that all about?" she asked Liam.

He shrugged, but said, "Shane's protective."

"Why? It was just a drink, not an offer to hit an hourly

hotel. Besides, Maggie introduced him as her friend, not boyfriend."

"Maggie doesn't drink."

"At all? Your family owns a bar."

Liam took her arm and pulled her toward a quiet corner. "A few years ago, Maggie was raped by her ex-boyfriend. She was drinking and he drugged her. So she doesn't drink."

"Oh, God. I had no idea."

"Don't worry about it. She's okay. Or at least getting there."

Carmen let Liam lead her back into the crowd in the living room. The beat of the music had her dancing without thought. Liam didn't move much, but he stayed close and she liked that. The night wore on and she drank more than she probably ever had, but she was having a great time.

Midnight struck and as the noise in her house rose and shots and fireworks went off outside, Liam pushed her up against the wall and kissed her. It was the kind of kiss a girl could never forget, one that changed her life and how she viewed herself. In that instant, Carmen knew, even with her alcohol-fueled brain, that she was completely and totally in love with Liam O'Leary.

BY ONE O'CLOCK, people started to leave and Carmen looked beat. As much as he wanted to take her to bed—and he'd wanted to do that for hours—she needed to crash. She was smiling and happy, but could barely stand up straight. He took her to her bedroom and stripped her. He knew she really had to have been drunk because she didn't protest for a second. Then he tucked her into bed.

"I can't go to bed. I have guests," she slurred.

"Your family had a great time. They're all heading home now. You threw a great party."

"But the mess…"

"I've got it covered. Get some rest."

She ran a hand over his chest and tugged at his shirt. "But I want you to come to bed."

"I'll be here soon." He kissed her forehead and went back to the living room.

Rosa was kissing people good-bye and ushering them out the door. He stood behind her. "Are they all right to drive?"

"They're good. Marco is driving the rest."

He nodded and turned to go to the kitchen to start the cleanup. Surprisingly, Rosa followed, carrying plates and cups to throw in the trash.

"You don't have to stay." He'd watched her drink a lot over the course of the night, and although she held her liquor better than Carmen, she had to be pretty drunk.

"I'm not leaving this mess for Carmen."

"I've got it."

"And I'll help."

If she wanted to clean, he wouldn't turn her away; the house was pretty trashed. They worked in silence for a while, but Liam had a feeling that Rosa was building up to something. He stood at the sink and began washing dishes.

Rosa set a stack of glasses next to him and finally said, "You're not good for her, you know."

"What?"

"You're not good for Carmen."

His hackles rose and he reminded himself that they'd both been drinking. "What makes you think you get to decide what's good for her? You know nothing about us."

Rosa shook her head. "I like you. I know Gus always liked you. But Carmen…she's head over heels, but it's not right." She huffed out a breath. "It's not you, so before you start thinking I'm a racist or shit, that's not it. I see that you make her happy, but this is supposed to be her time. Finally."

Liam dropped the sponge into the water and dried his hands. Rosa was serious. This wasn't some silly conversation about how he'd better not hurt her cousin. "What do you mean? If I make her happy, how can that be bad?"

Rosa ran her fingers through her hair and then scooped it up into a ponytail, tying it with a band from her wrist. "Look around. She has like five projects she started on the house that are left unfinished."

"That's because I needed help on the truck. It's temporary."

"No, it's not. Not for her. She put her entire life on hold when she came home to take care of her mom. When her mom died, she stayed and took care of her dad. She's never had her own life. This was supposed to be it, but now she's taking care of you."

"She's not—"

"She is and you know it. She never wanted to work on the truck. She did it because of you." Rosa shot him a look and crossed her arms. "Did you know she was supposed to go on a vacation? She planned to get away and have fun. Her first vacation ever."

His jaw dropped a little. He hadn't known. Why wouldn't Carmen have told him?

"Yeah, I didn't think so. She canceled her plans because you needed her. I get that your mom was in the hospital, but it shouldn't have been Carmen's problem."

Her words stung, but she was right. He had leaned on Carmen, but wasn't that what you did when you were in love? "She didn't tell me about her vacation or I would've told her to go. I love having her here, but I don't *need* her. I want her to have her own life."

The words in Gus's letter came back to him. Gus had

asked him to help Carmen find her freedom, to take care of her. Rosa was right. Carmen had been doing it for him.

Well, that would end right now. He sagged against the counter. "So, how would you like to work on the truck permanently?"

A smile spread on Rosa's face. "Yeah. But we need to figure out what we're gonna do about Heavenly Buns."

CARMEN ROLLED over and wished she could remove her head. The thumping beat a rhythm on her brain. She stretched her leg carefully behind her so she wouldn't have to roll over, and found the space empty. She slit her eyes open and saw sunlight, so she closed her lids again.

Liam wasn't in bed with her, but he never got up early, which meant it must be late morning. She tried to think of a reason for getting out of bed and came up empty. It was Saturday, so she didn't need to work. Of course there was always something that needed to be done, but nothing that couldn't wait.

Except her house was a mess. She knew her family well enough to know that they would've left a ton of crap everywhere as if she had a maid who would come through and clean. Knowing Liam, he was probably cleaning right now. It definitely wasn't his responsibility. It had been her idea for the party with her family and friends.

She gingerly pushed herself off the pillow and groaned. The thumping in her head picked up pace. She eased her eyelids open and glanced at the nightstand to see the time. A glass of water and aspirin with a note sat near her clock. She picked up the note and brought it close to her face.

Hey, Sweetheart—Had to take Maggie to the airport. Take the aspirin. You'll need it. Coffee's ready in the kitchen. Talk to you later. Love, Liam

She swallowed the pills and decided additional sleep was more important than coffee. Hopefully, by the time she woke again, the headache would be gone. As she settled back against her pillow, she tried to remember her night. Man, she'd drunk a lot.

Then she remembered her stupid jealousy being the reason for the extra drinks. She wondered if she'd done anything to make an idiot of herself. She scanned her memory, but came up empty. She danced with Liam. More like she danced at him, but he'd shown no signs of being embarrassed by her.

She lay there, willing sleep to come, but realized than once her brain was engaged, she couldn't fall back asleep. Gently sitting up again, she pushed herself to move. She took a long, hot shower and dressed.

By the time she walked into her living room, she felt a little better. What she found in the living room threw another shock into her. The entire room was clean. She checked the time again. It was only eleven. How the heck had Liam had time to clean everything?

The kitchen was spotless as well, clean dishes stacked neatly beside the sink. Rosa sat at the table sipping from a cup of coffee. One surprise after another. She was wearing some of Carmen's clothes.

"Did you clean everything?"

Rosa grunted, and then shook her head. "Me and Liam did it last night before crashing."

Her words poked at Carmen. She didn't like hearing it, but her reaction to the words bothered her more. "You didn't have to do that. I would've gotten it done today."

"We wanted to. You're always taking care of everyone."

Carmen poured a cup of coffee and sat.

"Liam hired me to work the truck with him permanently."

"What?" Carmen tried to keep her voice and her emotions calm.

"We were talking last night while we cleaned up. I know you thought Pete would work with him, but come on, it's Pete."

"I thought you hated working in food service."

Rosa set her cup down. "No, I hate working at the restaurant for my dad. Working on the truck this week was kind of fun. Besides, if I'm working, you can focus on getting a job you really want."

Anger poured through Carmen, but she wasn't sure why. Working on the truck with Liam was supposed to be temporary, until they could figure out something else. But they were partners. They were supposed to discuss things like this.

"Something wrong?" Rosa asked.

Carmen forced a smile. She couldn't be mad at Rosa. This was something she needed to take up with Liam. "Nope."

They finished their coffee before Rosa stood and stretched. "You might want to consider getting a new couch. That one is horrible to sleep on."

Rosa left the room, but then called over her shoulder, "What are your plans for today?"

"I don't know. I have some bookwork to do for the truck. Maybe I'll get some more painting done."

"You should have plenty of time to finish up your projects here since you won't need to deal with the truck."

Carmen nodded, not that Rosa was watching. Rosa came back through the kitchen holding a pile of clothes. She tugged at the shirt she wore. "I'll return this after I wash it. Thanks for the loan. Give me a call if you want to get together later."

"Sure."

Carmen walked through her house trying to decide what project she should do, but found she couldn't focus on anything. She put away the dishes from the party and then took a nap. Liam didn't call, but she'd hoped he'd be back so she could confront him. Even as she rested, she geared up for a fight.

She and Liam hadn't fought about much, but for some reason, she felt like this was something she couldn't ignore. Not if they were going to be partners.

CHAPTER 23

When she opened her eyes again, she had no idea what time it was or how long she'd slept. She heard noise in the other room, so she knew Liam had returned. She got out of bed. From her door, she heard him laughing. Not his usual quiet chuckle, but an outright laugh.

It startled her enough that it caused a hitch in her step. *Who made him laugh like that?* She turned the corner and he smiled at her.

"Yeah, sounds good. I'll see you there tomorrow then." He clicked his phone off. "Feeling better?"

"Fine. Who was that?"

"Rosa. We were making plans for Heavenly Buns."

Rosa had made him laugh? She grit her teeth for a moment to stomp on the jealousy creeping up. "Speaking of Rosa. How could you just decide to hire her permanently without talking to me?"

His eyebrows came together and that deep ridge formed between them. "Why would I need to talk to you? You brought her on and you said yourself that she was doing a great job."

"We're partners. We're supposed to make decisions together."

"You hired Pete without talking to me. And you brought in Rosa without any mention."

She waved her hand at him. "That was different. With Pete, I was trying to help you. He knows how to run the truck, and you had never done it before. I asked Rosa to help me *temporarily* because you needed time to be with your family. I didn't want us to lose out on having the truck on the street."

"I'm sorry I didn't run it by you. I never thought it would be an issue. She's your cousin and she's doing a really good job." He stood and came close to her.

She stepped back because if he touched her, she wouldn't be able to stay mad.

"You prepared me for running the truck. We talked about hiring someone once I got the hang of it."

"You still should've talked to me about it. And now you're making plans for Heavenly Buns?" That too should've been a conversation between them. Not with Rosa.

"Being partners doesn't mean I have to run every move past you."

"Oh, really?"

"Yeah, really. Kind of like you didn't tell me you had a vacation planned."

"I didn't tell you because I canceled it."

"But you shouldn't have canceled on my account. And if I had known, that's exactly what I would've told you."

"I canceled because you needed me here. I couldn't run off to the beach and leave you with your family emergency and no one to run the truck." She was borderline yelling at this point, but Liam remained calm. At least he appeared calm.

"I don't expect you to give up everything in your life for me. That's no way to have a relationship."

His words made sense, but didn't do anything to abate her anger. "I haven't given up my life for you."

"Oh, no? Look around. You had plans for this house you haven't completed. When was the last time you even looked at the want ads or filled out an application?"

She had no answer. She hadn't even thought about another job for weeks.

He took another step. "This isn't the life you wanted, and I was too selfish to see that. I have the truck handled. Go get the life you want."

What was he saying? That he didn't need her? Didn't want her? "I don't need you to tell me what I want in life, Liam. You barely know me." He opened his mouth, but she put up her hand to stop him. "I think it's time for you to leave."

"Carmen."

"I want to be alone. I have a life I need to figure out." She turned and went back to her bedroom. It wasn't until she heard the *click* of the front door that she felt like her life came crashing down on her.

LIAM HAD no idea what the fuck had just happened. He'd thought Carmen would be thrilled to have her time back and not have to work on the truck. Although they'd had a lot of fun working together, she was supposed to find her real career, something away from her family and the life she was forced into.

Why couldn't she see that?

Her reaction hit him hard. Something about it felt like it was more than a simple fight over him hiring Rosa. Telling him to leave felt like she was breaking up with him, getting him out of her house and her life. While he drove away, he tried to convince himself he was reading too much into it.

Carmen was upset, and while he was pretty sure that it was about more than him hiring Rosa, he knew she would calm down and then they could have a rational discussion.

By the time he got to his house, he realized he had nothing to do. He couldn't remember the last time he had a Saturday night off, and a holiday to boot. He'd spent all of his time with Carmen for the last month and prior to that, Jonathan had him working every weekend. Liam sat in his living room, unsure what to do with himself. He looked at the photo frame Carmen had given him for Christmas.

How could she accuse him of not knowing her? Her accusations drew up his anger. He didn't need this shit. He grabbed his phone and called Jimmy.

"Hey, Jimmy. You want to go out?"

"I don't know. Let me check with Moira."

"I'm not looking to go out with my sister."

"Okay. Sure. Where do you want to meet?"

They made plans to meet at O'Leary's because it would be halfway between their houses. Liam arrived first and sat at the bar to wait for Jimmy. Jenna was bartending.

"Hi, Liam. How are you?"

"Good. You?"

She nodded. Although he hadn't worked at the bar much over the years, he knew the staff who had been there a long time. Like the rest of the family, he always worked on Saint Patrick's Day. It was a family tradition. He'd have to figure out what to do about the truck that day. His family didn't ask much of him, so he didn't want to back out of the tradition.

He ordered a Guinness. When Jenna delivered it, she said, "Neither of your brothers are here tonight."

"I'm meeting a friend." He looked around the bar. Kind of

a slow night, but not too surprising since it was New Year's Day. Most people were probably still trying to get over their hangovers from last night.

A thump on his shoulder told him Jimmy had arrived. He took the stool beside Liam. "I'll have you know Moira is pissed that she was expressly not invited to join us."

Liam grinned. "Just like old times." He waved Jenna over to get Jimmy's order.

"And just like when we were teenagers, she was about ready to stomp her foot and try coming anyway."

"I knew you dating my sister was going to be a problem."

"Afraid she's stealing me from you?"

"Shut up."

Jenna delivered a beer for Jimmy and then he asked, "What's the occasion?"

"I have a Saturday night off."

"And? Why aren't you with Carmen?"

Leave it to Jimmy to jump right at the problem. "She told me to leave."

"That's not good. Never good when a fight ends with being told to get out." He drank from his beer and waited for details.

"Fuck. I don't even know what the hell the fight was about."

Jimmy chuckled. "Not surprising. You'll probably never understand. Just go apologize."

"I'm not going to apologize when I didn't do anything wrong."

"You'll regret that. Your bed will get mighty cold. Trust me on this." Another sip of beer. "What'd you do?"

"I hired her cousin Rosa to work on the truck with me."

Jimmy frowned. "And?"

"That's it. She got mad because I didn't run it by her first, but she brought Rosa in to work while I was dealing with everything with Mom. Rosa is a good employee. Hiring her means that Carmen doesn't have to work the truck."

"Hmmm."

"Not helpful."

"I've found that with women, rarely is the problem with the thing they say it is. There's always some underlying factor. The one time Moira told me to leave, I thought she was mad because I was bugging her about getting information on the story she was doing. After I left, I realized I hadn't respected her job. I had to suck it up and apologize."

Liam stared into his beer. What could Carmen's underlying reason be for being mad? "I have no idea what it might be. Things have been great between us."

"Trust me. You did something. Just accept it's always your fault." Jimmy slapped Liam's shoulder again.

That kind of logic would never work for Liam. He took responsibility for things he did. He refused to proffer fake apologies in an effort to create a phony sense of peace. No, he'd wait until Carmen was calm and then she'd tell him what was wrong. Plain and simple.

FOR THE REST of the night and through all of Sunday, Carmen worked on finishing all the painting jobs she'd started in the house. Her anger toward Liam hadn't dissipated. Part of her knew it wasn't right, but she couldn't help but feel mad.

She'd spent most of her life being told what to do, either explicitly or through implied expectations. Now that she no longer had her parents running her life, Liam seemed to want to step up and take over. How could he possibly know what she wanted?

She wasn't even sure.

But she'd been happy working on the truck. With him. That had been the key. She enjoyed the few days with Rosa, but working with Liam had made her happy.

And now he decided he didn't need her help to run the truck. He knew what he was doing, and he had Rosa to help.

That same prick of jealousy hit her.

She didn't like this side of herself and she needed to get over it. She wasn't some sixteen-year-old upset over a crush. She loved Liam and she knew he wasn't interested in Rosa. What did it say about her then that she kept having these flashes of jealousy?

All of Liam's words echoed in her head while she worked. He'd been right about plenty. She had all of these projects she'd started and left unfinished. She hadn't thought about starting a new career. She'd been avoiding all of it and claiming she was too busy with the truck.

That was why it was important for her to finish the painting. To prove to herself that she could. It also allowed for a whole lot of time to think.

Her next focus would be on doing what she'd told Liam she was going to do—figure out her life.

And it was something she had to do on her own. Because part of her avoidance of everything was because she was afraid of being alone. From the moment her relationship with Liam started, she'd been reminding herself that he would leave, that she only had a year with him.

Instead, she enjoyed the great month they had, and she'd leave first. She needed to be on her own without distractions to know what would be right for her life.

~

LIAM SPENT all of Sunday planning and scheming with Moira

to get publicity for the truck while trying to irritate Heavenly Buns. He and Rosa decided that a competition was in order. What better way to drum up business during the nasty cold winter months than to force Heavenly Buns to compete with them? If they thought they were good enough to steal business from the Taco Taxi, they should do it honestly.

Moira convinced him that a little fun shaming and goading on social media would be enough to draw them out, so she began the campaign. Liam remembered how much Carmen's trash talk during their friendly competition drew customers in, so he had little doubt Moira's plan would work.

Unless the Heavenly Buns people were total assholes.

In the meantime, he planned to meet Rosa at the restaurant early to talk about adding the new menu items he'd mentioned to Carmen. Although they had originally discussed waiting until spring, offering good walking food during the competition made sense. It would also act as a bit of market research to help them decide if they would continue.

He glanced at the clock. She was late, but he tried not to get irritated. He had corn cooking on the stove so they could make elotes. Churros would be next week's experiment.

While he waited for Rosa and the corn, he drank his coffee and thought about Carmen. She still hadn't called. He'd known his sisters to hold on to their anger for days. He'd hoped Carmen wasn't like that and given her usual sunny disposition, he'd thought she'd be done by now. After work, he would go to her house and make dinner for them. If she wouldn't come to him to talk, he'd go to her. But they *would* talk.

Rosa burst through the back door, slamming the metal against the wall. "What the hell did you do to my cousin?"

Her sharp tone was much too loud for the morning. Carmen had obviously told her about the argument. "I didn't do anything. She got mad because I hired you without talking to her first."

"You must've done something else because she asked me to come by this morning. She handed me her laptop and said you'd know how to handle the business stuff until she got back." As she spoke, one hand waved wildly through the air and the other cradled Carmen's laptop.

He'd been so busy watching her body language that it took a moment for her words to hit home. "Back? Back from where?"

She set the laptop on the counter. "She said she's starting in Mexico, but she's not sure where after that."

Liam took a slow breath. "So she's going on her vacation." Without telling him.

"If it was only vacation, would she be getting rid of her computer and the work that goes along with it? Isn't that something that could just wait until she got back?"

"She probably wanted to make sure we had the information we needed. That's all."

Rosa stomped closer to him. "You don't get it. She's leaving. She's not saying when or if she's coming back." She punctuated each word slowly. "What did you do to her?"

"Nothing. I did exactly what you told me to do. I told her to go get the life she really wanted."

A slow, steady panic seeped into him. After yelling at him over making a decision without her input when it was simple business, what did it say that she would make a personal decision without even mentioning it to him?

"You're overreacting." She wouldn't really leave and not come back. Would she?

"Shit. I don't even know the meaning of that. I react the way I need to. And you need to fix this."

He pulled out his phone and pointed at the corn. "Pull that off the stove. We're going to experiment with elotes today." The phone rang in his ear. After four rings, Carmen's voice mail picked up. He moved away from Rosa. "Carmen, it's Liam. Rosa's here and she's really upset. She thinks you're taking off and not coming back." He sighed. "I'm sorry we fought. Please call me."

He disconnected and turned back to Rosa. "She didn't answer. Did she say when she was leaving?"

Rosa shook her head. "She was in the process of packing, though."

He was torn. Part of him wanted to take off and go to her house and talk some sense into her in case Rosa was right. Mostly he wanted to kiss her and hold her and tell her to have a great vacation. But he needed to prep the truck and get out on the street.

"So what are you gonna do?"

"We're going to work, and I'll talk to Carmen when we're done. She wouldn't just leave." Not without saying good-bye. Not without making sure they were okay after their fight. Not without telling him she loved him.

Rosa shot him a disbelieving look, but didn't comment.

He focused on the task at hand. While they sampled different mixtures of cheese, mayo, butter, and chili powder, Liam filled Rosa in on his plans with Moira.

"We'll set it up as a dare. Ask them to go face-to-face with us."

"Like the food truck TV show. Whoever makes the most money wins. I love it."

"You watch cooking shows?" Why that was the first thing that came to mind, he didn't know.

Rosa shook her head again. "Nope. My dad does. All the time with the Cooking Channel or Food Network. He thinks he's going to discover the next big thing to expand into."

"He owns this place, right? Why does he want to expand?"

"He's like Uncle Gus. It's all about the American Dream, you know? They grew up with nothing and want to make sure they do as much as they can."

Her news made Liam revisit the idea of catering. If it was a joint venture, it might make it less risky for both of them. While he tasted another ear of corn, he made mental note to do some more research about catering and what it would take. When he saw Carmen, he'd ask her what she thought. She might know the business end, and she would definitely know whether it would be a good idea to approach her uncle.

Half-eaten ears of corn lay scattered on the table. He and Rosa couldn't agree on how best to prepare the elotes. Every time he slathered on the ingredients, she wanted to dump more chili powder on it.

"You're killing the taste of everything with that. It's just supposed to give a hint of spice, a little kick. You should still be able to taste the other flavors."

She ran her tongue along the corn. "I taste it all just fine."

"How about we make it my way, and if someone asks for extra chili powder, we add more? Doesn't that make more sense than overdoing it and having people complain? It's easier to add more than make a whole new ear." He began to gather the ingredients they'd need to make it on the truck.

Rosa disappeared into the storage closet. "Here," she said, shoving some Styrofoam bowls at him. "We can cut it off the cob and serve it in a bowl. It'll make it easier for people to eat."

"We have the ones we use for rice and beans."

"These are bigger, so they'll be easier to mix the stuff in."

"We can't steal bowls and lids from the restaurant."

"It's my dad's restaurant. We'll pay him back. It's not like he doesn't know where to find us. Besides, it's just a few bowls. He won't even notice them missing. If it works, we'll order our own."

She made another excellent point. He hadn't thought about serving in bowls, but it would make it easier for customers to transport the elotes. Once again, Rosa was proving she was an excellent choice as an employee.

CHAPTER 24

*A*s Carmen finished packing, she felt better about her decision to go. Liam had been right. While she hadn't given up her life for him, she had put everything on hold. For the first time, she had the freedom to do whatever she wanted. Before zipping her last bag, she tucked in the letter from her dad, the one she'd ignored for too long.

She checked the time. Liam and Rosa would be done on the truck by now. She'd expected the call from Liam this morning after Rosa came by. She ignored the phone to at least have the day to think about it. The problem was, she still didn't know what to say. Her packed bags sat by the door, ready for her flight in the morning. She'd cleaned out her refrigerator and put her mail on hold. She was ready.

When Liam pulled up, she'd been watching for him. She met him at the door. He already had his key out, but she had the door open enough to fit her body in the space. She wanted to get this over as quickly as possible.

"Hey," he said with a smile.

"Hi. I'm sure Rosa told you I'm leaving." Her grip on the doorknob tightened.

"Yeah. Can I come in? It's fucking cold out here."

"I'd prefer if you didn't."

The smile slipped from his face. "Why?"

Her throat tightened and she swallowed hard. "Because if I let you in, I won't be able to do this. You'll talk me out of it." She sucked in a halting breath. "You were right. I need to figure out my life. So I'm going."

"Is this because of our fight?"

"No. Yes. You made me think about a lot of things."

"Can't you think here?"

"That hasn't worked out well so far. I'm hoping distance might give me clarity."

"What about us?"

That was the question she feared most. She didn't have an answer for him. "I don't know," she mumbled.

His hands shook and she didn't know if it was the cold or his emotions. "Can I please come in? I'm freezing my balls off."

"You should go."

Instead of backing down the steps, he came forward and touched his cold hand to her cheek. "I love you, Carmen. I'll be here." Then he brushed a featherlight kiss to her lips before turning away.

She didn't watch him get in his car. She closed the door and let the tears drip from her eyes. Telling him to go was one of the hardest things she'd had to do. She wanted to cling to him and ask him to stay, but that wouldn't change her life. She'd continue to be guilty of exactly what he'd said.

The self-doubt gnawed at her. If this was the best thing to do, why did it hurt?

For the next two days, Carmen lay in her hotel room in

Puebla, where her dad was from, crying her eyes out. She'd boarded her plane and flown across the country and into another before the pain truly hit. She had left everything behind. Part of her felt like she was running away, but she didn't know why. It had simply felt like something she had to do. Now she was back to questioning her sanity.

With puffy eyes, she strained to see the time on the clock. By now, Liam and Rosa would be on the road, maybe even at their first stop. She thought of Liam with his sleeves rolled to his elbows even though it would be freezing outside. She climbed out of bed and pulled aside the drapes covering the windows.

Bright sun glared and stung her eyes. She blinked a few times. It was a gorgeous day. The whole point of her leaving Chicago was to figure out her life and what she wanted, but she was supposed to start with a vacation. Hiding in a hotel room crying about her boyfriend was not a vacation.

She'd never needed a guy in her life to be happy before. She didn't need one now. After taking a shower, she decided to hit the streets. There was no way for her to know what she wanted or needed unless she looked for it. Instead of going to the hotel restaurant for lunch, which would've been an adventure in itself after two days of minimal room service, Carmen got directions to a local family-run place.

Puebla was a big city, but she knew the food would be fabulous. This was where her father had gotten his start, where he'd developed his recipes.

Before leaving the hotel, she committed to not worrying about how much or what she ate. If Liam had taught her nothing else in their time together, it was that she could enjoy food without becoming obese. Her new sandals bit into the side of her foot as she stepped onto the street, but she smiled because Liam had taught her so much more than food appreciation. Thinking of those other things warmed her blood and sent naughty tingles through her body.

Her dress swished around her calves and sun warmed her bare shoulders. For the first time in her life, she felt like a woman. Not an overweight, unwanted girl, not a daughter devoted to taking care of her ailing parents, but a free woman ready to experience life.

Someone whistled and she spun toward the sound. A young cabbie leaned against his vehicle and smiled at her. *At her.* Although she knew she should've been offended, a big part of her blushed and enjoyed the leering as a compliment. She didn't encourage him with a smile or a wink, but tucked the feeling away.

When she got to the small taqueria, her stomach grumbled so loudly that she placed a hand over it as if the movement would ease her hunger. She hadn't realized how hungry she was. She sat at a small table for two and picked up a menu. Spicy smells filled the air, making her mouth water. Behind the counter, workers spoke the rapid language of her youth.

She remembered the one time her parents had brought her to Mexico as a kid. They spent two weeks of her summer visiting relatives that she'd never see again. Her dad had wanted her to know where he'd come from. Of course as a kid, all she knew was that she'd missed out on time with her friends back home.

But even back then, the language enthralled her. Her parents had taught her Spanish, but they'd always insisted that she speak English first. In the restaurant, it was acceptable to speak Spanish and it had been the waitstaff, dishwashers, and bus boys who had taught her the most colorful language.

Being surrounded by it now brought back memories of that long-ago summer. Back then, she wasn't as fluent in

Spanish and kids had made fun of her because she kept telling them to slow down. Now her ears picked up bits of conversation between the cooks, and she laughed at their jokes.

A waitress came to the table and Carmen ordered a Coke. It was a splurge but she remembered it was different here, like everything else. While she waited for the drink, she looked at the menu and decided on a combination platter. She wanted to taste a variety of foods from the region.

Then an idea struck her so fast that she felt dizzy. What if she did a tour of places, sampling foods to bring them back to Chicago? She had no desire to be a chef like Liam, but over the last couple of months, she found she did enjoy running the truck and cooking food that invoked memories of her childhood.

When the waitress brought her plate, she stared at the pile of food: an enchilada, a tamale, a taco, and a pork *cemita*, which was a sandwich she'd heard her dad talk about, but had never eaten herself. It smelled divine and she didn't know where to start. Her mouth watered and she itched to pick up the phone and call someone to talk about it. Who was she kidding? She didn't want to talk to *someone*, she wanted to call Liam. Instead, she snapped a photo of the plate and picked up her fork.

Today would be the first day in her adventures with food. As she savored the first bite, she began to think about the other places she would visit. She smiled as she realized she didn't need to confine herself to Mexico and its food. She could go anywhere, at least until she ran out of money.

Two days.

Carmen left two days ago and she hadn't called or

emailed or anything. Liam wasn't just worried, he was annoyed and terrified. He had no words. When she'd asked him to leave, there was no anger. It was almost like she was pleading and he couldn't understand. He wouldn't have tried to talk her out of going on vacation.

He thought about what Rosa had said. If Carmen planned to go and not come back, yeah, he would've tried to convince her otherwise. How could he not?

When he told her to get the life she wanted, he'd assumed he'd be a part of it. Never had it crossed his mind that she didn't want him.

The more he thought about everything Carmen had said, the more concerned he became. Everything he'd done was because he cared about her and wanted her to be happy.

He remembered working on the truck with her, imagined her smiling face, heard her laughing at him, and realized that maybe working on the truck had made her happy. He hadn't been trying to take that away from her. But what if she saw it that way?

As he and Rosa carried the remaining food into the kitchen for the night, he asked, "Have you spoken to Carmen?"

She shrugged. "She left a message telling me she was good, but she didn't answer when I called her back."

"So her phone works in Mexico?"

Rosa smiled. "Knowing Carmen, yeah. She'd make sure she had the right kind of plan or phone or whatever."

Liam wiped his hand on his pants. "Can you finish up here? I have some stuff I need to do."

Rosa's eyebrows scrunched together. "Sure. It must be *muy importante* for you to trust me."

"It's cleanup. Tough to screw that up."

She threw a towel at him, and he ducked before heading out the back door. He knew if Carmen wasn't taking Rosa's calls, she wouldn't take his either, but he could still send her messages. When he got home, he created a list of everything he knew about her. She'd accused him of not knowing her, but she was wrong.

He might not know what she wanted in life, but he knew her. He closed his eyes and thought about everything he knew to be true. By the time he finished a couple of hours later, he had pages of ideas. He would send them to her every day until he ran out or until she came home.

He sent his first text, not from the list, but from his heart.

I miss you.

CARMEN STARED at the text from Liam. She wanted to tell him she missed him too, but she knew that he would take that and try to convince her to come home. Liam liked to be in charge. It was one of the things she admired about him. He always seemed to know what he wanted and where he was going.

She wanted to be more like that. She needed to be more like that in order for their relationship to work. So she didn't respond to his message. But when she crawled into bed that night, she held her phone close and read it again.

Over the course of the next few days, Liam became harder to ignore. She never knew when to expect it, but he would shoot her a text. The first couple struck her as odd statements, but then she realized he was telling her every-thing he knew about her:

I know you love mornings because you wake up ready to take on the world.

I know you like to sleep with socks on because your feet get cold and when I peel them off, you use my legs to warm your toes.

I know you don't like the curves of your body because no one ever told you how sexy they are. (I dream of them every night.)

I know you approach life cautiously.

I know how important family is to you. (It's one of the many things we have in common.)

I know that if I kiss your neck, you go from zero to horny in seconds.

I know you're afraid of being alone.

I know you trap a little moan in your throat every time you eat something you really like, but that you think you shouldn't be eating.

Multiple times a day, her phone bleeped with a text and her heart would race, hoping it was from Liam. It was silly because they were always from him. She couldn't anticipate what kind of text it would be: sweet, sexy, funny. But she enjoyed them all.

Every night, he sent her the same one:

I miss you.

She shouldn't have accused him of not knowing her. They knew each other well enough to know the really important stuff, and they had plenty of time to learn the small things.

She spent a week traveling to different cities and towns in Mexico, absorbing the culture and tasting the food. For all her bravado when she arrived, thinking she'd travel the world, at this point, she was just tired.

More than that, she missed Liam. She wanted to go home, curl up in her own bed, and wake next to him. Even as she smiled and laughed each day, her heart ached for him.

She had a notebook full of ideas. She still wasn't totally sure what she wanted to do with her entire life, but she had a beginning. Business would always be her focus, but like her father, she enjoyed food. She liked knowing people came to them for meals. She wanted to stay in the restaurant business.

At least she was pretty sure.

Liam's texts were coming further apart, and she worried that he was giving up on her. And he had every right to. She'd pushed him away.

Before she could go back though, she had one more thing to take care of: the letter from her dad. She'd carried it for months and it was the only item from home that she'd brought, other than clothes. Sitting at a table at an outdoor café, she finally opened the envelope.

Dear Carmen, mi tesoro,

Just reading the greeting caused her eyes to fill. The childhood nickname reminded her that her dad had always made her feel like she was a treasure. She blinked back the tears and continued.

If you're reading this, I'm gone, and I'm sorry. I made many mistakes with you, but know that I always loved you. You were the best part of my life. You are a smart, hardworking girl, but you hide from life. Let the world see how wonderful you are.

Please don't stay in the house and let life pass. You did that too much after your mother died. Be sad. But then move on. Find love and happiness. Make a new life for yourself.

Tears cascaded down her cheeks and dripped onto her arms as the paper she held shook. Liam cared about her. He understood her in ways she never thought a man would.

By now, you know I made sure you couldn't sell the truck for a year. That wasn't meant to punish you, although I know you don't like the truck. I want you to have financial security. That is why I asked Liam to help you. I trust him. He'll make sure things go as they should. He'll give you the freedom to find your way without worry.

Now everything fell into place. Her dad asked Liam to

not only run the truck, but to take care of her. That was why he'd pushed her away. He was trying to set her free.

Liam wanted her to be free, but he was waiting for her. Time for her to make a new plan, one where she'd prove to Liam that being with him was better than any freedom her father thought she needed.

CHAPTER 25

*L*iam spent his days on the truck with Rosa, who was a constant reminder of how much he missed Carmen. Rosa was a good employee, but she wasn't Carmen. And Carmen had yet to respond to any of his texts.

So he spent his evenings at O'Leary's drinking far more than he should. He sat on the same stool he'd taken up residence on for the past week, and Ryan stared at him.

"You go nearly a whole year without stepping foot in here, now you're practically moving in. What's up?" As he spoke, he poured a beer for Liam.

Liam filled his lungs, unsure if he could even talk about it. His chest hurt with the pain of missing Carmen. He swallowed a gulp of Guinness to ease his throat.

"I know that look. It's woman trouble."

"What do you know about it?"

"Nothing that's worth having is easy. It's God's way of making sure we really want something. What happened with Carmen?"

"She left. Took off to Mexico."

Ryan leaned his elbows on the bar. "Why?"

"It started as a vacation, but now I'm not so sure. She won't take my calls or texts, and her cousin thinks she's not coming back."

"What happened?"

"I fucked up. I'm just not sure how. She said I don't know what she wants. Right now, she's right. I thought we were good." He shrugged. "Fuck it."

Talking with his brother was not going to fix this. Neither was Guinness. He slugged back the rest of the beer. "You got quiet. No brotherly advice?"

Ryan wiped down the bar. "I would've suggested going after her, but it doesn't sound like you know exactly where she is. Couldn't you have stopped her?"

Liam shook his head. "That's what she was afraid of. She needed to go. I told her I'd be here when she got back, but now I'm beginning to wonder how long that'll be."

"Does it matter?"

Liam thought about that and decided it didn't. He would wait for Carmen as long as he needed to. Even if he didn't want to wait, he couldn't just forget her. Nor did he want to. As he thought about ordering another beer, his phone signaled a text. In his heart, he hoped it was from Carmen, but given her track record, his brain told him not to hope. Sure enough, it was from Rosa. However, it held great news.

She's coming home.

Instead of texting, he called Rosa. "When?" he asked.

"I'm not sure. She called me to let me know she was coming home, but she wants to surprise you. So act surprised."

The irritation he felt at Carmen calling Rosa instead of him fled when he heard those words. She hadn't totally walked away from them. She was coming home to him. He knocked his fist on the bar as he stood to get his brother's attention. "I'm out of here. Carmen's coming home."

Ryan smiled. "Don't fuck it up."

"Not possible. I learned from all your mistakes." He turned and left the bar feeling lighter than he had in over a week. He itched to drive straight to her house, but he knew he shouldn't. Carmen wanted to surprise him.

Even as he had those thoughts, he found himself driving to her neighborhood. He'd missed her so much that just being in her house, waiting for her would feel good. He hoped it wouldn't be too creepy.

When he got to the front door, a piece of paper was flapping with the wind, tape barely holding it in place. It read, "I knew you would come."

His heart rate kicked up and he fumbled for the key. His hand shook as he opened the door into the dark living room. Dim light shown in the hall, but no sign of Carmen anywhere. He checked the time on his phone. Late, but not very. Maybe she was in bed. "Carmen?"

He locked up behind him and called her again.

"In the bedroom."

Liam paused in the doorway of the bedroom and just stared. Carmen sat on the edge of the bed, bundled in a fluffy navy robe. He didn't know what to expect, but part of him wanted to see her naked in bed.

"Hi," she said, with a gentle smile. "I got your texts."

He leaned against the doorjamb and waited. She seemed to be gearing up for something.

"I looked forward to getting them every day."

"Why didn't you respond?"

She tilted her head and her smile slipped. "I didn't know what to say. You were right when you told me that I'd put my life on hold. I thought I needed to cut everything loose in order to figure out what I wanted." She stood and took a few tentative steps toward him. "It was a mistake."

"What was?"

"Leaving you. Pushing you away."

Every ounce of tension that had been coiled and tangled and knotted in his chest since she left loosened. For the first time, he was able to take a deep breath.

"I did a lot of thinking while I was gone." She took another step.

He forced his feet to stay rooted even though every nerve pushed him to grab her and bring her into his arms. "Did you figure things out?"

"Some." Her smile returned.

CARMEN'S HEART thudded against her ribs. She'd prayed she knew Liam well enough to know that if Rosa texted that Carmen was coming home, he would show up even though she wasn't supposed to be here yet. She had a speech planned, but seeing him, being this close, made it difficult to remember the words.

"I like working on the truck with you, but I don't think it'll be enough for either of us in the long run. You need more than tacos."

"Carmen—"

She held up her hand. "Let me finish. We talked about maybe selling the truck in a year. We have plenty of time to figure that out. But I realized I like working in the food industry. It's not just that I'm used to it and it's easy for me. I went to school to learn to run a business. My family taught me about food. It's natural to put those things together."

"What are you saying? You want to keep working on the truck?"

"Sometimes, maybe, but I think you and Rosa have that covered. But I want to be included. When you and Rosa started making plans for the truck and the Heavenly Buns people, I felt left out and I didn't like it."

His eyebrows pulled together. "I never wanted you to feel bad. I wanted you to be free to follow your dreams. If you want details, I'll give them to you. We're going to have a competition with Heavenly Buns in two days. You want in?"

"No. I don't."

"What are you saying then?"

"I'm saying I love you. And I want you in my life. I want us to explore some other options as partners. Menu items, expanding, I'm not sure, but I want to think about it. Talk about it. I ate so many wonderful things while I was gone: *cemitas* and *tortitas de Santa Clara* and the elotes, oh, my God…"

"Anything you want. I have some ideas too." Liam pushed away from the door and took a half step toward her.

She held up a hand. "Wait."

He froze with a look of impatience.

"I had another Christmas present that I was too chicken to give to you. But I think I'm ready now." She tugged at the belt at her waist and let the robe gape.

His eyes widened and a genuine smile with teeth lit his face. The robe slipped from her shoulders and tangled around her ankles. The rush of cool air kissed her skin through the thin satin fabric.

Her skin pricked wherever Liam's gaze landed, and she realized how much she missed his touch. He licked his lips, but didn't move.

"Are you just going to stare at me?"

"Maybe."

She stepped over the robe and into his arms. "As much as I love the way you look at me, I prefer the way you hold me."

He wrapped his arms around her and pulled her close.

"Take me to bed," she whispered. "And leave the light on."

Thank you so much for taking time to read my book. I hope you enjoyed hanging out with the O'Learys in Chicago. Keep reading for an excerpt of the last book in the series, *Hold Me Close*, where Maggie O'Leary comes home to find love with her best friend. If you could spare a moment, I would appreciate you leaving a review of this book.

If you'd like to stay up-to-date on my releases and have the chance to win some prizes, click here to join my newsletter.

EXCERPT FROM HOLD ME CLOSE

Shane Callahan drove the loop around O'Hare again. He could've parked in the cell phone lot, or if he'd been smart he would've waited for Maggie to call him when she landed. But excitement overtook him. She was coming home.

Finally. For good.

He stayed in the left lane, moving like a snail, hoping he'd see Maggie emerge from the airport. Instead, another cab cut him off. He bypassed the terminals and curved left for another trip around. His cell phone buzzed. He glanced at the screen and saw the message from Maggie.

I'm here! Have my luggage. Be out in a few minutes.

His heart raced. He took a slow breath. He felt like a kid on Christmas morning. At least the weather made that believable. The city had been hit with another snowstorm last night. The nasty weather made February feel like the longest month instead of the shortest.

Shane shifted into the center lane until he pulled up at the international terminal. Maggie stood at the curb, stomping her feet. Her short jacket barely met her waist. And she had no gloves. Her cheeks were pink as the wind whipped her hair around.

She was a sight for sore eyes.

He stopped the truck and had nearly forgotten to put it in park before opening his door. His big smile stretched his cheeks in a way they hadn't been in forever. He rounded the back of the truck, and Maggie ran and jumped at him.

His first thought was that she'd lost weight again. She was nothing in his arms. But as she wrapped her arms around his neck and he breathed in her scent, he couldn't think of anything but Maggie. She was home.

"It's so good to see you," she said, muffled against his shoulder.

Even though he didn't want to, he released her and set her back on the curb. Looking at the suitcase at her feet, he asked, "Is that all you have?"

"Yeah. I shipped back boxes that'll arrive in a few days. I hope. I didn't want to worry about customs. I just wanted to get home."

He grabbed the suitcase and put in on the narrow backseat of the truck and offered Maggie a hand to step up into the vehicle. "Everything okay with your mom?"

"Yeah, I guess. Not that I would take her word for it. Ryan said the doctor has said she's doing well, and as long as she continues to eat right and take her meds, she can bounce back from the heart attack."

He closed her door and got behind the wheel.

"I wanted to be back here weeks ago, but I felt bad for my boss. I didn't want to leave him with no help, and then there was all the packing. I didn't realize how much stuff I'd accumulated over the last year and a half."

She rubbed her hands together in front of the vent, so he turned the heater up full blast.

"Not that I'm complaining about you finally coming

home, but are you here just because of your mom?" He flicked a glance in her direction when she didn't answer.

"Not really," she finally said. "I mean, that was a big thing. But as much as I loved traveling and meeting new people, it started to feel like I was still running away."

As Shane pulled out of the airport and onto the Kennedy Expressway, he smiled at the snarl of traffic. Rush hour would give him more time alone with Maggie. Her family would occupy her every minute as soon as they found out she was home.

"Running from what?"

"Everything." She turned the heater down. "I need to get my life back."

An uneasy sensation pricked the back of his neck. Whenever Maggie spoke with that kind of conviction, it usually meant she planned to do something other people wouldn't like. "How do you mean?"

She stared out the passenger window. "Let's stop for some coffee."

Shane made his way to the right lane and the nearest exit. He got off at Harlem and drove down the street until he came to the mall. Slush coated the street and mountains of snow were piled on the curbs. Shane pulled into the parking lot and found a spot.

Maggie jumped from the truck and didn't wait for him as she headed into the mall, her hands tucked tightly into her jacket pockets. Her hair was longer than he remembered. The dark strands flowed behind her. He smelled perfume in her wake as he caught up with her.

The mall wasn't crowded, and they found a coffee shop, ordered, and sat at a small table. Shane draped his jacket over the back of his chair, but Maggie kept hers on. The girl was always cold.

"Spill it, Magpie."

Her gaze shot up to meet his at the use of her nickname. Although her siblings had given her the name because she'd been so loud as a kid, he knew she'd become quieter over the last few years.

"When I left Chicago, Ryan was pissed. He accused me of running away."

"Big brothers can be like that." He'd lock his sisters up if they even thought about running halfway around the world alone.

"But he thought I was running from him. You know how he is. And in my mind, that might've been it too. But after traveling around and settling in with my cousins, I realized I was still missing out on life." She sipped her coffee. "Ever since Todd…" She paused, and Shane knew she did it to gather her strength because she hated talking about him.

Shane reached out and held her hand.

"He took so much from me, Shane. It's been almost five years since he raped me, and I've never stepped back in O'Leary's. It's my family's bar. I grew up there, and he took that from me. And my first apartment. I'm supposed to have great memories about my first apartment, but that's ruined."

"I know," he whispered. Guilt tugged at him.

Her fingers tightened on his. "I'm taking it all back."

"How?"

"I'm going to talk to Ryan and start working at the bar. And if there's an apartment available above the bar, I'm going to move in there."

Shane's lungs froze. Yeah, it had been nearly five years, but he remembered all the times where something would trigger a bad reaction in Maggie. She couldn't go some places or see things or smell things without falling apart. She had good reason to have stayed away from O'Leary's. No one expected her to go back.

He forced oxygen into his body. "Are you sure that's a good idea?"

"Something needs to happen. I'm better, Shane. I really am, but I'm still not myself."

He stroked his thumb along her knuckles. There was a time that even this small contact had been too much for her. She was better. He saw it all the time. But still. "Have you talked to Dr. Janzen about this?"

Maggie sipped her coffee again and shook her head. "I have an appointment later this week."

Great. So she dumped this on him before her family, before her therapist. How the fuck was he supposed to know what to say?

"Rushing into something like this isn't a good idea. You need to think about it and talk to Dr. Janzen. She's always steered you right."

"I'm not rushing. I've been thinking about it for a long time. I miss being part of the family business. Everyone tiptoes around me when it comes to the bar. They're all still afraid to even talk about the business in front of me. It's ridiculous."

"But living above the bar?"

"I don't want to live with my mom forever."

He could definitely sympathize with that idea. "I'm looking for a new place too. Why don't we go rent something together?"

"What happened with Joe?"

"His brother needs an apartment, so Joe asked me to move out."

"That sucks."

"So what do you say?"

She bit down on her bottom lip. "I need to live above O'Leary's. To know that I can."

Thoughts raced through his mind. "At least wait to talk to Ryan until after you see Dr. Janzen."

"She won't change my mind."

He already knew that. But it would buy him some time. "She'll talk to you about how to approach it, though."

Maggie nodded and smiled.

The knot of tension in his neck and the flurry of thoughts in his head disappeared. He'd seen her smile every time they FaceTimed or Skyped, but nothing could compare to the real thing.

"That's why I wanted to see you before I told my family I was coming home. I knew I could count on you to listen and not tell me I'm dumb."

"You're never dumb."

"Yeah, well, sometimes I do dumb things. And my family likes to point it out to me all the time." She finished her coffee, and he realized he hadn't even touched his.

He wanted to talk her out of this. It was a bad idea and had a ton of potential to set her back. He couldn't bear to see her go back. He couldn't imagine not seeing her gorgeous smile again.

"Thanks for the coffee. I think I'm ready to see my family now." She stood, breaking contact with him.

When he stood, she wrapped her arms around his waist and settled her head on his chest.

"I'm glad you came to pick me up. I needed this."

"Me too." He'd missed her something fierce over the months.

* * *

Maggie stared out the window as Shane took streets through the city to get her to her mom's house. Asking him to pick her up had been a good choice. She could've asked Moira, but her sister would try to talk her out of her plan. Shane was the best listener she'd ever known. He'd proven it again today. The guy even remembered the name of her therapist. Who did that?

Shane. Always Shane. He'd been there for her through the good and the really, really bad. Even when it was hard, and she'd tried to push him away because she didn't think she could be around any guy after being raped, he stayed. Not in an obnoxious *I know what's best for you* way, but an *I care about you* way. Without him, she probably never would have had the guts to travel.

After he pulled up in front of her mom's house, he put the truck in park but didn't turn off the ignition.

"Coming in?"

He let out a small chuckle. "You decided to come home without telling your family. Then you had me pick you up from the airport. They're going to have plenty to say, and I don't want to be caught in the crossfire. I think I'll head home."

"Chicken."

"Smart."

"Whatever." She yanked on the handle and jumped from the cab.

Shane met her and grabbed her suitcase. After setting it on the curb at her feet, he held her hand. "I'm glad you're finally home."

"You're gonna get sick of me."

"Never." He slammed the door. "Give me a call if you want to get together later."

"My family will probably fill my night. And then some. I'll call when I need to escape." She hefted the bag and stared at the front door. Although she knew Shane had gotten back behind the wheel, the truck didn't move.

Of course he'd wait for her to go inside. She waved at Shane and walked up the steps. The last time she'd made this trip, she entered a living room filled with her siblings all crying. Their mother had had a heart attack and was in the hospital. The whole episode made Maggie realize how much she was missing. Not just for herself, but with her family.

As the youngest, she'd always been able to count on having her family there. It had never occurred to her that at some point they might not be. She turned the knob on the door and found resistance. She fished out her keys and let herself in.

With the door closed at her back she paused and took a slow inhale. No dinner smells. And quiet. She couldn't remember a time when home was quiet.

"Mom?" she called, hoping her mom was there.

"What? Who is it?"

A relieved sigh joined the smile on her face. "It's me, Maggie."

She turned the corner and walked through the living room and dining room. Her mother stood at the door to the kitchen. The teacup in her hand shook. Maybe a surprise homecoming wasn't the best idea.

"What's wrong?" Eileen asked.

"Nothing. I'm home. For good."

Her mom set her tea on the table. "When did this come about? And without so much as a phone call."

Maggie hugged her mom and breathed in the scents of Jean Naté cologne and Estée Lauder makeup. Mom gave her a quick pat on the back.

"How do you feel?" she asked Eileen.

"Fine. Same as I have been every time you've asked. I've had enough of the coddling." She took up her cup again and sipped before sitting at the dining room table.

Yeah, Mom was back to herself. Even with regular reports from her siblings about Mom being fine, nothing could replace experiencing it. She sat adjacent to Eileen. "Is it okay if I move back in for a while? It'll only be for a little bit until I figure out what I'm doing next."

"Of course. I have this big house all to myself."

"Thanks."

Her mom stared at her with narrowed eyes. "What's wrong?"

"Nothing."

"Then why are you home?"

"It was time."

"*Psh.* You came back because of my trip to the doctor."

"That was part of it. I'm worried about you, Mom."

"I told you, no need." She pressed her lips so tightly, the pink line of lipstick disappeared.

"I needed to come home. I had a great time in Ireland, but it's time to move on. I need to start making a life for myself. Figure out who I am and what I want."

Her mother gave her one sharp nod in response.

"I'm going to go unpack."

"I'll make dinner."

Maggie tried not to roll her eyes. She knew her mom would be on the phone as soon as Maggie's foot hit the bottom step to go up to her old bedroom. "Can you tell them to give me a day before they descend?"

Her mom didn't answer, and Maggie knew she didn't have a chance. She lugged her suitcase upstairs and stood in the middle of her bedroom, the same bedroom she'd shared with Moira for years. Many of her things were still there, but there was no sign of Moira.

She tossed her bag on the bed and sat beside it. Would she want to live alone? Sure, she'd done it briefly. But even that hadn't been really living alone. She'd lived in an apartment above the bar. Her brothers worked downstairs. She always had family around.

Was that a good thing? Or bad? She made a mental note

to add that to the list of questions to talk to Dr. Janzen about. She got up and started putting away her clothes. Everything was exactly where she'd left it. It was as if no one had stepped foot in the room since she left a year and half ago.

As much as things didn't change here, so many others had. At Christmas, she'd been surrounded by her brothers and sister who had all fallen in love. She felt as if she'd missed out on something. It felt like waking from a dream, feeling like she was the same person but she'd time traveled. Everyone else was different.

It was another reason she was glad she'd seen Shane first. He was the same old Shane he'd always been. She liked being able to count on some things.

Just like when she heard a loud noise downstairs, she knew her big sister had come over. Knowing Moira, she beat everyone else there. Moments later, pounding on steps let her know Moira was too impatient to wait for her to come down.

"Maggie!" she screamed from the doorway. She squeezed her in a tight hug. When she let go, Moira tried for an angry look, but Maggie wasn't buying it. "Why didn't you tell us you were coming home?"

"Because I didn't want anyone making a big deal out of it."

Moira crossed her arms, which pushed her big boobs up, emphasizing them even more. Maggie wished she had a little more in that department. Moira had gotten more than her fair share. "So why are you home?"

"Why is everyone so suspicious? I've been gone for over a year. I figured you'd all be happy I came back."

"We are. But you always seemed happy when we talked. Did something happen?"

"No. Except Mom having a heart attack. That was a wake-up call. She's not going to be here forever." Maggie paused and debated how much she should tell Moira.

Moira threw her arms around Maggie again. "I'm so glad you're home. I missed you and I don't really care why you decided to come back as long as you're happy."

"I'm getting there. I'm at least trying."

"I'm here if you want to talk."

"Not yet. But soon." Maggie pulled away. "So how long do I have until everyone else shows up?"

Moira wrinkled up her nose. "Ryan and Quinn are on their way. So are Colin and Liam."

Maggie rolled her eyes. So much for having a day.

Moira nudged her shoulder. "At least Michael's on at the fire house, so he won't be coming."

"Whatever. You know this means Mom's cooking for everyone. You can do the dishes."

Hooking her arm though Maggie's, Moira turned them toward the stairs. "Only if you help."

As much as she wanted to be irritated, Maggie couldn't be. It felt too good to be home. Knowing that it was real, not just a brief holiday visit, but really digging back in at home with her family was nice. Traveling had been a great adventure, but it couldn't top the stability of her family.

She followed Moira down the narrow, winding steps and wondered how many trips she'd made up and down this staircase. The scarred wood and smudged wall looked the same as it had her entire life.

They reflected how she felt. Damaged, but comfortable.

RECIPE

Liam's Luscious Cheesecake

Crust:
    1½ cups graham crackers
    3 Tablespoons sugar
    4 Tablespoons melted butter

Filling:
    All ingredients should be at room temperature.
    2 packages (8 oz each) cream cheese
    2 packages (8 oz each) mascarpone cheese
    1¼ cup sugar
    2 teaspoons almond extract
    4 eggs

Preheat oven to 325 degrees Fahrenheit.

Mix graham crackers and sugar in a bowl. Add melted butter and mix with a fork. Press mixture into bottom and part of the way up the sides of a 9-inch springform pan. Bake crust for 10-15 minutes, until set and golden.

In a mixer, combine cream cheese and mascarpone cheese until blended. Mix in sugar. Add almond. Beat in eggs, one at a time, mix between each addition.

Pour filling mixture over crust. Bake for 60 to 65 minutes. Middle of cake will still be wobbly. Cake sets when cool.

Allow cake to cool for at least an hour. Wrap and place in refrigerator overnight.

Slice and enjoy.